PENGUIN BOOKS
THE HILLS OF ANGHERI

Kavery Nambisan is from the Coorg district of Karnataka. She graduated from St John's Medical College, Bangalore, and did her surgical training and FRCS in England. Since then she has devoted most of her working life to practice in rural India and has worked as a surgeon in Bihar, Uttar Pradesh, Tamil Nadu and Karnataka. She is now surgeon and medical adviser to Tata Coffee Limited.

Kavery Nambisan is the author of several children's books and four novels. She is married to journalist and poet Vijay Nambisan.

The Hills of Angheri

KAVERY NAMBISAN

PENGUIN BOOKS

An imprint of Penguin Random House

PENGUIN BOOKS

USA | Canada | UK | Ireland | Australia
New Zealand | India | South Africa | China | Singapore

Penguin Books is part of the Penguin Random House group of companies
whose addresses can be found at global.penguinrandomhouse.com

Published by Penguin Random House India Pvt. Ltd
4th Floor, Capital Tower 1, MG Road,
Gurugram 122 002, Haryana, India

Penguin
Random House
India

First published by Penguin Books India 2005

Copyright © Kavery Nambisan 2005

ISBN 9780143032717

Typeset in Saban by SURYA, New Delhi
Printed at Repro India Limited

This novel is for my teachers—
Hasmukh Mehta, Michael Bansod,
Sheel and Kamal Sharma,
S. Gyanchand and Sir Robert Shields—
who taught me the facts and influenced the fiction

prologue

Appa was already in the bus, carrying his string bag filled with turnips, onions and a coconut. He was returning from the market. I shoved my way to the seat next to him.

'Three rupees,' he said, staring ahead.

'Um.'

'The price of oranges.'

The bus lurched past the railway station, under the bridge and past Cheluvamba Park where children swung crazily on red-and-yellow swings. 'Beans one-fifty and avarekai four rupees. I did not buy any avare.'

'Um.'

His voice became stern. 'What's happened to you today?'

'Appa? It's . . . the laudable pus,' I blurted.

'*What?*'

'I drained a gluteal abscess. When the pus gushed out, Sripathi Sir said "laudable pus". That's a surgical expression—praiseworthy pus. Deserving glorification because it is out of the body.'

Appa gave me a severe look and I shut up.

A couple of hours earlier I had drained my cup of too-sweet coffee and picked up the white coat draped on the back of my chair. Mani the canteen boy scraped his feet and coughed his unique, toneless cough to remind me I had not paid. I handed him the fifty paise and made my way to the Theatre complex. Butterflies in my stomach played gaily with the coffee, my seventh cup for the day. I was three months into my internship and about to perform my first surgery, a gluteal phlegmon, more honestly called a boil on the buttock.

Twenty minutes, two reminders and endless pacing of the Theatre corridors later, the anaesthetist arrived. Without a word, he went to the doctor's room and was puffing on his second Charminar when my boss appeared.

I scrubbed, soaping lavishly to the elbows—once, twice, and then with the nailbrush. The yellow, stone-hard soap chafed my skin till it burned. 'What's she scrubbing for, plastic surgery?' said the anaesthetist, loud enough for me to hear. I battled with the gloves and got my index and middle fingers into the same opening. The world snickered as I struggled to get it right.

The ward boy swung the overhead light until it focussed on the abscess. Gloved hands held over my chest, I advanced towards the operating table and gazed admiringly at my medallion: suffused, glowing, its purplish hue enhanced by the pink antiseptic the scrub nurse had used to clean the skin. A comely little abscess. The boss nodded and the nurse held out the scalpel. I cut, pushing the tip of the blade through the skin. Pus oozed out, thick and queasy-green.

'Laudable pus!'

That was my boss, and he sounded pleased. 'Don't just stand there!' he said. 'Index finger in. Break the loculae. Sweep in. Firmly. Nurse, give her a ribbon gauze. Dip it in acriflavine . . .' Splendid smells of fruity, over-ripe pus filled the air. The anaesthetist gagged. The ward boy was grinning, I could tell by the bulges beneath his mask. The nurse acknowledged my thank yous and Sripathi Sir muttered approval. I entered details in the Theatre register as lasting proof of my surgical feat. Two hours later, I trudged to the bus stop, weary and exultant. The world cheered.

At home, I described the charming details of my first surgery until my sister Sujju said, shut up, we're eating, and you smell of rotten fruit. I had to bathe and change before I was allowed to sit at the table. Later, Appa told Sujju to have a proper talk with me about my future. Which, if you were a twenty-two-year-old from a traditional family, meant only one thing.

But I had already made the second important decision of my life. Laudable pus had done it for me.

part one

You can sometimes count every orange on a tree but never all the trees in a single orange.

—A.K. Ramanujan, 'A Poem on Particulars'

1

Nalli opened the door and peeped into the room. Sunshine streamed in and touched the bride. Hands on her lap, Sujju sat before the mirror while Amma and Chikkamma looped jasmine through her hair. How beautiful she looked, delicate and long-boned, with light eyes that took on the mauve tints of her sari. In less than an hour the groom's party would arrive.

Standing on her toes, Nalli was trying to get a look in the mirror. She looked beautiful too, though no one said so. In her parrot-green langa with its neat row of golden elephants, the tight-fitting blouse and the davani in flaming orange. Standing behind Sujju, she preened. Would anyone notice if she borrowed the lipstick and dabbed it on her cheeks and lips?

Less than half an hour for the wedding party to reach the village.

'Ajja!' Nalli stood in the doorway, holding the gathers of her langa to show off the elephants marching around her ankles. Ajja was busy adorning the wedding mandap with mango leaves, dasavala, jasmine and parijata. But he came up to her, rubbing his hands. 'Very nice,' he said.

In spite of being so old, Ajja had excellent taste. It was Ajja who bought the three and a half yards of green silk for the langa and the two yards of soft, best-quality georgette for the davani from Mysore. Nalli showed him her green stone earrings and her green bangles. She had just raised her langa to display the silver gejje on her ankles when she saw the look come into his eyes. Ajja had large eyes which swelled out of their sockets and now they looked like they might fall out. 'You have been painting your nails . . . and your face! And your lips! Kapi!' Hitching her langa, Nalli ran to the back of the house where Gaja the maidservant dabbed soot on her forehead to keep away the evil eye.

The wedding party arrived. The groom was handsome, the bride resplendent, the food first-rate. A perfect wedding, the guests said. It would be talked about for a long time. One by one they left, lips tinged with the pleasing red of betel nut. But Nalli was not happy. Ajja had endorsed her prettiness but Jai, back after ten long months in medical college, had ignored her completely. All because of that village lovely, the slant-eyed Veena. It was a custom in the village for the girls to serve the guests at a feast. The older women would replenish the vessels in the smoke-filled kitchen and hand them over. The men ate first, the women next, and the bride's family last of all. Jai sat with his friends and tossed out wisecracks for Veena to simper over. She blushed and minced about, serving pickle. Trust her to take the smallest dish while the other girls struggled with vessels of sambar and kootu.

Nalli in her beautiful green langa, her davani of soft georgette, and green bangles scoured with gold lines. 'Very nice,' Ajja had said. Who knew better than him? Jai was going to ignore her, was he? She would show him. Carrying the vessel of sambar, she walked past him. 'Sambar here!' Jai called. She smiled at no one in particular and served everyone else. Not that she was jealous. Ever since she could remember, her sister had bewitched Jai, as she had most boys. Now because Sujju was getting married, there was no need for Jai to start flirting with another girl. When she snubbed Jai that day, it gave her a bit of pleasure, not much.

Something more important happened after the wedding party left.

Ajja's younger brother Gappu Mava, his wife and their seven children had come down from Kolar. It was late afternoon when they sat down to eat. Even Ajji had come out of bed to sit with the family, which she did only on special occasions.

Gappu Mava said, looking at Nalli, 'So, it will be you in a few years.'

Nalli shook her head. 'I'm going to study to be a doctor first.'

She could ever recollect the moment when she said it and the thrill she felt each time she spoke it aloud, which was fairly often from then on.

Gappu Mava turned to Appa and said, 'You're not going to allow it, I hope. Beda kano. Five or six years of college and then it won't be easy to find a husband.' Appa was silent. 'It will be a mistake,' the old man persisted. 'She's pretty enough. She'll meet some useless sort in medical college.'

'How can a doctor be useless?' Nalli asked hotly, in defence of her husband-to-be.

Gappu Mava laughed his 'ho-ho-ho' laugh and went on eating. Appa reproached Nalli with his headmaster eyes and later that night told her that she should respect her elders. He left the matter alone after that.

But with Ajja it was not easy. Nalli sat on the lower step leading from the kitchen to the backyard, with Ajja on the top step. The last rays of the sun loitered on the rounded slopes of Jenubetta. Ajja poured coconut oil into his cupped palm and rubbed it into her scalp, a regular evening ritual. Nalli was not so young that she could not manage to oil and comb her hair; she was twelve. But neither saw the need to stop what they were used to. At dusk every day, she would sit on the back steps with comb and coconut oil and wait for Ajja. Sometimes Budhi sat with her, to have a few drops of oil poured in his ears.

Ajja's fingers were hard that day. He showed his displeasure by kneading her scalp and pulling at her hair as he combed. 'If God wanted you to be a doctor, you would have been a boy,' he said. Nalli kept her mouth shut. Appa had not been angry with her; that was enough. Her scalp screamed but she was stubbornly brave. Ajja could not get a wince out of her.

Ajja was a two-in-one grandparent. He had small hips, a smooth chest and a nubbed nose with fine red veins. His peppered-white hair came down to his shoulders when he left it loose. The way he styled his hair controlled his mood and behaviour. When he left it loose, he was grandfather: imperious and bossy. There was no crossing his path then. He walked straight in spite of his grotesque, callous-ridden feet with in-turning toes which looked as if they were being pulled by a string. His voice became deep and strong, his bulging, heavy-lidded eyes unyielding. If he tied his hair in a knot at the back of his neck, he was grandmother. He appeared to shrink in size. He clasped his hands behind his back and walked with a stoop, his telescoping neck rearing his head before him. He used timid, placatory words like 'nodona' and 'houdu, houdu', giggled like a girl, and little frills formed around his eyes. Ajja could be this person or the other by merely changing the way he styled his hair.

Healthy-looking Ajji, who was always sick, was their real grandmother. She was soft and fat, with hair that reached her hips. Nalli had memories of Ajji walking up and down the front room, teasing strands of her hair after her bath. She liked the just-washed smell of Ajji's hair and the feel of wet strands touching her face when she walked beside Ajji. That was a long time ago.

Ajji was twenty years younger than Ajja, and beautiful. She had a heart-shaped face, a delicate chin and lustrous eyes, which she lined with kajal twice a day. She had spent all her youth keeping herself beautiful. After three children she said she could not have any more, so Ajja got her some herbal concoction to prevent further pregnancies.

Many years ago, Ajji had fallen ill with a fever. Every morning after breakfast, Ajja laid her on a mattress in the sun which the Vaidyar said was a treatment better than any tonic. After a while she complained that the sun burned her skin, so Ajja put her in the porch. A few months later she decided that she would rather stay in bed. Ajji knew she could get almost everything she wanted by being sick: she could better control the family from her bed, which she asked to be shifted to the front room, and while the rest of the family used the toilet outside, she had the privilege of a commode. If a window was opened anywhere in the house, she asked that it be shut before she caught a chill. Ajja bathed and fed Ajji, combed her hair and dressed her in fresh clothes. Every afternoon he sat on the edge of Ajji's bed and listened to her endless complaints. When she called, he dropped whatever he was doing and went to her. Only once Nalli had heard him say, with a hint of irritation, 'I have just two hands, thanga.' Ajji became soft and plump, with pampered cheeks which looked like the petals of the pink dasavala near the hedge.

Ajji's mysterious malady stayed tantalizingly out of the reach of doctors. Ajja was willing to spend any amount of money to make her well. The Vaidyar, whose own wife Satyavati was a stubborn woman, understood Ajja's plight. He persuaded his one-time teacher, the Kuttanchery Moos, to come from Kerala to see Ajji. Moos stayed in Angheri for eleven days, examined Ajji and studied her urine in a clear glass every morning. He and the Vaidyar squatted beneath the tamarind tree, chewed betel nut and discussed Ajji's illness; they quoted from the *Ashtangahrdayam* and *Charaka Samhita*. Moos said the illness could be sloughed off in three weeks if she stayed on a diet of gooseberries and milk. In seventeen days she would moult, casting off hair, nails, skin and even teeth, and rejuvenate with new integument and her health would be restored. Ajji, who was extremely fond of food, flatly refused. Kuttanchery Moos went back to Kerala, defeated by Ajji's stubbornness. Ajji boasted that even the renowned Moos could not cure her.

For dinner Ajji joined the family at the kitchen table but at all other times she preferred to be served in bed. She ate more than any sick person could eat and she got the hottest rotis and dosais. What annoyed Nalli was the way she dumped her half-eaten roti on Nalli's plate, saying, 'Here, I'm giving you my long life,' before helping herself to a hot one. Nalli complained to Amma who said she should be tolerant of her sick grandmother. Once when Jai was having dinner with them, Ajji tried her usual roti trick on him. 'You're done with most of your life. What's there to give?' he asked, dumping the cold scrap back on her plate. Only Jai could get away with such cheek.

But Ajji's frailness was deceptive. She was like a spider in its web, ready to trap passers-by and spring questions on them. Visitors who came to pay their respects went away exhausted. When Nalli walked through the room ever so quietly, she called, 'Who is it?'

'Me.'

'Come here.' Nalli would reluctantly walk to her side. 'What's the time?'

'Ten-thirty.'

'Ten-thirty? Umm . . . what day?'

'Friday.'

'Friday? Umm . . . where is everyone?'

'Ajja is with the cows, Amma is in the kitchen. Appa at school, Vishnu . . .'

'Why haven't you gone to school?'

'I wasn't well.'

'Not well? Umm . . .'

Her curiosity amounted to nothing.

It surprised Nalli that Ajji did not quiz her about what she had said to Gappu Mava. If she had, Nalli would have told her: I will become a doctor and then I will make your illness go away.

But Ajji did not ask.

Worried about Nalli's health, Amma said Nalli should do something less difficult. She was the sickliest in the family, prone to fevers, backaches and fainting spells. Most young girls could swim in the village kere and float with their langas billowing; Nalli tried and failed. The only tree she could climb was the smooth, many-limbed guava tree outside Ajja's room. She would sit on one of its branches, look at the hills and dream her impossible dreams.

Oh, to be Sujju! Now that was an impossible dream. Sujju was slightly built with a fleshless frame and high cheekbones. Her thinness had a perfect symmetry; her hips were bony, shoulders small and sharp. When she bent to draw water from the well, you could count the little knobs of her spine. She had a dry voice that could become soft and sour-sweet delicious like ripe mangoes and a cackling laugh that died slowly in her throat. The way Sujju moved lent softness to whatever she wore. But it was the glance from her honey-coloured eyes which made her irresistible. Or was it the smile? The walk? The laughter?

Sujju sewed an amazing variety of things which adorned the house or were gifted away. Their house was unique because of her creations. While Amma sewed clothes that were useful, Sujju preferred delicate work. Ajja grumbled about Sujju's idle pastime but when he saw that it saved them having to buy gifts for relatives, he was appeased.

In school, Sujju was the most admired girl. Nalli, with her too-thick eyebrows, wide bones and skin which reacted violently to the sun, was ordinary. Her only assets were a stomach fortified by Ajja's food and legs toughened by endless walking on steep village roads. She envied her sister and at times was madly jealous. Nalli would be called names—kapi, kaththe, yemme or dodda donne by almost anyone, even Gaja. But no one called Sujju a monkey or a donkey or a buffalo or a big fat stick. No one whacked her on the head for any reason. Nalli was told to sit with her knees together because 'boys were looking', but no boy really looked at her.

Except Vishnu of course. Vishnu and Budhi, Amma's brother's children, had come to live with them after their uncle and aunt had died in an accident when Vishnu was nine and Budhi two. When no one was around, Vishnu told Nalli that she was too stupid to be a doctor. 'You? A doctor? Devare gathi! Only God can save us.' His God made her uneasy. Once when she was caught pinching a few coins from his coin collection to give Jai, Vishnu had scared her with 'God will never forgive you.' She had wanted to tell him that he was wrong but she had not been able to say it. With Vishnu it was always like that.

Ajja's gods were different. Ajja rose early every morning, bathed, offered flowers to them and finished his prayers, which were always either requests or threats, before the rest of the family was awake. In the evening he lit a lamp at the tulasi katte in front of the house, and the children, Amma and last of all Appa gathered for prayer. Ajji, who was not at all religious, claimed that she was too weak for the ritual and remained in her bed in the front room, occasionally peeping at them through the door. Not infrequently a minor scuffle would start between Nalli and Sujju as they josted for elbow space in the family circle until Ajja spanked them. After the prayers Ajja went to his room to read from the tattered Gita that was older than he, the others to whatever it was they were doing, and Nalli to the kitchen table to read a *Chandamama* and gaze at the giant shadows lunging on the walls. Appa prayed alone in the mornings, and silently. When they got a radio in the house, he listened to the news while praying and sometimes to film songs.

The way they were prayed to, with music, fights and all, Nalli grew up to believe that the gods were kind-hearted. Ajja, who had an excellent relationship with the gods, confirmed this. Nalli was sore that he was not willing to put in a word to them about her future. She was certain he had done it when Jai went to medical college.

2

Angheri huddled in a low valley at the foot of the hills which gave the village its name. The hills girdled the village all the way around except to the north where, twenty miles away, beyond the scrub jungles of Devarakaadu and Chinnakaadu, was Mysore. The riches of Coorg, the near-mythical land of brave men and fair women which lay beyond the hills, or the modernity of Mysore, the once royal city which was two hours away by road, did not touch Angheri till much later.

In the olden days the village used to be called Noorumane because of the belief that it was auspicious to have no more and no less than a hundred houses in it. If an additional house was built, it had to extend from an already existing house. If it could not be connected to any other house, it would be called a shop and no cooking done inside. Even a crumbling, broken-down house could not be demolished until a new one had been built to make up the number. So the hundred-and-first house was never built, nor was the number reduced to ninety-nine. Ajja's father had bought five acres of land for thirty rupees and on this land they grew ragi, paddy and coconut. Over the years, Ajja had also grown banana and orange trees and a vegetable patch and nurtured three successive calves to adulthood.

Angheri was a world where the women could not enter the kitchen on 'those days', where you could tell the prosperity of a household by the profusion of cow dung cakes on the walls or from the food the children took to school in their tiffin boxes, where the gods punished men for their misdeeds by withholding rain clouds, where for a long time—until Appa became the headmaster—the highest achievement for a student was Matric Fail. It was a world where the week's shopping for a family, including soap, jaggery and snuff, cost no more than twelve annas; a world where money was scarce and food plenty—it was the only thing they did not buy.

The hills made Angheri special. Ajja said that without the hills there would be no sunrise or the rising ball of the moon at night. On their strong shoulders the clouds nuzzled, thunder rolled and lightning crashed. The wind chased the clouds around their noble girth, beasts played on the lap of the hills and, time and again, armies going to war marched across. Ajja became quite poetic when he talked about the hills. Every myth or story that originated in Angheri had something to do with them. When people went away from the village, even for a short time, they longed for a sight of the beloved peaks.

Once, after a long spell of crying because of a fight with Sujju, Nalli complained to Ajja that she would be better off without a family. Ajja disagreed. 'How can that be? Even the hills have a family,' he told her. 'See . . . the three hills with the rugged peaks, sturdy shoulders and hard knees—Doddabetta, Hulibetta and Kadubetta—and Donkubetta with the crooked flank, they're the men. That rounded hill, Jenubetta, is the grandmother. She likes to be warm and the sun pampers her for a while longer than the rest. And there's the dark sister, Chinnabetta, standing a little apart from the rest of the family.'

'Where's the mother?'

'Gilibetta . . . that's a sad story.'

Did the hills not grow bigger, Nalli asked. They had finished growing, Ajja said. 'Are the hills as old as you? Older than the moon?'

'I think so.'

'Older than . . . time?'

'No, not older than time.'

'Who's older, the ocean or time?'

'If you keep asking questions, I can't go on with the story.'

Then, tying his hair in a knot at the back of his neck, Ajja told her the story of Gilibetta, the Mother Hill. Tens of thousands of years ago, hills and mountains could fly. They travelled the world and saw many things. They watched great armies marching to battle, they witnessed cities spring up and civilizations perish. But with all their flying around, they cast huge shadows over the earth and denied many lands their share of sunlight. Crops died and the weather became cold and miserable. On being beseeched by the earth, the hills agreed to settle permanently in different parts of the world. With time, their wings shrank and disappeared. But some errant hills, like Gilibetta, spurred by the wanderlust in them, would not do it. They kept flying. The sun saw that he was wasting his light and warmth because of them and became furious. He blazed on the hills until their wings were burnt to ashes and they were forced to the ground wherever they happened to be. That was how Gilibetta was lost to the family.

How did Ajja know all this? Little frills formed around his eyes. 'I listened,' he said.

Nalli cried every time she thought of the poor mother hill somewhere far away. Ajja told her that she could hear the hills if she listened carefully. She did not believe of course that the hills could speak, but when filled with any doubt she instinctively turned to them. Invariably her gaze fell on Doddabetta, the most magnificent of the peaks. Sometimes the sun walked lightly on his shoulders, or a shining white cloud belted his waist, and she thought she heard a voice that was very much like Appa's, telling her what to do.

Appa was the headmaster of the school and they never forgot this, even at home. If he entered a room, Nalli, Budhi and even

Sujju and Vishnu stood, as if they were in the classroom. When they brought their school reports home, Ajja would reward each of them with four annas, but Appa only said 'Good'. And he did not rebuke Budhi for coming forty-second in class.

The villagers called him Maestru. He went to school on his cycle, while Vishnu, Sujju, Budhi and Nalli walked the two miles. He was a Kannada scholar but he could teach history, maths, geography or science with as much ease. If any teacher was on leave, he took the class himself.

The Maestru was admired and feared. At the morning assembly he stood with his hands rigid by his side, his sternness enhanced by the sun glinting off his spectacles. Once, a boy came to school wearing shoes and Appa sent him out of class. The boy's father, the youngest of Angheri Naganna Gowdru's brothers, kicked up a fuss. The matter was solved when Appa permitted the boy to wear shoes to school but not into the classroom.

For Nalli, it was not at all wonderful. If she was caught eating gooseberries, the teacher said, 'On the bench! The headmaster's daughter! What will everyone think?' Nalli was more ashamed of being her father's daughter than of anything she had done to deserve standing on the bench.

Appa was not always stern. Nalli had faint memories of hopping about with him in a comic dance while Amma sang *Kaggalappana kanive olage*, of Appa playfully tugging the red stone earrings in Amma's ears and calling her 'my film star' when they went in a bullock cart to Panchavalli for a wedding. As she grew older, Nalli took care not to shame Appa. She learnt many things from him—about space travel and world wars, Hitler and Mussolini, Madame Curie and the climbing of Mount Everest. Appa taught them without preaching that there was a line between good and evil. Sometimes it was clear and sometimes hazy. Greatness was there, far away, shining and real. You could hear it, touch it and smell it. School notebooks displayed Gandhi and Nehru, Patel and Bose on the cover. Without saying it, Appa taught the children to identify with the courage of these great men.

If Appa taught of the outside world, Ajja was the first with local news—whose cow had foaled or which farmer got the highest yield of ragi. Curiosity was his teacher. When the first borewell was being dug in Angheri, he walked two miles to the site every day for the five days it took to complete it; he watched and asked questions. That was the way he learned. Having been to school for only two years, he felt that too much education was a waste of time. When Vishnu went to college, he grumbled that it was money wasted. 'Life is my cauledge and there's nothing wrong with that,' he said. He was shocked when he heard that girls were taught the same subjects as boys. Where was the sense in it? He believed that girls did well to get married after school. And this he reminded Nalli as he combed her hair on the day of Sujju's marriage.

Ajja tried to divert Nalli's mind from the crazy idea of studying to be a doctor. He taught her to milk cows without hurting them, to tend sick calves, cut sugar cane and husk paddy. All of it she learnt, but when he tried to show her how to cook, she was not interested. She was too fond of food to have the patience to prepare it. But she liked being with Ajja in the kitchen. In the afternoons when it was too hot to work outside, he would be busy stirring pots, instructing Gaja to peel, grate, grind and cook. He was bossier in the kitchen than elsewhere and stamped about, grumbling, 'No one listens to me,' but everyone listened to him. He was a genius in the kitchen. Be it ordinary fare like kootu, palya and sambar, or a delicacy like kesari baath, hebbittoo or kajaya, his was the best.

Ajja did not know his age, only that he had been married four years when the King of England visited India. As the eldest of ten children, his life had been tough. He knew the value of money; he liked money and was inventive in the way he made it. He laboured in the garden and grew vast quantities of vegetables; he walked miles to collect dung, made a compost pit and nourished the plants as if they were children. Once a month, he went to Mysore by bus with his produce and returned late in the evening with ten, fifteen, twenty rupees. He kept the money not in the bank (how could you trust strangers with your money?) but at home in a metal box, the key to which hung from a string around his waist. Once in a while he would beckon Nalli to his room, bolt the door and ask her to help him count. The notes and coins were arranged in stacks and they smelt of Ajja's snuff. Money made his teeth sparkle, his skin shine and his voice soft and girlish. It made his brain work like a computer at a time when computers were not heard of. He counted, computed, hoarded his meagre earnings; yet when the bangle seller came he was as eager as the girls and bought at least a dozen bangles, the best ones for Ajji.

Some days, Nalli went to the santhe with Ajja. Amma gave him a long list and Appa added things like a nib or a bottle of ink. Ajja was in first-rate humour when he was in the market and bargained over everything. His favourite was the corner shop owned by Sompa and his brother Ganapa, where he bought ribbons for the girls and talcum powder for Ajji. At the beginning of each year, the shop gave away calendars to regular customers. They stocked two varieties: the older men got calendars with gods' pictures on them, the younger were offered a different one, with scantily clothed film stars or apsaras. Every year Ajja was given the god calendar and each time he asked for the other type. 'I'm taking it only to remind myself how immoral the world has become,' he would say as he folded it away under his arm. In his room, he would hang it on the wall that was out of sight of the gods. If there was interesting gossip to be heard at the santhe, he lowered his voice to a whisper that Nalli tried hard to hear. At times he would break into an uncontrollable giggle and even if she begged him to tell her what was so funny, he would not. There were also times when she saw him wipe his eyes after speaking to an old acquaintance. 'It's all Igguthappa's blessings that we have peace in our home,' he said. 'Not everyone is so lucky.' The last stop was always at the jasmine seller's. He bought two and a half lengths for Ajji, Amma and the girls. He cut the lengths and apportioned them himself and then pinned the flowers in Ajji's hair.

Ajja loved animals. While he haggled over money paid to him for his vegetables, he did not take money for treating animals. 'My nakshatra, my tavare, my gubbachi . . .' he crooned while treating a sore or splinting a broken leg. Except for Karia the cock, which was Budhi's, they did not own fowls; but feathered families came from the nearby homes and pecked blithely at the paddy which Ajja scattered for them, calling, 'Koli, ba, ba, ba, ba . . .' He let other people's dogs jump over him and leave paw marks on his shirt. Every night he visited the cowshed before he went to bed. 'Bollu, Chondu, Ammi!' he called. 'Be careful. Be watchful. Sleep well. May Ishwara give you a long life.' He never chased away animals and birds that came to the backyard. 'Let them enjoy their short lives,' he said.

Only when the mice made an infernal din in the attic, he hitched up his dhoti and darted up the stairs shouting, 'Less noise, now! This isn't your home!' But that was as far as Ajja would go; he could not actually hurt the mice. If Jai offered to hunt them out and kill them, Ajja chased him away. 'Murderer,' he said and whacked him on the head. When Jai downed a chembooka with his catapult, Ajja splinted the bird's injured leg and punished Jai by denying him the just-made hebbittoo. But then he laughed softly and said, 'He's a good shot, that rascal.'

Ajja had a special fondness for Jai. When Jai played his wicked tricks on him, he took them like a sport. Ever ready with stories in which he was the hero, Ajja often told them of his daring exploits. He was barely eleven when, walking through the dense jungle of Chinnakadu with his grandmother, he came face to face with a bear. 'Did I run? Did I scream for help? Not me. I shouted at grandmother to hide behind a huge wild athi tree and broke a stout branch off the tree and fought the bear.' He had tackled ghosts, robbers, cut-throats and all sorts of evil at various times in his life.

Once when there was a crisis in Shanku Master's family, Jai and Vijai stayed with them for a month. Jai said he wanted to see how brave Ajja really was. In the night he crept beneath Ajja's bed and lifted it off the ground. 'Bhoota banto!' said Ajja in a pathetic whisper, burrowing beneath his blanket. He prayed to Igguthappa to save him from the ghosts. In the morning, seeing Ajja miserable, Nalli told on Jai and he was roundly

scolded for his wickedness. Jai said he was not trying to prove
Ajja's cowardice or anything, just helping lift Ajja closer to
heaven. The family felt that Ajja was entitled to his heroism and
they left it at that. Nalli had thought Ajja would never speak to
Jai again. But they remained close. Only when she was much
older did Nalli understand that Ajja and Jai were very similar
men.

3

Jai was the older brother of Nalli's best friend, Vijai. Their
father, Shanku Master, was a mean-eyed genius and the only
teacher in school more feared than Appa. He taught maths.
Master's time-tested method of punishment was to twist the ear
until his victim howled. He did it with obvious enjoyment, rising
from his chair, hitching up his dhoti and advancing towards the
victim with eyes full of predatory passion. Many students had
known the anguish of a red, bruised ear and the shame which
stayed a long time afterwards.

Shanku Master's family was poor, but then everyone in the
village except Angheri Naganna Gowdru and Bhimasena Nayaka
was poor. It was just the level of poverty which differed. Shanku
Master was poorer than Appa but better off than Gowru's
parents. He had two hundred battis of paddy and some ragi, no
workers and no bullocks. Jai had to absent himself from school
frequently to help plough the land and transplant paddy. His
two older sisters worked in the post office. On Sundays, Nalli
used to hang about their house, waiting for Vijai and Jai. If
Shanku Master was in his chair near the front door, she would
enter from the back just to avoid him. Vijai would be busy
washing clothes or scrubbing vessels while her mother swept the
front yard and collected dung in a basket. Shanku Master's wife
was pale and sickly; even when she smiled, which was rare, it
looked like she was suffering. Nalli wondered if she was a saint
of some sort, who never grumbled or got angry or cried or
fought with anyone. Nalli would wait for a game of cowries or

bugri, moving aimlessly about the house, which was always dark. Because this was the only Brahmin house she had seen, Nalli thought that all Brahmins lived in dingy houses and ate dull food; that their men wore thin dhotis and were clever and austere and never ate or drank in other people's homes. Only Jai was not like a Brahmin. He would eat anywhere, and anything that was offered. But in his dank home he too looked gloomy and distant. Nalli loved her friends, but never wanted to change places with them.

It was different with Gowru—Gowramma—who was Chowraiah's daughter. Chowraiah's family lived in the poorest quarter in a house that huddled, along with eight or ten others, at the edge of the village. Their neighbours were mostly Voddas, Kumbaars and Chamaars, so poor that they cooked once in two days. Chowraiah was slightly better off than the rest. You could see the smoke rising out of his kitchen every day. Chowraiah was a kumbaar and he worked at his kiln making mud pots. Having no land, his family had to buy everything they ate. In spite of the hardships, Gowru came to school cleanly dressed, her hair slick with oil and tied with two yellow ribbons. Her notebooks, made of the unused pages from old books and stitched together with thread were the neatest in the class. Her lunch was rice and lime pickle or a cold lump of ragi mudde. As she ate, she told her friends about the puris she had eaten for breakfast and the mutton curry they would have for dinner. She offered to take the leftovers from other tiffin boxes for the cows, dogs and pigs at home which her friends knew they did not have. Gowru was a clever girl. No matter how hard Nalli tried she could never wrest the first rank from Vijai, or the second from Gowramma.

Like Jai, Gowru decided early what she wanted to do—she would be a nurse, a matron in a white uniform with a red belt and a starched cap. And unknown even to herself, Nalli too had been straining towards her future, pushing in one direction, guided by her father, sparked into *doing* something by her grandfather and nudged by the raw energy of Jai.

Jai was five years older than Vijai and short—only five foot two. He did not see it as a problem. He could climb the tallest tree, run up to the atta five stairs at a time and reach the top of a haystack quicker than anyone. He had the stomach of an elephant—he once downed a Horlicks bottle full of gulab jamuns in one go. Nalli and Budhi were so impressed they forgot to ask for their share. They were even more impressed when Jai called them to the back of the house one night and showed them the best in his vast storehouse of tricks. He lit a bidi and smoked it with the lighted end in his mouth. It looked as though the bones in his face had been set alight. Nalli tried and burned her tongue. All pranks but the most innocent could be traced to Jai. Appa referred to him as a 'rogue elephant', which described him rather well. When he was in his final year in school, Jai suffered a dreadful blow when Appa appointed him the school monitor.

Nalli's friendship with him was capricious and frequently erupted in fights. If Vijai could not make peace between them, they went to Ajja. His judgement swayed unjustly in Nalli's favour and Jai was man enough to accept. No matter how often this happened, Jai's rapport with Ajja remained special. Ajja was among the first to know when Jai won a scholarship to the medical college in Mysore. He celebrated by cooking hulianna and vaangibaath. Nalli was furious and hardly ate that evening.

When the family objected to her decision, Nalli would protest, 'If Jai can, why not me?' Ajja of course was never swayed by this. Even Amma continued to say that it was not a good idea. Appa, as usual, was silent.

To Nalli it seemed that only Budhi understood. He was the gentlest of the children, with unhurried, thoughtful eyes and a smile which went straight to one's heart. When he walked, his hips moved as if he nursed a defect in his body, but Budhi was strong as an ox. Nalli, the sickliest, brought infections and fevers home and one by one the others succumbed; Budhi fell ill only once, and that turned out to be a boon for Nalli.

As a newborn, the boy's saintly eyes had prompted his parents to name him Budhi, Intellect. He turned out to be a slow learner, absorbing knowledge as deliberately as the earth soaks in water. He sat all evening with his maths homework but could do just one or two of five sums. When he read a book or the newspaper, he started at the beginning and went through till the end. If he could not finish reading a story or a piece of news at one sitting, he read it again from the start.

Budhi's closest companions were Karia, the twelve-year-old rooster and Kapi, the cat. They were his. Any complaints about the high-stepping, imperious fowl or the roguish cat had to be addressed to him. And there was the pumpkin vine which sprang up from a seed he had planted behind the kitchen. Nourished with dung and water, the creeper climbed the wall and spread itself over the soot-stained tiles of the kitchen roof. It put forth three blazing yellow flowers each the size of a hand. One survived to fruit. Budhi covered it with a piece of gunny to keep away lawless squirrels. In a couple of weeks the pumpkin swelled into a beauty of enormous size. Amma said it would ripen in time for Ugadi.

'You're not talking of *my* pumpkin, are you?' asked Budhi. Amma assured him that she was only suggesting.

'Your pumpkin is being fattened for sale. Ajja plans to sell it at the santhe . . .' Vishnu teased him.

That Sunday Budhi climbed on the roof and sat on the pumpkin and refused to come down until Ajja promised not to touch it. The pumpkin thrived; there was an intense debate on its future. The family was not so wealthy that it could ignore such an asset to placate Budhi's whim. When Satyanarayana Puja was to be performed in Bhimasena Nayaka's house and they were looking for a prize pumpkin, the painful decision was made, Budhi was spoken to and the pumpkin hauled away in a cart. He bore the loss in silence but refused to eat pumpkin ever again.

The evening of Sujju's wedding, after Ajja punished Nalli while combing her hair, she sat on the steps, moping. Her scalp still hurt and she was miserable. Budhi came and sat by her side. 'Akka, you won't give me injections, no, when you become a doctor?'

'You think I'll be a good doctor?'

'Yes, akka.'

Nalli promised that she would never inflict injections on him. Then she went in search of Jai.

She found Jai at the well behind their house with his trousers rolled up his calves, washing his feet. Stooping, she held out her cupped hands and looked slyly at him. He poured from the pitcher, and she drank. Of late he had become grown-up and aloof, preferring the company of elders. But that day he seemed to know that she wanted to talk. Seeing him smile, she knew he would listen. They sat on the grassy slope near the well; Jai leant forward and looked sideways at her.

'I'm going to be a doctor,' she said.

'I heard.'

'They're all against it.'

'I know.' He was looking down at his feet which were wet from washing. '*I* can't see why you want to. All for a degree that'll be an ornament around your neck.'

Nalli wondered if he was joking. 'When you come back here and start your hospital, I'll help,' she said.

'What a crazy idea. You'll soon be someone's wife.'

If you are angry, the best thing is to get up and walk away—so Ajja had advised Nalli although he did not practise it. She got up and left but not before darting her tongue at Jai. 'How can you be a doctor when you're so stupid?' she said, and hitching up her langa, ran. Jai had a temper too.

After the initial objections, the family left Nalli alone, confident that she would change her mind. She nursed her dream through the high-school years. She thought about it while listening to the owl on the jackfruit tree, while peering into the black depths of the well and while trying to spin a bugri on her palm like Jai. She gave up admiring herself in the mirror and forgot trivial fantasies.

Her only contact with the medical world besides Jai was a fat book, *The Home Doctor*. It had been left behind by a relative, a clever young man studying law in Bangalore. For some strange reason he had given up halfway and come to stay with them for a while. He sat all day with his back stooped and bony elbows protruding awkwardly. He smoked constantly and looked as if the world was just about to end. No matter how interesting the conversation, he had nothing to say. The family had given up hope of his ever leaving; then one day he asked Appa for a hundred rupees. 'Going to get a job in Bangalore,' he said. 'I'll return the money in a few weeks.' Appa gave the money without even asking what the job was. It was the last they saw of the young man. He left behind a thermos flask and *The Home Doctor*. Whenever Amma asked about it, Appa told her what the young man left behind was worth more than a hundred rupees. Turning the pages of the book, Nalli hoped it would help her when the time came.

Jai, of course, had been a major influence; but Nalli could trace the beginning of her ambition to the intestinal gurglings of Appa's friend Sompa. He was tall and stooped, with wide swinging shoulders and red eyes, and was a frequent visitor in the house. Nalli used to sit on his lap and listen to the ting-ting noises in his belly, wondering at the secrets of the body which produced the sounds. The mystery of those sounds—those tinkles dying away like bells, the drumbeats, the dancing feet of apsaras, the claps, sneezes, hisses and thuds—filled her with a curiosity about the body. Sometimes she even thought she heard words.

There was also the proximity of illness. Ajji's, her own. And there was the doctor who visited her when she was ill. Known to everyone as the Mysore Doctor he was a learned, nose-in-the-air type who belonged to another world, one of knowledge. Nalli did not know if he was paid for his visits in money or in oranges. He was certainly the most important person to come home; the house was readied for his visit. Nalli's bed was neatly made, her face scrubbed and hair plaited, and a pan of boiled water, a piece of soap and a clean towel were kept apart in the porch. The doctor came and prodded her belly with his thick fingers; he uncoiled his stethoscope and listened to her chest, looking out of the window as he listened. He told her to 'breathe in, breathe out, hold your breath'. He knew all the secrets of her insides, and Nalli wanted to be like him.

Four years after Nalli had declared her ambition to them, the family was still not in favour of sending her to medical college. Then came Budhi's one-and-only illness which changed all that.

Nalli had been ill with fever for a week and it turned out to be jaundice. With rest and a light diet the jaundice cleared and she began to recover. Just then, Budhi fell ill and within days the yellowness deepened. He could not keep any food down. Appa brought the Mysore Doctor. He prescribed pills and a bottle of glucose by drip every day. For Budhi, who was in mortal terror of needles, it was terrible. Even when the drip was over for the day, he would cry in anticipation of the next ordeal. The fever and the vomiting worsened. For three days the doctor came, peered into Budhi's still-yellow eyes, listened to his chest. On the third day Appa asked the doctor why Budhi had not improved.

'I cannot save every patient,' the doctor said.

He was being paid for his travel up and down and the treatment was turning out to be expensive. Appa said politely that he would like to consult the village Vaidyar about a remedy. He had brought the Vaidyar home in the hope that the two experts could discuss the case and decide what was best for the boy. The doctor started to put away the stethoscope in his bag. 'Try your hocus-pocus if you must,' he said, eyeing the dhoti-clad, bare-chested Vaidyar. 'It's none of my business.' He snapped his bag shut and left.

The Vaidyar treated Budhi with a kashayam which he made himself. Two weeks later Budhi was up and about, eating normal food. 'He will be strong enough to go to school next week,' the Vaidyar said. He was in the porch with Appa and Ajja. Amma served coffee. 'Our village needs doctors,' the Vaidyar added. 'But the right kind, who aren't afraid. Of what use is a doctor who fears the skill of others?'

Appa looked steadily at Nalli. His eyes were thinking.

4

'I've decided.'

Nalli was ecstatic to hear Vijai say it. They were sitting beneath the parijata tree, stringing kanakambara flowers. While she waited for Appa to say something about her going to college, Vijai too had made up her mind to be a doctor. Nothing could be better than that. Vijai was Nalli's friend in a grown-up sort of way. There was no giggling and holding hands and whispering behind cupped palms for them. Vijai with her square jaw, serious eyes and plaits swinging high from behind her ears, always came first in class. She was the best sprinter in school, after Sujju. It was thrilling to watch her win races, running with her resolute face thrust forward, her long skirt flapping at her calves. Nalli felt her own decision strengthened by Vijai's. They would be in the hostel together, sit in the same row in class and come home for holidays. Everything would be perfect.

'What does Jai think about it?' she asked.

Vijai grimaced. 'He knows it's the only way I can get away from home.'

'You want to get away from home?'

Nalli knew that theirs was not a happy home, and not just because the rooms were small and dark. Shanku Master beat his wife. He had done it for years, always behind the locked door of their room. When he came out, he would be smiling or chanting a sloka. The beating seemed to put him in a good mood. 'I don't like your father,' Nalli had told Jai once and he laughed, as if he knew it already. It was the day after Shanku Master punished him for some mischief in class by twisting his ear. He wrung hard but Jai would not let out a sound. Infuriated, his father hit him on the side of his head with such force that he sent Jai reeling against the wall.

Vijai's eyes were dry but her voice was thick with tears when she told Nalli.

'Why did Jai not stop him? He may be short, but he's strong.'

'Unless our mother protests what can Jai do? She doesn't say a word. It is as if she doesn't care.'

Jai had quarrelled with his father about it and for some time the beating stopped, but it started again once Jai went to college. The two older sisters were terrified of their father. Shanku Master did not want them to marry. He could not bear the humiliation of looking for a match. 'Will they earn the dowry money?' he asked. 'By the time they do, they will be crones.' A few years earlier, their eldest sister had been bold enough to start a friendship with a colleague at the post office. 'Marry him and you will not step into this house,' Shanku Master warned her. She did not have the courage to do it.

'I'll ask father when Jai comes home,' said Vijai. 'I won't end up like my sisters. I'll leave the house somehow.'

Nalli was certain that in spite of his cruel ways Shanku Master would be pleased to send Vijai to college. After all, she was no less brilliant than Jai.

⊷

It was a month since the girls had finished school. They were confident but also nervous. Neither of them knew how to go about applying to medical college. *The Home Doctor* was their Gita. Every evening, once she finished work at home, Vijai went to Nalli's house and they sat on the porch with the heavy book between them. They read of enemas and sitz baths, fomentations and poultices. Images floated before them. They smelt sickness and cure in the pages of the book. Tincture iodine, carminative mixture, permanganate, plaster of belladonna and turpentine. The words were so grand and redolent of curious smells. The mustiness of the pages did not matter, nor the frangible leg and wings of a dead cockroach glued to the flyleaf of the book. The girls preserved the legs as though they were part of the sacred knowledge. They read page after page but coyly skipped the reproductive system with subheads like PUBERTY, PERIODS and SEX. Later, each of them would read it furtively and feel confused.

Will we both go? Or will it be one? If one, which one? The thoughts nagged Nalli as she prepared herself to ask Appa.

Many times she peeped in through the window of his office, the small room where he worked when at home. He was always preoccupied with reading or writing. Pausing in the midst of work, he would lean back in the chair and stare at the wall before him, nodding to himself. He watched Nalli slipping past the window, sometimes lurking around outside it for a while, but said nothing.

One day Gowramma's father, Chowraiah, was seen waiting outside Maestru's office. They talked, and when they came out of the office Appa had an arm around Chowraiah's shoulders. A few weeks later when Gowru got admission for nurse's training at the nursing school in Mysore, she told Nalli, 'Maestru helped me.' Nalli asked Amma if Appa would do it for her too. He only helped those who needed it, Amma said.

When Jai came home on leave he kept away from the girls; he was in no way interested in his sister or Nalli studying medicine. We don't need him, the girls said, excluding Jai from their world of anticipation.

One afternoon he found them on the porch, reading the *Home Doctor*. It was open on a page titled THE HEART AND ITS FUNCTIONS. He stood behind them and read a few lines, then stepped back, smiling.

'So you think you know everything about the heart?'

'Of course,' Nalli shot back. 'The heart pumps blood to every part of the body. It carries oxygen and . . .'

'If you know so much about the heart, tell me, what are the chordae tendinae? Purkinje fibres? Sino-atrial node? Atrio-ventricular node? You'll have to read chapters and chapters before you know anything about the heart. *Home Doctor*!' He glared at the girls. 'Waste of money. Stupid girls going to medical college . . .'

With the girls suitably subdued, he strode away. Vijai watched him go, tears pricking her eyes. She knew she could not depend on him for any help.

In the end she picked up courage to ask her father. That day Nalli had gone to their house and when she saw her friend's face through the fat bars of the window, she knew. Jai was at home.

Seeing Nalli, he came out to meet her. 'Father refused,' he said. 'It would not have been possible for her anyway.' The look in his eyes said it would be better for Nalli too to give up the idea. She walked away quickly before he said it.

It was late afternoon. After a short burst of rain, the sun glinted on the just-washed leaves of the athi tree behind the house. Nalli stood by the tree, pressing her fingers on the rough bark till they hurt. Now she was alone, utterly alone.

Next evening, the two of them sat on the porch. Vijai shook a set of cowries in her fist and scattered them on the floor. She told Nalli she would learn tailoring at Chadkan's shop. Nalli was angry with her for not having tried hard enough to convince her father.

'If your father says no, you won't be able to go,' Vijai said.

'Appa won't say no. If he does, I'll explain to him and he'll understand.'

'If my father was your father, you would not be able to explain,' Vijai threw the words at her as if it were a possibility. Nalli shuddered at the thought of Shanku Master as her father. 'It will be a waste of time going to medical college,' Vijai said, with an angry thrust of her chin. 'You'll end up getting married, anyway. And you're snatching a seat from some boy who needs it more than you.'

'That's what Jai's been telling you,' said Nalli. 'Who said anything about getting married? I'll work.'

Vijai gathered the cowries in her palm and scattered them; gathered and scattered them.

Lonely in her predicament, Nalli sat in her favourite corner by the window in Ajja's room. Here she had a windowful of sky to herself. She could look beyond the jackfruit and the guava tree, beyond the paddy fields and mustard, at the hills. It was late evening and the hills were a deep blue. Doddabetta wore a lacy collar of mist around it. Only Jenubetta, the stout, rounded peak which stood apart from the taller peaks, was tinted a green-gold by the sun's last rays. In a short while Amma would call her to light the lamps.

She needed time to think. She slipped out and went to the

spot behind the well where the land dipped steeply to a rocky ledge overlooking the fields of paddy. The greenness stretching into the distance was fringed by coconut and areca palms. It was her hiding place. She dug her toes into the soft ground and looked across at the peaks of Angheri which were now very dark. There was no point praying. God could not do much. Only Appa . . .

Jumping up, she went home. Her heart raced as she heard the creak of the bicycle and then saw Appa come in through the gate. He propped the cycle against the wall and picked up the chombu of water. Never before, not even during the worst moments in school, had she felt so nervous, so afraid of her father. 'Appa,' she stammered. 'The application forms . . .'

He was pouring water from the chombu on his feet, and did not answer. She waited till he had washed his feet and hands and face and wiped them with a towel. Before she could speak again, he said, 'Magu, I want to talk to you.' It was a long time since he had called her Magu. Little One. When she was young, if she fell and bruised herself or had a fever, he would take her on his lap and call her Magu. Now he said it gravely but she sensed an urgency, an excitement in his voice. It was going to be all right. After all the fears she had had about the family opposing her, Appa was going to make it all right!

He told her to wait in the porch, went in and spoke to Amma. Beyond the areca palms, the light had softened. Shadows stretched over the front yard. The sky was lit with magic. Russet and orange, pink and gold, and then darkness. Gaja moved inside the house with the lamps. Appa came and sat next to her, and Amma stood leaning against the door.

'Magu,' he said. 'Six years of study and then a lifetime of hard work. You aren't strong.'

I can do it, she said. They sat for a long while, talking. Appa, one tired foot tucked under him, rubbed his knee. Amma brought two steel tumblers of coffee. This was the first time Nalli was being served coffee in the porch like an adult. Appa said the rains had been dismal for two years and they were struggling. Medical college meant a lot of money. There was this offer, a respectable family from Shimoga, brilliant boy. Just what they had in mind for her.

But she wanted to be a doctor, had always wanted it.

A good offer like this one could not be ignored. And, if she were to become a doctor, how would they find her a husband? Shimoga was a big town. She could go to college, do Kannada literature. She was good in Kannada, she had won a prize. She could be a lecturer, even a professor.

Angry words struggled on her tongue. She saw the look in Appa's eyes, pleading with her to understand. Her strong, admired, always-right Appa begging her to agree. Unknown to her, they had been looking for a match. She had been made to sit for a studio photograph, decked in a Mysore silk with Sujju's jhumkas dangling from her ears. The photo must have made its rounds. Horoscopes, job potential, background, everything must have been discussed behind her back. And now a suitable match, all ready, and only she to be told.

Nalli remembered Sujju's wedding. How glorious her sister had looked in the beautiful mauve sari that belonged to Amma's grandmother. Now she could wear it for her own wedding. What could she do but accept? It was the right thing to do, to stand by the family. She felt virtuous doing it. But something rebelled inside her. It said, What about *that* thing which you wanted? What about *that*?

They would travel to Shimoga so the boy's family could see her. She was to wear the pink silk sari with silver dots that Ajja had bought in Dharmasthala when he went on a pilgrimage. He had also had a gold chain with a pendant and two gold bangles made for Nalli. He had known, he said, that she would wear them soon. Ajja was particular about jewels. He would sit on the edge of Ajji's bed and hold them out for her to see. 'Half a sovereign . . . one sovereign . . .' Nalli liked wearing the chain and bangles but they did not give her as much pleasure as something so expensive should have done.

Two days later they travelled by the night bus to Shimoga. Amma showed Nalli the photograph. He was fair, with a straight nose, a slim moustache and a strong chin. The glare of the studio lights had set his lips into a tight smile but he was good-looking. With a woman's mind, Nalli thought of him as her probable.

Raghu.

In the morning they booked two rooms at a lodge near the town and went to meet the family at eleven. Studying herself in the mirror, Nalli was pleased.

It was a newly built house with a concrete roof, big rooms and windows with curtains. The floor was polished with red oxide, the doors painted cream. The men talked about the heat in Shimoga and the train accident the previous week; Amma and Sujju spoke to his mother. Nalli steamed graciously in her silk sari and ornaments. They were served Mysore paak, mixture, rava kesari and coffee. She was aware of being scrutinized, but managed to steal a glance herself and caught his eye. He was *very* handsome.

'Why don't you two talk for a while?' his father said.

A cosy room with a sofa, a small round table and chairs. Nalli headed for a chair and Raghu said, 'Here,' pointing to the sofa. She looked into his laughing eyes and her nervousness vanished. He talked fast, as if he did not have to think about what he was saying. Once it was all fixed, could he visit her? They could go to see a film. Did she like films? Books? As she answered him she thought she had never before sat so close to a boy she barely knew; their arms were touching. His voice was melting her heart. When they got up to join the others, she saw the two hollows made by their sitting so close to each other on the sofa. Instinctively she bent down to smooth the impressions they had left and he laughed, holding her hand for a second.

She returned to the lodge with her family. Everyone was happy. Raghu had no objection to her studying after marriage. Sujju and Amma talked about the wedding being fixed soon after the monsoon. Nalli sat by herself, remembering every word, every gesture that had passed between them. Raghu and Nalinakshi. Husband and wife. He was trying to go to the US, he had said. That night she lay in bed, thinking womanly thoughts, about marriage and America, and jeans and dark glasses and lipstick.

Next morning Appa went to their house to finish the negotiations. He returned quickly. 'If we hurry, we can catch the bus at ten-thirty,' he said. He did not look at Nalli. In the bus, Nalli pretended to sleep and spared the family the pain of trying to console her. Amma said something about planning it better next time. 'No more interviews,' Nalli said, looking not at Amma but at her father. She would not see her family abased again.

Back home, she tried to laugh about the failed interview, but inside she was not laughing. Amma said it had nothing to do with her appearance but Nalli knew. If it was something other than that, why did *he* not tell her? He had taken her up, up, up to the skies for the split second of an evening and then flung her down. The last thing she did when they were alone in the room was to bend down and straighten the folds on the sofa.

A week went by before Appa applied for two days' leave and took the early morning bus to Madras. He returned late on the second day with the application forms and filled them in his lamp-lit office room. 'The best university in the south,' he said to Nalli. 'Many girls are studying there. Let's see if you can get a seat.' He took a great deal of care with the forms, dipping his pen in ink and testing it on the blotting paper before he wrote. He put the carefully filled-out form in a brown envelope and sent it the next day by registered post.

From then on Nalli's future was talked about often. The family sportingly accepted that she would be studying in Madras. But first she had to get admission. Nalli's mood swung between euphoria and dread. She had no idea how to prepare herself. Jai she would not ask, on principle, because of the way he had spoken that first time. But when he came home a few weeks later, he told her, 'You have the marks. All you need is luck.'

Chikkamma—Fat Aunty—who lived in Hunsur, came to Angheri for two days. She said the family should feel proud of Nalli. 'She will serve the poor. She is dedicated,' Aunty declared, squashing Nalli in an embrace. The family, not having such a high opinion of Nalli's intentions, were wise enough to refrain from praise. Fat Aunty told Nalli that her father had enough 'influence' to get her a seat in Madras. He knew senior doctors who had studied with him in Mysore. 'Just a word from him will be enough,' she said. Nalli spoke to Appa. 'I got the application forms and even filled them for you,' he said. 'That's all you can expect from me. We will see now if you have the merit.'

Two months into her sixteenth year, Nalli received a brown-paper envelope containing a typed letter of admission. She was going to medical college!

5

The future brimmed with promise, and even Vishnu's barbs failed to rile Nalli. The rice was fragrant, the curds thick as cream, the oranges full of juice and the water sweet and cool in her throat. Everything was faultless.

Even Ajja had accepted what was now inevitable. When Nalli's admission was confirmed, he took her to Ajji.

'Nalli is going to cauledge to be a doctor,' Ajja said. 'In a few years she will have new medicines to make you fit.'

'I'll be gone before that,' Ajji said smugly.

Protests were voiced, with assurances that Ajji would live for a long time. Ajja coaxed her to her feet. 'Give your blessings, thanga.' She stood up for Nalli to touch her feet and then got back into bed.

Nalli dispensed with praying. In the evenings, after her bath, she stood dutifully at the tulasi katte with the family. She had never had the stillness of mind for prayer and her thoughts wandered. The hierarchy of gods and their varied personalities confused her—she invoked them hastily, or clubbed them together. They existed merely to grant her favours: God, let me come first in class. God, let there be avarekai palya for lunch. Sometimes she bargained: Make Ajja bring me pink ribbon and I will not fight with Vishnu. If she got the ribbon, the promise faded away. When she was desperate to get into medical college, she had prayed earnestly for months. Now she would stop disturbing the gods.

There was only one prayer which came without effort. Looking across at the hills from the guava tree or helping Gaja with the rotis and struggling to get them perfectly round, it would ring suddenly in her mind. 'Give me *that* thing, God. Only *that* thing and I won't ask for anything else. Please, God, give me *that* thing . . .' She did not know what it was she asked for, did not dare approach it with words. But in the core of her being, somewhere, she knew.

⌐

Five years earlier, it had been big news when Jai, the favourite son of Angheri, declared that he would be a doctor. No such enthusiasm greeted Nalli's decision. She was a girl. Moreover, one had to be exceptionally clever to get a seat. Or someone had to use influence. Jai got in because he was clever but he would have been applauded even if it was influence which got him there.

Angheri had three doctors: Dr Ravikumar, who had worked as a compounder in Mysore, Dr Janardhana, LMP (Passed), and the Vaidyar. Each claimed his group of faithful followers.

Dr Janardhana was popular because he would see patients at any time of the day or night. He won them over by playing on their guilt. 'You're suffering now because you ate too many mangoes in childhood.' When the unlucky patient swore he would never eat another mango, the doctor said, 'It's too late now, but I'll try and save you.' Patients were blamed for their dietary indiscretions, for sleeping with the window open, for having too many children or too few.

Dr Ravikumar had his clinic in the busy market area. He attracted customers by claiming that an English doctor had trained him. Everything he prescribed came with the tag 'English Medicine'. Three stethoscopes hung from the wall in his clinic with different coloured tubes and labelled Re 1, Rs 2 and Rs 3. The patient could choose the instrument with which he wished to be examined. His rainbow-hued penicillin injections also came with price tags. Naturally, there was rivalry between the two doctors. Ajja said the only way to get the best out of either doctor was to praise the talents of his opponent.

The Vaidyar was a class apart. He was at least as old as Ajja, with young shoulders and a few strands of silver hair on his head. His ears were long, with fleshy ear lobes. He drew water from the well, carried buckets, hewed wood and, in the evenings, prepared his pastes and kashayams. The Vaidyar asked many questions before treating a patient. He wisely desisted from being too harsh about the diet, knowing that patients did not follow such advice. Once, an excessively fat man went to him with multiple problems resulting from his obesity. He said he was willing to take medicines but could not cut down on his eating. 'I have a treatment which can cure you but I cannot prescribe it,' the Vaidyar told him. 'It has to be taken for six months.' 'I'll take it for six months,' the man promised. The Vaidyar shook his head. 'I might as well tell you. You'll be dead before that, in three, if not two months. It is certain.' The man went away, shaken. Preoccupied with the thought of his impending demise, he was too miserable to eat. In three months he had lost most of the excess weight and his problems vanished without any treatment. The Vaidyar believed that if we did not poison ourselves from within and without we could live to be a hundred and seventy, or even a hundred and eighty.

He treated Nalli when she fell ill, which was often. If the fever refused to go away, the Vaidyar advised that she should be taken to Mysore. He was of that rare breed, wise enough to acknowledge failure. Once, when he declared Nalli's fever to be beyond his reckoning, Ajja took her by bus. All morning they waited to see the doctor at the government hospital. It was hot and the waiting area brimmed with people. Nalli's fever soared. At one o'clock, when the crowd melted and they hoped their turn had come, the doctor went for his lunch. He returned at three and began to see patients but Nalli's name was not called. When Ajja objected, the ward boy said with a sly smile that 'something' had to be given to the doctor if he was to see her before five.

Carrying Nalli on his hip, Ajja walked into the examination room. 'Dactre!' he said, loud enough for all to hear. 'Duddu beka? You want money? From an old man and his sick grandchild, when you're paid to treat her? Here, take what I have, our bus money, and I'll walk the twenty miles to Angheri with this sick child. If anything happens to her, I'll come back with all the young men in our village!' He began to fumble with the pouch fashioned from his dhoti at the waist. The doctor saw Nalli at once and gave them all the medicines free of charge.

Many sick people journeyed to Mysore by bullock cart, tractor or bicycle. Once there, it was hard to pay for the treatment. So Jai getting into medical college was wonderful news.

A few days before he had set out, the important men of the village met in the open space between Raghavendra Stores and the Bank where such gatherings took place. Bhimasena Nayaka, Naganna Gowdru, the Maestru and Shanku Master were all there. Naturally, people came to listen.

Nayaka spoke. 'Our Jayanth has brought honour to the village by deciding to be a doctor. He will come back to Angheri and start a hospital. We must help him with the land, the building and all those important things . . .' He waved his hands vaguely to indicate the important things. The words X-ray, blood testing and injections were prompted from the crowd. 'Yes, yes. All those things which help to keep us healthy. We must help Jayanth in whatever way we can.'

Naganna Gowdru cleared his throat, ready to make his importance felt. 'Shanku Master's son is the jewel of Angheri. Let him choose the land for the hospital. I will pay for it and help start this most noble cause.'

Jai stood next to his father, solemn and modest. The Maestru, who was instrumental in everything that Jai had learnt, said nothing; but he was as pleased as everyone else.

The news of Nalli's going to medical college, however, only puzzled the village. The Maestru was letting his daughter study in a college with boys? That meant problems, surely. It would not be easy to find her a husband afterwards. And where was the money? The Maestru had married off his elder daughter only four years ago and there were Vishnu's college expenses to be met.

Nalli knew that Appa would have wrestled with his doubts before giving in. The doubts of other people did not matter too much.

The day before he left, Jai had come to their house sporting white trousers, a new black belt and black chappals. The way everyone talked it seemed the only thing that mattered was Jai's future. College fees, books, hostel food. Nalli was disgusted and refused to sit with him on the bench. He hardly noticed, so busy was he being serious, leaning forward, talking to Appa. She looked at him slyly and saw him glance sideways, past her into the distance. He furrowed his brow like an adult. For a moment his eyes went very still, and they were filled with dread. Jai, with his laughing, restless eyes—what was he afraid of? Nalli got up and walked away. Ajja noticed and asked her later why she was being rude.

Where was the justice in it? But no one understood.

Early in the morning she went to her hideout behind the well to be alone. Who was she going to spin the bugri with, who would join her in playing pranks on Ajja? Becoming a doctor was all very well for Jai but it was going to take five and a half years. She dug her feet into the soft soil and pulled the grass viciously with her toes. She decided there and then that when Jai asked her to marry him she would refuse.

There was a thud as he jumped down from the ledge and landed by her side. Nalli sat with her face cupped in her hands. What did he want her to say, what did he think she would do?

'You're angry with me? My bus leaves in an hour . . . I'll be coming home in six months.'

Six months. What was she going to do for six months? 'Go away,' she said.

He climbed back on to the ledge and walked away. That was not what she wanted. Then she heard something patter and fall on the ground: Marbles, dozens of them, bounced and rolled around her. She jumped up and scrambled for them in the dirt. There were so many marbles, she could not carry them in her hands. She heaped them together and ran home to bring Budhi. Together they took home Jai's going-away gift, and some of her sadness vanished.

Amma accepted Nalli's going with pragmatic composure. She was a plain woman with blunt, unremarkable features, flat hips and a capacity for work. Ajja was very fond of his daughter-in-law and consulted her on all matters. Ajji and sometimes Appa were jealous.

Amma was artless in her honesty. Nalli despaired when she went to the shops with her. She would ask for a certain colour of cloth at Chadkan's shop and, when he showed it and declared it cost three rupees a yard, say, 'Very kind of you to sell it so cheap. I thought it would cost at least four rupees.' The next time, Chadkan would oblige with a higher price. 'Amma, don't say that you thought it would cost more,' Nalli would say. Amma would agree, only to forget the next time. Nalli once heard Appa say, 'Kami is the only person I know who is so completely honest.' It was true, though Nalli did not really appreciate her mother until much later.

Besides her four half-saris, Amma gave Nalli three saris to take with her: a green handloom, a blue cotton printed with pink flowers and the orange silk that had belonged to Amma's mother. Amma sat at the sewing machine with bits of coloured cloth trailing all over the floor. She sewed relentlessly until the sheets, pillowcases, petticoats and blouses were ready. It was like having a tailor in the house. Nalli grumbled about the underwear made of coarse cotton. She begged Amma to make them with frills and elastic the way Sujju did for herself, but Amma did not know how.

Appa's tin trunk was brought down from the attic, cleaned and painted a bright cream with Nalli's name on the right-hand corner in green. Nalli arranged her clothes in the box and put in dried neem leaves to keep insects away. Several times a day she rearranged her things with needless care. Lying in bed at night she went over them in her mind: the petticoats and sheets were at the bottom, then the towels, the saris and blouses. She would be carrying with her a little home to live elsewhere, not for one night or two but for five and a half years. She breathed the smell of the newly painted trunk, the smell of her future, and felt dizzy.

As the day of leaving neared she felt an uneasiness somewhere between her chest and solar plexus. She wandered aimlessly, checked the clothes in her trunk a dozen times and was rude to Ajji who plagued her with questions. She sat still, doing nothing, while her thoughts leapt about in chaos. She stood beneath the jackfruit tree and let water drip from the leaves on to her lashes; she squinted at the sky watching the droplets form a rainbow. She peered into the smooth blackness of the well and whispered her thoughts to her mirrored self. *Nalli* . . .? Her thoughts echoed back from the well's clear depths. Her mind was tangled in excitement and indescribable fears. She had been selfish, and a little brave. This yearning to do something intensely and well. To work, work, work with the high purpose of being a doctor. It was hers, this yearning.

Advice was freely given, but she only half listened. 'Drink boiled water.' 'Don't talk to the boys.' 'Study early morning, not in the night.' She would not get enough to eat in the hostel, Ajja said. She must buy milk every day and set fresh curds in her room. She could live without milk or curds! She could live without anything!

Vishnu came home from college for a few days. He was still against her going. He found her alone near the tulasi katte and blocked the way. 'I know why you're going to medical college,' he jeered. 'So you can be a tail to that Kulla. The shorty.'

Sompa sat in the porch with his hands on his knees and looked closely at her with his coal-red eyes. 'So . . . college . . .?'

She nodded. She was used to his strange, staggered speech. Two or three words in a sentence.

'Umm . . . how long . . .?'

'Five and a half years.'

'Mathe?' he asked. 'Then? You'll be coming here?'

'Yes.'

Appa did not say anything.

One evening, as she knelt beside her box, rearranging her clothes, Nalli was aware of him at the door. She stood up, abashed. He had not chided her, not even when she went to the shops half a dozen times just to buy coconut oil, soap and tooth powder.

'This is for you,' he said, handing her a diary.

It was bright red, with a hard shiny binding and a different page for every day of the year. Beach Aunty's husband had given it to him. On the first page Nalli wrote, 'Nalinakshi. Medical Student. First Year' and, feeling important, put it away on top of her clothes. That evening she took the diary out again and wrote what she felt. She could manage only three sentences. Writing helped to still her mind for a while, until she slept. It would be some time before she wrote in the diary again.

Two days, and she would be gone. How slowly they dragged. Jai came from Mysore late on Saturday evening, lugging a bag. 'Books,' he said, and withdrew four heavy tomes bound in green rexine: Gray's *Anatomy*, Samson and Wright's *Applied Physiology*, *Biochemistry* by Kliner and Orten, and Grant's *Atlas*. The books did not come cheap and Nalli was grateful. It meant that Jai was no longer against her going. She spent all of the next day putting together the books inside a cane basket, refusing to let even Budhi touch them. She lifted Gray's and looked inside. Every detail of every part of the body crammed into hundreds of pages in small, small print. On the flyleaf was Jai's name, in his tapered, elegant hand.

Jai's writing was attractive, without the monotony or severity of ordinary neatness. The jet black ink lent brightness to the page, the same way his eyes lit up his face, his presence lit up a room. Holding his books in her hands, smelling the print, she was happy. Each time she opened one of his books she would remember that Jai too had turned the same pages. It was a link she did not wish to snap. But she was still angry with him for all sorts of reasons.

She would never forget the day Jai had told them that he would be a doctor.

He was ten and had been knocked unconscious in an accident of which no one knew the details. Head injury. Shanku Master had rushed out of the house carrying the senseless boy in his arms and shouted for help. Jai was operated on at the government hospital in Mysore. He stayed there three months and had three operations.

When Jai was back in Angheri, Nalli overheard him talking to Sujju and some of his friends in a corner of the school playground near the athi tree. She was there learning to spin a bugri and listened to every word. In the first operation the surgeons had opened Jai's skull (on the left side of his head behind the temple) and removed a large blood clot pressing on his brain. Two weeks later he became feverish and pus began to pour out of the wound. A fragment of bone the size of a folded handkerchief was found eaten away by infection and had to be taken out. In the third operation a piece of metal was inserted to replace the dead bone. The doctor told Shanku Master that the left lobe of the brain controlled the right side of the body. That explained Jai's peculiar stiff gait and his way of moving the right arm and leg in a wide arc when he walked. But for this, he was his robust self.

Jai described his hospital experience in juicy detail. 'The man in the bed next to me, he had a stomach full of water. He looked just like a drum. His face was small and his legs thinner than . . . Sujju's arms. I thought he would rise like a balloon and float away.'

'Did he?'

'He would have if the doctor hadn't come and stuck a needle, as long as *this* and as thick as *this* into his stomach. It was only kanji water and it poured out, all over the doctor, the nurse and the ward boy. The nurse connected a tube to the needle and they got two buckets of kanji out of him. They served it to the patients for breakfast next day and I made sure not to drink any kanji for some time. The man wept when he found that his big stomach had disappeared, gone. He looked at the buckets next to him and sobbed for hours. Died off the same night.'

'Ooooh . . .'

'Another man had worms coming out of his nose. They poured turpentine into his nose. It killed the worms and the patient.'

'You'll make me vomit,' Sujju said, holding her throat. 'Tell us something nice.'

'Let's see . . . There was a peon who doled out "special" tablets in exchange for bidis. And one very pretty nurse. She sat on the table in the duty room and let a ward boy paint her fingernails and another her toenails.'

'You're bluffing,' said Sujju.

'I'm not. The doctors fought about who would take her to the canteen for coffee.'

Sujju did not want to hear any more about the pretty nurse. 'I want to feel that plate in your head,' she said.

Jai let her. 'Me!' 'Me!' 'Me!' pleaded the others. They had their turn. Nalli sneaked up from behind and put her hand on Jai's thick hair. Her hand sank into his hair and touched the plate. It was the size of her palm, slightly concave and fixed to the bone with knotted wire at three or four places.

Sujju leapt up and pushed Nalli's hand away. 'Go away!' she screamed and slapped Nalli's arm. Nalli left, hurt by Sujju's anger, by the feel of metal in Jai's head and by the softness of his hair.

Jai told them then that he had decided to be a doctor. Not an ordinary doctor but a Brain or Bone Doctor. It was typical of Jai to be so sure of what he wanted and to not waver from his dream. He got a seat on merit, studied medicine in Mysore and treated patients in the ward in which he had stayed three months.

Nalli had admired and loathed Jai by turns. She had burned with warlike thoughts for him. And from the day she touched the plate and the wires in his head and felt the softness of his hair, she became truly possessive.

When the moment came, saying goodbye was not difficult. Ajja looked dour. He stood in the front yard with the others, his rubbery goose-like neck thrust forward. It was a dull morning but the dew on the grass shone like crushed glass. The mist clung thick on the hills, nestled in the hollows and rolled down over the paddy fields. The parijata and guava trees were dissolved in mist; under the umbrella of a cold white sky, the hills slept. Thoughtlessly, Nalli said nothing to the hills, not even a silent farewell.

Appa waited near the cart. Budhi was brave and dry-eyed. He would not say a word and he would not smile. Nalli bent to touch Ajja's feet. 'Siva, Vishnu, Venkatesa . . . look after our Nalli,' he mumbled in his crazy whisper. 'I have made an offering to Peggala Swami to make you a clever doctor,' he assured her. The cream-painted box and the cane basket with her books were carried into the bullock cart. Ajja brought a bag crammed with thindi—kajjaya, chakkuli and rava laddus. Nalli saw him smuggling in a jute sack tied with string. 'Four bunches of bananas,' he said. 'When you're hungry . . .' She declined firmly. No bananas.

Amma touched her arm lightly. 'Go and come,' she said.

6

Chellaiah drove fast; the bus lurched, complaining, over the patched-up roads. Instead of the khaki uniform, he wore a yellow shirt with the sleeves rolled high on his thick arms. There was a 'No Smoking' sign above the steering wheel but he drove with a bidi between his lips. When the bus stopped at Hunsur, Appa went up and told him not to speed. He was risking lives. Chellaiah grinned and spat out of the window. 'Sir, I am not a student in your school,' he said and, grabbing the wheel, drove faster. Appa came back to his seat, his ears flushed red.

The bus spilled over with baskets, chickens, sacks of ragi, and villagers; a man put his little boy and a bundle of onions next to her and her knees were squeezed between baggage and seat. Appa gave Nalli the middle section of the *Prajavani* to read but the words swayed before her eyes. Her stomach churned like buttermilk. In spite of everything, the smile stayed on Nalli's face. She was going to college!

Mysore bus stand. Sujju's husband, Kaviraj, at the window, with two paper packets of uppittoo. How could she eat? They would change buses in Bangalore, reach Madras in the evening and, next day, college. Everything else was a blur.

After what seemed like ages, they reached Madras. The city with its unceasing, purposeful activity, its noises and smells, whirled and spilled about her. Appa paid the fees and bought her books and stationery, spending nearly four months of his salary. He counted the money in his purse. Twenty rupees. Nalli told herself that she need not concern herself with money matters. Appa would manage somehow. He would take a loan maybe or sell Amma's jewellery, or Kaviraj might help. It was not her business.

The medical college was a red brick building on a large campus opposite the railway station. They would start the first year with anatomy, physiology and biochemistry. Jai had told her that the first eighteen months were the most difficult. They would dissect human bodies and experiment on frogs, mice and dogs. If they passed in all three subjects, they would start seeing patients.

'I'll leave you at the college after lunch,' Appa said. 'We'll go to a hotel.'

'Appa, I'm not hungry. I'll go now.'

He left her at the entrance to the girls' hostel. She was conscious of a group of boys not far away, staring at her as she touched her father's feet. 'God bless you,' Appa said and stroked her forehead. Then he turned and walked away and she was on her own.

She went up the stairs to Room 3 and pushed open the door. A girl in a yellow dress was dipping a razor in a mug of soapy water and drawing it expertly along her long legs. Nalli stared.

'Hi, I'm Carol,' the girl said, not looking up. 'You must be Nalinakshi.' She waved her razor at the other girl in the room. 'Suguna, first-rank holder from Stella Maris and niece to Dr Bad, the anatomy prof.' Suguna, with a thin face behind pink-rimmed spectacles, was huddled on her bed, reading. Her curly, spring-like hair was tied in a long plait as thick as a bamboo pole. If straightened it would reach her ankles, thought Nalli, envious.

Shaving done, Carol got up. Her yellow dress was scandalously short, tight at the hips and without sleeves, the nails on her fingers and toes were painted maroon, her short hair fell in a curtain over her eyes. By her bed was the framed photograph of some boy, grinning. Nalli sat at the edge of her bed not daring to look. Later that evening, Carol shocked her by pointing to the photograph and saying, though Nalli had not asked, 'Gerry Fernandes, my boyfriend. Works for a bank in Bombay.'

The girls helped her carry the tin trunk and bags up the stairs. At eight o'clock they went to the Mess. Two boys who knew Carol joined them. Three more pulled up chairs. Nalli was hungry, having eaten nothing since breakfast, but the boys were sitting so close, on either side of her! Trying to lift a piece of chapatti into her mouth with a fork, she dropped the fork and the chapatti.

I'll get you another, said the boy with black-rimmed glasses and the rrrrr accent.

No, I've finished.

She pushed the plate away and reached for the water. Carol was chatting loudly and no one heard Nalli's throat making noises as she drank.

The boys asked many questions. Where are you from? What marks did you score in the entrance? Know anyone in college? Nalli answered nicely, but fidgeted with her hands, pushing back her plaits, swinging them forward and back again, scratching the paint from the edge of the table. Two senior boys were approaching. One with pants so tight, how could she not look? A new rule had been introduced, they said, to ban ragging in the college. Instead, there would be a party next day to welcome the new students.

More people joined them. Carol said she was doing medicine so she could emigrate to Australia with her family. Suguna wanted to do an easy teaching job at a medical college so she would have enough time to read 'novels and stuff'. Nalli told them about 'the brother of my friend who is very-very clever and in final year. Mysore Medical College.' For some reason they found this funny. A few days later, Renu, who was in their batch, asked her, 'This very-very clever brother of your friend . . . what's he like?' She was hurt, and showed it by walking out of the room. They kept off teasing her, at least for some time, and by then she herself was slowly changing.

The rest of the evening was spent disagreeing on what to wear to the party.

Nalli had decided on the blue sari with pink flowers and her cream-coloured slippers, but just as she had finished tucking in the last folds of her sari, Carol said, looking at her feet, 'They don't match. Wear your sari an inch lower. Like this.'

The Mess was transformed: the tables had been removed and the chairs arranged along the walls; music boomed from the gramophone. Surely the whistles were not for her? Could it be the slippers? She pulled the sari lower to hide her feet. If they stopped staring, she would be fine. Not-so-tight pants was standing on a window ledge, hands on hips, smirking. 'There's been a slight mistake,' he announced, shouting to be heard above the din of music and voices. 'Ragging has been banned from *next* year. This is the last batch to be ragged, so you'll be ragged in style!'

Some suffered more than others. Carol had to climb up and down a window sill a dozen times, saying, 'Next time I'll do it in a tighter dress.' Nalli was crowned 'Junior Queen' (the crown looked something like a shoe box), given a thigh bone to hold in one hand and a scapula in the other. Two senior girls twisted her hair in a bun and fixed it with a rib. She was garlanded with a loop of intestines. She sat on her throne with her feet in a bucket of murky liquid—Dead Man's Mouthwash and Enema Fluid, they told her—and burst into tears.

That night, Nalli lay awake, not sleeping; not needing sleep. Cold, she pulled the blanket up to her neck. Then, hot and sweaty, she flung it aside and pushed it with her feet to a corner of the bed. She sat up and looked at the sleeping figures of her roommates. How could they sleep, how could anyone sleep with the jarring, whirring noises that did not stop even at night?

She lay back thinking how much she had seen and heard and done in two days. At home, sitting in lamp-yellow brightness at the kitchen table, Nalli had listened to Appa talk about the struggle for India's freedom. When Appa was nineteen he had wanted to join the freedom movement. He wanted to give up studies and join the thousands who faced British lathis and were flung in prisons. He brought home a charka and started spinning, but Ajji put a stop to all that. There was disappointment in Appa's voice when he spoke about it but he never blamed Ajji. Nalli hoped it would not happen to her, that no one would snatch away her dream. Would her future be her own? The thought scared Nalli. She wanted to know, but she did not want to know.

7

Dr Badrinarayan was short, dark and bellicose, in bush shirt, unironed trousers and sandals that squeaked. He observed them with eyes the brown of tamarind seeds. 'Great anatomists and surgeons' had to make do with animals,' he said. 'Susruta learned on monkeys, Galen on apes. *You* have the human body.'

They were in the room next to the dissection hall, just big enough for sixty fidgety students. 'Brace yourselves and consider your good fortune. Eighteen months. In eighteen months you'll learn everything there is to learn in anatomy.' The professor lowered his high-pitched nasal voice to let his reassuring words sink in. 'You'll be familiar with *every* one of the muscles in the four layers of the sole of the foot, each with a name so long you can't say it in one breath. You will know, *intimately*, the nine nerves that supply the skin of the buttock. And the *eight* little bones that make up your wrist. And I'll tell you if you haven't already heard, there *is no Sunday in medical college*. Monday starts with the weekly test.'

The breakfast of idlis shifted uneasily in Nalli's stomach. She backed to the wall, fixing her eyes on the professor's sandalled feet and saw without looking the cadaver on the table with its arms crossed over its chest, covered in transparent plastic. Grinning, the professor pulled away the plastic. 'First we will go through surface anatomy. In other words, the situational geography. And then we move to the axilla—the armpit.'

The bodies were stored in giant-sized tanks filled with formalin. Two attenders lifted them out and placed them on the double row of cement-topped tables. On Saturday evenings they lifted them back into the tanks. They did it cheerfully, with professional pride. Nalli wondered how men whose job it was to lay out dead bodies could be so jovial.

One cadaver for six students; ten in all. Armed with her box of instruments and Cunningham's *Manual of Dissection*, Nalli joined her batch: Carol, Sister Leema Rose, Mani, Manjunath and Velangiri. She did not have the courage to get close to the table but knew the cadaver like a photograph: withered skin and laddered chest, saucer belly and shrivelled genitals. A man finished, but not quite.

Carol flicked nervously through the manual. Mani looked out of the window and Manjunath fidgeted; of Velangiri there was no trace. He had opted to be ill and stay in his room. Sister Leema Rose went up to the body and poked it with a hesitant index finger. The boys followed, touching and prodding. They christened him Subbu and joked about preserved human meat. Nalli thrust her nervous hands into the pockets of her new white coat and suffered.

For Nalli, the ordeal was not confined to the dissection room. Subbu followed her everywhere. She could smell him in her hands and nails and hair. He sat with her at lunch. At dinner he was an enduring smell in the sambar. At night she shut the window next to her bed but Subbu lurked outside her mosquito net. When she went to the toilet, there he was, sitting on that dreadful wooden ring of a seat until, with trembling fingers, she switched on the light. A week later he left, smell and everything, and Nalli was forgetting to wash her hands after dissection.

It was much more difficult to be rid of the city smells of boiling steel, mortar and petrol, of hot brick buildings that clutched the sky, of dust that clung to green leaves turned brown. The deep-fused smells burned in her mouth and settled as nausea in her stomach. Unlike Subbu-smells, they refused to go away. She told Carol, but Carol said it was the cadaver and formalin that had upset her.

'This smell is different,' Nalli argued. 'I feel it on my tongue and in my stomach.'

'It's in your mind,' Carol said. 'That's where it is.'

Once she had touched the lifeless skin and cut through the meat and grease into blood channels where the dark clots sulked, it ceased to matter. The precise knowledge of what lies beneath the skin, and where, was captivating. She had her wooden box with the scalpel, dissecting forceps, scissors and probe, and like other students dissected without gloves. Her unskilled eyes failed to see the fine pathways between one tissue and the next. Clumsy fingers cut nerves and veins that were not meant to be cut. The axilla alone took three weeks.

There was no way out but to study, and Badri kept them at it. The anatomy hall and lecture room were his universe. He cycled to work and stayed back long after college hours, tormenting the students. In the lecture room he wielded a foot-long knee hammer to indicate details on charts and slides. He barked his questions, fixing his eyes on an unhappy victim who attempted to deflect the question by looking at a neighbour or turning to the back row. Badri set things right by striding up. 'Esss?' He sat on the table holding his lethal weapon of a hammer beneath his chin. Stupid answers provoked peppery abuse in Tamil and then his stamping out of the room, to sixty sighs of relief.

Dr Bad they called him, but Bad was really good. He steered them, not through the straight course laid out by textbooks but along gutted routes which stretched the imagination. 'You're young but your minds are constipated,' he grumbled.

When they did their best, Bad told them to do better.

The years were divided by the half-term and the semester exams. And just as Badri had promised, there were the Monday tests to ruin every Sunday. Nalli knew that only hard work would see her through college. She had grown up not resisting discipline, so in some ways it was easier for her.

After the first few months, their link with Subbu became close, almost intimate. Nalli would sit with her arm resting on his chest and chat with Manjunath. It amazed Nalli how a dead person lacked sexuality. The female lost her soft contours, the male his hardness; breasts became empty sacs, the penis a dried up twig and the scrotum disappeared. When they started on the genital system, it was Nalli's turn at the scalpel. She pretended a severe cold. Carol and the boys said 'sorry' and stood back with their arms folded across their chests. The long-suffering look returned to Sister Leema Rose's face as she took the scalpel from her workbox. 'Read for me,' she said to Nalli. Plump and purposeful, with a cross hanging over her white bosom, she set to work and convinced the others to get going. In two weeks they had learnt everything about the male perineum.

The face was more difficult; cutting into the eyes, the ears and the nose was a hideous experience. When they started on the mouth, the smell was so dreadful that Carol got sick. They hacked away: thorax, abdomen, pelvis, head and neck. With uncomplaining dignity Subbu let go of his axilla, groin, upper limbs, lower limbs. The brain remained, to be taken out of the large glass bottle in which it was stored—sliced in neat sagittal and coronal planes—and worked on in painstaking detail.

Months of immersing herself in the dead man's parts had Nalli constantly thinking about him. She imagined Subbu to have been the previous owner of the little shop across the road from the hostel where the boys went to buy cigarettes. He had a wife and four kids and lived behind the shop in a shack made of corrugated iron and wooden planks blackened with soot. He was forty when he died. How did he die and what happened to his wife and kids? Did they know that he had ended up on a slab of stone to be cut into by students? She thought about the living Subbu and the dead Subbu and her mind filled with the saddest thoughts.

Subbu had had his share of bellyaches; his bowel was filled with roundworm. He had a skin disease on the sides of his neck and it must have itched badly, for persistent scratching had abraded the skin and encrusted scabs had formed. Nalli could see him in his shop, reaching back towards the itchy patch on his neck; she could hear his grunts of annoyance. When she looked across the road at the little shop, through the window next to the dissecting table, she could see the present owner handing over change to a customer. Now dead, Subbu had a dignity all his own in the way he submitted to crude, ignorant hands. Lying on the cement-topped table or floating in the formalin tank, he was like a god enshrined in holiness.

Anatomy was difficult enough without Badri insisting they learn the origins of words. The tongue was 'lingua', derived from the same root as 'language' and 'linguistics'. 'Rectus' meant straight and had the same root as 'rtam', 'rekha', 'erect', 'rectify'. The abdominal muscle with fibres running vertical was the rectus abdominis; the terminal, straight portion of the alimentary canal, the rectum.

The textbooks weighed a kilo or more and were tiresome to read. When Badri sensed that their minds were under severe strain, he abandoned the lecture. 'Now for some history, to limber up your brain cells,' he said. 'By understanding the past, we can live our futures better.' From him they learnt about Hippocrates and Galen, Celsus and Paracelsus; Susruta, Charaka and Semmelweis. In the Monday tests, in the midst of short notes on the superficial temporal artery, the soleus muscle and the navicular bone would be a question on Avicenna or Maimonedes, Charaka or Cushing. 'Just to get the rust off your minds,' he said, rubbing his hands with pleasure. 'The mind gets clogged as easily as a drain,' he told them. 'Too much manure is bad for the plant.' Knowledge did not come from heavy tomes which strained the elbows or from the wickedly fine print that ruined the eyes. Nor did it come from the far end of a microscope. 'You need eyes on the top of your head, on the soles of your feet, in your ears and on your tongue. You should see the back of the kidney from the front, the inside of the heart from the outside. You must *visualize.*'

Physiology was altogether different. The professor, Salamat Ali Khan, with his thin, sharp nose, gentle eyes and arched eyebrows, was stylish. He wore a tie, smoked a pipe, and for important events turned up in a three-piece suit. They called him 'the Nawab'. He was as good a teacher as Badri. There was an unspoken rivalry between the professors. A peculiar antagonism. Students showed their preference for one or the other in the way they dressed. Ali Khan's fans became posh and even tried smoking a pipe; Badri-diehards wore scuffed sandals and unironed bush-shirts and made free use of Tamil invective.

When Badri lectured, he forgot the time, especially when he talked history. 'Dig deep, dust those shelves of memory which have grown musty. Everything that has happened before will shape the future. Leave your past unattended for too long and it will rot away . . . When I tell you about your ancestors, file it away neat and clean. You shall not *write* it down. Do you write down your grandmother's stories?' He went on, forgetting the time, until the Nawab appeared at the door in time for his class. He waited at the door with an amused smile. '*If* you don't mind . . .'

'I beg your pardon,' Badri would reply with excessive civility.

Once, as Badri was leaving, the Nawab remarked, 'Now that you've finished with history, we can get on to more important things.'

It was a war without rancour.

For Nalli, intimidated as much by Badri's unpredictability as by Ali Khan's sophistication, it was a difficult choice. If pressed to take sides she would have voted for Badri: not because of his sandals and bush-shirts or even the creak of his bicycle, but because of his wife, the wonderfully eccentric Guruvamma. Guru, with the big buck-toothed smile and a PhD from Cambridge, was the biochemistry professor. She wore deep-hued Kanchipurams which she washed at home and ironed by placing them beneath her mattress, a trait that endeared her to Nalli from the start. Guru invited the students home sometimes and served sliced mangoes or boiled groundnuts, and coffee in steel tumblers. She talked to them about Hindi and Tamil movies, which she loved and Badri abhorred. She went alone to the theatre once a month and bought three tickets so no wicked men would jostle her.

Once a year the professors asked the students home for tea. Khan's tea party was eagerly awaited. There was delicate lace and expensive china. They glutted on pastries, mutton puffs and Monaco biscuits served with diced cheese, listened to Western music and admired photographs of the Khan and his wife when they were in the US. They came away with dreams of living abroad.

Badri's parties on the other hand were defiantly informal. Badri himself—in a banian and dhoti, smelling of oil and fried mustard—opened the door. 'Three volunteers this way, to chop cashew and peel cardamom,' he said, pointing to the kitchen. 'And three more to slice chillies and fry vadas. Come, come.'

'Leave that to the men,' Guru said to the girls with her buck-toothed grin. 'All we have to do is lay the table and relax.'

The boys, hands and faces begrimed in oil, sweated in the kitchen. Two hours later the medu vadas and kesri baath were ready to eat. 'Sit where you like,' Badri said. 'And use your fingers, please. We're not royalty.'

Badri told them about his great-great-granduncle who had joined Madras Medical College in 1851. Students then came from every part of the country, travelling great distances in bullock carts. Twenty-five years later, his son graduated with a gold medal and went on to become a professor of medicine. The family tradition of doctors continued with Badri's grandfather. Badri's father followed, as the first Indian professor of anatomy.

Badri loved anatomy but vowed that he would not learn from his father. He went to King George's, Lucknow, for post-graduate training in anatomy. That was where he met Guruvamma, married her, and together they came back to teach in Madras. Their two sons became engineers. 'I used to boast that we had broken the monotonous streak of doctors in the family. Then I found this niece of mine had fallen in line,' he said, meaning Suguna.

Badri told them what it was like being a medical student before Independence. The swadeshi fever afflicted most youth. 'We weren't impressed with Gandhiji, I can tell you. He seemed so puny and pathetic. We laughed at him, ridiculed ahimsa and backed violence, which was manlier. But somewhere along the way, the magic of his genius became obvious.' He bit thoughtfully into a vada. 'We used to have raging debates about the pros and cons of Satyagraha. The girls started the khadi revolution. I don't know if it was their conviction or courage, but they looked beautiful in khadi.' He winked at Guru. 'We even organized a bonfire to burn European clothes. But better sense prevailed. How would we buy new clothes?'

One afternoon the rivalry between Badri and the Nawab surfaced into a verbal duel. No one knew what the provocation was. Badri's voice rose first and then Khan's, until other faculty members stepped in to calm them.

A few weeks later, the faculty lecture was held, as usual, in the auditorium. It was a monthly event which showcased knowledge and no professor could resist dwelling on a pet topic, often boring the students to tears. The students listened to Rosario on toxicology, Nayak on brucellosis, Bhansali on basal fractures of the skull, and Khan on neurotransmitters. This time it was Badri's turn. Everyone expected he would choose a topic to prove a point over his opponent.

The hall was packed. Badri's acolytes came early and captured the foremost rows behind the faculty. The Nawab turned up in a beige suit with a maroon tie but his pipe, for once, was absent. Badri was no less impressive, in his black coat, dhoti and turban (his attire for special events).

'I will be speaking about that renowned bastion of learning,' he said grandly, 'the Hyderabad Medical College. We have the good fortune to have one of its brightest alumni with us.' He bowed towards Khan. 'He may not know its history though,' he added with a smirk, 'and I hope he won't mind my elaborating a little.'

Badri described how the college had come into being. In 1836, the then Nizam of the princely state of Hyderabad was seriously ill and none of his famed hakims could cure him. Alarmed by his condition, the British Resident asked if he could get an English doctor. The Nizam agreed reluctantly, stressing that on no account would he agree to take any allopathic medicines, which went against his beliefs. Dr MacLean was summoned. He examined the Nizam. 'I will not prescribe any medicines, Your Highness,' he said. 'But I entreat you to follow a strict diet for three months. No sugar or sweets, no fried food and no meat or eggs.'

For the Nizam, who had delighted in epicurean feasts since childhood, it was not easy, but he agreed to try it. In three months his symptoms disappeared and he was healthier than he had ever been. The doctor had diagnosed diabetes and, knowing that the Nizam's rich diet was the main culprit, had advised the simple strategy of diet restriction. Impressed by the powers of modern medicine, the Nizam sanctioned the establishment of a medical college and entrusted to Dr MacLean the task of getting it started. The Nizam picked ten students who were studying science, after carefully checking their family background, intelligence and their ability to sustain themselves for seven years. He presented each with a knife, an inkpot and five quires of paper, and they were ready. Though many dropped out in the first few years, unable to stomach the sight of the skeleton or cadavers, the first batch of hakims graduated from the college in 1854.

'Some distinguished themselves as able physicians,' said Badri. 'The best among them was Dr Mohammed Nooruddin, a great-granduncle to our professor of physiology.' He paused, for another bow towards his rival. 'Nooruddin was a versatile surgeon who could tackle anything—from a nephrectomy to a cataract—and he was given the name of Arastu Salar Jung by the Nizam.'

Badri related how the surgeon was once called upon to do an appendicectomy on the son of a nobleman, not in the operating theatre but in their house. The surgery was successful and when the Nizam wanted to visit the boy, the father insisted that his son wear the bugloos—a gem-encrusted belt—over his surgical wound in deference to royalty. An argument ensued between the surgeon and the father and it was the Nizam who sorted it out by visiting the patient unannounced.

The college had even pioneered research in anaesthesia. Badri recounted how it became known all over the world after a team of doctors, which included Dr Naidu, Sarojini Naidu's husband, went to England to demonstrate their technique of using chloroform.

'In India it is second only to the Madras Medical,' said Badri, beaming at the Nawab. He ended his lecture with the remark that he hoped he had not wasted anybody's time with his 'lesson in history'.

At tea-and-bondas, which followed the talk, the Nawab walked up to Badri. 'Excellent oration,' he said, raising his cup of canteen tea. 'You don't drink alcoholic beverages, so I'll raise a toast with this.'

From that day on, the Nawab became more tolerant of his rival and Badri less abrasive. Their enmity faded; the following year they hosted the party for the students together, and it stayed that way.

The experiments in physiology took some getting used to. The effects of low oxygen, too much carbon dioxide, hypoxia, monoxide poisoning and brain damage from injury were tested on dogs and mice. Dr Venkat, who performed the experiments, had the looks of a film star, and an indifference to the dogs and to all the students except one—pretty, round-faced Vrinda Sadashivan. Venkat addressed every word he spoke to Vrinda alone, in a velvet voice, as if he was courting her. Vrinda sat in the first row and scribbled away.

The day Venkat was to demonstrate the famous Cheyne-Stokes respiration, Vrinda was absent. Joylessly, he injected the animal with a narcotic drug and, when it was asleep, laid it supine on the table. He cut into its throat, put in a tracheostomy tube and drilled holes in its skull, explaining the procedure in a dull voice and looking out of the window as he spoke. When it was over, he injected the dog with a lethal dose of scoline which paralysed every muscle and stopped its breath. The students were awed, but Venkat looked desolate, like a stage actor whose audience had deserted him.

For frog experiments, the animal was anaesthetized from the neck down by 'pithing', that is, by piercing just below the back of its brain with a needle to disconnect the brain from the spinal cord. Students had to pith the frogs themselves at the start of the experiments. Gripping the slippery, stippled frog by the throat and aiming the needle at the exact spot was a skill Nalli could not master. The rest of the class was well into the experiment on involuntary muscle contraction when Manjunath finally pithed the frog for her. She was also prone to dropping frogs, which resulted in chivalrous males running around the lab to reclaim them for her. Carol said that Nalli dropped frogs like other women drop handkerchiefs.

Knowledge toughened Nalli's mind. This is a Golgi body, this the myelin sheath. This is the CO_2 cycle. This is how food is digested, absorbed. These are bile pigments, these mitochondria—all meticulously defined, with no blurred edges.

Monday's tests led on to Wednesday, when the marks were declared, to feel happy or unhappy about. When Nalli scored poorly, she was summoned: 'Professor wants to meet you in his office.' She stood outside the door with several other unfortunates. Bad could make her cry with a mere glance or a sigh of disappointment. The Nawab hinted, with a stylish lift of an eyebrow, that she must do better. 'If you don't feel the commitment it's better to drop out,' he said. Nalli bit back her tears. Could she be more committed? Ceaseless study had hemmed her in like a wall. Nose in a book, she would go on for weeks without noticing the outside world. Five-year plans, UN meets and the cold war went by. The world was sighted now and then through movies. Only when the first heart transplant and later the war in Bangladesh came along was she jolted, but only for a moment.

At odd moments, like during a lecture, dissection or experiment, her mind lifted away from the pressure of study, from the facts about the body being crammed into her mind. If only she could have a week at home, a few days when she could sit on the porch with Kapi. She would trace the silken brown streak all the way from the top of the cat's head, over his back, between the shoulder blades, till the tail. She would observe his fussy ritual of cleaning. (Once she had watched him lick his paw thirty-six times.) She would hold his paw with its indrawn nails, feel the gentle sharpness of his teeth on her palm and peer into the green wells of his eyes. How peaceful, how trouble-free and uncomplicated had been her life. And now this, this which she had fought for and wanted so much. Nalli closed her eyes, fisted her hands and pushed her feet into the floor as if hugging it with her mind. *I want it. I want it.*

8

Of all her classmates, Balan intrigued Nalli the most. Two years their senior and having failed twice, he was still in their batch. The teachers disliked him. He sat through lectures, even Badri's, looking bored, while everyone else listened. Balan smoked bidis, wore pressed trousers to college and bright lungis to the Mess. With girls he was coldly polite, with the boys a hero. He was not interested in studying. All he wanted was to be a doctor, he said, no one had told him that he had to *study* to be one. His father owned a hotel in Madurai and Balan got whatever he asked for. In the evenings he zoomed out of the hostel on his Jawa, wearing a red helmet. Suguna said he was arrogant. Carol declared that he was too hairy. Nalli felt his walk was put-on. In short, every girl was in love with him.

When the boys played their tricks, it was Balan who set them up to it. Nalli's slippers disappeared to the back of the class and she knew who the culprit was. Sister Catherine put her hand in the pocket of her coat one afternoon to find a bit of pulpy liver. Suguna walked out of the dissection hall with a withered finger dangling from her plait. The pranks were puerile; but the sight of students stooped over cadavers, deep in study just five minutes later, lent a certain nobility to the silliest pranks. Underneath the frivolous attempts at fun were minds tuned with serious intent. That purpose was never switched off.

Carol knew a lot about boys. They did not make her feel flustered like they did Nalli. She talked about her boyfriend, Gerry Fernandes. She even read aloud from his letters.

Within three months of joining college, however, Carol forgot Gerry and started going out with Prashant. She was out with him for hours together and came back late. Nalli worried.

'We must warn Carol,' she told Suguna. 'He may try to get too close. He may even try to kiss her.'

'He'll be up to more than that,' said Suguna in her matter-of-fact way.

Carol went quickly through three boyfriends. She discussed each of them with her friends. They debated Gerry's foreign prospects, Vidya's mush versus his mushless face, Domingo's need for a cigarette before a meal, Prashant's passion for pastel-coloured shirts. When dropping a boyfriend, Carol was at her wisest. 'A guy can't be tied down. It isn't right, it isn't ethical. I told him he's free to go.' She would get over the romance soon enough, but the boys suffered. Domingo grew a beard and took to smoking bidis; Vidya paced outside the girls' hostel; Prashant scribbled love poems during dissection and sent them to Carol through one of the 'dead body' attenders. During the short period between boyfriends, Carol was depressed. 'In Bombay there's no sitting around in your room on a Saturday evening,' she sighed. 'People are so considerate, they're always asking you to a party or something.'

But for all her worldly wisdom, Carol was not frivolous. She had opted to be a doctor so she could earn money. Her father had been a clerk in the railways and her mother worked in a hairdressing saloon. She was the eldest of six. Carol said that by the time her father retired she would get every one in her family to Australia. She was sure about her future and talked of it all the time. This yet-to-happen Australian connection added to Carol's glamour.

When Nalli told her friends about the village hospital, they were puzzled. 'How can anyone live like that?' asked Carol, who felt a life without comforts was worthless. Suguna thought she should aim higher. Nalli hugged her dream and did not talk about it any more.

It had been Jai's dream before it became hers. He had come home from college for a few days and they were standing near the guava tree. Jai held on to the branch overhead as if he could pull it down with one wrench. It had rained all morning. The air was silky, the ground beneath them soft. In the distance, the hills stood clean and white against the sky.

'I've found the ideal place for our hospital,' Jai said. *Our hospital*. Nalli nodded dumbly. He had asked without asking if she would be a part of his future, just like that.

They walked the four furlongs to the land next to Naganna Gowdru's rice fields, where the stream staggered ribbon-like before disappearing into the marshy ground. 'Half an acre. Gowdru will sell it for a reasonable price. The panchayat has agreed to buy it for us.'

Jai was climbing over the bamboo stile into the land and she followed. 'See . . . the front area will be the outpatient complex.' He cleared a portion of the ground with his feet and, picking up a stick, drew lines on the soft mud. 'The wards will be on both sides with a passage between them—here. The Theatre at the back . . .' As he drew the Theatre, a worm wriggled into it. 'Uhh—our first patient.'

He looked up at her from where he squatted. Grabbing her wrist he pulled her down to kneel beside him. 'No matter what it takes, we'll have this hospital in Angheri. We'll have patients from everywhere, as far as Yelwal, Mandya, Hunsur, even Coorg.'

'The building should be cream in colour,' she said. 'The windows and doors blue, like in Naganna Gowdru's house. That will show up nicely against the grass and the trees.'

'A hospital is always white,' said Jai. 'A good hospital always is. A pure, shining white.'

No longer was it a bare patch of land overgrown with weed and grass. Before them was the hospital, white as milk, with clean floors, mile-long corridors and an operating theatre where Jai performed surgery. There she was, walking from ward to ward, checking on patients, instructing nurses, reassuring anxious relatives. If there was an ideal world, it was this. Never would she belong anywhere else.

But she could not explain it to her friends.

Appa's letters always began with 'My dearest daughter . . .' He always gave precise news—about the school or some important happening in the village. He was more eager to find out how she coped in college. He advised her not to study in poor light and to ensure that she got enough sleep every night. When she thought of home, it was Appa she missed most of all.

Ajja filled five or six pages with his scrawl that looked as if a crow had dipped its feet in ink and then dragged them over the page. On her birthday he sent two rupees by post, with a paper twist of bhasma from the Peggala temple. Nalli glanced through Ajja's letters telling herself that she would read them later, but always forgot. She hardly thought about home except when the letters came. When she read them she felt an acute loneliness, as if no one in Madras was interested in what happened to her.

Her days were filled with study and she had friends in whose company she was never bored, but it was nothing like home. Nalli figured it was the smells that made the city so unlike Angheri. No scents here of orange, jackfruit, hay and dung. No paddy ripening in the sun, no marigold or parijata and no knee-weakening fragrance of Ajja's magic from the kitchen. Here it was petrol and concrete, formalin and acid, and the seductive smell of cigarettes.

And the gods were absent. It came to her one evening when sitting on her box seat with Best and Taylor's *Applied Physiology* on her lap, she heard the call for prayer from the mosque. The mosque was miles away but the voice was so clear it started in Nalli a fierce yearning to be home, standing before Ajja's gods. The gods who were there, silent, moving in the background, listening and not listening, helping, punishing. Or being punished.

Ajja had a healthy, belligerent relationship with the gods. Twice a day he lit the brass lamp and talked to the six gods lined up on the shelf in his room.

'Can you see to it that I make two hundred rupees from bananas?'

'Kindly ensure that the cows step up the milk yield. From ten seers to fifteen.'

'Nalli must get a good husband. I leave it to you.'

'Vishnu has done well. With your help, he can get a job here.'

It was important to make one's requests specific and clear: gods had many requests to attend to. Due to Ajja's positive frame of mind and sometimes due to the generosity of the gods, many of Ajja's wishes came true. Occasional lapses he was willing to accept, but when an important plea was ignored, he became angry. 'You don't listen to my prayers because I'm a poor man,' he would say. 'When this poor man offered you coconuts and payasa made with ghee and a seer of jaggery, you didn't refuse. I'll stop this pampering.' He put the gods on a diet of plantains. The agarbattis were reduced in number, the garlands he offered were of coarse marigold rather than jasmine. The harsh measures were relaxed when the gods relented. 'Ah, Ishwara! You heard my prayers, then, that Chondu give more milk!' Ajja would sigh, and the payasa and the pampering would begin all over again. Ajja had a perfect sense of justice.

Reminded of Ajja's gods by the muezzin's call, Nalli jumped up and, opening her box, searched till she found her red diary.

There between the pages was a calendar cut-out of Ishwara. She cleared a corner of her shelf and put him there. She resolved to buy agarbattis and light one every day for Ishwara, and to pray. But Ishwara looked awkward there, leaning against her mirror, which reflected the room strewn with books and bones and towels and clothes, so she put him back in the diary.

She had been four months in college when Appa came to see her. He was wearing a khaddar bush-shirt, thick rubber chappals and that absurd cap of his. He stood stiff and straight with his hands at his side, the way he did at school assembly. How should she greet Appa? It would not do to touch his feet; the boys were looking. She could not take him to the Mess for coffee. That would be ridiculous. Was everything all right, he asked. College? Food? Did she need money? He handed her a packet wrapped in newspaper and, in a short while, he was gone. Nalli went to her room and untied the string. Kodubale, holige and rava laddus. That night she lay awake a long while, remembering the warmth of Appa's touch on her brow.

Carol's father was different. Mr Suares was a wiry man with a lean, lined face and muddy teeth. He was unselfconscious with the girls. Every time he visited he took the three of them for tea at Royal Bakery near Moore Market. They ate cake and puffs, drank Fanta and listened to his tales about being a railway clerk in Thane. The trains were not so frequent those days and he used to take his guitar to work. He played tunes to amuse his colleagues and serenade the girls who hung around the station just to hear him. He joked that that was how he got to marry in spite of his awful teeth. The coal dust from the trains gave him asthma, so he took early retirement and moved to Bangalore. He worked as a sales representative for a plastics firm and travelled to Madras several times a year. Mr Suares was proud of Carol and, like her, confident of making it in Australia.

'Dad's keen on Australia for a special reason,' Carol said.

'Come now, it's my asthma really.'

'Not true!'

'Too many people here,' Mr Suares explained. 'Australia

has plenty of space. You know . . . elbow room. Every family has a house and garden. When our Carol gets a job there, we'll have a ranch, or a sheep farm.'

'Dad, I'm going to tell them if you won't!' She turned to her friends, her eyes laughing. 'He read somewhere, in a novel I think, about a hero who's Australian eating a breakfast of ham, sausages, bacon and four fried eggs. He wants to sit down to a breakfast like that every morning!'

Suguna's parents did not visit often but they sent her books, food and whatever else she needed. Murukku, chips and til laddus arrived by the tinful for Suguna to munch as she turned the pages of some novel she was reading.

Ajja had written that he wanted to visit Nalli, but she dissuaded him by telling him about the frightful weather, the terrible sea, the noise and the food. It was unthinkable that her friends would see her barefoot grandfather with his calves peeping through his dhoti.

About a month later, Renu, whose room was on the ground floor, came up to tell her that she had a visitor. 'I think it's that brother of the very-very good friend of yours,' said Renu, with a wicked grin.

Jai! Nalli flung aside the humerus and the osteology notes, combed her hair, adjusted her dupatta, put on Carol's fake silver earrings and went down.

There he stood: in navy blue trousers and a new check shirt with cuff links, his hair fragrant with oil and in his hands a parcel. She walked slowly towards him. They sat on one of the long wooden seats provided for visitors. He said that Ajja had sent him. He had taken the trouble to carry the parcel all the way for her. When she asked about home, he answered carelessly, as if it was not important. Vishnu, with his prune-like handsomeness that would last forever. Vishnu, whose coming she had anticipated all along and hoped would not happen.

He had chosen a seat hidden from view by a pillar. 'City life suits you,' he said, flicking her earring with his fingers. If only the colour of her cheeks did not give her away. Everything about Vishnu filled her with dread. His furtive fingers stroked her shoulder and slid beneath her arm.

'Don't.'

His hand moved upwards and she shivered. 'Why . . . don't you like it?' he whispered. 'Tell me if you don't like it, and I'll stop. I'll get up and go away.'

Why did she not stop him? She did not want it and she did not not want it. She could have escaped, but there was the parcel, with Ajja's kodubale, laddu and hebbittoo, which Vishnu cleverly kept on the other side of the seat.

'You must learn to enjoy life.' His voice so mellow, it cut her like a razor blade. 'If you don't, all this studying is of no use.'

'Please . . . someone might see . . .'

'No one will catch me.'

True. Vishnu was far too clever. But she was not. Her guilt would show on her face. If she was to be found out by anyone, *anyone*, she would kill herself. Her parents so honest and noble, and she so depraved. That evening she went for dinner with stooped shoulders, unable to meet anyone in the eye, unable to connect with the dining table chatter. Even in her misery she was nursing a sweet pain, a wicked delight. Vishnu brought darkness into her life but it was a darkness she could not shun. That night the gods were subjected to a double dose of her prayers. Never again, God, never will I give in to such cheap thrills . . .

For weeks afterwards she was afraid to meet anyone from the family. But in the end Girija Chikkamma could not be avoided. She was angry with Nalli for not visiting them. Nalli's protests that their house in Tambaram was a long way off from college were brushed aside. She promised to visit the next weekend.

Amma's sisters were as different from her as they were from each other. Girija Chikkamma—also known as Beach Aunty— had wielded as much power over Nalli's childhood as Fat Aunty.

Fat Aunty descended on the family more often than any other relative. She was a quarrelsome, religious woman. Her fatness and her extravagance with food took the sting out of her mean ways. She carried a small bottle of Ganga water in the cleft of her bosom; her eyes shining with belief, she handed out packets of bhasma gathered from the temples she visited. She was always accompanied by her equally plump daughter Jalaja, and brought all sorts of home-made thindis—syrupy jamuns and whorled, biscuit-flavoured kal-kals which only she knew the recipe for. Jalaja was a year older than Sujju but generous enough to play hopscotch with Nalli. The sight of Jalaja's breasts bouncing inside her blouse as she hopped used to alarm Nalli—breasts which sometimes looked like bags of rice, pointing east–west. When Nalli's elbow brushed against Jalaja, she was afraid that the bag would spill its contents on the floor. Worrying, she lost the game.

Appa suffered Fat Aunty but he did not like Beach Aunty and her husband who did 'business' in Tambaram. He believed that anyone who worked with the intention of making a profit was suspect. The rest of the family waited keenly for their annual visit. Beach Aunty brought satin ribbons, bead chains and plastic belts and old issues of *Femina* for the girls. Sujju and Nalli read every copy and got thoroughly educated. Aunty never let ten minutes pass without talking about the splendours of the beach—the miles of sand, the sea, the ice cream cart and the coloured soda in bottles. Nalli imagined the beach to be something close to heaven, especially when Aunty said she had spotted Gemini Ganesan in a white suit and Padmini in a red sari and sleeveless blouse at the beach.

Every time she came, Beach Aunty brought something new to tempt the family with. She gave Nalli her first footwear, a pair of 'Hawaii' rubber chappals with blue straps, packed inside a cardboard box. Nalli walked on the porch, luxuriating in the springy softness and learning the skill of keeping the grip with her toes. She let Jai, Vijai and Budhi try them, but only to walk on the bench. Nalli resented Beach Aunty only when she told her, 'Don't chew with your mouth open.' Eating with her mouth closed took all the fun out of eating.

Once, she brought a packet of tea for Amma to introduce the family to tea-drinking. She showed Amma the art of brewing tea and serving it in cups arranged on a tray. Nalli added five spoons of sugar to mask the awful smell. Amma and Appa drank their tea out of politeness, but Ajja refused. He said it gave him a dry mouth and constipation, and stuck to coffee. Another time, she brought a cutting from a money plant which she said was a must in every house. Sujju planted it by the side of the porch. It grew fast, into an ugly plant with wide green leaves and no flowers, devouring inches of the wooden pillar and heading up along the tiled roof. It did not bring them money or luck.

Beach Aunty's son Vittala was nice enough, but Vimala, her daughter, was soppy. As a little girl she had crisp short hair—bobdare—and tender feet encased in shoes and socks. Everything about Vimala was unattainable. Even her fears reeked of superiority. In Angheri, she was afraid to use the toilet outside and she cried her lungs out every time she needed to go. Nalli showed her a caterpillar on the lemon tree but it only set her weeping more. When she exhibited a spider's web with the spider in the process of devouring a fly, Vimala howled louder, and when she showed her the calves Kanike and Malli in the cowshed the girl covered her nose and ran to her mother. Nalli lost patience and left Vimala to tackle her problems by herself.

One day, Nalli took Vimala to school. Vimala's cheeks were pinched by everyone and she was carried around like a baby. 'Bobdare and bukkal shoes,' the girls whispered, envious. They listened to Vimala's tales about her doll with golden hair and blue eyes. She taught them an idiotic game in which you held hands in a circle and sang 'Linga, linga, losses, pocket fulla horses . . .' and, every once in a while, squatted on the ground. In the classroom she sat primly in her yellow dress with the yellow ribbon in her hair and her feet encased in yellow socks and buckled shoes. During the maths class Appa happened to stop by to speak to the teacher and he saw Vimala. 'Who permitted you to bring her to school like this?' he asked Nalli. They were sent out of class. Appa said he did not believe in students going to school dressed in costumes. It resulted in Beach Aunty and family cutting short their visit by two days. Aunty got over the incident but Bukkal Shoes had been a hostile relative since.

On Friday, Vittala came to fetch her home. He hardly spoke during the long bus ride to Tambaram. Vittala was Jai's age and the quiet, serious type. He had not been like that when they were young. Nalli remembered them going to Raghavendra Stores when it first started to sell ice cream. Jai, Vittala, Sujju, Budhi, Vijai and Nalli. A pink ice cream cone had been painted outside and next to it a pink-faced girl eyeing it with greed. They sat on benches outside and ate the pink, runny ice cream which made their teeth hurt. Vittala and Jai whispered to each other and laughed. Nalli wanted to know what was so funny. 'Fukked!' Vittala said, and laughed meanly. 'Do you know the meaning? Fukked!' Sujju blushed furiously. Nalli felt tears starting in her eyes without knowing why.

Beach Aunty and Uncle lived in an upstairs flat in Tambaram with rosewood side tables in the front room, a refrigerator in the kitchen and potted plants crowding the balcony. Vittala left Nalli with his mother and disappeared with his friends; Vimala made a brief appearance and then shut herself in her room, but not before Nalli had made sure she had seen the red polish on her toenails. When Beach Aunty attacked Nalli with questions, she talked with a Bombay accent like Carol and giggled a lot when she spoke about the fun they had in college. Vimala, she was sure, would be near the door, listening.

9

There came a time when everything about herself felt wrong to Nalli. Her hair was too flat on her head, her cheeks were shiny, her voice too loud and her clothes dreadful. A few girls in college dressed like her, in half-saris, and they were happy being themselves. But Nalli was unhappy. She wanted to be a city girl.

Something had to be done about her clothes. Ajja had said she should wear only half-saris but Amma reasoned that it was all right to wear skirts if they reached below the knee. She had brought three skirts with her, and three blouses. Except for the creases that formed at the neck and around the armpits, her blouses were all right. Her skirts were held at the waist with press buttons. Once, when she got up from a chair to leave the class, the skirt she was wearing snapped open. Nalli resorted to using a safety pin, with her white belt to conceal the pin.

'Why don't we open out that blue-and-black striped skirt of yours and convert it into a kameez?' Carol said.

They argued about the style and Carol came up with 'cap sleeves, U-neck in front, V at the back and stripes running vertical.' They took the bus to Moore Market and found a tailor. Two weeks later Nalli walked into the Mess in salwar kameez. She felt as smart as the others but her joy lessened slightly when Velangiri asked, 'Wasn't that a skirt the last time you wore it?'

There was much to learn. Angheri had not taught Nalli about rock 'n' roll, the Beatles or the twist. And she could not speak English without getting it wrong.

'I don't think I can cope up with the Monday test.'

'Not cope up with. It's cope with.'

'I didn't use your lamp, Carol did. She's trying to pass the bucket on me.'

'It's pass the buck, not bucket!'

'Who's your favourite actor?'

'Rajkumar, in *Bedara Kannappa*. Best pitcher. And Sivaji Ganesan in *Veerapandiya Kattabomman*. Too good, no?'

'It's pic-ture, not pitcher. And we're talking about English films.'

Carol told Nalli that there was no need to shout across the room. 'None of us is hard of hearing, you know.' Nalli was hurt. At home she called to Gaja in the backyard or to Ajja across the fields or Budhi near the well. No one accused her of shouting.

Nothing was as tricky as using the 'sitting' toilet. In the village, right until Sujju's wedding, a deep pit cordoned off from the fields by bamboo poles and gunny sacks was where they 'went'. Twice a day they made their way across the fields with a chombu of water. When they did build a toilet inside, it was a comfortable squatting type. Here, she had to accept the ludicrous method of sitting on a cold wooden ring.

Nalli also tired of the food in the Mess in no time at all. At home, the mere mention of eating meat was unthinkable and she had been a vegetarian all her life. Time and again she had heard Ajja and Sompa argue.

'How can you eat a carcass?' asked Ajja.

'Just the way you eat nuts and grass,' Sompa replied.

'Look at me with my vegetable bones,' Ajja said. 'Am I not as strong as you?' There was no arguing with him.

Being vegetarian, she got a dull-looking cutlet for dinner every day. Carol said it was made from potato skin. Nalli wished her friends would offer her some meat but they never did. One evening she pointed to what was on Carol's plate and whispered, 'I want to try some of that.' It tasted like jute and smelt uriniferous. Nalli shut her eyes and held her breath as she swallowed the chunk. Nothing untoward happened. That was how she started, with a small piece from Suguna or Carol slid slyly on to her plate and concealed beneath a heap of rice. Pretending to be vegetarian, she ate meat every day.

Carol had gained two kilos after joining college. 'Because the food in the Mess is so horrid,' she said. 'If they served good food, I'd be satisfied with less.' She walked the length of the corridor carrying Gray's in one hand and Kliner and Orten in the other, weightlifting to burn calories. 'That peanut bar you're pigging on, it's two hundred and twenty calories,' she would remind Nalli. 'I'm having eggs without the yolk from now on. That's minus fifty calories.'

She was for ever telling them about some magic diet. 'Just read about the boiled-egg-and-cucumber diet. It's foolproof. Steamed and without salt . . .'

'Just the thing for you, Calorie—I mean Carol,' Suguna would say flatly and go back to her books.

Her friends had everything she wanted for herself: Carol's bobbed hair, short dresses and high heels that looked and sounded grand; Suguna's memory and love for books.

Suguna read all the time. She missed dinner and sat up till one or two in the night. In the morning she was late for breakfast. Four days out of six she went to college on an empty stomach. For Nalli it was unthinkable that she should miss a meal in order to read a book. 'Time to get ready,' she would remind Suguna every morning, though it seemed to fall on deaf ears more often than not. Suguna spent whole afternoons explaining why one had to read Gorky or Mauni. Worrying about Monday tests started for her a little after lunch on Sunday. She put away her novels, picked up the textbooks and read, with her pink-rimmed glasses perched on her nose. After dinner she had to go back to some 'light reading'. She concerned herself with boys only when she wanted to borrow books.

Suguna was brilliant. And Carol was just as studious as she was fun-loving. Her textbooks were never out of reach. Even when she was getting ready for a party she would pause while doing her eyes or brushing her hair or polishing her nails to flick through a page or two. She was disciplined.

Suguna's table and bed were littered: dozens of paperbacks, packets of murukku, and the bones which they studied in osteology. She did not see the sense in tidying up.

'Why don't you make your bed in the morning?'

'Make the bed?'

'Fold the blanket. Tidy the sheets. Put away the mosquito net. *Make the bed*.'

'Why, when I've to un-make it again at night?'

Carol grumbled about the clutter, but Nalli was not particular. When Suguna's parents visited, her mother insisted on seeing the room. As she climbed the stairs, Carol and Nalli would do a frantic tidying-up. Once, when an aunt who lived in Beirut came along to see her niece, she was shown Carol's bed and desk. Pleased, she reported to Suguna's parents that their daughter had changed for the better. But she had a roommate who kept her things in a mess. She did not even make the bed, and there were bones, human bones, on her desk!

When Nalli studied, she sat on her box with the pillow to lean on. At home the pillow was a luxury she did not have. When Sujju made two soft pillows stuffed with cotton for Ajji and Amma, Nalli too wanted one. 'The important thing is to know how to sleep without a pillow,' Ajja told her. 'Then sleeping with a pillow will be easy.' Now that she had a pillow of her own, she found she did not need one, although it did come in handy to lean on when she was studying. Nalli read, visualized, and committed facts to memory, only to forget next day. Study one organ, muscle, nerve or tendon. Learn everything there is to learn about it. The mind struggling, creeping, looping, inch by inch, over the folds and creases, borders and surfaces that made up the body.

The impending Monday tests troubled Nalli less and less. She observed Carol at her desk, flicking the pages, checking notes and drawing diagrams. Suguna sat on her bed with a novel, dipping into a handful of murukkus balanced on a scapula. With a rib, she scratched the back of her neck. If Nalli had a doubt she asked Suguna.

'The posterior surface of the scapula. Is it . . .?'

'Haven't got to the posterior surface.'

'Does the suprascapular nerve pass above or below the ligament?'

'Below, and stop pestering. This is a thriller and I'm on the last-but-one chapter.'

'Suguna, the way you're using that rib. It's disgusting.'

'Why?'

'It belongs to a dead man.'

'Not a man, a woman. See, its lighter . . .'

'It could be carrying germs. You'll get an infection.'

'The top of that table is more likely to carry bacteria than this desiccated rib.'

By eight or nine in the evening Carol flung aside her book and the bones, stretched out her legs and clutched her pillow. 'I'm missing breakfast tomorrow.'

Nalli was battling with the scapula. For Suguna, who missed breakfast most days, it hardly mattered.

'I've finished scapula. Ask me.'

No more than an 'umm' from Nalli. Suguna's auditory responses were wonderfully selective, she did not hear.

But Carol had a better hook: 'Guess who's taking me out on Saturday?'

'Who?'

'Who?'

The evenings could drag on and on. When Carol found it impossible to take in another word, she came out of their room and sat on the stairs between the first floor and the second to comb her hair or trim her nails. One or two more girls soon joined her. Their voices drew others out of their rooms and books were ditched for the rest of the day. But all those hours of not studying were when learning happened; while they talked about boys, about restaurants and films, knowledge was settling slowly, like sand in water.

On some evenings, after classes, the girls took the bus into town to shop. Nalli bought a lipstick, powder and face cream (fifty-one boys in class to be impressed), or they went to the beach. Nalli liked the beach, but not the sea. The unending expanse of water, the seeming calm and then the crashing waves, frightened her. While the others splashed and made merry, Nalli sat well away on the sand and watched the catamarans sail away in the distance. The vastness of the sea seemed to stretch her thoughts, and she became sad and reflective. She longed for a sight of the hills, steadfast guardians of her home.

Her village coarseness was going. Or so she thought until the day she heard Renu telling Carol about someone in the class being 'countrified'. She knew they were talking about her. What did they mean, she asked Suguna.

'Countrified?' Suguna pushed back her glasses and scratched the tip of her nose. 'When someone behaves like a villager. Lack of sophistication, that type of thing.'

'They were talking about me,' said Nalli. 'Suguna, you too are from a village, to start with. You told me. But no one will say you're countrified.'

'Don't worry. So what if you're countrified? What's it to Carol and Renu?'

But Nalli worried; she wanted to be the opposite of countrified. She felt unlucky to be born in Angheri; her origin stuck to her like a stain. Something of her was trying to break away from her past, but then who was she? The Angheri-born, langa-wearing village girl or a smart English-speaking, lipstick-wearing medic who said 'haaai' and 'baaai'?

Nalli tried harder. She plucked her eyebrows and shaved her legs. She refined her accent, stopped gesticulating when she talked and learnt to control her voice. She put on a seductive walk, until Carol asked what she was trying to be—a camel?

Sometime during the first six months it became clear that Manjunath nursed a special affection for Nalli. He came to the girls' hostel one evening and offered her a bar of Cadbury's and followed it up by asking her to watch *Vamsavriksha* with him. It was the first time a boy had asked her out and Nalli was flattered.

Unlike Nalli, who was confused and a little smug about her new graces and stitched-on sophistication, Manju had remained the simple, dignified person he was when he first came to college. Some of the boys had been easy targets for the city-bred bullies, but not Manjunath. He was from Nuggehalli and the only one in college to have even heard of Angheri. He wore white drill trousers with a shiny belt. His shirt was buttoned at the neck and at the wrists, his hair oiled, his manners coarse. His mother and younger sister had come from the village and lived with him in a rented house in town. In fact he proved to be cleverer than the others thought. He devised a simple trick with which to silence the boys: he scoffed at the limitations of living in a city. 'You get just one type of banana here. In Nuggehalli, we have six varieties.' 'The rice here is fit for the buffaloes. We eat a superior quality in Nuggehalli.' 'You call this rain? In Nuggehalli, this would be a mere drizzle.' He left the guys perplexed, chasing their own tails, and unable to mock him. Manju was a rustic and Nalli felt comfortable with him; he was an ally. But she also understood what Carol meant when she said that no girl would ever fall madly in love with him.

Nalli went for the movie, taking Carol along with her. Manju bought peanut bars and coffee for them. During the movie, he sneaked glances at her. When he tried to hold her hand in his sweaty palm, she pulled away. She was embarrassed, not so much by his holding her hand but because she knew she would soon learn to reject him.

As the three of them walked from the movie theatre to the bus stop, a middle-aged woman with a young girl accosted Manju: his mother and sister.

They were pleased to meet the girls. 'Is this Nalinakshi?' asked his mother. 'And this? Oh . . . Come. We're going home.'

Nalli saw the distress on Manju's face. Till then bright and smiling, it closed up with anxiety. 'Amma, they have to catch the bus. They can't be late. Hostel rules.'

'Simply you are saying. Rules, rules. Some caafee and thindi. Come, come.'

Their house was on a narrow back street that spilled over with shops, vendors, stray dogs and women selling onions and potatoes spread out on gunny sacks. It was a converted garage— small and tidy. Boxes and cardboard cartons had been made into seats; Manju's books and bones were neatly stacked on the window sill, the bedding was rolled up in a corner. Everything was in its place. They drank coffee that smelled of kerosene and ate 'khara'.

On the way back to college Nalli told Carol not to tell anyone about the visit. She knew Manju did not want everyone to know how he lived. 'Why? Because they're such drips?' asked Carol. 'So what? They're sweet.'

Like her and Manju, there were other misfits, being swept along—learning, changing, adjusting—until their separateness ceased to matter. There were Kamal, Mathew and Ranjit who were always together. They went about with hands around each other's shoulders, talking conspiratorially in a way that made others jealous. There was Velangiri, a sad case of perfection where none was needed. He was pale, with dark lips and hair trimmed neatly above the neck. His white coat was Robin Blue white. He had a memory as sharp as Suguna's but his intelligence was blunted by the need to be perfect. And of course there was Balan, who considered himself exclusive.

Vally admired Suguna and before long his admiration

turned to love. But it was a sour, languishing sort of love. He walked past the hostel and looked up at the window to her room with sheep eyes. He wrote hopelessly inscrutable poems. On Valentine's Day the boys would call out, 'O Vally, a happy Tyne Day to you . . .! Any luck with Brilliantyne?' Suguna was truthful enough never to encourage Vally.

Unrelenting, the boys played a cruel joke on Vally. They sent him an invitation which requested him in an official, respectful tone to judge a beauty contest in the women's college in Nungambakkam. They made it appear that Suguna would be there with other girls from their college. Velangiri went in a borrowed suit with the hope of impressing Suguna. The watchman at the gate said he had not heard of any beauty contest. He went to the Principal's office where he was spoken to and sent back. For three whole days Vally stayed in his room and suffered.

However, Vally turned out to be smarter than he appeared. One evening he came to the girls' hostel lugging a cardboard box. He asked to see Suguna. Nose-deep in a Georgette Heyer, Suguna said 'no'. Carol and Nalli persuaded her: she could at least see what he had brought in the box. When fifteen minutes went by, they crept to the edge of the stairs to spy. Suguna and Vally were sitting together, with the carton between them. Suguna was talking breathlessly, a novel clutched in her hands. 'I'd like to borrow just a couple . . .'

Half an hour later, she came up. 'It's books,' she said, breathless. 'A cartonful! Durrell, Graves, Tagore, Basheer. Help me carry them up.' She had accepted the whole box.

Vally started to spend all his money on books. He invaded bookshops, befriended roadside booksellers and cajoled anyone he could to part with books. Then he started smuggling love notes between the pages. Suguna was upset. 'I'm being selfish,' she said. 'I've got to stop this.' That evening she spent a long time with him and when she came up she was empty-handed. Vally looked paler than usual for a few days. He continued to bring her books, but the missives stopped.

One day, after the biochem class, Pavan asked Nalli if she would go with him to a party.

A party!

Studying the central nervous system in Best and Taylor that evening, she could not take in a single word. She sat on the box, hugging herself with excitement.

'What's up?' asked Carol. 'You bitten by something?'

'Pavan . . .'

'He bit you?'

'He's asked me to a party on Sunday.'

Carol closed her book. 'We'll have to get you spruced up,' she said. 'We have two days. Wash your hair tonight and tomorrow. I'll teach you to dance. The rest's easy.'

Nalli borrowed Suguna's midnight-blue kanjeevaram, the blouse and the lace-edged petticoat. It took three girls two hours to get her dressed. Suguna made her eat a few handfuls of banana chips so she would not be hungry.

Pavan, handsome in a bright yellow shirt and tapered jeans, came to take her. The son of a coffee planter from Coorg, Pavan awed Nalli with his money and his glamour-filled life. She enjoyed the proximity of his deep voice and the heady smells of cigarettes and gin; she loved the way Pavan looked at her. The party was fantastic until drunken fights erupted among the older men towards the end. The boys were noisy and brash but they did not misbehave with the girls. Nalli was not sure if it was because they could not afford to drink like the older men or if youth really was more honourable.

A week before Diwali came the chance to go to another party and Nalli grabbed it. With more lessons from Carol her dancing had improved. She wore her new hip-hugging kameez, clip-on flower earrings and a generous spray of Carol's perfume. They were to go with the boys, in four autos. Special permission to stay out late had been asked for and granted. At the sound of approaching autos, Nalli went tripping down the stairs with Carol, Renu and Shyla. The boys were waiting. Somewhere behind them someone cleared his throat. Nalli, one foot in the auto, looked up to see Appa, wearing his ridiculous black cap, standing ramrod straight, his hands clasped behind him. She stumbled out of the auto and towards Appa on her high heels. 'We're—going out,' she blurted.

'Will your friends be kind enough to let us have an auto?'
He spoke with deliberate slowness, turning his eyes from Nalli
to the boys. No one said a word. Walking up to one of the
autos, he said, 'Anand Lodge. Mylapore,' and climbed in.

Her own father had kidnapped her! How she hated him.
She wept; Appa held out. He offered no explanation, no apology.
For dinner that night they ate rava idlis with sambar; enormous
idlis, with bits of carrot, coconut and chillies. Every mouthful
stuck in Nalli's throat. For years afterwards, she would never be
able to eat rava idlis without recollecting her humiliation.

Appa left the next day, and life continued as before.

There were movies, picnics and flirtations, a change in
sensitivity. Nalli knew that her family, and Jai, would disapprove
of the way she had changed. Earlier, with Appa as her reference
point, choices used to be easy; when faced with a dilemma she
would decide on her course by imagining Appa's reaction to it.
Now all that had blurred. Only rarely, when she imagined Appa
riding off to school, so straight and dignified on his bicycle, did
her guilt surface. But she did not want to think about it. She was
enjoying herself.

A few weeks before the first-year finals, Nalli quarrelled
with Pavan. It had started a month earlier when she cut her hair.
He had shown her a photograph of his older brother's family in
America. His brother's wife was pretty, with stylish short hair
curled around her ears and neck. 'I'll be pushing off to the US
as soon as I finish here,' Pavan said as he showed her the
photograph.

Nalli began to think of Coorg and America and, two days
later, begged Carol to cut her hair. Was she sure? Yes. Carol
obliged. When her long hair lay scattered in soft heaps around
her, Nalli panicked and refused to go to the Mess for dinner,
although her friends assured her that she looked fabulous.

It was Suguna's birthday the next day and the three of them
went to watch *Doctor Zhivago*. The queue for the show at half-
past-three was almost all college students and it snaked well
beyond the gates of the cinema house. Some boys who had come
early offered to get their tickets. During the interval, Vivek

bought coffee and was very attentive towards Nalli, and they went for ice cream to Dasaprakash afterwards.

The next morning Pavan greeted her with a scowl and asked if she had enjoyed the movie. And what about the ice cream afterwards? He did not say a word about her hair. Back in her room, Nalli studied her reflection in the mirror and decided that short hair did not suit her. Pavan continued to disregard her and she him, and three weeks later she saw him walking towards an auto with Renu. She was hurt but the fast approaching exams diverted her mind and, after a while, Pavan ceased to be important.

Now exams were the only thing that mattered. She got up early every morning to study with Sister Leema Rose who lured her with the promise of coffee which she made with an immersion heater in her room. She dragged herself out of bed for the coffee, and her day ended a little after midnight with a question-and-answer session with Carol and Suguna. Her brain was dulled into a machine that devoured knowledge. Her back began to assert itself; it ached all the time. Doubts assailed Nalli. She sat with the petrous bone in her hands and wondered how she had got herself into this. Her mind was fat with knowledge, and weary. She was done with hacking cadavers, pithing frogs and thumbing through grease-stained pages of Cunningham's *Manual*. She could not wait for the exams to be over. After that it was four weeks of parole from the prison of lectures and books, and then she would be in the wards, seeing patients.

The exams came and went, bringing to an end Nalli's first eighteen months in medical college. Now, she could go home.

10

It was evening when the bus skirted the bamboo grove and reached the village. The bus manoeuvred on narrow, twisting roads, and Nalli saw the fields of yellow mustard running away and up the slopes. She saw the sameness of Angheri and felt sharply her own transition; she so anxious for change, but the

village and its people content in their sameness. Nalli sat up
straight. She would take them forward; she would show them
what it was like to be modern.

At home, she was first plied with kajaya and kesari baath,
then with questions. There were many things to tell and much
to hide.

On her second day at home she heard Sompa say, 'She used
to be a pretty girl. What happened to her?'

'That's what comes of letting girls go to cauledge,' Ajja
replied.

The coldness in Appa's eyes showed that he too was
displeased. Amma made her wear half-saris, part her hair in the
middle and deck it with kanakambara. 'You look better this
way,' she said.

Nalli tried to impress her family by taking out her set of
bones on the pretext that she must brush up osteology. Far from
being impressed, Ajja forbade her from displaying the bones
anywhere but next to the pathaya at the back. Nalli's learning
to be a doctor was one thing but bringing home the bones of a
dead man was in bad taste.

Nalli had lived sixteen years without electric lights but now
she found the dim yellowness of lamps tiresome.

'When will we have electricity here?' she asked.

'When everyone has enough to eat,' answered Appa. 'This
year too the rains have been scanty. The poor feel it all the time,
in their stomachs.' It was the third consecutive year that Angheri
had suffered a dismal monsoon. More young men of the village
had headed through the rugged paths over the hills to Coorg to
find work in the coffee and pepper plantations. The daily wage
of three rupees was good money and easier than labouring in
Angheri, but Coorg offered work for only a few months in the
year. 'Compared to them, *we* are well-off,' said Appa. 'We have
food enough to eat; there is smoke rising from the kitchen twice
a day and always a chombu of coffee ready near the fireplace.
Don't complain about luxuries.'

Nalli had been home for a few days when Vijai visited with
her husband. Most girls from her class in school were married,

or about to be. Vijai had escaped the tyrannical clutches of her father and married an electrician, a quiet man and happy with a wife who stayed home. Nalli was saddened by the gulf between her and Vijai. The childhood bond had not been strong enough to withstand the disparity of their lives. She remembered the brief, wonderful phase when they had dreamed of college together. They used to sneak into Appa's office room and study the map of the world that hung on the wall. With inquisitive fingers they identified countries: This is Russia, this is China. England, America, Germany, Iceland. In the triangle that was southern India they searched for the city of Mysore. Where was Angheri? Here, it must be here. In their minds they saw their village, as famous and important as Madras, Delhi or London: Angheri!

Nalli was embarrassed to ask Vijai about her husband. He seemed like an intrusion. They talked about the family, home, relatives. And then? Their closeness was fading like a photograph and there was nothing they could do about it. Vijai sat on the bed with her knees drawn up to her chin, looking slender, almost beautiful. She smiled as she talked and her fingers played constantly with the silver toe-ring, worn only by a married woman; a sumangali. She did not ask Nalli about college. Talking to her, Nalli missed Jai with an anger she could not understand.

With nothing else to do, Nalli went about the house wrapped in her dreams. She played with Kapi, who gazed at her with unblinking, lime-green eyes. She looked at the family photo that hung on the wall in the bedroom and saw the transformation in herself. Gone was the plumpness in her cheeks. The long hair, which she used to plait high up behind each ear, was now shoulder-length. She had pink polish for the nails, shampoo for the hair and Lux (the beauty soap of film stars) for her face; she used toothpaste instead of tooth powder. Conscious of the privilege of education, she sat with one knee crossed over the other and ignored Ajja's scowl of displeasure.

Nalli sat at the window, looking beyond the valley, at the hills. In the foreground and partly screening the hills were jack, guava and parijata trees. The dark, shiny leaves of the jackfruit contrasted with the paler, ribbed leaves of the guava. With its effeminate trunk and spreading branches, the guava tree was the easiest to climb. The pink flesh and curious sweetness of the fruit attracted parrots, chembookas and children. Squirrels skidded on the highest branches of the jack in a frenzy of eating, until the ripe, spiky fruit crashed to the ground. Ajji, whose illness had never prevented her from eating, was the first to smell a ripe jackfruit and ask that it be plucked. A branch reached out from the guava tree and interlocked with the leaves of the jack. They were like friends whispering secrets. The parijata stood aloof, wreathed in flowers which it shed with limitless wantonness. By dusk the ground was scattered with white flowers which shone like stars on a purnima night.

Was it the trees that gave beauty to the sky? Each time she looked, the sky changed colour. It was a soft blue in the morning, a smoked gold at dusk and of varied hues in between. As light faded and night fell, the leaves of the jack turned from deep green to black, and the sky beyond it to white. Nalli watched the trees melt into the darkness. Once the birds returned to their nests, the chirping crickets engulfed the silence. Nalli strained to decipher to their monotone, to break it down until she could discern the varying notes, stops, squiggles, exclamations, serenades and lullabies. Later in the night came the sound of the owl, a soft and noble gnnnn . . . sawing at the wooden quiet. She never failed to hear it, however soft. She could tell the different tones of the three owls that lived in the bamboo grove at the back. At such times it was as if she belonged as much to the world outside the window as she did inside.

The hills, her old friends, were in the distance—listening, speaking, telling her many things. And Ajja, who knew that it was important to dream, never called her away from her perch at the window. Her dreams matched the shiny white parijata flowers. But were her dreams really as pure as she imagined them to be?

How dull life seemed, and how trivial the daily chores. Gaja picking stones from the rice, Amma at the grinding stone, Ajja in the porch haggling over the price of bananas. Karia the cock, haughty and majestic with his blue-black plumes, high-stepped across the yard in search of worms. Kapi, who knew that Nalli was idling, jumped on her lap and bit her wrists. She hid her hands behind her back and he chewed her langa. She flung him on the ground and he climbed back to paw her ankles. Then he curled up on her tummy and she watched his body relax in sleep and his face twitch with the visions of his dreams. The sun hung lazily overhead. Beyond the gate, half a dozen crows began a noisy conflict over lunch. The world left her alone.

'Akka . . .'

She withdrew her knees to accommodate Budhi on the ledge. 'How many dead bodies have you cut open?'

'One.'

She had blurted the truth and he was not impressed. 'Only?'

'How many have you cut up?' Nalli challenged and went into grisly details of dissection. She showed him her instruments— the rusted scalpel, the forceps, toothed and non-toothed, scissors, probe and artery clamps, all stored in a wooden box.

'Have you seen the ghost of that man you cut?' he asked.

Of course. She had seen Subbu's ghost and the ghosts of all the other bodies in the dissection room. Medical students called for help from the ghosts when they could not understand some anatomical detail.

Pointing to the heap of coconut shells under the neem tree, she said, 'See those scalps lying there?'

'Those? They're not scalps, they're coconut shells.'

'You see coconut shells but I'm trained—in medical college— to identify the ghost scalps among them. One, two, three . . . seven. Seven ghost scalps.'

'You're bluffing,' said Budhi, drawing closer to her. 'Do they live in your hostel?'

'Not exactly. They come to the Mess when they're hungry. Subbu is fond of cutlet so I save it up for him.'

'What is cuck-let?'

'Cut-let. Looks a lot like the round cowdung cakes that

Gaja uses for the fireplace. Cut-let means you cut and let out the mess of vegetables inside. Only fit for ghosts to eat.'

Budhi never forgot. When he did not want to eat something, he said, 'It tastes like cut-let.'

Nalli described in lurid detail the lives of ghosts and the ghosts of dead ghosts, until Amma said that was enough. Badri's history lessons were fresh in her mind and she told Budhi about the history of medicine. About Greece before the time of Hippocrates; about the Oracles and their advice to sick persons.

'Akka . . . what is Greece?'

'A country, far away, in another continent.'

'That way or this way?'

'That way, beyond Donkubetta. Shut up and I'll explain.' She told him stories of her medical ancestors.

Budhi was a willing listener. But when Jai came on leave and she told him, he said it was the future that was important, not the past. 'The past is boring,' he said.

'It isn't. Don't you want to know how Susruta removed stones from the urinary bladder? And about the tumour in the abdomen which was removed on a kitchen table, without anaesthetic?'

'I'd rather learn how to do it now.'

The past is boring, he had said, and she had disagreed. But sometimes watching her family she wondered if the past was all good. If yesterday had been today, if Angheri had been Mysore, Ajja would probably have finished school and—provided he improved his handwriting—been an engineer or a shop owner. And Appa with all that knowledge could have been prime minister.

Life still centred around the kitchen table where they ate and the porch where the family spent a lot of its time. Vishnu ate the fastest, washed his hands and sat on the window ledge. Nalli knew without looking that he was staring at her, just as he used to earlier. She gulped down her food and got hiccups. 'A meal not slowly eaten will cause wind,' admonished Ajja. When Appa who was the next to finish left the table, there was an immediate shift in mood. Amma and Ajja talked about breakfast the next day. Should it be uppittu or idlis? Should the mango pickle be brought down from the atta, or the lime? Budhi was always the best behaved. 'Ajja, the chutney is *too* good,' he would say. 'The payasa is first class!' He was not greedy but scrupulous: pickle should be on *this* side of the plate, palya on *that* side. He pressed down the heap of rice on his plate to form a crater and waited for the sambar to be poured into it. If it was not, he looked up with such hurt in his eyes that nobody ever repeated the slip. On Sundays, lunch ended with betel leaf, chunna and areca nut, with sugar added for the children. However much Nalli tried, she could never get her lips wonderfully red like Ajja's. Now, after eighteen months in the city, she did not even try.

The porch was the most important part of the house. It extended along the front to the door that led to the kitchen. It had a sloping roof, floors made of cow dung and a parapet wall, two and a half feet high, skirting it. The wall was topped with a wooden ledge, broad enough to sit on. Five wooden pillars rose from the ledge to the roof and were so spaced that you could sit on the ledge and lean against the pillars.

It was here that Ajja bargained over the price of bananas and coconuts. The easy-chair with its long smooth arms and the seat made of gunny was reserved for him. When Ajja was not around, Appa sat on the easy-chair, looking pleased with himself. He was heavier than Ajja and the seat sank alarmingly close to the floor when he settled into it. Nalli had tried to grab the privilege of the chair when she thought no one was looking, but Vishnu shooed her away. He said it was not meant for girls. Vishnu preferred to sit near the door leading out, so he could slink away unnoticed. For Nalli and Budhi the favourite perch was on the ledge between two pillars, their legs extended, feet touching. Sujju sat two pillars away, working on her embroidery. When Jai and Vijai came, the four of them used the bench or the more comfortable reed mat. Amma stood leaning against the door jamb between the porch and the front room. She never stayed long. There was always some work inside to pull her away.

Sompa came visiting, as usual. When Nalli was small Sompa used to lift her up and then swing her down. She liked to sit on his knee, look into his coal-red eyes and smell his strong breath. She listened to the men, and when they were silent she listened to the sounds that scratched away at the silence: Gaja pounding grain in the backyard; dry leaves of coconut tickling each other; the rumble in Sompa's belly. She watched the areca palms arching, curling and swooping as if to lift the house up, the way Sompa lifted her. When she grew older, the space on his knee was not enough and she had to sit with the older children.

When the three men were together, there were arguments. Ajja would spring out of his chair and stamp around the porch, his hair streaming behind him, his arms beating the air. Appa and Sompa waited for him to cool off. When the conversation was at its interesting best, Ajji would call out to Ajja. 'Yes, thanga . . . what is it?' he would ask, and go in.

Nalli was often bored by their talk but she must have listened because she remembered. They argued about business, capitalism and social justice. And Gandhiji. Appa was an admirer, Ajja a critic, and Sompa neutral. Appa believed in ahimsa, austerity and the abolition of the caste system. Ajja said, 'There was a lot of foolishness floating in Gandhi's brain. Show me one god who wears rags like your Gandhi.' Appa said India would progress if we followed Gandhiji. 'This Gandhi is corrupting our household,' Ajja grumbled. Sompa listened with suppressed amusement. About austerity, everyone knew, he was inclined to agree with Ajja, but he never took sides. He was as respectful and tolerant of squabbling men as he was of the women who bargained noisily at his shop for a bit of elastic, plastic beads and coloured buttons, or Afghan Snow. Goods in his shop were cheaper than in Raghavendra Stores. If a customer was short of money, Sompa sold things on trust. Ganapa, who was more shrewd, lamented that one day the shop would have to close because of his brother's generosity.

The children—and even Amma—sided with Ajja. He was the one who brought them bangles, ribbons and balloons, while

Appa frowned on such frippery. Nalli sided with Appa out of loyalty rather than conviction. 'I believe in ahimsa and simple living,' she once said to Jai. Jai demonstrated the foolishness of her belief by pulling her plait and giving her his famous 'electric shock', a slap with the edge of the palm which caused a painful weal, and Nalli promptly abandoned non-violence.

Nalli liked to be near Ajja when he was angry with someone else. 'Shani! Dodda donne! Kaththe!' he cursed. If he was really angry, the words became exotic. 'Thayi-thinda sule magane! Shani Mudevi!' If Ajja was angry with her, she only had to say 'Ajja . . .' in a pleading voice. His eyes would soften and he forgot what he was angry about.

The worst quarrel between Ajja and Appa happened when Nalli was six or seven. A month after Vasu Sir, the new Science Master, had joined the school, Appa brought him home for lunch. Vasu Sir was short and spectacled, with bony shoulders that moved awkwardly when he wrote on the blackboard. He sweated all the time and had to take off his glasses every few minutes to wipe his face with a handkerchief. He looked a lot like a startled rabbit, but he was a marvellous teacher.

Appa took the chombu of water from the ledge and offered it for the guest to wash his feet and hands. Vasu Sir looked happy. 'Sujju, tell your mother we have a guest,' said Appa. 'Our Science Master has come.'

Ajja sprang up from his easy-chair. 'You can't bring him inside,' he cried, grabbing the chombu from Vasu Sir. 'You want to feed him, let him sit at the back.'

Vasu Sir let go of the chombu. Appa's face turned the colour of the dasavala near the gate. He said something in a low voice and stamped away, with Vasu Sir following him. By the time Amma came to receive them, they were gone.

When Appa came home late in the night, Ajja was pacing the porch. 'I suppose you'll want to bring Chowra through the front door next!' he shouted. 'I will die before I accept this equality nonsense.' Appa shouted back. Then he went to his room and banged the door shut. Neither of them came for dinner. Amma persuaded Ajja to eat in his room but Appa refused to eat.

Chowra. Chowraiah. Gowru's father. Nalli began to cry. 'Why did Ajja say that? Who was he talking of when he said *them*?'

'Ssh . . .' said Amma.

'Gowru doesn't come because they live so far.'

'I know . . .'

Nalli woke next morning hoping that it was all over, but it was not. Ajja and Appa would not talk, they would not look at each other. After a few mouthfuls of avalakki, Nalli gave up. Sujju and Budhi were dejected too and Amma was putting up a brave front, Nalli knew by the way Amma snapped at her for no reason. Only Vishnu, who kept darting glances at the two men, ate a hearty breakfast.

In school, she asked Gowru why she did not come home. Gowru laughed her loud, gong-like laughter, like the gongs they beat in the temple. But she would not say why.

The quarrel went on for a long time, or so it seemed. One evening Nalli came home from playing with her bugri to find Ajja on the easy-chair and Appa next to him on the ledge. Amma served coffee and uppittoo. Nalli flung her bugri in a corner and jumped on Ajja's lap. 'You're too big,' Ajja said, patting her head. She got down, nuzzled her father and hugged him. 'Mind you, don't spill my coffee,' he said. She ran around laughing in a silly fashion until Amma told her to wash up and eat. She sat with the plate of uppittoo in her hands, not listening to anything that was being said, blessedly happy.

They were so unlike each other. Ajja was homely and he made up for Ajji's lack of grandmotherly attributes. Appa, preoccupied with school matters, seemed distant and aloof. Appa admired virtue, while Ajja was charmed by something else. As with Akkamma Teacher. When she visited, Ajja disappeared into his room and dabbed on some of his precious scent. He liked Teacher very much. Such a perfect mix of beauty and good breeding, he said. When the children asked him about his marriage, he became shy and giggly. He said that he used to send letters to Ajji scratched on a banana leaf. 'Only once,' laughed Ajji. 'And he only wrote "thanga" on the leaf.'

Not that Appa was less ardent. Nalli slept in the same room as her parents where two cots were joined together for Appa, Amma, Nalli and Budhi. Early in the morning she could hear Appa's endearments: 'Kamu, Kamugi, Kamugini . . .' He whispered about Amma's 'soft warm waist' and 'tender feet . . . so beautiful . . .' Not so loud, the children might be awake, Amma said. Amma, beautiful? It was so funny. But for her parents' sake Nalli hoped that Budhi was truly asleep and not pretending, like her. On those days of the month when Nalli had to wake early, bathe and wash her underclothes, she went to the kitchen for coffee. Appa and Amma would be there, seated on the windowsill next to the fireplace. Amma poured jaggery coffee from the brass chombu kept warm by the fire, using the edge of her sari to hold the hot chombu. Nalli sat on the three-legged, wooden stool with her coffee and watched Amma run her fingers along the outer ridge of the chombu as she talked to Appa. Appa drank two cups of coffee and Amma one. Nalli's being there never interrupted their conversation.

There was another week of holidays to go before college reopened. Appa came home late one evening. She heard the ring of his cycle bell and saw him ride through the gate with the newspaper rolled up in his hand. He walked into the kitchen and spread the paper on the table near the lamp. The family milled around him. Appa moved his finger over the columns, his lips worked in silence. He was searching for her number. Nalli could feel her cheeks tremble as she waited. And then everyone was thumping her on her back. She had passed.

'Appa wants to talk to you,' Amma said the next evening. They sat in the porch; Appa with one foot tucked beneath him, his face inscrutable. Outside, behind the jackfruit tree, the sky was turning softly pink. The light had dimmed and a red glow like a blush rested on the grandmother hill. Wildfowl set up a committee meeting in the guava tree and their cluck-cackle filled the air. Soon they would be asleep on their perches and the crickets would take over. Nalli was nervous. Appa had not had a serious talk with her since she had joined college. Appa began in his headmaster voice: 'If you're given a gift what will you do with it?' She was about to speak when he said, '*Think* and answer.'

He wanted to reward her with a gift! A sari would be nice, or a gold chain, or a stylish leather bag like Carol's. But they could not afford anything like that. Just a handbag, then. If only Appa would let her choose the gift.

'I don't know what you want to give me,' she said, shyly. 'I promise to look after it well.'

'A reasonably good mind, Nalli,' Appa said. 'You already have it.'

Such a strange thing to say. A good mind? What good mind? It was hard work that got her through the exams. She waited for Appa to explain, but he simply got up and went for his bath.

11

Clutching her stethoscope Nalli approached the young man with the groin hernia. She looked at him in confusion, scratched her nose and tugged at the buttons on her coat. 'His heart and lungs are normal,' said Dr Bansali, pre-empting her. 'Request him to undress. You cannot examine a hernia when the patient has his clothes on.' The hapless patient undid his trousers and pushed them down a few millimetres. 'Ask him to drop his pants *and* his underwear,' snapped Bansali.

The professor of surgery was an eccentric sort. He was polite with his scrub nurse, considerate to patients and savage with the students. He had a no-nonsense, practical approach to surgery. They had to think clearly. What will you do if a patient comes vomiting blood? If there is a hot, tender lump in the neck? A stab wound in the abdomen? He countered ignorant answers with fine-tuned sarcasm. The students preferred to stay clear of his mordant tongue.

'What will you do for a patient with fracture patella?'

The question was for the students in general but no one

would bite. Nalli had never seen a case of fracture patella but had read about it. This, she decided, was her chance to impress. She described how the surgery was done, how holes were drilled and screws passed through the fracture fragments. With encouraging nods from the professor, she described every intricate detail with the breathless ease of one who did not understand it too well.

When she had finished, Bansali asked, 'May I ask where you got all this information from?'

'*Operative Surgery*, Chatterjee, sir.' Chatterjee's was a readable book with guidelines that were easy to memorize and therefore popular with students.

A lopsided grin appeared on the professor's face. 'Miss Nalinakshi,' he said. 'I suggest you throw that book in the wastebin and come to Theatre. That's where you'll learn about fracture patella.' Nalli's patellae buckled beneath her.

With their stethoscopes snailed around their necks, the students entered the wards every morning. They raced along the hospital corridors trying to acquire the harried look of the medical tribe. Patients were wheeled and sometimes threatened into subjecting themselves to the students' learning hands. Bellies were made sore, hernias tender and limbs painful by unskilled prodding. They learnt from the doctors, every one of whom had a peculiarity.

Dr Ninan, the senior physician, was a small, stylish man trained in the best British tradition. He walked with little hopping steps, smiled sweetly at patients, and offered advice. He told them to have soups, puddings and jelly with cream. The patients, who survived mainly on kanji, listened in respectful silence. Ninan liked the association of disease with food. He taught the students about red-currant-jelly stool and ground-coffee vomit, pea-soup diarrhoea and anchovy-sauce sputum. These pithy metaphors of body effluents were made with a beatific smile while the staff nurse held out the specimen in a bedpan, sputum cup or emesis basin for the students' benefit.

Dr Rodrigues—better known as James Bond—taught forensic medicine. He lectured in loving detail on bodies mutilated by

murder, suicide and accident. James Bond did everything with
the style befitting his epithet. As he entered the class, he would
stub out his cigarette with the air of a martyr who had to wait
an entire hour before his next puff. Dr Mahalingam peppered
his public health talks with jokes, which were easier to remember
than details of latrines and sewage disposal, and Ponnamma,
who taught microbiology, kept male interest alive with her
tiered hairdos and audacious cholis.

⟿

Eighteen months of learning on a dead man had not equipped
Nalli to deal with patients. How could dead Subbu have taught
her to treat the living? Every sick kidney or heart, liver or limb
was attached to life and that was the difference. Surgery was
anatomy applied to a sick person; disease was physiology gone
wrong. As her insides toughened, the smell of living blood failed
to nauseate and she was able to pass by suffering and not think
about it.

Only once, for a period of several months, it was different.

Her friendship with Alagu just happened. He was forty-plus
and good-looking, with fine eyes and a smile that lingered
beneath his bristling moustache. When he first came to see
Bansali, Alagu was dressed in a red check shirt and tapered
trousers. He had a swelling in his groin which had been growing
bigger and had now become painful. Hernia, the doctors said;
it must be operated on. Alagu said he did not believe such
nonsense. He had spent more than a hundred rupees in three
months on doctors' fees and the swelling had only got bigger.
All he wanted was a belt to hold the swelling down.

It was a large hernia, the size of an orange, starting in the
right groin and going down into the scrotum. Bansali explained
that the hernia was no longer reducible and in danger of
obstruction. A belt was not the answer. It would only harm him.

'Why did the other doctors not tell me it was serious?' asked
Alagu in a voice pitched higher than necessary. 'They told me it
was serious but not that serious. They should have said it
clearly, that my life was in danger. Doc, you better pull them up,

they're not doing their job well enough.' He was angry and frustrated. 'About surgery being necessary, it's a good joke. But I happen to know someone, an old man who comes to church, who's been wearing a hernia belt for years now, specially made for him. Just measure me for a belt, doc, and give a prescription. I'll stop bothering you.'

'Let me put it in plain words and then you can decide for yourself,' said Bansali. He tore off a page from the prescription pad on his desk and started to sketch. Just then a nurse came with an urgent message from Theatre. Excusing himself, Bansali hurried away. Alagu saw Nalli who was posted in the clinic that week. 'These doctors go to any extent to bluff their way through their own bungling,' he said. 'They tell me I need an operation when a belt will do the job.'

Bansali had taught them hernia the previous week and Nalli knew it well enough. She showed Alagu on the piece of paper how his hernia was in danger of obstruction. 'At first it refuses to go back into the abdomen. Later, the blood supply can get cut off and that's serious. It's safer to operate before the complications set in.'

'I'm not a fool that I'll agree to be cut up so easily,' Alagu said with a short laugh. 'I'll find doctors who know what they're doing.'

He returned in little over a month. For two days he had been in constant pain. 'Isn't there some other treatment?' he asked. 'I'll agree to anything but an operation.'

He was admitted. The pain did not go away and reluctantly he began to think about surgery. That evening Nalli found him brooding and still indecisive. 'I hate to think of being in bed at a time when my life's *going* somewhere,' he said. 'I'd be mad to submit to blood-thirsty surgeons.' She explained again the risk of keeping an irreducible hernia. He was miserable. 'The pain's quite bad at times. Even my son said I should have it done . . . Listen, I'm not going to let them do anything without their explaining every detail. No one will operate on my hernia without properly justifying the reasons.'

After a week in hospital, he made up his mind. When the

anaesthetist checked him over, Alagu was found to have another, bigger problem: a saccular aneurysm of the left ventricle. The senior anaesthetist came to check him and more tests followed. Alagu was told that he was a high-risk case.

'You mean you can't guarantee that I'll survive the operation?' he asked.

'Nothing of the sort,' said the doctor, who was embarrassed by words like 'guarantee'. 'A spinal anaesthetic should be safe enough.'

'Why're you asking me to sign a high-risk consent form? Is it because you don't have confidence in your ability or because my heart's not going to stand what you're going to do?'

Alagu asked for more time to think. The pain from the hernia was now constant and it had made him irritable. Nalli would often stop by his bed. Alagu put on an act of being brave but his distress was obvious.

One afternoon he told her, 'My wife died two years after we married and I brought up our only son. He's now in college and can look after himself. I've led such a lonely life. That's what led to my smoking a pack and a half a day. But six months ago, I met a wonderful woman. Sings for the church choir with me. Name's Maria but I call her Myna.' Anger flashed in his eyes. 'After a long time I find myself happy, and then this.'

Myna, a quiet woman, had been coming every day. She sat by his bedside, reading from a book of jokes, or they walked in the garden outside the wards. They were very much in love. The son, a shy serious boy, joined them in the evenings. They were so happy together that Nalli was sure everything would work out well.

The doctors gathered around Alagu's bed every morning; they spoke in low tones about his perfusion, arterial oxygen and lung capacity. Alagu turned away, his eyes puzzled.

It was afternoon. Nalli saw him behind the surgical block, smoking. 'This is the last one, I promise,' he said with a weak smile. He had lost a lot of weight in one week. Through the open neck of his shirt she could see that the hair on his chest was turning grey.

'I've decided to go ahead with it,' he said. He was worried. 'Everyone tells me, be confident, it's going to be all right. I have this awful suspicion it won't be. Doctors are known to make mistakes—they even operate on the wrong side or leave an instrument behind. You'll be around to make sure they don't do anything foolish, okay?' He had asked Dr Bansali what his chances were. Would his heart condition remain stable during the surgery? Bansali told him his chances were fifty-fifty. 'How does he know it's fifty-fifty? Has he done four cases like mine and lost two, or done ten and lost five? What if the chances are one to nine?' He flung the cigarette butt on the grass and stubbed it out with his foot. '"You have to take the risk" he told me. But *he* doesn't have to take the risk.' There was fear in his voice. 'You must be my son's age,' he said. 'Don't lie to me. You think I'll make it?'

'Of course,' she said. 'You have a good chance.'

He threw up his hands. 'You have a sneaky feeling that I might die.' She flushed at the truth of his statement. 'I can read people,' he said. 'Not always, but a lot of the time. Dr Bansali lied about my chances because he has to get me into the right frame of mind for a surgery which is inevitable. The nurses lie because they think it's their duty. And you, because you pity me. I said to Myna yesterday I was certain I would come out of it. I lied because I love her.'

Then Myna came and the three of them went back to the ward. Alagu went on talking. 'The padre from our parish came last night and you know what he said? He asked me to pray. Prayers don't work for me. Devotion to another human being is enough. What do I need God for?' He put an arm around Myna and squeezed her shoulders. 'Death can be a positive experience, the padre said. I've never heard such nonsense. I like everything that's happening in my life, except for this lump. I want to live. A world without me, it doesn't exist. I can't imagine people coolly going about their lives when I'm gone. The choir in which I sing—no matter who takes my place, it will always be without me.'

That day it was late afternoon when Nalli left the surgical

ward. She had missed the forensic lecture. As she went out, she met the hospital matron near the entrance to the ward. 'Just a minute,' she said, stopping Nalli as she walked past. 'I want to have a word with you.' Turning around, she led Nalli to her office. Years of giving orders to the student nurses and admonishing various staff had brought an unerasable sternness to the matron's face. It was never easy to guess the emotions behind those tightly pursed lips. Now she glared at Nalli from behind her desk. 'You're spending too much time alone with one of the patients.' She said 'alone' as though the word had some disgusting connotation. 'It isn't proper for a medical student.'

'He has a serious problem and he's afraid. He needs to talk about it.'

'I can send a male orderly or a ward boy to talk to him.'

Who was the matron to tell her not to speak to a patient? Nalli decided not to heed her warning. The next day when the matron told her that she was wanted in Bansali's office, she wished she had listened. Bansali heard the matron's complaint and then Nalli's faltering attempt to explain: 'Sir, this man, he lost his wife years ago, sir, and is just planning to get married again after many years. He's afraid of surgery, sir. He needs to talk to someone outside his family. Sir, I only listen to him. He has a son and Myna and the priest who comes but . . .'

It was the first time she had talked at length to the professor. He listened until she finished and then turned to the matron. 'She's doing what you and I don't have the time or the capacity for,' he said. 'I suggest you leave her alone.'

On the day of the surgery, Nalli could think of nothing else. Alagu was first on the list of operations and she hurried to the ward to see him before he was wheeled into Theatre. As she entered the male surgical she saw the commotion: doctors and nurses rushing about, dragging suction machines and oxygen cylinders.

She managed to get into the ward, now overfull with doctors, nurses and machines. Cardiac arrest: Alagu had coughed up a kidney tray of blood, and collapsed. At the door, Myna stood terror-stricken. Alagu, white as the wall behind him, struggled to breathe. Through the oxygen mask that covered his nose and mouth, Nalli could see his eyes wide open, accusing: *You're going to let me die. You know I'm dying and you can't do anything about it.*

When it was all over she watched the nurses carry out the 'dead body routine'—close the eyelids, tape the lips, bandage the jaw, tie the big toes together, plug the orifices. The doctors, all of them, had left soon after the death was certified. Nalli walked out of the ward and through the hospital gates. She walked past the bank, the shops, the town hall, the police station, with the sun stabbing into her eyes. On the narrow, quieter road behind the police station was a patch of grass. On the grass sat a young man, cross-legged, swaying back and forth as he read aloud to himself from a book. Not ten yards away the crows fought over an empty lunch packet. In the police grounds beyond the lawn, a batch of trainee policemen marched to *left-right-left-right-left-right* . . . Nalli did not see the young man or hear the crows fighting or the policemen quick-stepping to their daily routine.

In the morning, Bed No. 21, neatly made by student nurses with white sheets and a red blanket, lay empty. For an entire day it stayed bare as if no one had the courage to use it. Death was an embarrassment, and too recent to dismiss. On the second day Nalli saw a young girl scheduled for a tonsillectomy seated on the bed, reading a magazine. Later that day, Nalli was asked to meet Bansali in his office. It had not been long since the matron had complained. Wondering guiltily what this could be about, she went.

He was sitting back in his chair, looking out of the small window of his office. She stood before him, shifting uneasily on her feet. 'The patient who died on Tuesday . . .' he said, in his usual abrupt way. 'He was a fine man and I'm sorry. I appreciate what you did for him.'

Nalli was embarrassed. She had not done anything except talk to Alagu. 'The opportunity to wait on a dying patient does not come too often,' Bansali was saying. 'As doctors, we run away from death. You were there with him till his last day.'

'I wasn't there in the end,' she blurted. 'I didn't know . . .'

'Even if you knew, even if you were there, you couldn't have helped him. None of us could have, but that's not what I'm talking about. I had one such opportunity when I was an intern at a hospital in a small town near Rohtak, a few years older than you are now. I had to wait on a father and his sixteen-year-old son, both dying of cholera. The doctor—he was the only doctor in the hospital—told me that they would both die and I would have to sit there till the end. I protested, saying I was very tired and they were dying anyway. You know what he said? "It's a rare opportunity to be able to wait upon the dying. We're so eager to wait upon important people, on royalty. The dying are royalty." The father kept telling me he was happy I would save his son. He died first, and the boy six hours after him.'

Bansali looked out of the window again and was silent. Nalli was scared to interrupt his thoughts. Through the window she could see students hurrying to the classroom for the forensic lecture. 'It's time for your class, isn't it? You can go,' he said, reaching for the stack of case sheets before him.

Nalli was puzzled by what Bansali said. She did not understand the importance of his words until much, much later.

12

That year when Nalli went home for the holidays, she took her stethoscope instead of the bones.

'Our kutty dacter,' Ajja said. Cows with boils, blisters and wounds which Ajja had managed for years merited her opinion. Neighbours asked her advice for aches and fevers, cough and cold. Nalli protested that she was inexperienced. 'She's being modest,' they said, and kept coming.

At the santhe on a busy Sunday morning, Kenchi, who sold jasmine, was knocked over by a lorry. It had skidded as it took a turn at the entrance to the market where the road narrowed. Kenchi's leg and her basket of flowers got caught beneath the wheel. They brought her on a bamboo stretcher, a portion of her sari torn off and wrapped around the protruding bits of bone.

Nalli knelt beside her and spoke soothingly but could not bring herself to look at the leg. What should she do? She sprang up, went to the kitchen and stirred several spoons of sugar into a glass of water. 'Drink this, Kenchi,' she said. 'It will give you strength.' When the woman raised her head it brought fresh waves of pain and she retched violently. 'Come, just a sip . . . it's good for you,' Nalli said, averting her eyes from the wound through which blood seeped steadily. Her words sounded pathetic.

Ajja squatted by the injured woman. 'Get me a clean dhoti,' he said to Amma. 'Kenchi, breathe deep and think of Ishwara. I'm going to look at the wound.' He folded the dhoti until it was a long strip, about eight inches wide, quickly peeled away the rag and wrapped the dhoti tight over it. The blood soaked through but the folded dhoti was good enough to stem the bleeding. 'Vishnu, hold the foot at the ankle. Now pull!' When the fractured ends were better aligned, Ajja supported the limb with a splint made of bamboo and secured it with strips of cloth. By the time the jeep came to transport Kenchi to Mysore, the bleeding had stopped. She was pale, but her jaws were no longer clenched in pain. She moaned softly and breathed easy.

Splint. Clean dressing. Pressure to stop the bleeding. Why had it not occurred to her? A medical emergency right there at her doorstep and she had been witless. Drink sugar water, she had said. Could anything be more ludicrous? Ajja had saved the injured woman's life. No one, not even Vishnu, ridiculed her, but she was ashamed. Five years of college and she was unable to give first aid to an injured woman. Kenchi reached Mysore and had surgery on her leg. Every time her name was mentioned, Nalli flinched as if it were her own leg that had been broken. The doubts fed on themselves until she wondered if she could wriggle out of the mess she had got herself into. She did not want to be a doctor. She could be something else, like a teacher or a tailor. Two boys in her batch had dropped out, but for her it would not be easy. Appa had taken loans and spent a lot of money. She needed a solid reason.

As if to assist her devious intentions, her backache resurfaced

when she went back to college after the holidays. Nalli's back
had troubled her since she was a child. Ajja used to pour warm
coconut oil into his palms and massage her back, kneading,
punching, pinching the sore spots to make the pain go away.
When she was older, Amma took over but she was not as good
as Ajja. Nalli's back had left her alone for some time but with
the strain of standing in the wards and at operations, the pain
returned. She worked out the scheme in her mind and then
wrote home about her back: She had tried painkillers, a hot
water bottle, Amrutanjan and Tiger Balm. The painkillers caused
stomach upset and nausea; the salves burnt her skin. She could
not study. She had tried everything: she had moved her desk
close to the wall, stacked books on it to get a comfortable height
so she could lean against the wall and read; she had tried tying
a towel tight around her waist to dull the pain.

Lies, lies. She reasoned that her lies would hurt no one. Ajja
wrote that he was sending a medicated oil which the Vaidyar
had made for her. It smells but it will do you a lot of good, he
said. There was no point in dissuading Ajja. He would send it
anyway. And it would be Vishnu who came with the oil. He
would see through her fraud. She dreaded his coming, but also
waited for it.

When the visitor did come it was not Vishnu. Jai, along
with two of his friends, waited in the quadrangle. He was on his
way to Bombay where he was in his first year of post-graduation
in surgery. Ajja had urged him to take the three bottles of the
strong-smelling oil for her. It was the first time Jai had visited
Nalli in college and she was happy. They went to the Mess for
coffee and she got on really well with Jai's friends, especially the
boy with the pointed beard and the steel bracelet. She liked the
way his restless fingers played with the bracelet on his hairy
wrist. He was interested in everything she said. Nalli laughed her
newly cultivated laugh and moved her shoulders in that sexy
way she had seen in a film. Jai was quiet, almost dull. He said
he would start building the hospital soon after his MS. 'No place
to beat Bombay,' said his bearded friend. 'Why do you want to
hide in a village?' Jai said his village needed a surgeon. 'They've

managed all these years, haven't they?' argued his friend. 'Nothing like quack remedies to please villagers. Your surgical skills will be useless.' Nalli thought Jai's friend was very clever.

Before he left, Jai took out a pen from his shirt pocket. 'I've had a good nib put in and made it leak-proof,' he said, giving it to her. Back in her room, she put away the oil and looked at the pen. The second-best gift, after the bugri he had given her years ago. She would preserve it forever.

The oil did nothing but stain her clothes and smell terrible, she wrote home after a week. Appa told her to see a doctor. The orthopaedic surgeon ordered X-rays which showed she had scoliosis, an abnormal lateral curve of the spine. It was a birth defect and in her case very slight. The curve caused an imbalance in the ligaments of the back. The doctor put her through a course of physiotherapy and pain-relieving tablets. Nalli had hoped it would get worse and justify her quitting but the doctor dampened such hopes. He said that if she took good care of her back and avoided lifting anything heavy, it would not trouble her too much. She waited a month and then asked the doctor if he could recommend sick leave so she could go home and rest for a few weeks. Convinced that she was suffering, he agreed. Two days later Nalli was on a bus, heading for home.

Her coming home had the desired effect. All day she lay in bed making a feeble attempt to read the medical books she had brought with her. The family talked of little else. Prayers were offered at Peggala and Igguthappa temples. Fat Aunty came with holy water and bhasma. Appa said that if Nalli did not get better in a week he would take her to Mysore and talk to the doctors himself. No one saw through her fraud. Only Vishnu, who was briefly home on leave, looked at her through narrowed eyes. His glance said, I know, I know.

It was very early one morning when Nalli heard Ajja praying; his whispers and extortions, and then his weeping. He sobbed and lifted the edge of his dhoti to wipe his face, 'Devare! Nalli *has* to be all right. Her back should be as strong as a tree trunk. You know how hard she has to work. Our gubbachi has set her mind on being a doctor and only you can make her well again. Devare! Don't make her sickly, like thanga! I might forgive you any other lapse but not that! You hear me? You hear me?'

Nalli felt terrible. But before she could make up her mind to confess her lies, a crisis in the school distracted her.

If she had not been at home, she too might have blamed Appa.

A group of village spokesmen had invited the local MLA to a meeting concerning funding for the school. They petitioned him for a government grant of fifteen thousand rupees with which they would help students buy books. Speeches were made about the need to impart education to the poor. The MLA was applauded for the grant he had recommended two years ago, was hailed as a saviour and garlanded. He had grown up in a village and was receptive to the idea; he said it was a worthy project. But before signing his accord he consulted Appa with whom he had studied in college. 'What does Maestru have to say?' he asked with a genial smile. He was only being polite.

Appa cleared his throat. 'These men who talk about helping poor students will be the first to lick it all up,' he said. 'Ask them what they did with the previous grant of five thousand. I have the figures. Not more than eight hundred rupees was spent on books for poor students. The rest was licked clean, like honey. If you want to help, have the books purchased and distributed to deserving students. But please, no money.'

Without a word, the MLA got into his car and drove away. He looked annoyed. It was hard to tell if he was angry with those who had asked for the grant or with Appa for shooting it down. Everyone in the village was furious. Maestru had spoken the truth but he had also denied the village a share of the funds. Those who had long respected Appa became cold towards him.

Things worsened when Angheri Naganna Gowdru's nephew failed in the ninth standard. He was the same boy who had created a minor incident some years ago when he came to school wearing shoes.

Gowdru owned twenty acres of areca and paddy, thirty head of cattle and the mango grove, two carts and four bullocks.

His house, which was on the other side of the market, was one of the two double-storeyed houses in Angheri. His hitherto friend and now adversary, Bhimasena Nayaka's was the other. The two men had adjacent pieces of land, which were blessed with an abundance of teak. Their parents had abided by the law and refrained from cutting down the teak but the sons were ambitious. They cut the timber, sold it by stealth and amassed fortunes. As the two became wealthier, they grew more stupid. When Bhimasena Nayaka put glass panes in his windows, Gowdru got coloured glass for his home. When he had his doors and windows painted green, Bhimasena painted his a bright blue and extended the extravagance to include the veranda and gate.

Gowdru's nephew had failed by seventy marks. Pressured by his wife, Gowdru asked for a special favour: that the boy be given enough marks to get promoted. Appa explained that a few grace marks were permissible, but in this case it could not save the boy. It was bad enough for Gowdru that he had to ask a favour of the school headmaster; to be refused was unthinkable.

Ajja berated Appa for his stupidity. 'You have nothing to lose by giving in,' he said. 'The day will come when we will need help from Gowdru. What will we do then? How will we hold our heads high in the village?'

'We will always hold our heads high,' Appa said, and stuck to his decision.

Naganna Gowdru set to work, meeting higher officials in Mysore to complain about the high-handedness of the headmaster. Appa was accused of favouritism and prejudice against pupils whose parents he was jealous of and resentment against him increased in the village.

As if things were not bad enough, Appa got into trouble over the Independence Day function. Some students were to dress up as freedom fighters—Gandhiji, Nehru, Bose, Patel and Kasturba—and lead the singing of the national anthem. When word got around that a Brahmin boy was to be Gandhiji and Gowramma's sister would play Kasturba, Shanku Master was angry. He said it was wrong to mix castes. There were many high-caste girls who could be Kasturba, why had Maestru asked an untouchable to do it? Appa said his choices were intentional and went ahead as planned. Many were infuriated and openly reviled Maestru.

Hostile glances and murmured accusations pursued the family. Neighbours stopped visiting; friends kept their distance. Nalli prayed for some miracle that would solve the problem but it got worse. A memorandum was signed by the teachers about Appa's inefficient handling of school matters. He was stripped of the headmaster's post and his immediate junior appointed to the job. Nalli would always remember the groan of Appa's cycle as he came in through the gate that day. Amma, who must have known that a crisis was at hand, hurried out to meet him. He looked at her and shook his head in a hopeless gesture.

The family gathered on the porch in a moment of collective grief. When Appa said he would resign, Ajja became frantic. He walked the length of the porch and back and each time he came to Appa, he said, 'Beda kano, beda . . . Don't do it, don't.' Amma stood at the doorway. 'We have the children's education to think of,' she said. 'And Nalli's marriage.' They pleaded with him to stay on for the four years he had before retirement.

Nalli sat on the ledge and listened. She was confused and angry and also a little proud of her brave father. She did not understand why he had to suffer like this. He did everything with a conviction that was his. He could have made that small concession to Naganna Gowdru. He could have kept his mouth shut about the grant for the school. He could have got some girl other than Gowru's sister to be Kasturba. Now, because he had stuck so stubbornly to his principles, he was no longer headmaster of the school he loved more than anything else.

The light began to fade and shadows lingered and moved on the front yard. Ajja went in for his evening puja. Appa looked at her and his eyes spoke. *You understand, don't you?*

She should say something to her brave father, she thought; instead she went in to light the lamps while Amma stood where she was and spoke quietly to Appa.

Next day Nalli stood before Appa in the little room that was his office. He was planning to take her to Mysore for treatment, he said. She need not worry, her back would be cured and she would be back in college soon.

The words tumbled out of her. 'Appa . . . I exaggerated the pain. It isn't so bad. The doctor said it was a minor problem. I did not mean to lie, Appa . . . It's just that all the study and the work . . . bit too much for me . . .' She forced herself to look at him, prepared to face his anger.

The silence stretched for a long minute. 'Never mind,' he said. 'The important thing is that your back problem is not serious. But—do you really want to leave college?'

A week later, a chastened Nalli returned to Madras, determined to face the exams.

13

Orthopaedics was a busy department with injured patients coming at all hours. During her two-week posting there, Nalli first learnt the technique of applying plaster casts to broken arms and legs. It felt great to mould wet sheets of plaster of Paris around a limb, to feel it grow hot and hard and to then peel away the chalky flakes of white from her palms and nails.

Soon, she was assisting the house surgeon in simple cases. She helped in the reduction of a fracture forearm and applied the cast herself. That evening Suguna and Carol were treated to a step-by-step account. Suguna posed as the patient and Carol as assistant while Nalli showed them, using a thin towel, how the roll of plaster was moistened and wrapped around the limb: 'The elbow must be at right angles and the forearm semi-prone. There. Once the plaster has set—it's lovely to feel the soft plaster grow hot and hard—you wait a full five minutes, no movement, and then make a sling. The collar-and-cuff type, to support the arm. The plaster stays on for six weeks . . .'

Two days after her self-acclaimed ortho case, the patient was back in hospital complaining of a crawly sensation inside the plaster. 'It's because of sweating,' the house surgeon assured him. He came at least twice a week, imploring the doctor to make the itching go away, or remove the plaster. The house surgeon referred him to his senior. 'The bone won't heal faster just because you don't like having a cast,' said the doctor. 'You have to keep it for six weeks.' When the plaster was finally cut open, the disintegrating remnants of a cockroach were found inside.

Nalli, who was by then in paediatrics, heard about it from the patient himself. He stopped her on the stairs and told her what he thought about her skill in plastering.

The students were the pariahs in the wards. The interns bullied them, disgruntled patients cursed them and the doctors ignored them. The nurses watched pitying as they fumbled with newly learnt talents and hung about waiting to ambush the sick. History taking, examination, auscultation. Rectal, vaginal. Lie down. Sit up. Lean forward. Clench your teeth. The timid among the patients submitted to the indignity. Others grumbled, or reported to the matron, who shooed the students away. In the canteen, over coffee, they gloated over rare cases.

'A Huntington's Chorea in F ward. Coming?'

'The bilateral amputee's having two fingers chopped off . . .'

'A fabulous scrotal hernia, man. Hanging down to the knees!'

The clinical years, which were spent mostly in the wards, seemed to merge into one another. In five years every one of them had changed: taller, broader, leaner, plumper, balder. But not all the changes were superficial.

One afternoon, Bansali was about to begin his lecture on gall bladder diseases when he had noticed Balan at the back of the class with an unlit bidi in his mouth. Balan had just managed to pass the pre-clinical exams. Everyone had predicted that Badri would fail him even if Ali Khan did not. Nothing of the sort happened. He carried on as before, slouching in the back row during lectures as if he was doing everyone else a favour. With quick steps, Bansali walked up to Balan.

'I have an important topic to teach,' he said, loud enough for the whole class to hear. 'If I don't do it today, it will not be taught. Make up your mind. Will it be the lecture that will take centre stage today, or you?'

For a few seconds there was silence. Balan looked defiant. Then he pulled the bidi out of his mouth and sat up. When the class was over, the professor asked Balan if he would like to talk things over in the canteen. They went, stopping briefly to light bidis. They were in the canteen for an hour. Balan did not tell anyone what Bansali told him that day, but he became serious about his studies.

Mathew, Kamal and Ranjit were not so lucky. Kamal was a Bombay boy with a trembling smile on his lips as though he would burst into laughter or tears if he paid attention to what was going on. Ranjit was meek, round-faced and courteous with the girls. He walked them back to the hostel from classes, wheeling his cycle and stopping to chat for a few minutes before riding away. Mathew was a football player. When he played in a match, his two friends were always there, cheering him.

Kamal was a good student, but in the latter part of the second year he seemed to change. He no longer smiled; he dressed carelessly and often missed class. It was rumoured that he was experimenting with mandrax and methedrine, maybe something else and, one day, he was found dead in his room. His friends were questioned and the Dean spoke to the students about the dangerous world of drugs. Someone got a copy of *Valley of the Dolls* and passed it around. Nalli read it, but it did not help her understand what had happened to Kamal.

For Nalli, the sight of Kamal's family sitting swollen-eyed by his body brought memories of the only death she had known. It was an old woman in the village, a distant relative, who had died. The death had upset everyone. Ajji had wept all day, delicately and persistently. Amma sat next to her, sobbing. Even Sujju went about with wet eyes. Nalli was embarrassed by her inability to weep. When with effort she managed to squeeze out a few tears, she got carried away and imagined herself a tragic heroine. By evening it was time for the funeral and Nalli was disgusted with her own vanity. She declared that she was not going. 'Funerals depress me,' she said.

'We're not going for your sake, but theirs,' Appa said, angry, and as she began to protest, added, 'no, now you may not come, since you think it a tedious duty.'

The next day she went with Ajja, carrying a bottle of lime pickle and a plate of rava puttoo. For years afterwards she felt guilty when she went past the house where the woman had died.

After Kamal's death Mathew and Ranjit continued to stick together. A few months later, during the pharmacology exam, Ranjit was caught referring to a formula he had written on his palm. He was debarred from the exams for a year. He hanged himself in his room the same evening. For the rest of his days in college, Mathew stayed a loner.

Then there were the college romances that faded as girls opted to listen to their parents.

Suguna's marriage was arranged with a Delhi-based engineer.

'What's he like to look at?'

'He's all right.'

'How do you feel about marrying him?'

'Okay.'

Suguna's reaction to most things was lukewarm. It was not that she did not care. It was natural for her to play down everything. If asked what it was like to be brilliant, she would have reacted the same way.

For Carol, the blows had come fast. She had got through four boyfriends before she started going steady with Prabhu, a senior in college. When Prabhu was first seen wheeling his bicycle alongside Carol, no one believed it would last. He was a quiet sort who kept to himself. But it worked. Carol stopped dating others. No more late nights and parties for her. She was content to go for long walks or sit with Prabhu in the quadrangle. They were always together. Prabhu had an older brother in Australia, and he and Carol planned to emigrate when they finished college.

After completing his internship, Prabhu went to Australia as planned, to a job his brother had fixed up. He would come back and take Carol with him. But after a few letters from Australia, there was silence. A few months later Carol recieved a letter saying he had changed his mind. Carol did not shed a tear, not even before her friends. She studied furiously, sitting up late every night. There being no dearth of boys eager to please her, she went out on Saturday evenings and stayed out late. In the Mess, her laughter rang louder than before. It sounded as if she was laughing at herself.

The last semester came all too soon. With the final exams approaching, this was a time of mind-zapping study, of a battle with sleep and lassitude, and the fear of not knowing enough. You had to have knowledge, clinical acumen and a lot of luck. In the practical exams there would be a long case and two short cases in each of the three subjects—surgery, medicine and gynaecology. For the long case they would be given twenty minutes to take a medical history, do a complete physical examination, come to a diagnosis and write it all down. Then the examiner would ask questions. The student's future could be wrecked by a single case. And there were patients cussed enough to mislead a student with false symptoms.

In surgery Nalli's long case was an avuncular man with 'water-problem' and lumps in his groin that appeared when he coughed or sneezed. An easy case: enlarged prostate and bilateral inguinal hernia. In medicine it was rheumatic valvular disease with an abundance of clinical signs to help her along. But gynaecology almost finished her. The fat, garrulous woman could not stop boasting about the number of students who had failed on her illness. It was five precious minutes before Nalli could pin her down to answering questions. With luck, and generous hints from the kind examiner, she diagnosed endometriosis, a chronic ailment of the female reproductive organs.

One of the external examiners in medicine made a fuss because Carol appeared for the exam in a short dress. He said it was not suitable attire for a future doctor and then proceeded to ask her the toughest questions on a difficult case. She failed the viva by eight marks. The students were bitter about the injustice and planned to protest, but with the stress of the exams on them they failed to do anything. Carol took the exam again after six months, in salwar-kameez, and got through without a hitch.

Exams over, it was time for them to move on. Some eyes were fixed on foreign jobs; going abroad was the ultimate goal. Only Manjunath had no intention of working anywhere but in Nuggehalli. 'You don't know what poverty really is,' he told them. 'No water in summer, dozens of buffaloes dying before my eyes, girls I knew in school growing old in their twenties. I don't need a foreign degree to work in my village.'

'Cardiology for me,' said Pavan. He was sure one needed a foreign degree to be recognized, even in India. Not that he had any plans of coming back. Like many others in the batch, he was taking the ECFMG exam the following month. If he got through, he would be in the US by the end of the year. 'Five years of slogging as a trainee resident in Boston, and then I'll be earning enough to buy a house with a swimming pool. When I come to India, I'll stay at the Taj in Bombay and the Ashok in Delhi.' Listening to Pavan, for whom she had once shed tears, Nalli wondered: Was he a realist or a mere braggart?

'If I have to slog, it will be right here, not in some other country,' said Balan. 'You *can* be successful without a foreign degree. I might even get that house with the swimming pool before you.'

'Doesn't matter where you live as long as there's lots of money,' said Carol dreamily. She steadfastly stood by her ambitions to be in Australia. And Suguna, who had decided on pathology in the first year of college, had not changed her mind either.

Nalli envied her and the others the firmness of their decisions. Her own future seemed a blur. Her dreams flickered—sometimes dimly and at other times bright—and deep inside she was confused.

The farewell party in the Mess was a sober affair. Tea, going-away mementos, speeches. The faculty members seemed less intimidating and more friendly. Badri, the Nawab and Bansali stood together, chatting with a bunch of the boys, Balan among them. Dr Ninan listened intently to Manju tell him of his plans to work in Nuggehalli and offered advice. Nalli, like everyone else, made promises about writing letters. She exchanged her address with dozens of her classmates. When it was time to go she stood alone for a while, distracted by the unsureness of her future, embarrassed by the goodbyes. Given the uncertainties of the next few years, she knew that few friendships would survive.

14

Back home from college, Nalli wished she could talk to Jai. The last time they met, he had been serious and aloof. Before giving her the pen, he had touched her cheek with it. Then he had looked back and waved as his bike turned the corner.

He was in Bombay now and it worried her. What if some girl, a no-good type, snared him? Nalli examined her feelings and decided she must write everything to him; free herself of anger and guilt. In college, she had told Carol. Did she want to marry him, Carol asked. No. 'Then why're you worried? Can a guy live in Bombay without girls?' 'Lots of guys live without girls,' Nalli said. Confusion churned her mind and in the end, ignoring Carol's advice, she wrote to Jai. All she was doing was giving him a friendly warning. But she wasn't honest enough even then.

Jai wrote occasional letters in reply, all very serious and never mentioning her letter. The villagers had been disappointed when he decided to specialize in surgery, which meant another three years. They urged him to come back and start the hospital. Six years of learning was enough for a doctor.

Jai could convince people better than anyone. 'There's not much use in a hospital where operations cannot be done,' he reasoned. 'This going from Angheri to Mysore for everything must stop. I'll ask an anaesthetist friend in Mysore to come a few times a week. I'll do all the surgery in Angheri. Some surgical experience is what I need, and then I'll be back for good.'

'Patients respect doctors who specialize,' he wrote Nalli. 'You must decide during internship and do your post-graduation. In *something*.' Even though she would then work in the village? Even then.

The thought of further study filled Nalli with dismay. She was angry that Jai was not there to talk to, that he could not sense her dilemma. As a child she had confided, argued and fought with Jai. She fought because it was her right. One hot afternoon (at ages six and eleven) they had been married. Nalli hated the game. She had to sit with her head draped in a red davani and a curtain wrapped around her. A twig of bougainvillea was stuck in her hair. Jai too was bored. The others, playing guests and family were making merry with the avalakki and jaggery filched from the kitchen. Nalli set it off by kicking her groom in the shin with her curtain-draped foot. He kicked back, she scratched, he punched, she bit, he slapped. The marriage ended with Nalli chasing Jai, the curtain trailing her. But Jai did not let her forget their matrimony. 'You have to obey me, you're my wife,' he said.

Like Ajja, Jai had a genius for living. Something of the charmed energy of Ajja and Jai had infected Nalli. In college she used to read his letters and feel unhappy because they were so serious. It was difficult to reply to those letters. What would she write? I am well. Exams are coming up. Beach Aunty visited last week. What was the point? It did not mean a thing. The questions storming her mind remained unasked.

When she used the pen Jai had given her, she remembered all his gifts. The marbles, matchboxes, cigarette wrapper, feathers; and the bugri, which she had once used against him.

Gowru's father had made the bugri, taking all of one morning to finish the job. They had watched as Chowraiah shaved the soft wood into a cone, cut the grooves with a knife and rubbed the upper surface with sandpaper. It was beautifully etched, and the peg was as sharp as the sharpest nail. Chowraiah painted it in blue and green. It was the first real gift she got from Jai. Usually he gave her something when she threatened to tell on him for some wickedness. 'Here, take this,' he would say, pulling it out from his pocket. Always a bribe. Only the bugri had been spontaneous.

Jai taught her to spin the bugri and then lift it, still spinning, on her palm. She carried it everywhere, gripping it, feeling the grooves and the sharpness of the nail on her palm, the cord wound around her wrist and fingers. Amma objected to her playing with it in the house, so every evening she hung it on a branch of the guava tree.

Remembering, she took the bugri out from among her things. The blue and green paint on the grooves was just as fresh, and the nail as sharp as ever. Could she have forgotten the skill of spinning it? Quickly winding the string and holding the free end taut, she flung the bugri with a quick movement of her wrist and watched it spin, with a whir so soft that she had to bend low to hear the sound. As she lifted the bugri on to her palm she remembered the one big fight between her and Jai, the fight in which the bugri had played a part.

It all started in defence of Appa. Jai, like Ajja, believed that Gandhiji had ruined the country by glorifying simple living when everyone knew that if you had any brains you tried to get wealthy. Jai taunted Nalli by ridiculing Appa's belief in austerity and ahimsa. One Sunday afternoon, after a savage fight in which two of Nalli's front teeth had begun to wobble, Jai came back to make peace. Nalli and Vijai were playing a cowrie game near the jackfruit tree. Jai stood leaning against the tree trunk. With him was Rumba, the stray dog he had befriended months ago. Nalli scowled and continued playing.

'I'm going for some mangoes,' Jai said.

'Where?'

'Naganna Gowdru's grove.' He slurped with anticipatory greed. Nalli had already put away the cowries. Gaja overheard Jai and they had to plead with her not to tell. They gave Budhi the slip (for quick forays into forbidden territory, he was a handicap) and set out.

It was a long way off, and hot, but once they had climbed over the stile into Gowdru's land, it became cool. Jai led them to the tree, strong and squat with branches dripping fruit. The girls waited below while Jai swung himself up with the ease of a monkey. Nalli held up her langa to catch the fruits as Jai plucked them. Vijai put them in a heap beneath the tree. When they had enough, Jai climbed down and they sat to eat.

Halfway through the feast, Jai pointed to the beehive on the athi tree opposite. 'If the bees come near, keep absolutely still. If you get excited, they'll sting you to death.' Both Vijai and Nalli knew how painful a bee sting could be and how the skin burned for a long time after the sting was removed. Rumba watched with a grin. Greedy children! With the mango juice matting their hair, sticking to their faces and legs and arms, they ate. Rumba's tongue hung long with disbelief. When they had had their fill, they washed at the narrow brook which was more stone than water. They rubbed the moist stones against the skin and wiped themselves dry with their clothes. Jai stretched out beneath the mango tree while Vijai and Nalli raced around the tree, with Rumba chasing.

'Stop it,' Jai said crossly. 'I want to sleep.'

They went on playing. Rumba barked and ran about in that entirely pointless way of dogs. 'Stop it, Rumba!' Jai screamed, but the dog was in no mood to obey him. 'Vijai, Nalli, stop it, and stop that dog!' Nalli stuck her tongue out at him and Vijai laughed.

Jai leapt up from where he sat, dragged Rumba to the athi tree and tied him there. Walking a little distance away from the tree, he lay down and covered his eyes with his arm. Rumba barked and jumped in protest at being deprived of the game he so enjoyed. Sure enough, the commotion disturbed the hive and a bee stung him. Rumba jumped and barked all the more. That set the hive alive and in no time Rumba was being stung by bees, hundreds of them. The girls, who had been running and laughing till then, pleaded with Jai to untie the dog. Jai uncovered his face, now dark and expressionless. 'Gandhi is an idiot,' he said. 'I'm showing you. Gandhi is an idiot.' He covered his eyes again but Nalli pulled his arm away. 'Jai! Jai!' She hit and kicked and implored him to set the dog free, but Jai would not move. Vijai started to weep. Rumba barked pitifully until he was exhausted and his barks dwindled to a moan. Only then did Jai get up and untie him. The dog limped away, his face swollen, eyes almost hidden, looking at Jai with puzzlement. It was the last they saw of the dog.

Jai looked sheepish. He looked from Nalli to his sister as if waiting for them to say something. 'It's only a dog,' he said. 'He wasn't letting me sleep.'

'I hope it happens to you one day,' Nalli said. Jai laughed a strange, strangled laugh and it incensed her. She hit him with the hand that held the bugri. Jai's hand rushed up to his face in defence and when he took it away, his fingers were streaked with blood. The nail on the bugri had split his cheek.

'I'm bleeding!' Jai screamed. 'Do something!'

Nalli pushed him away and ran; she climbed over the stile and ran all the way till she reached home. Vijai must have helped Jai. Nalli did not meet either of them for a week. After that when Jai came home with an inch-long scar on the side of his face, Nalli would not say sorry, she could not forgive him.

The Rumba episode revealed to her a Jai she did not understand. She had noticed earlier how he sometimes pulled Rumba's tail or kicked him with a meanness that was unnecessary. Even with his pet turtle Peshwa, Jai did strange things. He would tie a string with a stone to one leg and watch the turtle struggle to move. Peshwa was fond of greens and pieces of fruit and most of all of marigold petals. Jai would strew some a distance away and watch the turtle painfully moving forward, and this continued till Peshwa became lame. It was hard to figure out this madness because at other times Jai was thoughtful and considerate. He was the only one among the older boys who did not tease Budhi and was ready to fight off anyone who tried.

Nalli put away the bugri; it reminded her of that ugly afternoon and her mind clouded with disappointment and anger. Why did she trust Jai to share her dream? He had mocked her ambition once, and he had done nothing to support Vijai when she wanted to join medical college. Yet it was not Jai she was angry with, but herself.

❧

In the years Nalli had been away Angheri had changed. The village folk struggled through the harsh, rain-starved months which dried up their crops, they worked for a few months in the year in Coorg and earned some money, and they allowed the invasion of Angheri by visible comforts that were hard to resist. Bojaiah's son bought a second-hand motorbike which grunted with pride along the gutted roads and filled their nostrils with smoke. Plastic toys appeared in the shops, aluminium and steel vessels in the kitchens.

Even after being stripped of the headmaster's post, Appa continued to go to school, regal on his bicycle, and taught the way he always had. He cared about language the way Badri did about anatomy. He had taught more than twenty-five batches of students and they never forgot him. Long after they left the school and the village, they returned to talk to Maestru about their jobs, marriage and family. Appa listened; but since they were no longer his students he did not believe he had the right to interfere. Ajja made up for it by freely airing his views, giving advice, with his goose-neck thrust forward.

Vishnu returned from Shimoga after completing his BA. He impressed everyone with his neat trousers, full-sleeved shirts and shoes that squeaked grandly when he walked. He had a flair for pleasing people, for saying what was expected of him. Everyone in the family, even Ajja, was a little afraid of Vishnu. He was exacting, respectful and secretive.

Jai was the brightness in Nalli's life, Vishnu the darkness. She pursued brightness, but it fled; she shunned the darkness and it thrust itself on her. Many times her dreams began with Jai, the two of them doing something together, but then inexplicably he became Vishnu.

Jai and Vishnu were opposites. They hated each other. Once, on their way back from school, they had a terrible fight in the open ground not far from home. The ground was marshy after the rains and a fine drizzle persisted. The boys fought, lunging and grappling, slipping and falling in a confusion of mud and slush. Budhi ran home shouting that they were killing each other. Being smaller, Jai got the worst of it but he would not give in until Appa came and pulled them apart. They were both bruised and cut, Jai more than Vishnu. Shamed by the defeat, Jai avoided his friends for weeks.

Later that night Nalli overheard Amma talking to Sujju and realized that her sister had caused the fight. Amma was telling Sujju what girls should and should not do. Sujju looked sullen and unrepentant. When she saw Nalli standing at the door, she ran up and shoved her away, screaming, 'Hoge! Kapi!'

'If you were angry with Jai you should have told him yourself,' Nalli said, as she ran off. 'If it was me, *I'd* have fought and not asked Vishnu to do it!' She knew that Sujju would punish her for this. She would mock her about something, like her Book of Poems or Book of Good Thoughts, two notebooks she had carefully been compiling since she was ten. She was proud of them but did not want anyone to see what she had written. She hid the notebooks behind the palambu in Ajja's room, where Sujju had found them. Nalli begged her not to tell anyone but now, of course, Sujju would.

Once, Nalli provoked a fight between Jai and Vishnu. Nalli, Vijai and Budhi were busy shaping mud, stones and twigs into a model of Angheri beneath the parijata tree. They had spent all of Sunday morning at it. They built a wall of stones around the village and with soft mud they built shops, houses, the school and the post office. Nalli patted a large chunk of wet earth into shape next to the post office and declared it The Hospital. She hoisted a flag made out of a twig with flowers. Vishnu came along and saw their make-believe village. 'This is Jai's Hospital,' Nalli said, pointing.

'That Kulla, the Shorty, he'll build a hospital? I'll show you what I can do to his hospital.' A vicious kick, and the hospital was just a clump of mud and stone. Jai heard about it soon enough. He waited for Vishnu near the school and hit him with his hockey stick. The bleeding would not stop in spite of a poultice of sugar and coffee powder and Vishnu had to be rushed to Mysore for stitches on his nose.

Vishnu jealously guarded what was his. No one could touch his school bag or borrow his pen. Everything he did was secret. He half-covered the food on his plate with his left hand as if eating was a sin to be committed in haste. He sniffed whatever he ate. If he liked the food, the family was delighted, almost grateful. 'Vishnu likes it,' was the ultimate compliment. Whatever he ate, he left a small portion unfinished on his plate. When Nalli tried to do the same she was scolded for being wasteful.

Nalli disliked Vishnu but meeting him after a long time, she felt attracted again to his sneering handsomeness. She was uneasy in his presence, and he knew it. That Vishnu was not to be trusted, she knew. She remembered the shameful incident years ago in Fat Aunty's house. The family was visiting Hunsur. Aunty served vadais and a wonderfully sweet pumpkin halwa. Nalli finished the three vadais and the halwa on her plate. When Aunty asked if she would like some more, she shook her head coyly, very sure that Aunty would insist. But Fat Aunty just carried on telling Amma about the Subramani temple she had been to and did not ask Nalli again. The table was cleared and everyone went to sit in the front room. Nalli could not stop thinking about the four pieces of halwa that remained and had been cleared away. Pretending interest in the garden, she wandered out and crept to the back door, which was open. She slipped in, grabbed two pieces of halwa and crammed them into her mouth.

'Stealing . . .'

Turning around, she saw Vishnu blocking the door. Fat Aunty was summoned. 'Silly girl! You said you didn't want any,' Aunty said, laughing. 'Come, come, I'll give you some more.' As if that was possible. 'I don't want it, it's horrible,' Nalli sobbed, as hot tears filled her eyes and the sweet halwa gummed her teeth.

It was always Vishnu who found her out. When she passed into middle school, Ajja gave her three rupees to buy notebooks. She went with Vijai and Gowru to Raghavendra Stores. Six shiny new hundred-page notebooks, and a pencil. Two rupees, twelve annas. She put the new books in her bag, and the girls walked home. They tarried as usual outside the corner shop. The jars filled with coin-sized peppermint sweets, pink rubber sweets, black-and-white rounds and toffees wrapped in silver paper were hard to ignore and her palm was moist from clutching the four annas change. It was not a difficult decision to exchange the coin for three rubber sweets, six wrapper toffees and a paper cone of roasted groundnuts. When Nalli reached home, she had finished everything but her share of toffees. At the gate she popped a toffee in her mouth, licked the sticky remnants from the wrapper and in her haste swallowed the wrapper. Rinsing her mouth, she went in. Coffee was drunk and kajayas eaten without anyone asking questions. Relieved, she sat down to cover her books with newspaper.

Ajja stood looking over her shoulder. 'How much?' he asked. 'Three rupees.' It was easier than explaining about the four annas. She had two more toffees in her bag and was suddenly afraid that Ajja would get suspicious. 'I need more newspaper,' she said and Ajja sent her to the atta, reminding her to take it from the old pile near the pickle jars. Nalli hurried out of the room.

'Are the books hundred pages or hundred-and-fifty?' Vishnu stood leaning against the door to the front room.

'Hundred.'

'You should have four annas left. Where is it?' Nalli pleaded with her eyes for him to shut up, but he grabbed her arm and took her to Ajja. A dreadful scene followed with everyone accusing her. Nalli walked away to where the hay was stacked and climbed one stack, clutching fistfuls of the straw till she was on top. Ajja came to call her but she refused to answer. Grown-ups did not climb the haystack, it would not take their weight, so she stayed there till Jai climbed up and brought her down later in the evening. Vishnu's shadow was in the doorway, watching.

Now Appa's friends had become fewer, but Vishnu gained in popularity. His newly acquired style, his suave manners and edification were much admired and talked about. There was always more to Vishnu than was apparent. When he said that he wanted to be a teacher like the Maestru, Appa was surprised. He advised Vishnu: 'Do what's right for you and learn from your mistakes. It's foolish to follow in anyone else's footsteps.' But Vishnu already knew that walking in Appa's footsteps and avoiding the mistakes he made would be the foolproof method for him. Soon people started dropping in at home to see Vishnu instead of Appa. Young men sat in his room till late in the night. Naganna Gowdru's son was among them.

As she waited for the results, the days seemed to slow down, and Nalli had more time to think and remember. The day of Sujju's marriage, when she had declared her intention of being a doctor, was also the day she discovered a truth about herself.

Her parents had gone with the wedding party to the temple near Nanjangud. They would return late, after the puja. Ajja, Ajji, Vishnu and Nalli had stayed at home. She, because it was one of those days when she was forbidden to go to the temple. The guests had left and Nalli was deprived of the chance to feel pretty for a longer time. She decided to stay in her green langa and orange davani and delight in the softness of silk. Snapping off a length of jasmine from the wedding mantap, she pinned it on her hair.

Jai had said that being a doctor was not for girls, and she had walked away angry. Later in the evening he had come home and they were friends again. They sat near Ajji's bed in the front room and talked about the wedding, the food and the guests.

Jai said that if he could not get the plot of land next to Nagappa's grove, he would buy the site near the post office for the hospital. 'Father says I can get a loan from the bank,' he said. 'The building will be double-storeyed. OPD, X-ray and lab on the ground floor, wards and OT on top. Thirty beds. Six nurses.'

Nalli listened to Jai spin his dreams and her anger vanished. Jai, a doctor. His hospital right there in Angheri. Having declared her intention for the first time that day, she felt herself a part of his dream. She wanted to listen forever. Vishnu stood leaning against the door, a bored expression on his handsome face. He did not appear to be listening. After a while, he walked away.

Daylight was fading; it would soon be dark. Nalli went to light the lamps before the others returned. She paused for a moment near the window from where she could see the last of the light and a patch of sky over the grandmother hill, a tender pink. Happiness hummed inside her. She placed a lamp next to Ajji's bed and carried another to the bedroom which she shared with her parents.

He was seated on the bed, alone. 'It's so dark,' she said, placing the lamp on the window ledge.

Without a word, Vishnu leaned forward and pinched the wick of the lamp. She could see nothing. 'I'm not afraid,' she said. It was a lie. She hated being in a dark room. She was always a little afraid in the evenings when she went round with the lamps to each room. The glow from the lamp would offer a circle of timid brightness but the rest of the room would be pitch. She was afraid of dark corners, of the ghosts that lurked in them. Moonlit nights were better, but that night there was no moon and the darkness was deep.

He was near her now. Wordlessly, he reached out and touched her face, her neck. His hand moved over her shoulders, gripping them. His fingers pressed gently, painfully, against her nipples. His mouth was on her neck, his breath scalding her skin. She did not scream. Instead she pushed her palm against his face, prised open his mouth and pulled his lips, tugged his hair. It must have hurt, because he backed off, and she ran out of the room, bumping her head on the bedpost as she ran.

'Nalli?' She had run straight into Ajja. 'I . . . was frightened,' she gasped, rubbing her forehead. 'Aiyo . . . come, pour some cold water, or it will swell,' said Ajja.

Later that night, the family gathered around the kitchen table and talked about the wedding. Nalli went into the bedroom and closed the door. No one, not even the moon had seen anything. Nor the lamp whose wick had been killed between his fingers, nor the bedstead which had no eyes in the dark. No one knew; but she felt a deep guilt like she had never felt before. And then, as the hours passed, it changed to a chill, steaming pleasure at the knowledge of what might have happened if she had not fought him. Nalli stood before the mirror with the lamp in her hand. In the yellow light she saw it written in her eyes; she saw it. The thrill spread upward until it burned her cheeks and singed every hair on her scalp. She changed her clothes and put them away. Later she would wonder what made her fold that yellow blouse, the green, most beautiful langa with the elephants and the flaming orange davani which had flapped around her like a banner all day, what made her fold and hide them at the bottom of her box. Sometimes she took them out and ran her fingers over their softness. The locked-away memories jumped out and came at her with their talons. It was the first of many such nights. Always in the same room at the same time, with him sitting in the dark and she with the lamp and he snuffing it out . . .

As she lay in bed, awake, her senses sharpened, her mind swam between delight, fear and disgust. Sometimes more delight than fear and then more disgust than delight. She touched her throat with icy fingers, stroked it gently, lovingly. A strange hunger burned in her guts. Was it pain or pleasure, joy or sadness, revolt or submission? She unbuttoned her blouse, slipped her hand in and pressed her breasts. She wet her fingertips with her tongue and touched her nipples. She remembered reading in a book once: 'They sank to the floor and made love.' She had wondered what it meant, to make love . . . sinking to the floor to make it. How? What exactly? Now she knew. She knew what would happen on Sujju's wedding night, oh yes, she knew everything. All about the hardness and the softness and the cruelty of it.

Sujju . . .

Nalli was very young when she realized that Jai was in love with Sujju. Nalli was accustomed to boys looking at her sister and Jai was no different. Sujju did not encourage Jai and she did not discourage him. Her cold eyes, her smile, her laughter, worked their magic. The way she moved about in her most ordinary clothes imbued her angular body with an alluring softness. If she entered a room when Jai was holding forth to the rest of them, his tone changed. He would not look at Sujju but whatever he said, it seemed to be for her. With a faint smile in her eyes Sujju sat on the window ledge, her fingers playing with her hair. Then she sprang up and walked away, her plait swinging behind her. Their silent games bewitched Nalli. She noticed when their eyes met, she listened slyly when they talked. She was jealous. Oh, to be Sujju.

The incident in the atta happened when Nalli was ill with one of her fevers, a childhood affliction with its predictable pattern. Her head throbbed, her calf muscles ached, her eyes and mouth burned with fever. Vijai who sat next to her in class touched her arm and it hurt all over. When she came home, Amma felt her brow, dropped what she was doing and carried her to bed. Sometimes she succeeded in spreading it to the others, but this time she suffered alone.

When Nalli was ill, Sujju had to vacate her room below the atta and sleep on a mattress near Ajji's bed. Nalli's sick mind unfurled and wandered all over the place; it filled with fantasies and nightmares which made her heart race. When the fever abated she enjoyed the aching sweetness of convalescence and reigned briefly like a queen. Ajji felt that her importance as the sickliest in the family was being snatched away. She got out of her bed and peeped into Nalli's room, sniffing with disapproval. 'Fever? Um.'

Ajja was fussy about what Nalli ate and how much she rested. He called her 'gubbachi' and pampered her with hot tomato rasam. He bought a pineapple for her although it cost a rupee, cut it into rings and sprinkled sugar on the pieces. When the fever stayed away two days, he boiled water with gaali soppu for her bath. She bathed and changed into fresh clothes and sat at the table to eat. Ajji's sovereignty was restored. When she went back to school, for the first few days Appa let her ride on the crossbar of his cycle.

This time, after five days the fever had almost left her. It was late afternoon and Nalli was in that state of lazy half-wakefulness which comes from spending days in bed. The sound of some children far away, enjoying a game of seven tiles, reached her ears. How could they be happy when she had almost died?

It was the season for drying hay and Amma and Ajja were out near the haystacks. Budhi was in school and Sujju had come home early because she was studying for the tenth standard exams. Everything was peaceful, and then Nalli heard footsteps and whispers in the kitchen. Jai's voice. Happy, she started to get out of bed. Then she heard footsteps going up the stairs to the atta. They were unmistakably Sujju's. That was odd because Sujju hated climbing the narrow stairs. She did not like salted mangoes or puffed rice. Nalli peeped, just in time to see the edge of Sujju's langa disappearing upstairs. Jai followed her. Nalli got back into bed and pretended sleep. She heard the stealthy, muffled sounds tap and move above her room. They were there a long time, maybe half an hour. Then they came down and everything was silent.

Because she was ill, Nalli had kept the bugri with her, under the mattress. She took it out and squeezed her palm over it until the grooves bit her skin and the sharp nail dug into her flesh. She wound the string round and round and with a swift movement flung it—bugri and string—out of the window. She climbed up the steps on unsteady legs and stood in the middle of the atta. It could not have been the salted mangoes they were after, it could not have been the puffed rice in its wooden box, it could not have been the old books or newspapers. The atta, which had been her domain, suddenly seemed less friendly. She beseeched the jar of salted mangoes, the old books, the single spider struggling up its web to tell her the secret but they would not.

Budhi found her bugri and brought it back. 'Akka . . . you left it hanging on the tree and it fell,' he said. She did not contradict him.

Her fever came back that day and she was in bed another

week. When she returned to school, her position dropped from third to eleventh. Everyone said the illness was to blame but the illness had nothing to do with it, it was in her heart that she suffered. When they played marriage, she had been Jai's bride. When he acted as Rama, she was Sita. When he was Nala, she was Damayanti. When he made bows and arrows out of bamboo he gave the sharpest arrow to her; he taught her with infinite patience to spin a bugri on her palm. Once he even let her join the older children in their escapade up Chinnabetta to fly kites. Now her beautiful sister was threatening to ruin her universe. Everything became clear: Sujju had sewn a bag with satin-stitch embroidery and given it to Vijai. Why, when Vijai was Nalli's friend? Embroidered on the inner lapel of the bag was 'ViJai' with the J in capitals. Nalli now knew whom the gift was meant for.

Nalli prayed for some serious illness to befall her sister, whom she had begun to hate. Ajja became suspicious of her sudden devotion to the gods. 'If you want favours, you must learn to behave better,' he said. 'Igguthappa does not approve of girls who sit with their knees apart.'

When a young man from Mysore joined the bank, her mind set to work. Kaviraj, with his Jawa motorbike, tapered trousers and cooling glasses, was a sensation. He was the only person in the bank who could use a typewriter. The magical dexterity of his fingers and the quickness of his brain enabled him to produce a neatly typed letter in five minutes. The Typer, he was called. He had gracious ways and so much style, all new in Angheri. Walking past the bank with Sujju one day, Nalli saw the Typer getting on his motorbike. He was staring at her sister. Sujju walked on without looking but Nalli could tell that she was conscious of the young man. In a flash Nalli knew that something would happen between them. She would help to make it happen.

She schemed. The next day when she went to the market on an errand for Ajja, she lurked near the bank till she saw Kaviraj come out on his way to lunch. He was already astride his Jawa when she went up to him. 'My sister said you're very smart,' she blurted.

He looked at her, obviously pleased. 'That your sister, in Raghavendra Stores yesterday?' She nodded, yes. He kick-started his motorbike and rode away, smiling.

Nalli raced home. Sujju was in the porch, sewing. 'The new man in the bank,' Nalli whispered, 'the Typer, with cooling glasses and the motorbike. He said to tell you you're the most beautiful girl he has seen.'

Sujju covered her smile with her hand. 'Did he . . . say anything else?'

'He said you are the Dhruva nakshatra of Angheri,' Nalli offered.

The next step was to arrange a meeting. 'Tomorrow at one-thirty,' she told Kaviraj. 'She'll be waiting, behind the Mysore bus.'

'She said she'd meet me?'

'Yes.'

Nalli carried dozens of letters to and fro. They met in secret, and she kept watch. When it was certain that they were in love, she began an artless conversation with Ajji, casually mentioning Kaviraj more often than necessary. Ajji grabbed her wrist and pulled her closer. For a woman who was frail and ill, her grip was strong.

'What was it you said?'

'Nothing.'

'About that boy, you just now said—'

'Which boy?'

'Kapi! That boy in the bank. With the motorcycle.'

'Oh . . . The Typer . . . he . . . asked me if I would . . . he told me not to tell.'

'You must tell!'

Sujju quickly forgot Jai. When Kaviraj sent a formal proposal through his parents, the family approved. He was from the same community as theirs. His family was well off and not too concerned about the dowry. He had come to Angheri on a year's rural posting in the bank. When he returned to Mysore, the match was fixed.

Jai took it like a sport, at least outwardly. It was his first

defeat. He always had to be the best in everything, and he had
wanted Sujju. He never talked about it, nor did he find out
about Nalli's crime. He knew that The Typer with his Jawa and
a job in the bank had outstripped him. Jai showed no rancour
towards Sujju but she was always uneasy in his presence.

Nalli wondered how the meanness had come to her with
such ease. All her other sins paled in comparison. Ajja sometimes
said, 'Nalli is a good girl.' But she was not.

15

Nalli visited her future in vague details, almost furtively. A
thousand times she walked the corridors and entered the wards
in that gleaming white hospital, now pausing to listen to a
patient, now bending down to speak to another, now peering at
an X-ray or looking through a microscope at a sample of blood;
discussing a difficult case with Jai; explaining to patients. It's
typhoid. It's TB. No problem, we'll cure you. Your son needs an
operation but don't worry. Dr Jayanth is the best. Her mind
waxed happily. Even her dreams were blissful.

Marriage she wished for, and children, though she would
not allow her mind to dwell on the specifics. In any case that
would have to wait. Most girls from her class were married, or
about to be, and Appa was anxious. But he was considerate
enough not to talk about it yet. Perhaps he was waiting for the
results. He only insisted that she do her internship in Mysore
because Sujju and Kaviraj were there and she would be closer
home. Nalli understood that he feared she might drift away
from the family. She knew that she would not. Even now, her
transition from a village girl to a yet-to-be-hatched doctor
seemed unreal. She, a doctor. The irritable patients, putrid
smells, haranguing seniors and gaping wounds, temperature
charts and electrocardiograms, tubes and catheters and drugs
with complicated names, the rattle of spittle in the throats of
dying men—in Angheri all of it seemed far away. Life in the
village was settled in its quiet certitudes. The interminable

mornings, empty afternoons and the comfort of laziness was hers for now. It calmed Nalli but sometimes it annoyed her. She was confident that she had passed the final exams. It was the practicals which tripped students and she knew she had cleared them. After the results came she would get on with being a doctor. Now, for two months, respite.

She was laying the table for lunch one day, when Appa called from the gate. With him was Madheva the farmhand who worked for Bhimasena Nayaka. His son was ill with stomach pain and vomiting. He wanted Nalli's advice.

'I can't prescribe medicines without seeing the boy,' she said.

Half an hour later the boy was there lying on the bench in the porch. Nalli's mind was a blur. She looked at his tongue, felt his pulse for a full minute, prodded his belly and palpated his liver. She would have liked to sit down and think and maybe refer to her textbook. But Appa and Madheva were waiting. Mumbling something about the digestive system, she said, 'I'll give you a prescription.' Buscopan tablets. She had not taken a proper history. What had he been eating, were his bowel movements regular, had he been treated for worms? She had not asked. It was good fortune that the boy recovered and her stupidity went undiscovered.

Her apparent success with Madheva's son gave her some confidence. With a year's experience as an intern in Mysore, she would be good. But it was a long wait, first to complete her internship and then for Jai to finish his surgical training. Appa sensed her impatience but could not guess the reason. 'You can treat patients while you're here,' he said. 'People will be happy to get some advice for free. These are hard times for the village.' The prices of ragi and paddy had not recovered and the rains threatened to fail them again. Still, the thought of treating patients worried her and she asked for time to think. Appa was quiet. Days passed. Late one Sunday morning Appa beckoned her to his office and sat down. She knew that she was in for it. One of his speeches would follow. She stood before him, hands clasped nervously at her back. But instead of advising her, Appa spoke about his childhood.

When he was a young boy, they had lived on the fringes of poverty. The village was poorer then and he studied in the thatched hut which was the school. Later he went to high school in Nanjangud and came home twice a year on holidays. When going back to school, he used to be woken at three in the morning so he could walk to the market to catch the only bus, which left at five. There were no lights anywhere and he used a coconut-frond flare to light the way. Once when his fees had not been paid for months, he was sent away and not allowed back until Ajja could pay. He did his teacher's training in Mysore. Gappu Mava accompanied him the first time. He wore Mava's black coat over his dhoti for the occasion, and the fact that he was barefoot did not matter; few people had shoes in those days. The day he started college he was sad because he had wanted so much to be a doctor. 'We could not afford the medical college fees, and I was fortunate to be able to study at all. Chowraiah was not so lucky. His father needed him at the kiln from the age of seven. Mudda was with me till second standard and then he became a sweeper, just like his father and his grandfather . . . I think about these things.'

Nalli understood what Appa was asking of her. He said she could use his office room to see patients. It was small, with a table and chair and a wooden rack on which his books and files were stacked. After being stripped of the headmaster's post, he used the office less. On the table was a bottle of ink, a nib and holder, a blotting paper and notepad. If you went past his office room when he was at work, you could hear the nib scoring paper. For more important letters, he used the priceless, glistening black Pilot which was clipped to the pocket of his shirt; an essential part of his attire. He cleaned the pen himself and filled it with ink from the bottle without using an ink-filler, without spilling a drop.

Nalli made excuses. 'Appa, it's better that I wait for the results. I don't know if I've passed.'

'You had no doubts till now.'

'I'll need things. Drugs, instruments, an examination couch.'

'Make a list,' Appa said, pointing to the notepad on the table.

Seated in his room with the empty page before her, Nalli wrote:

1 stool for patient to sit on
Blood pressure instrument
Stethoscope
Syringes: 2 ml, 5 ml, 10ml
Needle—size 20 to 23
Cotton, gauze, bandages
Latex gloves
1 basin, towels
1 tongue depressor
Drugs: Aspirin, Analgin & Sulfa, Pentids, Lasix, Coramine injections
Dettol, Spirit

What about sterilization? Appa inquired. The metal and glass syringes could be boiled in a saucepan, but gauze and bandages? So she added Autoclave. (How did one operate an autoclave? She did not know, but could not tell Appa that.) And she needed an examination couch—two benches covered with a mattress would do it.

'What if the patient vomits?' asked Appa.

1 kidney tray.

'If someone has had a heart attack?'

She could not do anything. Just check his blood pressure and pulse, give a painkiller and send him to Mysore.

'If a woman comes for delivery?'

No. Definitely, no. She would not conduct any delivery.

They started coming before she got the essentials in place. Basappa's wife with diabetes, Nanja with chest discomfort, Anni with a tender lump in the armpit, Maregowda with a wheezing attack. Anni's problem was the most trying. Appa asked what had caused the lump and she explained in detail about hair follicles and sweat glands whose secretions were blocked, causing bacteria to thrive. Penicillin, eight lakh units a day. When she gave the injection in the arm, Anni complained that she could not draw water from the well. Nalli worried. Had she boiled the syringe properly? What if she had injured the radial nerve with her needle? It was better to give the injection in the buttock and, hopefully, she would not hit the sciatic nerve. When she gave it, Anni grumbled that she could not walk.

Obstetrics was not Nalli's strong subject. The common sense required for a safe delivery seemed to elude her. Most women managed to deliver at home but they were ignorant about diet and exercise. Pregnant women were denied milk and pulses. They were not seen outside their homes once the condition began 'to show'. Home delivery was common and afterwards the women were not allowed out for six weeks. The prolonged inactivity inevitably led to ill health. Nalli advised women to go to Mysore for their delivery and was glad that at least a few of them agreed. She wanted to keep clear of problems she could not handle.

One day Budhi came from school and said the Vaidyar was waiting at the gate to speak to Nalli. The old man stood near the tamarind tree. 'My wife's had a fall and is unable to get up,' he said. 'It's her hip. She won't let me touch it.'

Satyavati, the Vaidyar's wife, was known for her rasping voice and mean temper. The old woman lay on a mat in the front room of their house where she had fallen. Her right leg was turned outwards and shorter than the left. Nalli knelt down to examine: fracture neck of femur. 'She must be shifted to Mysore,' she said. 'For surgery. They'll put in a nail to hold the fractured ends together.'

'To be handled by butchers who must cut me up first to put me together again?' cried Satyavati. 'No nails will be put inside me. I'll die instead.' With her mouth closed in a fist, she turned away.

The Vaidyar knew that no potions could heal the fracture. 'Can you not do something?' he asked Nalli. 'If the bone knits together and she walks, it is enough.'

The bones could unite without surgery but there would be shortening of the limb, which would give her a bad limp. 'So there *is* another method,' the Vaidyar said. 'I'll provide you with anything you need as long as she doesn't have to go to hospital.'

She, still a medic, treat a fracture femur? The Vaidyar believed she could do it. Surely, people with broken bones could heal without operations?

Nalli needed time to think. The Vaidyar's wife groaned with pain, so she got an injection ready. When she approached her, Satyavati refused to reveal herself in any way. 'If you have to give me the poke, do it through my sari,' she said. Nalli's protests that it could cause an infection were refuted with: 'My sari is clean, I wash it every day.' So Nalli injected the painkiller through her clothes. In a while, the Vaidyar's wife said she was feeling better and Nalli did not feel too much of a quack.

Back home she sat in Appa's office with the notepad before her and thought frantically back to her two weeks in orthopaedics when she had seen more than a dozen cases of femoral neck fracture. There had been an old man who was unfit for surgery. The surgeons treated him with skeletal traction: a steel pin passed through the upper end of the tibia, attached to ropes passed over pulleys and connected to weights. The foot end of the bed was raised on blocks to counter gravity and prevent the patient from slipping down the bed. Instead of the steel pin passed through the bone, you could apply traction by using adhesive plaster on the limb.

Nalli sketched a diagram and explained it to the Vaidyar. 'We'll need a cot on which she can lie down. A strong rope, a pulley, ten pounds of weight, a roll of plaster and crepe bandage.'

The Vaidyar obtained everything in quick time and summoned Nalli. But there was another hurdle. Satyavati was adamant that she should be treated by the Vaidyar alone, no one else. Pleas and threats were of no use. Nalli had an idea. She asked the Vaidyar if he would apply the traction. 'I'll be your assistant,' she said, and explained what he would have to do.

The Vaidyar agreed. Going up to his wife, he said, 'Satya, I'm going to treat your fracture myself. I don't trust anyone else. I've asked Nalinakshi to help me hold your leg while I do it.' Satyavati was appeased. She was coaxed to lie still. Following Nalli's whispered instructions, the Vaidyar stood at the foot end of the bed and pulled the leg firmly. A scream of pain from the old woman, and the leg was straight. With the Vaidyar holding the leg and 'telling' Nalli what to do, she quickly applied the traction and attached it to a gunny bag filled with sand.

Satyavati complained all of that day and night but by next morning her pain had lessened. For two weeks she lay flat in bed while the family attended to her needs. Daily, under the apparent supervision of the Vaidyar, Nalli checked the alignment of the rope and pulley; she looked for bedsores. When she finished, the Vaidyar would offer her a steel tumbler of coffee. She drank while he plied her with questions. If antibiotics killed bacteria, what happened to their dead bodies? Surgeons did heart operations for which they cut open the breastbone. How did they close the bone? She could only answer a few of his questions.

In two weeks the Vaidyar's wife could sit up. Six weeks later the weights were removed so she could turn in bed and hobble to the toilet. Her leg was short by an inch and a half and the limp obvious, but the bone had healed. Satyavati made it a point to tell everyone about her good fortune. 'I'm able to walk because of the expert hands of my husband,' she said. 'If it wasn't for him, God knows, I'd have been a cripple.'

'No matter what she thinks, it is your triumph,' the Vaidyar told Nalli.

⟿

'Daactriddara? Is the doctor here?'

It was Gowramma, waiting at the gate, her eyes smiling as usual. She had finished her nurse's training, got a job in Mysore and was home on leave. 'Come in,' said Nalli, grabbing her hand.

Gowramma shook her head. Nothing had changed for her in Angheri. 'There is a patient,' she said. 'Poovi's son. You know Poovi, she was with Sujju in school till the fourth—it's her son. He's very sick.'

Gowru explained as they walked to the ukkada settlement, the cluster of huts where the family lived. 'It's blood dysentery.

Poovi has been taking the child to Dr Ravi who gave a pink injection for three rupees and when that did not work, a yellow one for five. And tablets. It's been going on for a month.'

Poovi was outside her hut, splitting firewood with an axe. Her youngest son sat naked on a gunny sack next to a pile of wood. Poovi saw them, put down her axe and, bending over her toddler, warned him, 'You move from there and I'll break your legs.' Then she led them into the ramshackle hut.

Inside, it was dingy and dark. Nalli could see an older woman, the mother-in-law, squatting next to the sick boy. He must have been about five years old but weighed not more than twenty pounds. His face was dried up like an old man's and his hair was the colour of turmeric. His eyes were quiet with suffering. He did not resist Nalli's examining hands. Poovi said she had stopped going to Dr Ravi. Instead, listening to her mother-in-law, she kept the child on a diet of jaggery coffee.

Nalli told her to stop the coffee and feed the child kanji with salt and sugar. She prescribed medicines. Two days later the child's father, Mara, who had been working in the coffee plantations of Coorg came home. He blamed Poovi for the boy's illness and said that if anything happened to him, he would kill her. He accused Nalli of 'poisoning' him. He stopped the medicines, proclaiming that he would take his son to be seen by big doctors in Mysore. But first, he would rest for a few days. Before Mara felt rested enough, the boy died. Poovi not only lost her son, but had to take the blame for his death.

Nalli told Gowru of her plans to work in the village with Jai, once both had completed their training. 'No child will die of a simple illness like dysentery,' she said. 'Jai and I will take care of everything.'

Gowru listened, silent.

16

With barely a fortnight remaining for the results, she wrote to Jai again. And waited.

It was longer than any letter she had written him before. Being in Angheri for two months and falling into the old rhythm of her life had something to do with what she wrote. She said everything she wanted to. Or did she? What was it that came in the way, between her thoughts and her words? Who would she be sincere with, if not Jai? He was sure to write and sort out whatever it was that threatened their universe. They would sit on the bench in the porch and Jai would tease her about those 'lectric shocks'. She hit back, but his metal-hard body made her hands sore. She used to hate him for a long time after the red, burning weal stopped hurting. Now she could laugh.

She remembered every detail of his last visit—the way he wore his brown shirt, sleeves folded halfway up his forearms. She remembered his stubbornness, and that look of dread in his eyes. What was it, the fear in his eyes, as they looked sideways at her and then away into the distance? She had first seen it when he came home before going to college and then again when he visited her in the hostel. His brow was scored with lines. Nalli could not look at him now without remembering that look in his eyes, and those lines. She had to ask him what he was afraid of.

Nalli was in the kitchen helping Gaja cut mangoes for a pickle when Ajja said there was a letter for her. Nalli washed her hands, took the envelope from Ajja and was walking away as casually as she could, when Ajja said, 'Here's a letter from Hari Chikkappa. Read it to Ajji.' She read out the four-page letter about Chikkappa's transfer to Gulbarga, his new job in the telephones department, and about their daughter's marriage. Then she strolled out of the gate to the yard where the hay was stacked for drying. She wanted to be alone. Leaning against the hay, she read.

She sat there a long while, with the dry dust of hay choking her lungs, the twigs scratching her skin. She had known that it would turn out this way and yet she had allowed herself to believe otherwise. She longed to scramble back in time to before the letter came. How happy she had been then. She looked up at the white sky until her head swam. The sun burned her cheeks and reminded her that it was time for lunch. She went home, laid the table, ate and got through whatever else the day involved. She put the letter away beneath her clothes in the box, never to read it again.

'That letter,' Ajja asked in the morning. 'It had nothing to do with the exams?'

'It was from a friend about her marriage.'

'Something to be happy about, then. It won't be long before we have you settled.'

For Ajja and for Angheri there would soon be something more to be happy about. The trees had been thirsting for water, the streams and wells running dry. Hot winds blew down from the hills whose slopes had been flogged an arid, dusty brown. Ajja had already cautioned his gods: 'This is the final warning, I'm telling you . . . There must be rain, and plenty of it within a month, or you'll regret it.'

After Ajja's fourth and most severe warning when he threatened to stop praying altogether, it started to rain. It went on ceaselessly, for fourteen days. The roaring of the water robbed people of sleep. The fields were deluged and the mud ran off the roads in a saffron-coloured stream. The stream filled and overflowed, carrying away half a dozen goats. Moisture seeped through walls and floors, slime ate into everything, and a hut in the ukkada was washed away. Clothes refused to dry, even with tins of glowing coal placed beneath them. Umbrellas leaked. The school and post office stayed shut. Children, at first happy that the schools were closed, got bored as they had to stay indoors with racking coughs and streaming noses. Ajja said it was the result of everyone asking the same favour from the gods. 'It's enough for now, can you hear me?' He shouted so the gods would hear him through the din of pouring rain.

For a few days, as the clouds slouched and dragged themselves over the hills, the rains lessened to a grumbling on the roofs, a hiss in the leaves. Angheri was bright and dry again. Children escaped from their homes to make the best of what was left of their holidays. The village pulled itself back on its feet. Umbrellas were put away and people came out on the roads. Ajja resumed his visits to the market.

When the post office reopened, Shanku Master got his letter and the news became known. Jai had decided to marry a girl in Bombay and stay there for some more time. Shanku Master appeared to have accepted the news bravely. In fact he was happy. This rich girl would keep his son tethered. He was the only one besides Vishnu who was jealous of Jai. He had wished his son to be no more than a teacher or a pujari but Jai had gone and done better things. The probability of Jai staying away from Angheri pleased Shanku Master.

Everyone else was shocked. With so many beautiful girls in and around Angheri where was the need to look elsewhere? His father could have swung the horoscope in favour of any beautiful and worthy girl Jai wanted. Jai, the favourite son of the village— would he ever return now? Shanku Master reassured them that his son would fulfil his promise about the hospital: he had said so in the letter. With time, the villagers accepted it.

'Bela is beautiful. You'll like her,' Jai had written in his letter to Nalli, making her mind up for her. Bela was from a wealthy Parsi family and had studied in the best school in Bombay and then in America. Jai sent a photograph. Nalli looked once and put it away but all through the day the photograph smiled at her. Bela in ankle-length trousers and a sleeveless top, showing off her white arms, her hair combed back in a knot, her eyes a soft brown. A girl from another world. Nalli wanted to hate Bela but knew even then that she would like her. It was those eyes.

Jai said that Bela was eager to live in Angheri but Nalli had doubts of it happening soon. He said nothing about her letter to him. Perhaps he wanted to spare her needless pain. He had suffered and now it was her turn to be punished for her spite of long ago. It was hard to pretend happiness. The family thought she was worried about her results. Ajja guessed. He would sidle up when she was alone, look mournfully at her and walk away muttering, 'Shiva . . .'

Sujju came, along with her twin girls and advice. She thought Nalli was still hurt by the rejection from the boy in Shimoga before she went to college. That was years ago and it happened to most girls, she said. Nalli bristled. It did not happen to Sujju, *she* was always lucky. Her husband and his parents doted on her. Nalli remembered how envious she had been when Sujju was expecting the twins. Sujju's thin frame had looked thinner and could just about support the protruding belly. The pulse beat faster in her throat; her voice became soft and her movements slow. She looked lovelier than ever. Kaviraj too was perfect for her. He had the timidity of one who knew that no matter what he did or did not do, his life would be comfortable. He chose easy options and was happy to let Sujju do as she pleased. Not one to sit at home and be lazy, Sujju had made friends in the neighbourhood. She managed the twins, embroidered, and made trinkets out of beads, lace and ribbons to impress the neighbours with.

Nalli's results were announced while Sujju was still at home, and Nalli returned to Mysore with her.

Mysore she remembered clearly, from her first visit as a child: the clip-clop of horses pulling tongas, cars speeding on the hard black roads, the ornate lamp posts lit with moon-sized lights and the moths that swarmed thickly around them. Years later they had gone again to buy saris for Sujju's wedding. Ajja, Amma, Sujju and Nalli.

They saw the palace, gawked at every store, and bought saris. In one of the shops there was a sign: *Two shirts for the price of one. Buy any shirt and get another free.* Ajja darted in and selected a white shirt and started putting it in his bag when the shopkeeper said, 'You can take another shirt, and you'll only be paying for one.'

'I'm taking the one that comes free,' Ajja said. 'I don't want the other shirt, the one that costs money.'

It took a great deal of convincing to make him accept that he had to pay for the first one to get the other. 'Cheating,' he grumbled. Amma got the shirt out of his bag, returned it to the shopkeeper and led Ajja away. Nalli could still recall the bafflement on the shopkeeper's face as they walked out of the shop.

They ate in a hotel called Indra Bhavan. Ajja ordered four plates of dosai, four of idli with vadai. 'It costs eight annas!' Ajja said and insisted they finish everything. They ate some more but three idlis remained. Amma said it was all right to leave what they could not eat but Ajja would not hear of it. He spread his kerchief on the table and wrapped the idlis. Then he twisted a piece of paper into a cone and poured all the sugar from the bowl that was on the table. He said it would come in handy during the bus ride back to Angheri.

Amma was embarrassed. She took it out on Nalli, scolding her for staring at people. But Ajja was worse than Nalli. His rubbery neck worked overtime. He was curious to see what the other people ate. He stopped a waiter who was carrying some dishes to another table and was aghast to find that one was a plate of sliced cucumber. 'They came here to eat cucumber and pay for it?' he asked. 'Four annas a plate?' He turned to Amma. 'Let us sell vegetables to this hotel.'

In Indra Bhavan they saw a dorai with his wife. Nalli had only heard about dorais and dorsanis. Ajja was at the counter paying the bill when a blue car stopped outside, doors opened and banged shut. A man and a woman got out. The woman was dressed in trousers and a blouse without sleeves, held up by straps the width of the ribbon on Nalli's hair. Her skin was pink and her short hair yellow. Her shoes were a shiny black with stick-like heels. Behind her came the man, pink like her and dressed in striped shirt and khaki shorts. Shorts! Nalli giggled and was silenced by a slap on the head from Ajja. They sat two tables away and each time the woman threw her head back and laughed, her hair shone like a flag of gold. When she talked, strange words poured out of her red mouth. Sujju said it was English. Ajja stared just as hard as Nalli and said it was wicked to dress like that. To Nalli it seemed that the woman was having a lot of fun being wicked.

Now coming back after eight years, Mysore seemed more like an overgrown town. It was propped up by the splendour of the palace and the little that remained of a well-bred culture. Not that any of it mattered to Nalli. She did not care very much where she worked or where she lived. Internship. Patients. Diseases. Cures. There was nothing special about any of it. With a feeling of emptiness that was devoid of any pleasure, Nalli began her internship.

17

'Dactre! My wound hasn't been cleaned for three days,' said a young man, lifting his banian to reveal a wad of darkly stained bandages on his belly. 'Please . . . today.'

'Amma, just one injection for my husband. He's been burning with fever all night.'

'Staying in this hospital is like being thrown in a gutter.'

'Catheterization for Bed 21. The duty-doctor at night was too busy.'

Nalli plunged into the anxieties of her job in the government hospital, where she was in charge of thirty male and thirty female medical beds, and ignored everything else. There was little time to relax and, thankfully, less time to be with the family.

In the house where Sujju and Kaviraj lived, in a restful neighbourhood full of austere Kannadigas, Nalli had a room to herself. Each morning she got a bus right from the doorstep and got off in front of the hospital gates. From the moment she put on the white coat and entered the wards, it was work: patients to examine, lab reports and X-rays to check, injections to give. At nine, Dr Das and his team gathered for ward rounds. When the rounds were over and the doctors had left the wards, the interns headed for the canteen. After coffee and Mysore bondas, it was back to work until lunch and then a second round of injections in the afternoon. If she was lucky, she finished by six-thirty or seven.

Nigam, the other intern in medicine at the hospital, was a good sort, chubby and unperturbed, with a weakness for cigarettes and the strong coffee from the canteen. He wore garish shirts and trousers that strained at the knees. When he smiled, his mouth opened in a tiny circle, revealing his incisors. Nigam was balding and the few scanty hairs on his head were combed back over the scalp. He smiled through the tensions of work; nothing upset him. Two days after Nalli joined, she was subjected to his Intro Lecture.

They were in the canteen. Nigam smoked, slurped his coffee and talked non-stop. 'A prestigious hospital, man. Thousand beds, fifteen departments. Big, bungling and mismanaged. A ten lakh-budget and most of it siphoned off. No medicines, no staff, no blankets, no water. A government hospital should be free, man. Except for cough, carminative and diarrhoea mixtures, is anything free? It's not just drugs. Service comes with a price. One rupee for the use of a urinal, two for a bedpan and three for a dressing done by the ward boy while picking his nose. The only thing that's handed out free is food.'

Twice a day a peon wheeled in a huge trolley and handed out plates heaped with rice and vegetable curry. The poorest came for the food as much as for the treatment they might or might not get. Many recovered because of the rest and a full stomach. 'It's a rusty wheel, this hospital,' said Nigam. 'If efficiency improves, it'll upset some . . . bank accounts. Strings have to be pulled only *so* much and in *such* a way. Perfect disorder.'

At work, Nalli had little help. The nurses, unable to see their work as anything but punishment, were rude and callous. At the top of the heap was Ponnamma Matron, a fat little woman with a ghee smile and a cap that sat like a starched napkin on her head. She was a ball of energy and avarice. She was everywhere, berating sweepers, punishing ayahs, scolding nurses and ignoring the interns. But when the senior doctors entered the ward she became an angel whose sole aim was to serve the sick. In the afternoons she sat in her little office and held court as patients 'paid their respects', which meant an envelope dutifully offered.

The assistant matron too merited the use of the starched

cap. Sridevi was rail-thin, buck-toothed and severely myopic. She smiled about three times a month. Brusque and unfussy, Sridevi had a temper to match the broad red belt around her waist. If the matron was like a deeply entrenched rock, her assistant was a rugged cactus and not to be meddled with. Ponnamma Matron and Sridevi battled it out in silence. They did not speak to each other; not a word. The matron never stopped trying to influence her assistant to be like the rest of her pliable, crooked staff; she was afraid Sridevi would contaminate others with her goodness. Of this there was no chance because most of the staff and even the interns and doctors who might otherwise be less than honest, shied away from Sridevi.

When Nalli was a few weeks into her job, a little girl was admitted with high fever. Blood tests confirmed typhoid. With intravenous fluids and antibiotics, she recovered within a week. The evening before the girl went home, when Nalli handed the discharge summary to her mother and was advising her about diet and rest, the mother pressed an envelope into her hands. In it were five crisp notes of ten. 'Doctors don't take money here,' Nalli said, returning the cash. The mother produced another envelope from the folds of her sari. 'Will you give this to the Dodda Dacter?' she asked, referring to the assistant professor who had treated the girl. 'He will be very angry if a patient tried to pay him,' Nalli said. 'He's paid a salary by the government.' Obviously relieved but hiding her surprise, the woman put away the money. Just then the matron rolled up. 'I'll be in my room,' she told the woman and walked away.

The next day, Nalli related the incident to the assistant professor. 'She tried to give me an envelope with money in it for you. I told her how angry you'd be.'

The doctor's face became queerly rigid. 'Patients want to show how grateful they are,' he said. 'It is good for our prestige. I never refuse.' Nalli thought he was joking, and smiled. 'You do something stupid and think it's amusing?' he shouted. The other doctors turned away, embarrassed. The matron stood by dripping her ghee smile. 'When a patient gives me money, especially when they give it unasked, it's a measure of how good I am,' he said.

'I once had a patient pay me a bucketful of notes for operating on his peptic ulcer. A bucketful. Gratitude must never be turned away, remember that.'

'Disgusting, isn't it?' Nigam said later, in the canteen. 'Why on earth did you tell him? Should have kept your mouth shut.'

'I've a good mind to complain. It's malpractice, to take money from patients.'

'Start complaining and you won't know where to stop. There's the spurious tonics being sold at the chemist's across the road. Flavoured, coloured sugar water. Worth two or three rupees and sold for ten times the amount. They vanish from the shelves like the canteen bondas. If you prescribe two hundred bottles, the company will gift you a clock. Tablets and syrups with PHYSICIAN'S SAMPLE, NOT FOR SALE are sold over the counter. No one cares, man.

'We must look at it this way,' he said, wisely. 'For every money-grabbing thug, there are other doctors who're different. Dr Das sees patients in the clinic long after everyone's gone to lunch. He doesn't take money. The professor of obstetrics, he's been around for years, he still comes to work on his rut-phut Bajaj after dropping his son at school. He refuses lavish gifts. "Give me a ball pen or a scribbling pad," he says to the medical reps who try to bribe him with gifts, so he's not obliged to prescribe their drugs.'

Listening to Nigam, Nalli wondered whom she would complain to and where she would get the proof. She was confused and angry, more so at Nigam because he did not feel as strongly as she did. And whenever she thought about the assistant professor, she imagined a bucketful of rupees by his side.

In the outpatients', Nalli and Nigam sat at one table, with the patients pressing from every side. 'Dactre . . .!' A ward boy guarded the door allowing eight or ten to shoot through every few minutes. Some jumped the queue by slipping a coin into his ready palm. They saw patient after patient, sometimes not even caring to look up. Cough. Fever. Toothache. The very sick merited a glance or a feel. Lift your arm. Unbutton your shirt.

Lower the trousers. Cough. Cough once more. With no running water in the vicinity, washing hands was dispensed with. It saved time. For the sick who came to the hospital it was an ordeal: buy medicines, pay doctors, keep the ward boys and ayahs happy, placate the nurses, and of course the matron would be waiting.

After admitting ten or twelve patients, Nalli went to the wards to write down case histories. When the evening rounds were done, there were new orders to be followed and at least a dozen injections to give. It was chaotic. The seniors snapped at the interns, the interns at the nurses, the nurses at student nurses and they at ward boys and ayahs, who took it out on the patients.

For Nalli, it was easier to keep working. She did the minor procedures in the duty room: tapping of ascitic fluid from the abdomen or fluid from the chest with the terrified patient sitting on a stool, a ward boy restraining him in a firm grip. She inspected wounds, removed sutures and spent disgruntled moments waiting her turn with the syringe. In the duty room, six syringes and an assortment of needles boiled away in a sterilizer the size of a shoe box. The interns jostled for their turn while ward boys, ayahs and various hangers-on walked in and out. The two 5 ml syringes were in constant demand. If they were in use Nalli had to make do with a syringe too small or too big and needles with mutilated tips which guaranteed abuse from the victims.

It was hard work. Interns were entitled to ten days' leave in the year. The professor doled them out like a miser handing out cash. They had to explain, exaggerate and lie in order to get a few days off. A sick grandparent or a nubile sister was freely invented.

Though she did not make many friends at work, she was on good terms with most interns, especially Nigam. He could turn a grim situation into a funny one, and never lost sleep over a mistake. When Nalli told him that she wanted to do surgery, he smiled his peculiar smile, revealing only the incisors.

'You don't think I can do it?' she asked.

He only said, 'Me too. It's surgery for me.'

'You'll have to work harder,' Nalli said. 'And cut down on those cigarettes and canteen visits.'

Nigam squashed the cigarette stub on the edge of his saucer. 'Why punish myself? Surgery or no, I'll do my best and forget about it.' He smoothed the hair on his head. It surprised Nalli that he was not in any way embarrassed by his thinning hair. 'You haven't noticed but I've cut down smoking from 27.5 to 25.3 cigarettes a day.' He lit another to reward himself. 'You're too serious, man,' he said, as if the thought had just occurred to him. 'The way you go about your work . . . As if there's someone holding a knife to your back. Relaaaax!'

At home too, Nalli kept to herself. Sometimes she talked to Sujju about the hospital, but the utter lack of interest on her sister's face soon shut her up. By choice, she met few people, said no to picnics and parties. She had doubts of a different nature now. She wondered why she felt more for one patient, less for another and almost indifferent towards someone else.

It was one of those cluttered days in the outpatients'. Nalli had seen dozens of patients and still they kept coming. Around eleven, Nigam took off for coffee. Nalli directed her frustration at the patients and was needlessly snappy. She saw a woman holding a child in her arms trying to push her way through. A scuffle followed and the woman had to step back and wait her turn. 'My son is very sick, dactre!' she wailed. The boy was at least eight or nine years old. A fuss over nothing, merely to jump her turn, Nalli thought, and decided to see the others and make the boy wait his turn.

An hour later when the boy's turn came, Nalli saw that he was drowsy. A bright red cap was perched incongruously on his head, long black lashes swept his pale cheeks. 'He sleeps all the time, it's been three days now,' the mother told Nalli. 'When he wakes, he screams that his head hurts. He vomits everything, even water.' His skin burned with fever. When the mother laid him down on the examination table he turned to one side, drew up his limbs and tried to sleep. He had the telltale rigidity of neck muscles.

Nalli hurried to the next room where the registrar sat at a table, besieged by patients. 'I think it's meningitis,' she said. 'Will you see him?'

'Send him to the ward. I'll see him in the evening.'

'He's semi-conscious.'

'Is that my fault?'

'Should I put up a drip?'

'Dextrose saline. Analgin half ampule, i.m. Now leave me alone, I have serious patients waiting here.'

When Nigam returned from the canteen, she went to the ward. The boy was curled up on the edge of a still-occupied bed. It was some time before the drip could be readied and the injection given. In the evening the registrar saw the boy. 'You didn't tell me he was critical,' he snapped. 'The boy is near death. Quick, we must do a lumbar puncture.'

By the time she got the instruments ready the registrar had cooled down and he let her do the lumbar puncture. Her first. She inserted the long spinal needle into the space between the third and fourth lumbar vertebrae and drew a few millilitres of fluid into the syringe, then squirted it into a sterile bottle. The registrar studied it, shook the bottle and showed her the light grey strands forming inside. 'Straw-coloured, with cobwebbing. Tuberculosis. Start the triple drug regimen and tell the relatives his chances are fifty-fifty.'

Nalli was getting used to telling the relatives about the prognosis of a disease.

'The cancer has spread through the blood, there is little we can do.'

'An operation *may* help but in the first three days after surgery anything can happen.'

'We have tried everything . . .'

It was unpleasant business.

Now she had to speak to the boy's mother. Venkamma was used to fighting battles. Some years ago the boy's father had been coughing up blood for a month before they came to hospital. He died in spite of treatment. She listened to Nalli tell her that her son had the same illness and it had affected his nervous system. Venkamma did not flinch. 'He's in your hands, dactre,' she said. 'I'll bring whatever medicines you want. You save him.'

Nalli examined the boy twice a day for signs, good or bad. Toppi—so called because he insisted on wearing his cap all the time, even in bed—began to respond to the drugs. He became alert and was able to keep liquids down without vomiting. He lay in bed, his pale face peeping over the red hospital blanket which he clutched tight with his hands. It was precious property, the blanket. Not every patient in the ward could get one. Venkamma had used threats, bribes and persuasion to get Toppi his.

Toppi hated his daily injection of streptomycin. 'Check the needle, akka,' he pleaded each time. 'The blunt one hurts too much.'

Venkamma was true to her word. Any medicine asked for, she produced within the hour. In the first week when Toppi's temperature soared, she sat all day by his bed mopping his brow with a wet cloth. When he was able to eat, she brought him boiled eggs, milk and groundnuts. Toppi was something of a spoilt brat and rude to his mother. Venkamma coddled him beyond her means. He refused to eat the hospital breakfast and asked for buns every morning. He wanted bondas from the canteen and hot tea in the evening, which his mother never failed to bring, denying herself to please him.

Toppi had dropped out of school after four years and worked in a hotel, washing dishes and cleaning the tables. 'He never liked school,' explained Venkamma. 'Now he earns money but it's never enough for him. If I don't give what he wants, he stops eating.' It was unthinkable for Venkamma that her son should go hungry. He had learnt to smoke from his father and that was why he became ill. 'I will take him to the temple when he's better,' she said. 'I'll break a dozen coconuts to Chamundeshwari.'

Her own diet was leftover scraps after her son had eaten,

and a handful of boiled peanuts. Venkamma was about thirty-five but her face was heavily lined. The skin on her arms hung loose. When Toppi improved and did not need her ministrations all the time, she bustled about the ward, checking on others. She was an optimist. 'Do as the dactre says and you'll be all right. See my son. The dactres pulled him out from the clutches of Yama.' She could bully a patient to eat, or to move a stiff limb, or withstand a painful procedure. She brought them tea or plantains from the shop near the gate. Every morning, she greeted Nalli with 'Namaste dactre' and then reported the night's happenings. 'Naga has a fever. Boraiah coughed all night. Mandappa went to the bathroom twelve times. Blood in the stool every time.'

For Nalli, Toppi was a trophy to feel good about. When she entered the ward, the sight of the pale face peeping over the blanket buoyed up her mood like nothing else. At home, Sujju and Kaviraj listened to detailed reports about the boy with the cap whose life she had saved. So it surprised Nalli, as she got off the bus one morning, to see Venkamma waiting at the hospital gates. 'Toppi has fever,' she said. Nalli hurried to the wards. Toppi's temperature was 104. She prescribed tablets and told Venkamma to sponge him with cold water. 'Only a fever, it's nothing,' she said.

The fever raged. The doctors reviewed Toppi's treatment, added more vitamins and gave him blood. Weakened by the illness, his body refused to fight back. He lay in bed, his thin fingers clutching the red blanket, his eyes large in his face. He stopped eating. Day and night Venkamma sat by his bed, sponging and fanning with her pallu. Toppi struggled for a week and then sank into a coma from which the doctors could not revive him. Venkamma squatted by the bed, covering her mouth with the edge of her sari to hide her pain. She looked at her son whose beautiful eyes were closed forever. Hours later Nalli saw her walking away along the hospital corridor and out of the hospital. In her hand she held Toppi's cap.

Some people at the hospital said they had always known the boy would not make it. They had known because Shiva had said so.

Nalli's meeting with Shiva was unavoidable and it happened soon enough. Shiva had the uncanny ability of zeroing in on a soon-to-die patient. He predicted death even when it was days away. He squatted at the tea shop near the gate, his back to the hospital, puffing a bidi or drinking tea, showing no apparent interest in the problems of those who walked in and out of the gates. But when they talked, he listened. In the evenings he hung about near the barred entrance to the wards, baring his rust-coloured teeth in greeting to anyone he knew. Doctors, unsettled by the sight of Shiva, avoided him. He was also the unofficial disposer of dead bodies in the hospital. Rumour went that there was an understanding between him and some doctors in the anatomy department, but it was never proved. Some mornings he could be seen lying in wait on the corridor alongside a ward. If he entered the ward and paused near a bed, it was ominous for the patient. Yama would soon be there.

If the family members were told, 'Shiva has been here,' they hastened to seek him out. Over a steel tumbler of tea he would tell them the end was near. In nine cases out of ten, he was right. Shiva did not criticize the doctors but when it came to death, he was an authority. When a patient died, he was there, a silent figure amidst the wailing, chest-beating relatives. When the acute grief was over, he consoled them, lifted the burden of their guilt. Everything they had done was in order, he reassured them. 'Good thing that you brought her here,' he would say. 'The doctors did their best. Her time was up, that's all.' Then he went about arranging the funeral rites, for a fee, always reasonable. Whether it was a cremation or a burial, and whatever religious rites the family followed, he arranged for them with painstaking care.

No one knew where Shiva lived and how. He came and went by bus and did not speak about himself. Nalli saw him approaching her at the bus stop one day and quickly turned away. He coughed in greeting. Hiding his bidi-held hand behind him, he coughed a little more until she turned round. 'Boraiah— Bed 24—he's in a bad way?'

'It's a curable illness,' she said. Boraiah had been in the

ward for more than a fortnight, with bronchiectasis. A chronic, debilitating condition of the lung, it was not as serious as Shiva seemed to think. The patient had received a customary course of strepto penicillin and since it did not seem to work, he was put on tetracycline capsules. 'He should be out of the hospital in a week,' she added.

'A week,' Shiva said, taking up her last word. 'Yes, that's what I told his brother. Not more than a week.'

'You understand nothing about the disease,' she said, and stepped into the bus which had just arrived.

As the bus moved away, she saw Shiva shake his head sadly.

Two days later, Boraiah began to vomit blood. A small amount at first and then copiously, filling a sputum cup in half a day. The doctors transfused two pints and started ampicillin, the latest of antibiotics. He lasted nine days.

Nalli was there to certify the death. She checked Boraiah's now-still heart and taking the earpiece of the stethoscope out of her ears, started to tell the relatives. They who had hung on her every word, now looked at her with reproach. Her hands, which had felt so important a while ago, hung like pieces of wood by her side. The medicine trolley, the intravenous line, the tubes, catheters, injections and blood pressure cuff were all useless now. Of all the difficulties a doctor must face, this was the worst. The certainty of death, the mysterious end to a life with that last, stumbling breath.

Without looking she was aware that Shiva was standing behind her. His work would now begin.

18

'The patient was sitting when I did it. Two kidney trays of pale, watery liquid gushed out . . .'

Sujju, who was stirring the sugar syrup for gulab jamuns, dropped the spoon. 'Don't touch anything till you've bathed,' she cried in disgust.

Nalli could not stop bragging about her surgical triumph. 'If you don't position the needle right, you can hit a blood vessel. Or worse, puncture the testes.' She embroidered her limited skills with detail and avoided the truth: that she had succeeded after the fourth try, with help from Nigam.

She did not tell them about the other patient with a bigger hydrocele, who was to undergo surgery. He was an assistant manager in a bank and had taken a special hospital room. Nalli had read about the way doctors in America obtained an 'informed consent' from patients before surgery. So the day before the operation she stood by his bedside and explained the procedure and the possible complications. 'Sometimes there's profuse bleeding after the surgery. It forms a haematoma inside the wound which can be very painful and has to be drained with a large-bore needle and then bandaged tight. Of course, it can get infected, in which case we keep you in hospital a while longer and prescribe antibiotics. It's very rare that the testis gets damaged and has to be excised . . .'

The banker's smile faded and disappeared. When she came half an hour later with the consent form for him to sign, she saw him sitting on his bed, fully dressed, tying his shoelaces; his wife hurriedly stuffed clothes into a suitcase. Without looking Nalli in the eye, she mumbled something about a family emergency. Her husband would come back later for the surgery. It was the last they saw of the banker.

And there was certainly no point in telling her family about the appalling disaster the previous week.

When she started the three-month posting in surgery she had hoped that she would be in Unit Three, where the chief had a reputation for kindness. But she got Unit One and Nigam, forever lucky, landed Three. The balding professor of Unit One looked a lot like Sardar Patel and was difficult to work with. He was a loner; the demands at work distanced him from everyone. With the patients he was brusque, with the juniors a despot. When he smiled, which was rare, it looked like he might relax and reveal something of himself. But the smile died quickly and he walked over to the next bed, the next case. A few years back he had been in the reckoning to be Dean but many of the faculty members had lobbied against him.

On her first day in Theatre, Nalli tried to impress the Sardar by scrubbing for a colectomy. The registrar was first assistant and she would at best get to hold the retractor. She was only doing it to impress him. As she started to soap her arms, the Sardar saw her. 'Who's the stupid girl?' he shouted. 'She's scrubbing with her bangles on!' Nalli began hastily to remove the two bangles on her wrists. 'Out! Out!' It was two weeks before he let her go back into Theatre. On a Sunday afternoon a post-op patient fainted in the toilet after Nalli told him it was all right to walk. 'Shape up or you won't find a job after internship,' the Sardar yelled.

Nalli wanted desperately to please him. Her moment came one day at outpatients' when she made a brilliant diagnosis. A drunken labourer had been brought in with severe pain in his right arm. It was grossly swollen all the way up, a dusky blue and pulseless. Nalli's mind raced to a photograph and description of venous thrombosis in Bailey and Love's *Textbook of Surgery*: Phlegmasia Cerulea Dolens. She wrote the diagnosis in the case sheet in bold letters and produced the patient before the professor. In her haste and eagerness she started to tell him about the condition. 'Phlegmasia Cerulea Dolens,' she said grandly. 'Venous gangrene. It's more commonly seen in the lower limb, and is often a clue to a malignancy somewhere in the body. In the upper limb, it's very rare. Mortality and morbidity are both high . . .'

The Sardar looked the patient over and asked her whether she had taken a proper history. 'He's come after a drinking binge, sir. Some people found him where he had fallen, by the roadside.' Did he complain of pain anywhere? 'His left shoulder, sir.' Had she examined the injured part?

The shoulder was dislocated and pressing on the main artery to the arm. An hour later, the joint was put back in place under anaesthesia. The hand regained its colour and movement and Nalli's precious Cerulea Dolens vanished. She heard clearly the professor telling the anaesthetist, 'I wonder where these idiots come from!'

Stupid errors and irritations recurred. Failed diagnoses,

difficult procedures, sleepless nights and missed lunches. Each morning Nalli resolved to be polite to every patient but, ten cases later, she was snapping. In spite of initial embarrassments, she stubbornly spent more time in Theatre.

There were plenty of small cases, too insignificant for the seniors to bother with. The Minor Theatre, also called the Septic Theatre, was the annexe to the Main Theatre. Dr Sripathi, better known as Cut Dactru, handled abscesses, lumps and bumps here. Sripathi was a veteran. At four every evening the ward boy announced his arrival: 'Cut Dactru has come!' Like the Pied Piper, Sripathi led the assortment of cases to the Minor Theatre. He walked with his back stooped and his half-finished cigarette held behind his back. A dozen patients squeezed on to the bench outside and others stood, marking the already stained hospital walls with sweat. Outside the Theatre he paused to acknowledge the namaskars, pretended not to see the rupee notes clutched in nervous hands. With a few murmured words to the ward boy, the Cut Dactru disappeared inside. He worked at breakneck speed, despatching victims until the bench was empty but for a whimpering casualty or two. He charged a uniform ten rupees for every case, any case. If someone wanted to pay more, he did not refuse.

Sripathi was a busy man; he had no time to teach. When he paused for a cigarette between cases he let the interns do a few, but always stood by and muttered advice. Circumcision was the most common surgery and there was a circ list twice a week. Young boys waiting their turn cringed as they heard the shrieks from inside and watched the just-operated victim hobble out, face contorted with pain.

Nalli's chance at circumcision came soon after her first case, the winning gluteal abscess. Having assisted Sripathi on several cases since letting out all that Laudable Pus, she was confident she could do them on her own.

The brothers Murad and Abu, aged seven and six, waited on the bench with thin towels wrapped around their waists. Just as their turn came, Sripathi was called away to the Main Theatre and Nalli offered to fill in. Murad walked in bravely and, refusing help from the ward boy, climbed on to the table. The nurse whisked the towel away and painted his lower abdomen with the pink antiseptic. His sharp unsmiling mouth trembled a little. Nalli muttered reassuring words which she was in need of herself.

The scrub nurse was annoyed because the unskilled hands of an intern would take twice as long as Cut Dactru. Her annoyance showed in the way she flung the green drape called the eyelet towel—hole towel, the nurse said—over Murad's belly so that only the operation site was exposed. She positioned the table of instruments and the ward boy adjusted the overhead light to shine on Murad. As Nalli took the syringe of xylocaine to inject around the penis and numb any pain, the boy went pale. He pressed his thighs together in an effort to shelter his dignity. 'Relax, it won't hurt,' the nurse fibbed, patting him through the drapes. Nalli finished without a problem and Murad limped out with the hunched shoulders of an old man.

Abu came in whimpering and then broke into loud sobs. The masked faces, the piercing smell of antiseptic, the instruments and the light compounded his fear. He saw Nalli's masked face and tried to jump off the table. The ward boy pinned him down. Abu was past caring if it really hurt. His screams were loud enough to be heard outside the gates. Nalli finished, and his father carried out the shrieking boy. Instructions were given, medicines handed out. It was over.

Two days later Murad came back with painful scabs and purulent fluid in the wound. Abu was brought in the day after, with bleeding from the wound. The unlucky brothers were admitted and everyone talked about the 'complications'. Murad's wound settled with penicillin injections and dressings. But for the first few nights when the erectile tissues of the penis swelled, he would wake, crying in pain. He sobbed through the night and dark rings of sleeplessness formed around his eyes. He needed a heavy dose of phenobarbitone to help him get through the night.

Abu continued to bleed. He lay in bed, tense and unmoving. Nalli changed the dressings three, four, five times that day. The same night Sripathi took the boy back to Theatre and stopped the bleeding under a general anaesthetic. A week later Abu came out of hospital, still hunched in misery.

It felt terrible, more so because the father of the boys thanked her for having saved his son's life. She told herself that the scrub nurse had not checked that the instruments were sterile, the ward boy had given her 0.5% xylocaine instead of 1% and then he had continued a loud conversation with the boy and distracted her, and Sripathi had not stressed the need to stop minor oozing. The real reason was her ineptitude.

Medical college had not prepared Nalli for this: The sudden bleeding that could follow surgery, the bead of pus in a wound, the sutures that gave way. In Toppi's case she had blamed herself when it was not her fault and, after the circumcision disasters, tried to transfer the blame. Nalli suffered when she need not have, was nervous when she should have been confident. She dithered, suffered the heartache of knowing too late that she should have chosen another drug, another suture, another method of treatment. Medicine, she realized, was as imperfect as the doctors who practised it.

Demands at work pushed personal pain to the back of Nalli's mind. She did not think about Jai too much and, when she did, told herself that all she had ever wanted was to work with him. That had not changed. She would finish her internship, train in surgery and join him. Their dream was on the move, it was taking shape.

⌇

Sometimes lessons came in unexpected ways, as from the incident of Sabari and Seethu.

Nalli met them first when she went to the market to buy brinjals, on her way back from the hospital. As she entered the noisy marketplace, a barrage of foul invective greeted her.

'Offal-eating pariah dog!'
'Horse!'
'Buffalo!'
'Lice in your pubic hair!'

'Worms in your backside!'

Sabari was a jasmine seller and Seethu sold vegetables. Sabari was dark and attractive, with a nose-ring glittering over her betel-stained lips. She sat near the entrance to the market and sold lengths of jasmine which she measured on her forearm. She seduced women with her neatly strung, fragrant flowers. When Nalli declined to buy, she said, with her lovely eyes sparkling, 'In Mysore a woman is beautiful only when she has wound a length of jasmine in her hair.' If a man came alone, she insisted he take a length home. 'Only thirty paisa, anna. Your wife has been waiting all day for it. For thirty paisa you can make her happy.'

Seethu was a raw-boned woman. Her face and arms were often marked with cuts and bruises; it was widely known that she had a drunkard husband. She had a far sharper tongue than Sabari's but she sold quality and never cheated. If she saw a customer pick an ageing bendekai or a withered carrot, she said, 'Let me choose fresh ones for you,' or 'The bendekai isn't worth buying, amma. Come tomorrow, I'll give you tender ones.'

It was not often that Nalli went to the vegetable market, but every time she went she saw them at it. No one knew what the two women fought about. Usually their fights followed a pattern. When they started voicing obscenities it was a sign that the fight had neared its end. Their fight had escalated only once, when Seethu had chased Sabari through the market with a knife, causing a great deal of panic.

Late one afternoon, having missed lunch, Nalli was in the canteen eating her second bonda when Nigam came in, dragged up a chair and sat across from her. He ordered coffee and idli-vada, lit a cigarette and told her about a case he had scrubbed up for the previous night. 'A wall collapsed and a woman was trapped beneath the rubble. Ghastly chest wound, it bled litres. It's lucky she's alive. My boss is on leave so I called the Sardar. An open, sucking pneumo-thorax, five crushed ribs, a mangled lung and a messy wound on the thigh.'

He ordered another plate of idli-vada. 'Sardar was terrific. Thoracotomy. First time I've seen the chest opened. He cut away the crushed portion of the lung, sutured the bleeding vessels, put two drains in the pleural cavity and connected them to underwater drainage. In and out in forty minutes.' He finished his coffee and leaned back. 'I was wondering if you could do the dressings for this woman. She doesn't want a male doctor to do it. Poor woman, she was selling jasmine in the market when it happened . . .'

A jasmine seller? Nalli gulped her coffee and hurried to the ward. It was Sabari. Pale and rather breathless, she greeted Nalli with a weak smile and allowed her to change the dressings. As Nalli walked out of the ward, she saw Seethu with a glass of tea in her hand. She had brought Sabari to hospital in an auto and then gone to find her husband. She told Nalli how Sabari had been sitting in her usual place near the market entrance when the wall collapsed and crushed her along with her basket of jasmine. It had taken them six hours to extract her from the debris. 'Will she be all right?' Seethu asked, worried. 'She'll pull through,' Nalli assured, but she wasn't really sure. The wounds had been badly contaminated, so there was a high chance of infection.

Sabari's husband appeared briefly in the evenings, hovered around his wife and went home. Her young daughter stayed back to look after her. Seethu came daily with food and medicines. When, after an initial recovery, Sabari started to cough and complained of chest pain and breathlessness, the doctors suspected a haemothorax. An X-ray confirmed that there was a massive collection of blood in the pleural space which envelopes the lung. It had got infected and the resulting pus was too thick to be drained through a tube. The Sardar had to cut away a three-inch segment of the fifth rib below the armpit to let out the pus.

The post-op period was stormy. Sabari's haemoglobin had dropped to 4 grams. Her husband and three brothers were asked to give blood and they promptly vanished. Two days later they brought a donor, pale as chunna, and willing. The man sold his blood once a month. ('Blood money,' Nigam laughed. 'It's good income and easier than toiling as a porter at the railway station.') He was sent away with iron tablets. Sabari struggled on until one of the doctors volunteered to give her blood.

On the tenth day, when the sutures were removed, Sabari's wound gaped open. Weakened by lack of nutrition, it had failed to heal and had to be resutured. Sabari willingly submitted to the countless insults of post-operative routine. A few days after her wound was sutured a second time, she began to complain of sleeplessness. 'She says the wound itches too much,' Seethu told Nalli. 'As if something live is crawling underneath.' Nalli took away the dressing. The stitches were giving way again and the raw pink surface of the wound crawled with shiny white maggots, the size of rice grains.

Sabari was isolated in a corner of the ward near the toilets. She became known as The One with the Maggots. Patients from nearby wards stood at the door and watched as she tossed about in bed, pleading that the dressing be changed. But gauze and bandages did not come free and Seethu had sold her earrings to pay for the medicines. Nalli sent the ward boy to the main store for extra dressings and if he could not get them, went herself. Sabari's husband and brothers stopped coming. Only Seethu and Sabari's daughter came every day with medicines and food. Nalli changed the dressings, fighting the sickly sweet smell from the crawling grains of rice. Sabari watched intently as she poured turpentine over the squirming maggots and cleaned them away. It took three weeks for the wound to be rid of maggots and yet another for Sabari to walk a few steps.

She went home a month later, a frail shadow of herself, leaning on Seethu for support. The two women were almost rupeeless, but on the day of Sabari's discharge from hospital, Seethu brought a paper packet of jalebis for the nurses. Nalli was pleased to see that the crisis had ended their enmity. There would be no more fights between them.

Many weeks later, as she neared the main entrance to the market, she heard them again.

'Sister of a eunuch!'

'Perishable dog-meat!'

'Bag of dead bones!'

They were at it again.

There was Karthikeya, who walked into hospital clutching a stack of notebooks in his long fingers. He was tall and fleshless, with a face that was all teeth and smiles. His wife complained that he ate very little, only a few mouthfuls at each meal. He weighed forty-two kilos.

The Sardar being away at a conference in Delhi, the associate professor (who had boasted about the bucketful of rupees given to him by a patient) was in charge. He was known for his excessive display of bedside manners when it came to certain patients, usually those who opted for special wards. Karthikeya was subjected to an elaborate examination. The doctor then explained to his wife, 'I think he's suffering from a peptic ulcer. It has scarred the outlet of the stomach and narrowed it. That is why he's unable to eat.'

'Doctor, I thought an ulcer will be painful,' said the worried wife. 'My husband does not complain of any pain.'

'A silent ulcer,' the boss said, grandly. 'Not common, of course. We'll put him on medicines and see if he improves.'

The wife was impressed. My husband has a silent ulcer, she told anyone who came to see him, the doctor says so. She was always by his bed, coaxing: Drink this, eat this; take this and that and that. He turned his head to the wall, the muscles of his neck taut with refusal. When the doctors came on ward rounds Karthikeya sat up and subjected himself to their inquisitive hands.

'How are you?'

'He's very poorly, doctor.'

'Do you feel stronger after the drip?'

'He's so weak.'

'You must eat more.'

'He won't listen.'

Karthikeya had been in the ward for four days when it struck Nalli that he had not spoken a single word. The boss did not consider it important. 'We're concerned with the illness,' he said proudly. 'What does it matter that he doesn't want to speak?'

Karthikeya's silence was unobtrusive, it did not ask to be noticed. Every day Nalli found him writing in a notebook which he carefully put away when the doctors came. When they finished their examination and went out of the room, he reached for it again. Nalli was curious. What did he write, with such diligence, in those notebooks? A list of complaints about the hospital, perhaps. Or maybe he was writing a novel.

One day when his wife had gone home to get fresh clothes, Nalli went to Karthikeya's room to check his blood pressure when suddenly he spoke. 'Why do the doctors want me to eat more?' he asked. He wiped his hand over his forehead in a baffled gesture. 'I'm healthy and alert. All my blood counts are normal, the doctor said so himself. Then what's the problem?'

'With so little nourishment, you'll fall ill,' she said.

He smiled, a little sadly, his lips stretching over his teeth. 'I'll tell you why I won't be ill, if you have the time to listen.'

He had worked as an accountant in a government office. For forty years, eight hours a day. 'I loved my work. When I retired and closed all my official files, I realized that without the mental stimulation provided by the endless work, there was very little for me to do. Read the paper, pay the electricity bill, stand in queues, visit relatives . . . I wasn't prepared to shut the file of my life just yet.' He showed Nalli his notebooks: page after page of calculations, numbers in tight columns of antlike neatness. Figures multiplied, subtracted, divided, squared. 'I do these counts . . .' He looked apologetic. 'Every day I take up an assignment. Yesterday I was dividing the runs in every fifty-plus partnership in a cricket Test last year by the average of the ages of the two batsmen involved and working it out as a graph against the total innings score divided by the average age of all eleven players. Today, it is a correlation of the square root of the year of birth of every known king in Indian history with the number of wives he had.' Did he not need books to refer to for dates and figures? 'I don't forget such things,' he said.

He crossed one bony knee over the other and pulled his dhoti over his stick legs. 'It may seem entirely pointless, these mind games that preoccupy me. But the fact is that when I worked at the office, it was the same thing—mathematical calculations, which gave me a sort of strength. It was like nourishment. I always ate little. Just that my wife never noticed until I retired.' He waved his hand over his concave belly. 'I'm happier and healthier when I eat less. I wish you could talk to her, and the doctors, and make them understand.'

'Shouldn't you explain all this yourself?' asked Nalli.

'Doctors don't like it when a patient doesn't need their help,' he said wisely.

When the medicines did not work, the boss ordered a barium meal X-ray to confirm the diagnosis. It proved inconclusive but he said that the quality of the X-ray film was not good. Surgery was the only way out.

With a respectful shake of his head, Karthikeya refused. They tried feeding him with a tube passed through the nose into his stomach. He looked a tragic hero with the hospital gown pulled over his scrawny neck and the tube dripping from his nostril.

The boss managed to convince his wife about surgery. In the end, to please his wife, Karthikeya agreed. That evening Nalli told Nigam. 'Isn't it ridiculous? He's a little eccentric, that's all. And he's happy eating less. Does that mean we must label him with an illness and operate on him?'

'Just try telling that to the boss,' said Nigam. 'Or the wife.'

Nalli did. The boss was angry. 'There's no need to display your ignorance,' he said. The wife had full faith in the Big Doctor and would not listen to anything Nalli had to say.

So the surgery was done, but they did not find any ulcer or anything else wrong inside. Next morning during ward rounds, the boss cleverly camouflaged the truth with medical jargon. He said Karthikeya's problem had been attended to. 'Doctor, you will always be like a god to me,' his wife said, over and over again. The way the boss overdid his niceties with Karthikeya and his wife, it was clear that he expected a generously filled envelope. Karthikeya still ate next to nothing and when his wife complained that he was being stubborn, the boss dismissed it as a 'mind problem'. Later, Nalli told her not to force him. 'Now that his . . . problem . . . has been taken care of, let him decide how much food he needs.'

Two weeks later Karthikeya left the hospital, his weight unchanged. The only difference was that he now carried on his belly a scar. Nalli knew that Karthikeya was aware of the truth—the scar was nothing but the stamp of a surgeon's unconfessed ego.

19

A few stops short of the house, Nalli got off the bus. She walked slowly, not seeing the gulmohur bursting with flowers, not hearing the music that flowed from the homes where girls learnt to sing Thyagaraja and Purandara Dasa. When she reached home she stood briefly at the gate to shrug off her fatigue and walked round to the back door. Bath first and then some tea.

It was a cheerful, noisy home, but for Nalli there was no joy. She had left her happiness in Angheri, among the light green leaves of the guava tree, in the atta amidst the jars of pickled mangoes, in the sweet breath of the rice fields. Her prayer, her one prayer which had been ignored, she put away on the ledge next to the gods whom she had once implored with selfish fervour. Let it trouble the gods. Let them spend sleepless nights gnashing their teeth. She would never believe again.

Sometimes memories of home would slide before her eyes: Karia's scornful stare and Budhi's soulful one, the owl's hum and Ajja's ridiculous temper. She felt a vague disquiet, a resentment directed at everyone and no one.

Amma visited often and stayed weeks. She was caring and affectionate. If Nalli's back hurt after a long day at the hospital, Amma massaged it with liniment.

The family could think of only one future for Nalli. Appa came frequently to make her see reason; aunts and uncles brought more advice. She was sent on sari-buying sprees. If she was the least bit light-hearted, if she joked with Sujju's twins by calling them her 'knees' or wore a different pair of earrings, it was a good sign: Nalli is changing, she will be herself again. She had to pretend a dark, depressed mood, take care to dress carelessly and show no interest in anything outside her work to keep them from approaching her with any talk of marriage. She had constant arguments with Sujju, she snapped at Amma and avoided Kaviraj.

Staying in Mysore, Nalli could have been friends with her sister. But she pulled away and did not share with her a single moment of closeness. If anyone could have made their parents understand, it was Sujju. Instead she sided with them. She even implied that Nalli could have found a suitable husband herself: 'You meet men all the time. A romantic involvement is all right, when it is with the purpose of marriage.'

'You had nothing to worry about. Every boy was smitten by you.'

Sujju laughed. 'It wasn't like that. I developed the knack of attracting men without saying or doing anything. I sometimes wonder at you. If you'd only try a bit.'

It was a strange conversation to be having with her sister.

Sujju never let up. She was laying the table for lunch on Sunday. Nalli was at the sink, washing the Raspuri mangoes Kaviraj had bought with his usual lavish disregard for cost. 'So, have you thought about it?' asked Sujju.

'About what?'

'The young man from Puttur. His family is interested.'

'I'm quite happy not being married. I like being a doctor.'

'Like it! What are you going to do? Go to bed with your degree and your stethoscope?' She laughed, her dry delicious cackle which used to drive boys crazy. 'A few more years and no one will look at you. All this reading and learning that you want to do will frighten them away.'

'You're jealous that you don't have a degree,' Nalli shot back, banging the plate with the mangoes down on the table.

'I have a husband and a family. I have status. Do you know

what happens to women without a husband? I don't have to tell
you . . .'

Nalli was furious, all through lunch and until she had eaten
her portion of the Raspuri. And then, as always, she plunged
into her work and put it out of her mind. But the needling went
on.

Appa was the most difficult. He was no longer proud of her.
'Is it such a difficult thing I'm asking?' he said. 'We're not
forcing a husband on you.' He arranged for eligibles—doctors
mostly—to meet her. She told them she was not considering
marriage.

'You're my problem child!' said Appa. 'I expected the best
from you, spent more on your education than Vishnu's, and you
repay me with ingratitude.'

'When I get a job I'll pay back everything!' Nalli cried.

So much sorrow in one home and she the cause. Her
defences were not all that strong. Once, after a bad day at the
hospital when she had seen over fifty patients, she came home
to find everyone tense. Sujju took her inside and told her about
a match that Appa had set his mind on. 'An offer like this will
never come again,' she said. 'Appa will talk to you. Can you do
it, for his sake?'

Maybe it was the problems at work, or maybe it was her
affection for the family that won eventually. When her father
told her about the match, she said yes. She was ready. Nalli felt
a heaviness lift away, she felt clean and good. She had had
enough of loneliness; she had been stupid and selfish. It was a
wonderful feeling to make the family happy and, really, so easy.
They talked all evening about shopping, jewels, and about the
doctor she was to marry. A photograph. A young man with a
moustache. A blur before her eyes. Yes, yes.

Sleep evaded her that night. In the morning she rose and
went in search of Appa. He was in the garden plucking flowers
for his puja. 'I can't do it, Appa,' she said. Appa looked at her
with puzzled eyes and his chin trembled, as if he would weep.
Without a word, he turned and walked into the house.

Vishnu visited them one day. Having stayed the night, he

was to leave next evening. Nalli was conscious of his eyes following her. Eyes which said things she did not want to know. That morning she escaped early to work but he cornered her while she was waiting for her bus to the hospital, a short distance from home. 'Let's go to Cheluvamba Park,' he said. 'We'll take an auto.'

'I'm busy.'

'Too busy to spare a moment for me?' There was a mild threat in his voice. He stood close to her and she could smell the scented oil in his hair, see the smoothness of his shaved chin. 'You can take a few hours off. No one will know at home . . .'

Nalli felt giddy. It was such a long time ago that she had succumbed. She had never defined in her mind what happened between them in the lampless darkness of her parents' room. That would be getting too close to fire. They stood beneath a gulmohur near the canteen; a few of the falling orange flowers were caught in her hair and Vishnu brushed them off. He was smiling, a smile of triumph that made her stomach burn. He turned to call an auto and the bus came just then. She ran the few yards and got in; the bus moved on its way. She was afraid to look back, afraid of Vishnu revealing their wretched secret. But he did not have that kind of courage.

Each morning she escaped to the hospital and allowed herself to be engulfed by work. She did not go home for lunch but ate at the canteen. And on long, hot afternoons when there was a lull in work, she sat in the library, cramming her mind with knowledge. It justified her isolation somehow, made it less personal and selfish. If she tired of reading textbooks and journals, she switched to the history of medicine. Years after Badri's lessons, she learnt again about her ancestors. As she read, her mind raced back in time. In Greece, the sick were taken to the temples of Aesculapius and treated through a ritual called incubation or 'temple sleep'. They lay on the hides of sacrificed animals and followed a strict code of diet and morals which was written on the walls of the temple. In their dreams they were visited by the god who gave them advice, which they would follow to be cured. The temples were like the hospitals, and the inscriptions ancient case records.

With Hippocrates came perception and understanding. She imagined herself there, with Hippocrates, watching the way a patient moved, looked and sat, noting what deviated from the normal, listening to the patient and predicting the course of disease, mastering the art of taking the patient's history. From there she learnt the practice of listening first and then touching the patient. At a time when dissection of the body was unheard of, Hippocrates described four types of shoulder dislocation and two of the hip. When he said, 'Our natures are the physicians of our diseases,' she nodded wisely.

With Celsus, in Rome, in the first century, she discussed the washing of wounds in sugar and thyme oil, and the use of ligatures for arterial bleeding. She met Galen who by dissecting apes and pigs added to the knowledge of anatomy and physiology. There was Cordoba in the Arab world, who wrote an illustrated book of surgery; Avicenna who became court physician when he was eighteen; and Paracelsus who introduced chemical drugs in place of vegetable remedies. She read with amazement Fracastro's description of syphilis in verse.

Having travelled to Egypt where the mummies were found to have dentures and well-set fractures, she came back to India. Brahminism prohibited the cutting of dead bodies, so Susruta devised the trick of placing a body in a basket and sinking it in the river. Seven days later when the flesh peeled off he was able to study the bones, joints and ligaments. He explained the benefits of enemas, emetics, purgatives and sneezing powders. He showed her his surgical instruments made of forged steel and kept in a clean box wrapped in flannel. She watched him at an operation, removing faecal obstruction in the intestine. After surgery he covered the wound with ghee and honey. When the adulterous women of the day had their noses and ears chopped off by jealous husbands, Susruta did plastic surgery, using a bit of the cheek as a pedicle graft.

Each time Nalli closed the book after reading about her forefathers, she was filled with an eagerness to prove her worth.

Her commitment fascinated no one but herself. The need to *do* was strong, it made her heart race and brought tears to her eyes. She worked hard, observed the doctors in the hospital and saw that there was much to learn from each of them.

Dr Chandra Prakash, who was the nephew of an MLA, strutted in the wards and worked little. Devraj quoted expansively from textbooks. He saw patients as bed numbers with the disease attached: '21 is a prostate,' '29 has had another bleed in the night,' '34 hasn't passed urine . . .' And there was Nigam, with an ambition that matched hers and way ahead of her. She watched him do a venesection on a little baby. With sure fingers he made a tiny incision in the baby's ankle, found the vein and threaded a fine tube into it. He made it look so easy. Nalli was not sure of her own abilities. Was she good enough? She could be supremely confident one day and fumbling and awkward the next. With every patient it was different. Sometimes it all got too much for her and she went about her work with her shoulders stooped, her lips unsmiling.

She overheard the patients: 'She's no dacter. The injection she gave me yesterday, it still hurts'; 'Their injection-giving skills should be tested before they're given the white coat'; 'Dacter Nigam is too good. Can't he give all the injections?' When she approached the patient with her syringe that day, her hands trembled. She imagined savage glares following her as she walked the length of the ward. So Nigam was better. Of course. Everyone else was better. Surgery was teamwork, and she had become a loner. Perhaps that was the problem.

Sridevi, the buck-toothed, brush-browed assistant matron became Nalli's ally. During the lunch hour Sridevi sat by herself in her chair and ate from a small, round tiffin box. She went about her work with her teeth clenched firmly over her lip. The soda-bottle glasses made her eyes look like the deliciously large marbles costing an anna each which Nalli had coveted as a child. Sridevi, with her single-minded defence against the corrupt staff around her, reminded Nalli of the hills of Angheri.

Around noon every day Nalli waited for Sridevi to finish her work and they went to the canteen together. Sometimes

Nigam joined them. Sridevi was sharp. 'You doctors make clever diagnoses and use new medicines all the time. Where your common sense goes, I don't know. Karianna's varicose ulcer. He's been on penicillin for weeks and the ulcer's just the same. Soframycin ointment you put every day. Now you will give more antibiotics. Yes or no?' She grinned, showing wide white teeth. 'Try mercurochrome on the edges.' Nalli did, and the ulcer healed in a week.

'You're so clever, you don't ask us nurses. You know how to give enema? You know how to give a bedpan to a patient with fracture femur? A vaginal douche? Too proud to learn simple things. And bandages? How many types of bandaging techniques you know? Nurses can show you many things. We're with the patient all eight hours of our duty time. Doctors? Two minutes for a patient. Talking clever things, then walking off, leaving nurse to do everything.' Nalli protested that she spent a lot of her time in the wards. 'That is because . . . you're an intern. No? When you become a doctor, then?'

In her mildly aggressive way, the assistant matron educated her: Nalli learnt the eight different bandaging techniques, she learnt how to insert a stomach tube, how to safely shift an unconscious patient from stretcher to bed. She realized it was stupid for a doctor to not know these things.

Three months of work in a rural area, and Nalli would be through with internship. They were thirty-eight interns—eight girls and thirty boys—and they went by train to Mandya, where Dr Mallaiah at the district hospital was in charge of their training. Trains between Mysore and Mandya were frequent. They reached Mandya at ten one morning and went to Parimala Lunch Home for coffee and refreshments before heading for the hospital. Dr Mallaiah was mild-mannered and courteous. Had the journey been comfortable? Had they eaten tiffin? He passed the register around for them to sign. These important rituals over, he enlightened them for ten or fifteen minutes about soakage pits, septic tanks, family planning and immunization.

After which he said, 'It is late now. You had better catch the Express. We will start the village programme tomorrow.' So it was back to the station and into the train. But the sign 'Meals Ready' outside Parimala Lunch Home could not be ignored; a quick lemon-rice-with-pickle, and they stampeded to the station.

Six weeks went by until someone complained to the Dean: The interns were doing no work. Dr Mallaiah started to get them organized. They went in jeeps, in groups of eight or ten, to Nuggehalli, twenty kilometres away, to preach Health. A fortnight was spent enlisting women for family planning operations (the men cheerfully agreed to their wives undergoing the surgery), another in motivating mothers to have their infants immunized. They talked to the villagers about closed drains, clean toilets and a balanced diet. The villagers nodded, smiled, and went back to living the way they always had.

Nalli's group had to list the cases of infant diarrhoea in the summer months. In twos and threes they went, staying as long as possible in each house. The heat was intense and it was slightly cooler inside the thatched, mud-walled houses. The job was quickly finished and they had time to kill until two in the afternoon when the jeep would take them back to Mandya. As Nalli sat idly in the shade of the last hut she had visited, she heard that in one of the houses a woman was in labour. The dai (midwife) from a nearby village had been sent for and would be there any minute. Sanguine that her lack of expertise would not be discovered in the godforsaken village, Nalli offered to help.

The house was small with dark rooms and cool, dung-washed floors. The woman had bathed, changed into a clean petticoat and blouse and lay on the single cot in the inner room. Her neighbours bustled about, readying things, children peeped through the window; anxiety and expectation showed on every face. The pains were coming every two minutes. Nalli stood officiously by the woman's side and needlessly checked her pulse. Should she initiate anything or wait for the dai who would be more experienced? Better to wait.

The dai breezed in, went to the back of the house and washed her hands and feet at the well. She came back into the room and saw Nalli. One of the women answered her questioning glare. 'Dacter Amma from Mysore. She's here to see . . .'

The dai had a square, resolute face, her betel-stained mouth expressed authority. 'I won't put up with meddlesome dacters who know nothing,' she said.

Nalli stood her ground. 'I'm curious to see how you handle it. I . . . have enough experience.' A fib of course. Her knowledge of obstetrics was still shaky. She would not be able to conduct a delivery on her own.

'You want to test my skills? I have delivered every child below fifteen in this village and two others.' She plonked herself on the floor near the door. 'Let *her* deliver the baby. I'll watch.' She withdrew a pouch from her waist and, choosing a betel nut, tossed it into her red mouth.

The woman on the cot had begun to moan. The pains were coming fast. 'Go on, let us see how the dacter manages,' the dai said.

'I only came to see . . . I don't want to take over from you.'

The dai sat where she was, her eyes dancing. 'You think it's an easy job? Tell me, how long must a woman in labour be starved? How long before that should she eat only kanji with salt? What should you put on a tear that may be caused by a big head as it comes out? Sugar? Coffee powder? Turmeric? Tell, tell!'

A crisis was at hand. Nalli knew that she had to make peace, and quickly. 'If you let me stay and maybe give you a hand . . .' she said, politely.

The dai gave her a withering look, got up and approached the woman. Her expert hands probed the dome-like belly. She nodded to the two women in the room. They raised the head-end of the cot by placing bricks below the legs. The woman lay with knees fully bent so her heels touched her haunches and then held both heels with her hands. A string was tied to each hand and foot and then to the cot so she would not slip down.

The dai checked her equipment: a vessel of hot water, clean sheets, a towel, coconut oil and a length of jute string. She lubricated her hands with oil and, standing next to the patient, plunged her hand in. Fluid gushed out and she stepped aside smartly to avoid getting wet. Nalli got some in her eye. 'I've spilt the water,' she said to Nalli and then to the woman. 'Now all you have to do is take a deep breath and push down when the pain comes. Mukkamma! Mukku . . . mukku . . .' With her left hand on the belly to check when it grew stiff with a contraction, she sweet-talked the woman and sometimes threatened her. Each time a wave of painful contraction passed, the mother-in-law wiped the sweat off the woman's face and gave her a sip of water in readiness for the next contraction. Nalli stroked the woman's hand.

The baby's head appeared between the woman's thighs and, with the dai's help, the rest of the baby and then the placenta. The dai cut the cord with what looked like a knife from the kitchen and cradling the baby in a folded sari, handed the baby to the mother. Nalli, wanting somehow to make a good impression, asked if it was risky to use an unsterilized knife. The woman could get some infection, even tetanus. 'The knife's been washed,' said the dai testily. 'It's a vegetable-cutting knife and vegetables are not infected.'

The dai was not too pleased about it being a girl. She got only twenty rupees, two coconuts and some rice. If it was a boy she would have got fifty rupees, ten coconuts and maybe even a sari, she grumbled as she tucked the notes into her blouse.

During one trip into a village, the headman, who had the best house in the village, asked them home. The women of the house were perfect hosts. They served hot brinjal bajjis and tea. The interns ate their fill, drank tea and, thanking their hosts profusely, got into the jeeps that were waiting. Just then Nalli realized with dismay that she needed—urgently—to go to the toilet. She stopped the jeep and rushed back to the house where they had just eaten. She mumbled to one of the women.

'We don't build toilets inside the house,' the woman said, offended.

Nalli pleaded. Outside, the driver sounded the horn. Without a word the woman led her through the house to the back door and a vegetable garden, beyond which was the expanse of mustard fields with yellow-flowered stalks swaying in the breeze. She dipped a large brass lota into a drum of water and, handing it to Nalli, pointed to the shrubs beyond. 'Go there,' she said grimly. 'I will stay here till you finish.'

When Nalli came back, the woman poured water for her to wash her hands. Nalli thanked her; a smile flickered on the woman's face. Whenever Nalli looked back and recalled others she was grateful to, she remembered the woman with the brass lota, pointing to the shrubs.

The three months passed. Dr Mallaiah's efforts to snare the fledgelings with captivating accounts of sewers and soakage pits did not work. For the interns, the posting to Mandya and the nearby villages was a curse to be endured. So they endured it.

20

It was the last day of her internship. Nalli waited outside the Sardar's office, rehearsing the words in her mind. Fighting nervousness, she knocked and went in.

'Yes?'

'Sir, I wanted to ask if I may . . . if you will . . . if it is possible . . . for me to work in surgery for a while . . .'

He removed his reading glasses and looked up from the journal of surgery. An eyebrow rose, half an inch, on his grim face. Before she could figure out if it was surprise or ridicule, he said, 'Start on Monday.'

'Thank you, sir!'

'It will be honorary,' he added, putting his glasses back on. A nice way of saying she would have to work without a salary.

In the two weeks before starting the job, having nothing to do in Mysore, she went home. How restful, how contented the village, slumbering at the foot of the hills. It was for a sight of the hills that she had been thirsting when she was away. Sadly, home was not a happy place any more. Amma had a hurt look in her eyes, Ajja was peevish and Gaja answered her in monosyllables. With Appa, the rancour had settled into sullen silences and quick retorts. Nalli retaliated. She helped around the house when asked but with a total lack of grace. She went to the table when mealtimes arrived, and then to her room. She sat by the window and beseeched the hills.

When she was young, Ajja had weaved magic around the hills. They lived and breathed like humans and if she listened very quietly, she would hear them speak. Nothing was so great, so pure and so true as the hills of Angheri. Cleaning her teeth with a mango twig and salt, Nalli would look at the hills swimming in mist, or bathed in the glow of dawn. She saw them sprout wings and fly away, leaving the skies as bare as a bald man's head. Alarmed, she would rub her eyes and look again to reassure herself. The rock and mud of the hills, the mist-soaked trees, the scrub and stones were quietly telling her to do, do, do. But what?

Ajja was angry with her and he did not think it necessary to handle her with any gentleness. 'Your sister married eight years ago. Vishnu is waiting to bring home a wife. How can he when you're still at home? It is one year since you became a dacter . . .' It went on day after day. She woke to the sound of Ajja's carping voice somewhere in the house, blaming her for every family upset. When Akkamma Teacher visited them, he complained to her.

Teacher, who had taught Nalli in primary school, was short, shorter than most of her students in the fifth standard, and had a face like a succulent fruit. She talked in a breathless voice and walked with a lovely rotating movement of her hips. Teacher looked like she would topple if you touched her. She dressed tastefully in light-coloured saris with two red, gold-flecked bangles on each fat wrist and a red bead chain on her neck. She was Nalli's idea of perfection.

When Nalli was in school Teacher had paid them a visit every few months. Spotting her fat figure at the gate, Nalli ran out to welcome her. 'Ajja . . . Teacher!' Teacher thrust something wrapped in newspaper into her hands. Nalli raced back into the house. 'Amma . . . Teacher!' Nalli unwrapped the paper; inside were coconut sweets cut in neat little diamonds, richly fragrant, bright pink and glistening with sugar. Amma told her to empty them into a tin which Nalli readily did because she could then polish off the pink bits sticking to the paper.

Ajja greeted Teacher with a bashful eagerness. He placed the guest chair near Ajji's bed and went off to dab himself with perfume. When Ajji had finished asking her tiresome questions, Teacher and Ajja sat in the porch. Amma served tiffin—semia payasa with cashewnuts which Ajja kept cached in his room and eagerly parted with for the special visitor. Akkamma Teacher did not refuse anything and ate daintily, wiping the sweat from her face with a hanky. By the time she finished eating and reached for the coffee, she was pink in the face and slightly out of breath. Ajja watched, appreciative. He treated Akkamma Teacher as if she were made of glass. She was feminine and self-conscious in a way that appealed to him.

This time, when the snacks had been eaten and the coffee served, Ajja complained about Nalli. His cheeks quivered and the angry look came into his eyes. 'Her father should have been strict. All this going-to-cauledge. Even now I tell him, fix her marriage and get it over with. No one listens to me . . .'

Akkamma Teacher sipped coffee in that fetchingly delicate way of hers, put down the cup and wiped the sweat from her chin. 'Maybe you should leave her alone for some time,' she said.

Ajja stopped pacing.

'She's a doctor. She can look after herself. Young women these days—not all of them want marriage.'

'Hmm . . . hmm . . .' Ajja stopped pestering Nalli after that and the rest of her holidays went by without any scenes.

᠊᠊᠊᠊᠊᠊

Having married in Bombay, Jai and Bela held a reception in Bangalore. The day before the reception, Nalli 'remembered' she was on duty that night and there was no one to stand in for her. Nobody seemed to mind her not going.

That night she opened the diary Appa had given her. She turned to a fresh page and put the date in the top left corner, feeling self-conscious. Then, two blank lines down, she wrote 'SURGERY' and so made her decision irreversible.

She went to bed thinking vaguely of the reasons: Toppi and Sabari; Sripathi and the Sardar. The family's resentment. Laudable Pus. Jai. It was with her first gluteal phlegmon that she had decided to hitch her future to the scalpel. Even in the haze of approaching sleep it seemed strange to her to be analysing her life like this.

At the hospital, no one was particularly impressed with her momentous decision. Many young doctors went through wanting to do surgery. Only Sridevi was pleased. 'Nice . . . very nice,' she said. 'I think you can do it.' She clamped her teeth over her lower lip and frowned. 'Tell me, you want to be a surgeon, for what? To make a big name?'

'To help people.'

'They all say that. Don't feel bad to say the truth.'

'I'm not just saying, I mean it.'

Sridevi shook her head impatiently. 'They all mean it. Ask yourself every six months and see what answer you get. And whatever your reasons, if you become too clever or stupid, I'll tell you.'

That evening she told Sujju and Kaviraj. Sujju bent lower over the tablecloth on which she worked in elaborate cross-stitch; Kaviraj played needlessly with his watchstrap. They were not curious. Their silence, Nalli knew, conveyed dismay.

Appa tried to dissuade her. 'I've never heard of a woman surgeon,' he said. 'Surgeons have to operate all day and even at night. A surgeon should be strong.' When Nalli persisted, he did something despicable. He met the Sardar and requested him to discourage her. The Sardar told her with very little delicacy that she was not suited for surgery. Doing minor cases and leaving behind complications for the seniors to manage was all very well, but being a surgeon meant doing everything on her own. It demanded a certain manliness, an aggressive faith in oneself. Anatomy or pathology might suit her better, with fixed hours, holidays and no night calls.

Was she or was she not good enough? Nalli became self-conscious and clumsy at work. She thought for some time and decided to ask Jai. 'You know how awkward I am, physically,' she wrote. 'Everything I do looks ungainly, and surgery is so graceful and smooth. You did everything with ease, always, so it wasn't a problem for you. What about me?' Marriage had distanced him further but a question like this, he would answer. He would not lie to her. The reply came promptly: If you don't try, you'll never find out. At the bottom of the letter, he wrote, 'Remember the yellow flowers?'

She did. The yellow flowers by the stream which she had nearly broken her nose for. They came always after the first rain, bursting, exploding from the low green bushes that hugged the narrow strip of land which banked the stream. Those brightly screaming yellow flowers which she wanted, like Jai, to lean forward and pluck while standing on the opposite side of the stream near the rocks where the flow was but a few feet wide. Jai could do it without getting a drop of water on himself. He stood with his feet wide apart and leant forward like a vertical rod falling gently. His body angled and came so near the water it seemed certain he would fall. The bed of pebbles gleamed dangerously in the shallow, sun-drenched stream. Jai leaned until his face was inches away from the water and, reaching out with one hand, plucked a whole bunch.

They envied him, she more than Budhi and Vijai. When she tried, she ended up with her feet and her hands in water. She was too much of a coward to risk hurting herself. Reading the envy on her face, every time they went to the stream, Jai plucked the flowers and tucked them rakishly behind his ear. Nalli watched him intently and tried again. The flowers burnt before her eyes, inches away—and then she lost balance and fell. She wept bitter tears of shame and pain, from a rapidly swelling nose. Vijai helped her wash while Jai stood watching.

'You can do it,' he said, when her sobs subsided.

She sat on the rocks, pressing the edge of her langa to her nose, and glared at him. He was not teasing her. 'You're muddy and wet, your nose looks terrible,' he said. 'Best time to take another try.' He shrugged with apparent unconcern, moved

away and started to aim pebbles into the stream. It made the
water jump. Nalli went to the edge of the water. The blurred
reflections of herself and the others stared back. She wiped her
nose, took a deep breath and stiffened the muscles of her legs.
From the corner of her eyes she could see Jai watching. She
pressed her feet firmly on the ground and tightened her belly.
Holding her breath, she leant forward and got five yellow
flowers without touching a drop of water.

Jai's letter, reminding her of the flowers, heartened her. Yes,
her hunger was greater than her fears.

Nalli knew that without support from the Sardar, a post-
graduate seat was impossible. Madras was out too; it would end
with another round of objections from the family. On a Sunday
evening when Sujju and the others had gone to the
Chamundeshwari temple, she wrote to Dr Bansali, remembering
what he had said when she left college after the exams: 'Let me
know how you get on.' It was a strange letter to write a
professor. She said everything about her family background, the
pressure to marry, and her desire to do surgery. She asked,
naively, if he could help.

Silence for six weeks. And then a letter arrived, typed on the
college letterhead, just over a page long.

Dear Ms Nalinakshi,
It is always a pleasant surprise to hear from one's
students. I am happy to note that you have completed
your internship and have chosen to work in surgery.
You are working under a very skilled surgeon and a
good man. Make the best of it.

Here, in college, the batch of students who came
after you have just finished their exams. A new batch
has taken their place in the wards. We are under
pressure to increase the number of students from sixty
to one hundred in each batch. That would strain our
resources and affect standards. We're trying to fight it.
Some money has been sanctioned for the renovation of
the operating theatre and the surgical wards and we
hope to be able to complete work this year.

I have noted the contents of your letter regarding your personal life. You must understand that parents will always want what they feel is best for their children. You are at a difficult stage in your life, and about to make a major decision. It can alter the entire course of your future. Think hard and think honestly. Is it really what you want? Do you believe that you can sustain yourself through a lifetime of hard work? You strike me as a strong young woman, with a tendency, perhaps, to stubbornness. That is not always a bad quality. But be clear in your mind about what you wish to do.

You say in your letter that you plan to work in your village. I am happy to hear the confident voice with which you say it. If you are certain about surgery, I am sure your father can be convinced. I remember meeting him briefly when he came to the college once, and he struck me as a wise man.

About your training, you can try for post-graduation in India. Or if you like, I will ask a friend of mine in England if he can take you for training. Think it over carefully, discuss it with your father, and if you make up your mind, let me know. Once or twice in life comes a special moment, like a knock on the door. You must open the door, find its worth and seize it, for it may never come again.

With best wishes,
Dr Bansali

'Once or twice in life comes a special moment, like a knock on the door.' How could she refuse? How could she accept? She was pleased that Bansali had a good opinion of her. And sad because Appa would never let her go. She put the letter carefully in her bag and went to work. She always carried the letter with her, to cheer herself.

Jai did not announce his coming; he just stopped by in Mysore on his way home to the village on a short visit. Nalli was still at work and he came to say hello. It was their first meeting after those stupid letters she had written him. Had he laughed at them, or did they fill him with remorse?

They sat in the canteen in the heavy heat of the afternoon. Was it her anger, or the heat, or something else that made Nalli feel feverish? She asked for a Mysore bonda with her coffee even though it had been only an hour since lunch. Jai settled for coffee. Jai, who ate anything at any time, saying no to Mysore bonda. He looked handsome, the way men do when everything is going well. His movements were quick, his speech clipped and assured. He talked about his job, and about Bela. 'You did not come,' he said, referring to the reception for their wedding. She did not answer. Between them there could be no excuses. He would have to understand.

He drank two coffees and smoked three cigarettes. He asked what she was doing about her future. Nalli got up and washed her greasy fingers in the sink in the corner of the canteen. Then she took Bansali's letter out of her bag and showed it to him.

She watched as he read the letter, quickly. 'You've always been a bit stupid, but this beats everything,' Jai said, his voice rising. 'Two months since he wrote, and you haven't done anything?'

'Don't shout.' At the nearby tables, heads were turning.

Jai grabbed her hand and pulled her to her feet. 'I'll shout where no one can hear.'

They stood beneath the feathery branches of the gulmohur which was now bereft of flowers. 'Two months. Two months!' Jai was furious, and she was angry because he had called her stupid. 'You've forgotten how it is for me,' she said. 'Appa would not trust me to do my internship in Madras. You expect him to let me go to a foreign country?'

'Nalli, you idiot. I'll speak to Maestru, you said he's here in Mysore.' He looked at his watch and quickly took the letter from her. 'I've a train to catch at seven, I'd better hurry.'

They had not talked enough. She had not asked him when he was coming back to Angheri. But she knew that once Jai made his mind up about something, anything, he did it. She would have to wait.

Deluged with work she forgot her anxiety till late evening when she reached home. Jai had left. She heard about it from Sujju. When Jai spoke to Appa about her, he had told Jai to mind his own business. He did not need to be told what to do by someone young enough to be his son. The family wished to see Nalli properly married. It was a matter of honour and duty.

'Sir, what honour are you talking about if you cannot spare a thought for your daughter's happiness?' Jai argued. 'If you force her into marriage, it won't work. Where will honour be then? If it's surgery she's set her mind on, let her at least prove herself.'

Appa was not convinced. 'Her professor here says women are not suited for surgery,' he said. 'Nalli is weak and sickly. She has a back problem.'

Jai, who had been waiting for the right moment, showed him the letter from Bansali. 'See what this professor thinks about her.'

'Nalli, a surgeon,' Appa said slowly, his features softening as he folded the letter and handed it back to Jai. 'I can't see it happening. But . . . this is surely wonderful.'

'Sir, it's an opportunity I'd have given anything for.'

Appa was still wavering, when Jai slipped in a threat: even if he did not agree, Nalli could still go. The ticket money could be arranged.

Once Appa agreed, he talked of little else. The family dropped the subject of Nalli's marriage. No more resentful glances, no more debates about her future.

Things moved fast. Appa went with her to Madras. Nalli had outgrown her stupid pride and did not mind his going with her to meet the professor. Bansali greeted them politely and took them to his office. He spoke to Appa for a few minutes, ignoring Nalli. Then, with a glance at his watch, he said, 'I'll speak to the doctor, now. It's nine-thirty. If you could come back by one?' Appa left.

It was a few seconds before Nalli realized that the doctor Bansali was referring to was herself. Across the table, he eyed her grimly. With a weak smile, Nalli started saying how grateful she was for his help. He stopped her with an impatient wave of his hand. Leaning forward, he asked, 'Why do you want to go to England?'

'I . . . sir.'

'What will you do there?'

'I hope . . . I mean . . . I'll try . . .'

'When will you come back?'

She remembered how he spoke in that queer, choppy style when he was particularly worked up about something. She looked blankly at him, her thoughts in a tangle. The simple clarity of his questioning trapped her. He waited for her to speak, not taking his eyes off her. When she did not, he barked, 'Why did you become a doctor?'

'To give medicines to sick people and cure them.'

'In what way is a doctor different from a washerwoman?'

Silly thing to ask, but Bansali's questions were meant to be answered. This time he answered it himself. 'No difference!' he said. 'The washerwoman washes clothes, wrings them and hangs them out to dry. She folds them neatly and brings them home. A doctor has patients lined up for treatment. He sees them one by one, gives pills, ointment, injection, whatever, and cures them. Where is the difference? Washing clothes; servicing bodies.' He was shaking a finger at her, trying to make her understand. She could not make sense of what he was saying. 'You don't know and you're happy not knowing.'

He leaned back and said gruffly, 'No woolly-headed girl will do surgery on my recommendation. Surgery, my foot.' He rose from his chair and almost shouted. 'Listen! You're going to sit here and Think. Clearly. Why? What? When? I have ward rounds to finish.' He called his secretary. 'Give her a cup of tea if she wants it.' Then he walked out, shutting the door after him.

Nalli stared at the door that he had just closed, at the walls and the wooden shelves filled with books and journals; at the blotting paper, ink and paperclips on the table. Her cheeks stung as if someone had slapped her. When she was very young, during one of her fevers, the doctor had given her an injection of penicillin. It was horribly painful. Bansali's questions felt like she had had a penicillin poke and that too with a blunt needle.

She sat still in her chair. She recollected Bansali's words, and tried to feel her way through her doubts and fears. Her mind raced in confusion between wanting to speak her mind and somehow finding the words which Bansali wanted to hear. She felt muddled. Did he not trust her any more?

Two hours. When Bansali came back, still scowling, she was calm. She said that she wanted to train at a reputed university and obtain the fellowship of the Royal College of Surgeons.

'Oh? I *see* . . . And how *long* will that take you?'

'Two years.' A smile flickered on his lips. 'I'll be back in five years,' she added, quickly.

The smile faded. 'Not good enough. Five years in England is far too long.'

She promised to try to be back earlier.

'What are you waiting for? Get your passport ready. I am writing to Professor Ferguson in Liverpool. If he accepts, you should be able to get your visa in three months.'

21

When Nalli's going became certain, Ajja began to advise in earnest. She barely listened. She could look after herself. He warned her in particular about the perils of eating meat but she was unafraid of a sin already committed.

The ticket to England was a lot of money and Appa managed it with a loan from Beach Aunty's husband. Nalli said her farewells with less haste than she had when she joined college. She promised to bring lipsticks and creams for Sujju, a pink sweater for Fat Aunty, a camera for Budhi and a blue sweater for Amma. Early one morning in November, she boarded the bus to Madras.

This time when they met, Bansali was kinder, almost courteous. Tea was served in the office and Bansali chatted amicably about England, until she asked him if he had any advice to give her about living amidst foreigners. She had heard about racial prejudice.

'You can't be stupid enough to worry about that?'

In a show of confidence and self-assurance, she said, 'Sir, England is a different country. They ruled us for so long, now they resent us going there as equals.'

He shook his head in an angry gesture. 'Wherever you go in this world, you get the respect you deserve. No more, no less. Everything else, you sort out yourself. Don't come whining to me about prejudice.' She wanted to say something to justify herself, but he stopped her. 'Foreign! Do you understand the word? When you came to college from your village, was it not foreign? My coming here from a little town in Punjab where I grew up was foreign. Foreign and not foreign, it's all in the head. It's not because of geography or religion or gender. If you cannot understand that, you'll be miserable wherever you go.'

He drummed his fingers on the table and looked steadily at Nalli. 'Self-belief. That's the only thing.' He pushed a green, leather-bound file on his table towards her. 'Surgical notes that I made in England,' he said, his face relaxing. 'May come in useful. Be sure to bring it back.' He stood and with a slight nod of his head dismissed her.

She took the train to Bombay where she would stay three days before setting off. Jai and Bela came to the station to meet her. When she saw them, the pain of her hurt twisted inside. She should have hated Bela but she liked her, had liked her ever since that first moment when her photograph had fallen out from between the pages of Jai's letter. Any hope that she might find something in Bela to dislike melted away by the time the car reached their flat in Worli.

Bela was lazy in that feline way of beautiful women who need not work for a living. She dressed with a careless elegance knowing that no matter what she wore she would look lovely. Their baby was due in five months; Jai fussed over her all the time. He brought her lime juice to fight the morning sickness, propped up cushions for her to lean on and worried over her every twinge. He called several times from the hospital. In the evening he called once more to check if she wanted something from the shops. He sat with an arm around Bela's shoulders, stopping occasionally in mid-sentence to stroke her hair. Their little acts of love embarrassed Nalli but they were not embarrassed.

Their flat was elegant, with sleek furniture and soft lighting. In Nalli's room was a carpet in light beige, soft and deep, good enough to sleep on. Bela said she had taken it out especially for her visit. When she left, it would be cleaned, brushed, wrapped in plastic and stored away. Nalli could not bring herself to step on the carpet. She walked carefully around it. In England, it will be like this, she thought.

Bela was friendly, kind and eager to please. She invited friends who had lived in England to meet Nalli. There was plenty of advice.

'They work you to the bone but feed you well. A hospital breakfast keeps you going all day.'

'The food's terrible. Boiled meat, potatoes and boiled cabbage. My husband always came home to eat.'

'No matter how good you are it's your skin colour that matters.'

'The Brits don't walk, they run. They're obsessed with time. Even old ladies will beat you to it.'

Nalli listened and was confused. Alone in her room she took out her diary and read all that she had written. It gave her a surge of confidence to know that she believed in herself. She would do it, whatever the problems.

From where they lived in Worli, Nalli saw something of the city. While Jai worked non-stop, she and Bela drove around the city, walked about and shopped, mainly for non-essentials. Bela used an umbrella to 'keep out the sun' and, more important, 'not to be jostled.' It was easy to pick up diseases, she said and insisted that Nalli too shield herself. Nalli worried that they might injure someone with their umbrellas. 'We've just got to be careful,' Bela said and with apologies and smiles, ensured she offended no one. When they went to restaurants, Bela ordered endless cups of coffee which she never finished.

Nalli liked the city. It did not scorn strangers, it absorbed them. A few weeks there and it would be easy to consider herself a part of it. There was confidence in the people without the showing off. The only thing Nalli disliked was the milky coffee they served everywhere. When she asked for stronger coffee, the waiter looked at her curiously and brought a quarter-teaspoonful of the instant powder. After several attempts to get strong coffee, she settled for tea.

Once, as they drove through Mahim and stopped at the traffic lights, she saw two little children washing vessels in front of their shack in a slum. The girl was four or five and dressed in a thin slip of a dress. She squatted with the pans and plates stacked before her and scrubbed, her hands buried inside a saucepan, her dress curling up to her waist. The boy was naked and smaller than the girl. He watched her and struggled to wash a vessel himself. It kept sliding away from his little hands and he got up and carried it back beneath the tap and started again.

Bela was concerned about the slums and the poverty. 'It's heartbreaking. There are whole families living in one-room apartments. All over Bombay.'

'In the slums it must be worse.'

'Someone should write a book about it or make a film or something,' Bela said. 'I'm too much of a coward to go into the slums. Jai has studied poverty. I thought it was the worst thing in the world, but Jai doesn't think so. Poverty is necessary because it gives us a chance to do some good. Jai says we must be optimistic, we must do our bit for the poor and hope for the best.' She leant forward, resting her chin on her hands. 'Isn't that a brilliant way of looking at something so appalling as poverty? Whenever I can, I give sweets. That's what I do. It's not easy to find these poor people. They're not accessible. So, what I do is, every month when I go to my hairdresser I give sweets to the sweeper-woman. She has five kids, all in some school. They have money problems, naturally, and can't dream of buying sweets. I give a whole handful to her, every month. You should see the joy on her face. It keeps me going for one whole month. Jai teases me about being Mother Teresa . . . but I'm so happy doing it, I can't wait to do it again.' Bela had not seen the sweeper-woman's children. She did not know where they lived. And she herself did not eat sweets because they would ruin her teeth.

She could give money for their school books. Or to buy milk or clothes, Nalli said.

Bela frowned. 'Jai says the poor have short lives. They die of all sorts of diseases like worms and infections and dog bite and dysentery, which is nothing but an infection from the food they eat. They die sooner than most people. What do bad teeth matter? Let them enjoy something, let them have some sweetness . . .' She sounded earnest about it.

Bela loved to talk about Jai. 'He's made for success. He outshines everyone. "Young Dr Jayanth, he's too good," a patient of his told me the other day. Isn't it quite something, in a city that's full of super surgeons?' A few months earlier, an eminent surgeon had picked Jai to be his assistant. 'Jai has to reach the hospital an hour before his boss and get the patient ready on the operating table. The boss walks in only when the patient is under. "Get started," he tells Jai and then starts to scrub. When he's finished the main bit, he lets Jai close. Jai does the hard work and the surgeon gets the credit. It's good experience.'

Every day Nalli watched Jai and felt a sadness for things that had changed. He had honed his unerring instinct to achieve and lost his youthful abrasiveness, his fits of violent temper and the constant need for mischief. He thrived on the speed and madness of the city, coped with the stress of fourteen-hour lunchless days, and slept lightly. For Bela, who loved parties, the once-a-week Saturday night out was a must. Even when Jai finished late and was tired, he never refused her.

Nalli's sadness was partly mitigated by what the future offered. Jai was eager to discuss the village hospital. He had it all figured out: the building, staff, equipment and the bank loan. Bela, in her impractical way, talked eagerly about moving to Angheri. 'I wonder how easy it will be to get sweets, you know, to give away to poor children? Do you have shops and things or should I take a supply from here?' She was confident that they would be supremely happy wherever they went and pestered

Jai to take her for a visit. It was not a good idea to travel when she was pregnant, he said. And they should give time for the village folk to get used to the idea of his marrying out. It was the only thing they argued about.

'Bela deserves comfort, it's always been a life of luxury for her,' Jai told Nalli when Bela was not around. 'She isn't used to hardship.'

'How will she adjust to Angheri?'

'She likes to see me do well. It doesn't matter so much where we are. But we must plan everything and prepare ourselves for the job. Let's not hurry things. No false starts. You go to England, learn and earn. We'll do it when you come back.' Then he asked, abruptly, 'Why haven't you married?'

It was the way he asked, as if it was a trivial matter, that angered her. 'For reasons I'm quite clear about,' she snapped, not speaking the truth.

Bela warned Nalli that her suitcase might be too heavy. But everything in it was essential: Amma had sewn four thick petticoats, she had bought shoes in Bombay, and then there were her books, twelve of them, Dr Bansali's leather-bound notes, and the red diary. When she checked in at the airport, the suitcase weighed fifty kilos. Shamefaced, she let Bela and Jai help lighten the load. Out went a pair of shoes, some books and two bottles of pickle.

Then she walked across the tarmac to her future.

part two

Is there a surgeon anywhere who doesn't lose a patient once in a while? Why, some of those guys must tow a fleet of souls behind them.

—Saul Bellow, *Henderson the Rain King*

22

I spent my first night in London washing underclothes at the sink and struggling for warmth under an electric blanket which I did not dare plug in. The room was small, the bed sinking-soft and cold. The lime-coloured wallpaper with leaves falling in orderly disorder looked at me from every side. Through the windows, a myriad yellow lights squinted in the fog as the noise of traffic receded into the night. A sense of being torn away from everything that was familiar swept through me, stronger than when I had first left home for college.

Earlier that day I had stepped off the plane into the perishing cold of a November morning. The wind greeted me with an icy slap. Carrying my bags I struggled through the formalities that awaited a foreigner. No porters to help. Passengers pushed their luggage on wheeled trolleys with skilful speed, but I preferred to pant my way through, bags and all. The only hitch that arose was my slipper strap snapping on the wicked escalator. With help from a kindly fellow passenger, I stumbled off the wretched thing. In the midst of unsmiling strangers, there were two Indians. A woman in a long black coat and salwar kameez was sweeping the foyer. She paused to adjust the dupatta over her head and looked at me with cold eyes. A Sikh lad went by pushing a trolley and ignored me completely.

The strangeness of it all confused me. Everyone knew what to do; I did not. But the moment I stepped out of the plane and felt the punishing hand of the English weather, I had decided: I will not let anything stop me from what I have come here to do. Clutching my bags, I walked on.

Mr Mani, a friend of a friend of Bansali, waited at the exit.

He was a quiet and courteous man with a dark, intense Malayali face, quickly moving eyes and a prim moustache. He had booked me a room at Hotel Tarun for four pounds a night.

The Chhabras who managed the hotel did it with British efficiency, Punjabi homeliness and a Cockney-Punjabi accent. A Gujarati couple occupied the room next to mine. It was four days since they had come from Rajkot; they were to leave for Bradford in the morning to visit relatives. Over tea in the dining room they offered generous advice. Locking your hotel room when you went out was bad manners; you greeted people with a 'Good morning' or 'What a lovely day' or 'Cold, isn't it?' and nothing more; you said 'Thank you' and 'Please' to everyone, every time. I let their advice pass me by. I was sure I could handle things my way.

I soon found I needed Mr Mani to see me through those first bewildering days until I left for Liverpool. The next morning he took me to the office of the General Medical Council and introduced me to the woman in charge. 'Let her speak,' said the lady, eyeing me over her glasses. Mr Mani switched to a local accent when he spoke to the British but was perfectly normal when speaking to me. 'They find it hard to understand us,' he explained and advised me to speak like him. I did not like it one bit. I was no longer a foolish sixteen-year-old desperate to imitate others; I would speak in my own accent.

Mr Mani took me to the shops. With fifty borrowed pounds I bought a coat in deep purple, two skirts, blouses, polyester trousers and knee-length woollen stockings—blue, white and maroon. Mr Mani stood by, waiting for me to finish. He was not the meddlesome type. Later, when I saw how hopelessly out-of-fashion my choices were, I wished he had told me. Only matronly women wore the type of clothes I had chosen. Twenty-five pounds were gone; the rest of the money would have to see me through the month, before I was paid. But, that day, when I walked out of the shop laden with new apparel, I was pleased. In my room I changed into the brown skirt and yellow blouse. I practised the stiff-hipped walk of British women and laughed at myself.

Three days later, clutching the ticket (six pounds ninety-nine), I boarded the train to Liverpool. The near-empty stations, the sameness of the compartments, the plastic-wrapped sandwiches and the gentle contours of the countryside soothed my excited brain. The journey to Liverpool was three and a half hours long. I smiled at the other passengers; they smiled and returned to their newspapers. Children did not tear down the aisle or pester others; the little ones dozed in their prams with teething rings sealing their mouths. I was amused by the manner in which people stood and moved and spoke or did not speak. Young women wore dresses shorter than Carol's and higher heels, and their brown, yellow, red hair was all in place, as if fixed with glue; youths with tattooed arms and metal-studded sleeveless jerkins said 'fuck' at least three times in a single sentence; men read tabloids with strange headlines: LIVERPOOL FLAYS CHELSEA FOUR-NIL! ROYAL DAREDEVIL FINED FOR SPEEDING! LUCIFER QUOTES SCRIPTURE? SCANDAL IN CHURCH-RUN REFORMATORY! BIRMINGHAM BEAUTY BARES ALL!

The Royal Infirmary being five hundred yards uphill from the station, and my suitcase too heavy, I splurged on a cab. It was late evening when I stood outside the rusty iron gates of the hospital. The cabbie carried the suitcase in, accepted the fare of a pound, touched his cap and left.

The Infirmary was Victorian, a quarter of a mile from the docks and three storeys high, with a gate that led to Pembroke Street. My room was large, with a high ceiling and wooden floors. It was plainly furnished and the windows opened on to the road. Having eaten too many sandwiches on the train, I skipped dinner and went to bed. In the morning Patsy, the domestic, came to tidy the room. I watched her as she briskly went about with pail and swab and duster. Ajja would have been pleased with her strong, untiring arms.

Dressed in a sari, nervous and cold, I went to meet Professor Ferguson. He came round his desk and shook hands, and was a little taken aback when I gave him the pound of Coorg coffee powder and the sandalwood elephants which Appa had bought in Mysore.

The professor was a gracious Scot and genuinely concerned for my future. Bansali and he had been colleagues in the surgical department at the Royal Infirmary. They had even taken their fellowship exams together. He talked about my training: 'Casualty department for six months, six months of surgery, and then we'll see . . .' He advised me to settle down and take my time over the FRCS. Most foreign graduates took the exams in haste, he explained, and were frustrated by failure.

He took me to meet the doctors in casualty. Paul Smutch and I would be on the morning shift, Mike Mace in the evening and Vivian Mathews at night. Duties changed on Mondays, he explained. All emergencies went through casualty; minor problems were handled there and major ones admitted to the concerned department.

Given the British methods of training in India, the job was easy. I worked in earnest. Cuts, sprains, fractures, stomach ailments—a dull routine, often interrupted by a tricky case like chest pain, overdose, or a slashed wrist. Fractures were reduced, ingrown toenails removed and wounds sutured in the Theatre attached to casualty. On weekends we kept busy with football injuries. In the evenings we sutured cut heads of drunks who poured in from the pubs and were treated free by the benevolent National Health Service.

Slowly, I got accustomed to the regulars at the hospital—alcoholics, drug addicts and the tramps who came at night or were brought in by the police, just plain drunk, harmless, dirty and unwanted, in need of some kindness and a bed for the night. The doctor's job was to do a quick once-over and then it was up to the nurse to get the man undressed. The most difficult job was getting a tramp to take off his shoes. It took some coaxing or firm threats like 'Off with it, or I'm sending you right back.' It was wise not to venture in the vicinity when they were at last off. The nurse then got him to take a bath, gave him a scrub-down if needed and tucked him into bed.

When I finished with a patient, I summoned the next from a disciplined row of people seated in the waiting area. One card said 'Carlisle'. I called 'Caar-Lisslay!' No one stirred. 'It's *Carlyle*, doctor,' the nurse whispered.

The way most people talked baffled me, it was not English. 'I hate me thambe at wake . . .' said a burly dockworker. 'What?'

'I hate me thambe at wake,' he said, sticking his grimy thumb in my face. The nurse came to my aid once more. 'He's saying he-hurt-his-thumb-at-work,' she said, trying to keep a straight face.

Of the four doctors in casualty, Mike Mace proved to be the best. He had published a paper on recurrent appendicitis and was working on another. When he was not on call he went to the surgical wards with the registrars and tried to learn as much as he could. Vivian was more interested in student nurses than in his work. Smutch, who looked and behaved older than his years, was ploddingly purposeful. He asked me if I would join him in doing clinical research. He had discussed it with the orthopaedic surgeon and come up with a subject: 'The diagnosis of serious ankle sprains as compared to minor ones'.

The method was simple. You dipped the injured ankle in a basin of water, measured the increase in volume and compared this with the uninjured side. An increase of 33 ml was serious. Every morning Smutch and I sat measuring ankles. Old ladies, tramps and puzzled young boys were subjected to the cold ankle bath. Basins of water splashed everywhere. Old ladies peeled off their stockings, muttering, 'I just wanted some tablets, dear . . .' 'Bleeding madness,' said a brawny construction worker, hobbling off in search of his shoes. 'Water torture,' grumbled another. We persevered. 'Please dip your ankle in this basin . . . the sore one first. Now the other . . .'

The lunacy ended when Pat Nesbit, the nurse in charge of casualty, said she was not going to put up with the department looking like a waterlogged swamp. Smutch challenged her to try and stop him but eventually buckled, and the ankle research ended for good.

I was learning fast, and enjoying it. In spite of Professor Ferguson's warnings, I wanted to take the exams early and spent most of my time at the library, a few hundred yards from the Infirmary. It was comfortingly warm and lined floor-to-ceiling

with books. When I tired of study I read my letters and wrote
more. Sitting there one afternoon, engrossed in reading 'The
Tuberculous Lung' in Boyd's pathology textbook, I sensed a
stealthy, ever-so-soft sound which I might have missed if it were
not for the absolute hush. My gaze pulled sideways to the
window: it was snow, falling in a loose stream. It looked like
someone was showering parijata petals from above! The white
fluff covered the roads, trees and cars, and dulled the sharp
sounds of the city. Forsaking Boyd, I put on my coat and went
out to witness the magic. Two days later the snow on the roads
settled into ice and slush and even walking to the library was
difficult. Old ladies who fell on the slippery ice came in with
fractured wrists and ankles. I did not like the snow all that much
any more.

~

I battled with greed of many types.

I went for lunch in the doctors' dining room with Paul
Smutch and the maid asked, 'Cottage pie or beef casserole, luv?'

'Cottage pie,' I answered, not having a clue what it might
be.

'Suet pudding, or peaches and ice cream?'

'Suet pudding.'

I hacked away at the edges of an awesome pie made of
potatoes and mince, and gave up. The suet pudding was too rich
and too much. With time I found that soup and salad suited me,
and, whatever the dessert, I ate ice cream, unlimited.

Food shops snared me and I stood outside, tormenting
myself: cakes, ice cream, chocolate and the creamy mousse,
which came in little plastic tubs that were a bit too small—just
four decent mouthfuls (and another half spoonful if you scraped
the tub clean). The first time I asked for 'strawberry mouse', the
woman at the counter corrected me: 'It's *mooze*, dear.' It cost
five pence, like everything else. Yoghurt, ice cream, coffee, tea,
a scone or a pastry, everything was five-p. You could buy
brands which were more expensive but I was comfortable being
a five-p person. Ajja had bequeathed me his miserliness. I did

not throw away the little plastic tubs. Instead I lined them up on my window sill with some vague idea of taking them home. One day Patsy did a thorough clean-up job of my room and chucked out the 'rubbish' on the sill, leaving it bare.

The TJ Hughes Department Store I discovered on my own. It was a low-cost bargain shop where doctors did not shop. I bought three skirts and two lipsticks for four pounds fifty. I went every Saturday evening and walked among the shelves laden with goods, eyeing cosmetics, clothes, underclothes and nightclothes until I was dizzy. One day the security man in the shop asked in a clearly suspicious voice, 'Can I help you?'

'Just looking,' I said, smiling weakly.

With the cold my conflict was altogether different. I could not adjust. Outside the centrally heated hospital it was bitter most of the time, with harsh winds and a constant rain. I reinforced myself with woollen tights, knee-length socks, vest, sweater, overcoat, scarf, mitts and a woollen cap and fought my way into a pair of boots. With the shoulder bag and umbrella in my hands and several pounds heavier, I stepped out. I trudged down Pembroke Street and all the way towards the docks, then took a sharp turn to the shopping mall. It was bearable as long as I kept walking, huddled into myself. The wind pierced my clothes like needles and I struggled to hold up the umbrella, which habitually turned inside out. I must have looked ridiculous but no one seemed to notice. I rubbed my nose with mittened hands, tapped and twisted my toes inside the boots. Back in my room, I peeled the socks off my numb feet and saw that they had turned a deathly blue. When I washed them in hot water they turned red and at night they itched and burned. My toes were falling off, my panicked mind screamed . . . could it be frostbite? The next day I went to the dermatologist. 'Chilblains,' he said.

～

Most people minded their own business and I was content to be left alone.

About a month after I came to Liverpool, I got a call.

'Mountain speaking,' a leathery voice announced from the other end of the line.

Mountain?

'Colleague of Bansali. A bit under the weather right now or I'd have come over. Can you make it for tea on Sunday? Good. Agincourt Road, bus number 14. Get off opposite the children's hospital and take the first road to the left. House number 9 it is.' All week I wondered what Mountain might look like. A doctor with a name like that had to be interesting.

It was a twenty-minute ride on the bus, and the house easy to find. A sweet old man with moist blue eyes answered the door. 'Walter Mountain,' he said, with a warm handshake and a quivering smile. His voice was soft, meek. Who was the Mountain who had spoken to me? The mystery was solved when a familiar voice boomed from inside, 'Walter! Bring the doctor in here.'

Seated in the living room was a big-boned woman of unselfish girth, with a mat of greying hair and a face as broad as a hat. 'A bad touch of arthritis,' she said. 'Don't mind me sitting here all wrapped up. Make yourself cosy. The tea, Walter . . .'

Rose Mountain had been a student nurse when Bansali was in training. 'He was brainy, that one,' she said. 'Better than most. And a charmer, though he didn't know it.' She laughed. 'He had a crush on me!'

She had asked him to a dance once. He borrowed a suit and learnt some easy steps. When he did not turn up for the dance, she looked everywhere and found him near a sausage stand at the corner of Pembroke Street, all dressed up and nervously puffing a cigarette. She dragged him to the party. 'He was a terrible dancer,' she chuckled.

Walter gave us scones, walnut bread and a cream cake. He had worked as a baker for forty years, Rose said proudly. Now all he did was spoil her. In a neat reversal of roles, Walter cooked and tended the house; Rose saw to the plumbing and electricity, and tinkered with their Morris Minor. I liked the Mountains and I liked the cakes.

I visited them often, at least once a month. They had lived through the war years when there was very little of anything. They did not have the comfort of central heating in those days. How did they keep warm? 'Bed warmers,' Rose said, pointing to the two heavy iron pans hanging on the wall. 'Heat them on the fire and put them beneath the sheets half an hour before bedtime. You're as warm as toast.'

When I was with them I liked to talk and quite forgot the time until Rose looked at the clock and said brusquely, 'Time to catch your bus, dearie.' She had a mild air of bossiness about her.

At the Infirmary I often chatted with Stan, the ambulance driver who brought patients to casualty. He was small for an Englishman, with a beak-like nose, a sharp chin and straight hair that fell over his eyes. His smile revealed tiny gaps between his teeth. He was polite and mild-mannered but dealt firmly with tramps, drunks and dockworkers. 'Steady now, you chaps, this is a hospital. Keep your fights for later, please.' They listened to him. There was no cockiness about Stan. He had lived in Liverpool all his life and the farthest he had been away was to Blackburn for a weekend. When no one else was around, he talked easily to me. In company, he was content to sit quiet and sip his tea.

Sometimes a glance or a tone of voice reminded me of my distance from home, and also that home did not seem so real any more. The feeling usually passed soon enough, but sometimes it persisted.

One evening in casualty we were sitting in the tea room— four or five doctors and nurses—making the best of a lull in work. I drank tea and listened to Paul Smutch talk about his childhood in Tanzania. His father had worked there as a missionary and, along with other countrymen, set up schools and dispensaries. They helped the natives fight 'ignorance' and weird customs like occult medicine and other 'barbaric' rituals practised by the numerous tribes. Paul studied in a boarding school in England and visited Tanzania for holidays. When he was twelve, there was a political upheaval in Tanzania which resulted in his parents and most other white men and women leaving the country.

'My parents are still remembered there,' he said. 'Dad gets letters. Apparently, it's got terrible out there. One of his colleagues wrote, "I wish your government would send a planeload of your soldiers to take over this country. We'll welcome them with open arms, we'll celebrate their coming with a day-long feast."'

I was irritated by the conceit in his voice. But not knowing much about the political scene in Africa, I could not comment. Noticing that I was quiet, Paul asked, 'What's it like in Indiar, Nell? I hear that most people feel the same there. That they look back with nostalgia at the past when we were in control.'

I do not know what happened to me. The colonial days were well and truly in the past and it hardly concerned me. But something about what he had said about Tanzania, the way he said 'Africar' and 'Indiar' (and never Americar or Russiar), the way my name had conveniently been changed to Nell 'because Indian names are unpronounceable', the memory of Appa's conversations at the kitchen table—all of it led to my outburst, which I did not regret, nor repeat since.

'It's wishful thinking on your part,' I said. 'No people, African, Asian or Arabian, want you back.'

'They did ask my father,' Paul said, stiffly.

'Wherever the British went, they plundered wealth. They set local chiefs against each other, caused chaos and bloodshed and then cleverly offered to rule. That's how they did it in India and that's probably what they did elsewhere.'

'How about the hospitals and schools and . . .'

'Yes. And roads and railways and the postal service. But who wants to trade freedom for roads and railways?'

The painful silence was broken by the hiss of water boiling in the kettle and then the scraping of a chair as a nurse got up and switched it off. Mercifully, the siren of the ambulance sounded as Stan drove in through the gates with an emergency and we got back to work.

The next day I was in the dining room having a late lunch

when Paul came across carrying his plate of dessert and pulled up a chair next to me. 'Sorry if I offended you,' he began gravely. 'But you missed the point, Nell. I wasn't talking of forced occupation or empire-building. Let me assure you, that's never going to happen. But the Third World needs our help. There are millions of impoverished and ignorant people out there. We cannot ignore them.'

Again, I saw red. 'Paul. Will you stop calling me Nell? It's Nalinakshi or Nalli. And why "Third World"? Who decides which is First, which Second?'

He smiled but there was a tightness in his face. 'You know why some of the Brits resent the people who come over to this country? These people are so desperate when they come—*their* countries don't do anything for them but give them passports to get away—but when they've sort of settled in, they begin to crib about all sorts of things. Strange, isn't it?' He finished his dessert and got up. '*I* don't think like that, don't you worry,' he added, absolving himself of any invidious design. 'I'm always happy to have helped.'

Later the same day we apologized to each other. I mumbled something about not having been entirely fair; Paul said he would not rake up the issue again and promised to call me Nalli. It made me wonder if there was some truth in what he said. I had come to dredge their knowledge banks, to learn from them. I was taking with one hand and hitting out with the other. I felt depressed by my confused hurt and identity. Did my credentials start with being Indian, being Hindu, being a woman, a doctor, or as a rustic? Bansali had warned me against this sort of fencing off and yet . . .

I had other friends—Sushma, Ambili and Romeira who had rooms next to mine.

Sushma was from Chandigarh. She was short and buxom with her hair secured in a topknot by colourful pins. She wore saris to work and salwar kameezes when not on duty. She worked hard, was up at all hours of the night, but she never looked tired. On Sundays she cooked Punjabi food—pungent, greasy and ample—which we ate in the small kitchen adjoining our rooms. Sushma wanted to be the chief of obstetrics in Chandigarh and had given herself three more years in England. She said the only advantage for Western women was that they could stay unmarried without anyone making a fuss. Her family considered her a rebel.

'I'm like you,' I said. 'I don't want to get married.'

'A few years on your own and you'll wish you had a family,' said Ambili. She was a high-strung girl from the medical department and in love with an army officer in Bangalore. She wrote him letters every week and pursued him with an anxiety that seemed to be heading for a frustrating end.

Naturally I told them about the village hospital I was going to work in. Sushma was against it. 'You can have these big dreams,' she said, 'but you'll lose. What will you do there? You'll get defeated by the corruption and politics, even in the village.'

'There isn't a single doctor in our village.'

'If you wanted to be a village doctor, an MBBS was enough, na. A surgeon must be recognized. You'll have to be in a bigger centre. A medical college hospital, baba. And you'll have to work twice as hard as the men, do research and write scientific papers.'

Sushma knew what she was talking about. I was distressed by what she said but I was in no doubt that I could do it.

Romeira was an Iraqi, stylish and pretty. She had come as a post-graduate student in pathology and had wanted to go back after her two-year training but within six months she acquired an American boyfriend. He was a biochemist from Nebraska and in England on a year's fellowship. He was a loathsome man who found fault with all things not American. He was set on taking Romeira back with him. Once, I met him outside the Tesco supermarket unloading food from a trolley he had just wheeled out of the store. 'There's hardly any variety of bread here,' he grumbled. 'Back home we get thirty-six types.'

'All the more reason for you to go back soon,' I said. 'By the way, if you ever happen to come to India, better bring a supply of bread. We have only one type.'

When I had nothing to do I sought the company of the maids in the dining room. I was never sure if they were interested in listening to me or were merely being polite. I avoided the boisterous Friday night parties held in the doctors' wing because I was shy. But sometimes, listening to their noisy revelry or seeing gorgeously dressed nurses tripping off for a night out, I was envious. One Friday, Robert, the ginger-haired houseman told me at lunch—rocking his chair back and touching me on the shoulder—that the party that Friday was going to be the best, so would I come? On an impulse, I agreed.

I wore my pleated green skirt with the frothy white blouse and my green stone earrings. With the silver-sequined handbag in my hand, I studied myself from every coquettish angle. The mirror said wonderful things. As I came out of the room I met Linda, the house surgeon in anaesthesia. 'Robert said you're coming to the party,' she said. 'Hurry and get dressed.'

After hating Linda for a while, I changed into a pink silk sari and painted my lips a frosted pink. Remembering the flattering whistles during that first party in the college Mess in Madras, I wore the sari low on my waist; it had been a ploy to hide my slippers that did not match. Now I pushed the sari down as low as I dared and, oblivious of looking like a C-grade starlet, I went to the party.

The room was filled with smoke, jangled music and the sour smell of beer. I lurked in a corner. Where was Robert, where was Sushma? Vivian saw me and hollered, 'Hi, Nell! Have a drink?' No, thank you, I said, but gave in when he persisted. I could feel myself grow sociable and chatty. If it was not for Sushma, who firmly escorted me back to the room, I would have made a fool of myself.

I bought two more dresses, a pair of uncomfortably high-heeled shoes, a black leather overcoat, and rouge. I spent hours in the doctors' lounge trying to impress the tall and wickedly handsome medical registrar from Lahore. One evening there was a knock on my door. It was not the Pakistani but Winston, the pink-cheeked intern with pimples. That was the end of my foolish fantasy.

When he saw me in one of my new dresses, Stan said, 'A sari looks better on you.' I was peeved, and sulked for a few days. But Stan was being honest and somewhere within me I was grateful.

In spite of my social ineptitude, I remained focussed on what I had come to do. I spent my spare time in the library, poring over my books. Shopping, television and spending time with friends, even Stan, were secondary. I continued to be a loner because it suited my pursuit. It was a sort of selfishness that I was comfortable with.

23

Appa's letter arrived three weeks after I had reached Liverpool. Having finished duty I had come up to my room after a late lunch. Sitting on my bed, I read:

Dearest Nalinakshi,
We were extremely happy to receive your letter and learn that by the grace of Igguthappa Swami you reached safely and you are settling down well. We are all fine here. Ajja, Ajji and your mother send you their love and blessings. Budhi is writing a letter, which will be sent as soon as he has finished it. We have decided that we will write you by turns to save on postage. Ajja still refuses to send any letter to a foreign country but he listened eagerly when I read out the news from you.

Here life goes on as before. It will be time for harvesting in a few weeks and then we will be busy. Ragi crops seem to be slightly better than last year but paddy is worse. Ajja went to Mysore last week and made some money from his gooseberry pickle. The smaller farmers and the kumbaras, voddas and thotis in the ukkada will suffer greatly if this drought continues.

Right now I don't want to elaborate on this but will come to the main point I wanted to talk to you about. I could not express myself that day as you were leaving, but will try to do so now, in this letter. It will also give you a chance to think about it now that you are on your own. We sent you to medical college because it was your ardent wish to be a doctor. It was not an easy decision for me to make, nor was it simple to get the money to see you through college and internship. I did it with the full faith that you will not fail us in our expectations. You lived up to it and earned this great opportunity for higher training.

Then why am I disappointed? No, it is not your stubborn, obstinate refusal to consider marriage. With time, you will certainly come round to accept it. What worries me is the way your medical training has insulated you from the world. I noticed the change as soon as you went to college but hoped that you would soon see it for yourself and correct the fault. But I have not seen the change. You are immersed in this idea of being a doctor, in learning more, and you forget there is a world outside. What do you know about the Bangladesh war, about the drought in Bihar, or about the floods in Andhra? Did you read the newspaper while in college or during your internship? Do you read it now? I think not. I doubt if you read anything other than your textbooks. You were the most eager among our children to read the news in Prajavani, *you were the first to ask questions at the kitchen table when we ate. But when you were here last, in your own village, you showed little interest in anything that did not concern you directly. What has happened to your curiosity?*

Living in Madras, you became smarter, but it has unfortunately given you a falseness, which I tried to talk to you about. Such things can be set right. I am aware of your burden of work and study. But there is a world outside, a world that you must remain sensitive to. As the headmaster during your school years and as your father, I have a double responsibility. I beseech you not to go through life with your eyes shut.

Look after yourself. I hope you have bought the warm clothes that you need. Let me know if I should send money. We will await your weekly letters.
    God bless you,

Appa

I remembered the last few days at home before I came to England. Appa's enthusiasm about my going had faded away; I could not understand why. He hardly spoke to me and when he did, he was short. A few days before I was to leave, he summoned me to his office room.

He was seated in his chair behind his desk. His stern headmaster eyes made me nervous. He had uncapped his black pen, dipped it in ink and poked the blotting paper with it in an effort to get the words out. It was a sign familiar to every child in school, a sign of impatience. He poked away at the blotting paper as he tried to make me understand. I could not. He shook his head in despair, got up, and left the room. I stood looking at the blotting paper inked with dots. Now in his letter he had said it.

I sat with the letter in my hand, looking into the mirror and in it the window and through the window at the grey concrete of the dental college opposite. I looked at my white coat hanging on the door and at myself in the mirror until everything became a blur. I wept because I was hurt; I wept because what Appa said in the letter was true. I also knew that there was no way I could respond to the letter. Appa's letter had in some way disturbed the needle of my compass, the direction of my quest. In the days to follow the needle shifted surely, imperceptibly.

Budhi's letter came a few weeks later. Then Amma's, Sujju's and Appa's again. The letters sustained me for a few days and then I was back to checking my pigeonhole for light blue envelopes. I wrote home about the snow, the supermarkets and the British obsession with time: 'They visit friends by appointment. They walk so fast even old ladies race down the streets. Young men don't loiter, friends never hold hands!'

I remembered Angheri in loving detail. The dark rooms and

the wooden beams of the roof that enhanced the darkness; the cowdung-washed floor cool against my feet and shadows weaving their magic on the walls. I breathed the burning smell of the lamp wicks and the sharpness of Appa's ink. I felt the fat coldness of the window bars and the grooved contours of the bugri on my palm. I heard the gnnnnn of the owl, saw Ajja's peppered white hair, Amma's honest eyes and my beloved hills, white and sturdy against a clean sky. In England the lights were shadowless, plastics smell-less, flowers without fragrance; it was all cold steel and cold cleanliness.

It was the flowers that bothered me the most—gorgeous, gaudy, abundant and without scent. Every house boasted a radiant garden. In the hospital, bouquets of perfect loveliness were everywhere. At first I used to bend over and breathe in the smell, only to find that however beautiful the flowers, they were as fragrant as a plastic imitation. I missed the heady perfumes of jasmine, rose, sampige and savantige, mango and the wild lantana blossoms which spread their unique scents.

It rained here, but this was not rain. It did not pour as it did in Angheri, where when it stopped after several days at a stretch Ajja grumbled that he could not sleep because of the silence. The sun here was weak and non-existent for days. It was not the sun of Ajja's stories.

'Ajja . . . why is the sun red in the morning and evening and white during the day?'

'How little they teach you at school,' Ajja had said, sitting back in his armchair while Budhi and I listened. 'When the sun sets he sinks into the earth and sucks blood from the creatures living inside. He has a big stomach and needs a lot of blood which is used up as he moves across the sky. When he rises in the east, the hills are soaked with the blood dripping off him.'

We were ready with more questions. 'Then how is he red again in the evening?'

'The earth knows that the sun may perish without blood so it waits with pots and pots of blood to drench the sun with.'

'What about the moon and the stars?'

'They live on dew and mist and that is why they are cold and bright.'

Budhi asked questions that only Ajja could answer.

Awake at night, reading a letter from home, I thought about how far away from Angheri I had come. My life seemed unreal to me. And yet I did not feel very different from the Nalli who longed to plough the fields, cut grass and tie hay in neat stacks, like Jai.

My mind went back to the day before I had left for England. It was a few hours after lunch and I had gone to Appa's room with coffee. He took the coffee and because I continued to stand there, expecting him to say something, he spoke. I remember every word, his every gesture, the colour of the sky through the window and the sound of Ajja's voice speaking softly as he ministered to Ajji in the front room.

'I was younger than you are now and visiting Mysore for the first time. We stayed at a lodge and Ajja had sent me out to buy tea. I came across a pile of stinking garbage and quickly crossed the road to get away from it. I saw a man in a tattered banian and a cloth tied around his waist crossing the road at the same time. He was heading for the rubbish heap. He squatted, picked out bits of food from the rubbish and put it in his mouth. He didn't bother to check if it was edible, he just picked up bits from the filth and ate.

'Then he found a packet. I think it was rice wrapped in banana leaf. He untied the string and, springing up, crossed the road again to where his wife sat with five children. The oldest must have been eight or nine. They shared the rice and each of them got a mouthful. He must have been an affectionate father, it must have been difficult to bear the humiliation of providing so little to the family. So many years, and I still remember. He was so thin, I could have counted his ribs through the banian. He had such fine eyes.'

Appa's voice was suddenly harsh. 'So? What have you to say?'

I was embarrassed. 'It's very sad . . .' I said. Poverty was common enough, there was no sense in talking about it.

'Sad? But whose fault is it?'

'I—I don't know whose fault.'

'Don't know? You don't know why a man with a wife and five children has to eat from a rubbish heap?' He looked hard at me. 'I hope you'll find out some time.'

I felt like asking him why he was telling me this when I was about to embark on the most important journey of my life. It was unfair to burden me with a guilt that was not mine. I was going away to study and do important things. I said nothing. Outside, darkness fell rapidly. The hills were no longer visible; the leaves of the guava tree shone briefly in the twilight.

'It's a strange world,' Appa said. 'The only thing we can do is not forget.'

It was early morning and still dark when I left home. I had hoped Appa would come to the bus stop to see me off, but the night before I left Vishnu had come home on leave and he offered to take me. I pretended it was all right. Luckily, Budhi came too. Vishnu hardly spoke to me except to say that I could bring him a cassette player from England. He said it as if he was doing me a favour.

When I went to say goodbye, Appa was at his prayers. I bent down and touched his feet. For a fleeting moment he put his warm hand on my forehead. 'Seri, seri,' he said, his voice gruff. 'You better leave now. You shouldn't miss the bus.'

The touch of his hand on my forehead stayed with me all day. The confused anger I had felt towards him for telling me about the man at the rubbish dump faded away. I put the image out of my mind but it came back to trouble me at the oddest moments. Just like that, in the midst of something unconnected with home or with poverty, I would see the young man with fine eyes and matted hair squatting by a pile of garbage. Damn. It was not an image that I had wanted to bring with me to England. His eyes, Appa had said. What was the look in his eyes which had moved Appa so?

24

Stan lived with his parents on the other side of the Mersey. I was thrilled when he invited me home for the family Christmas lunch. Partying had begun a week earlier in the various departments of the hospital but I did not feel a part of it. I was puzzled by the whole frenzied build-up to the big day. It was most peculiar. The nurses went on a diet from October; they starved, smoked excessively and survived on lettuce and coffee in order to shed a few pounds, and they put them back in a few days of binging. I could not see the sense in it.

I avoided most parties, but with Stan it was different—I wanted to go. He had asked few people. The only other doctors were Badal Singh, the orthopaedic registrar and his wife Parveen. I disliked the couple but when Badal offered to give me a lift in their car, I agreed. It was easier than taking a bus. I took with me a sandalwood Saraswati for Stan's parents. Badal, nicknamed Cloud, came alone in his car; Parveen had somewhere else to go. 'Will you hold on to this?' he asked, giving me the dish wrapped in a kitchen towel. 'Fried rice. Main ingredient, half a tin of Pathak's chilli powder. Sure to give them ulcers.'

Cloud had a destructive streak which impelled him to be nasty. His good looks had not been ruined by his excesses. He had not acquired any of that leavened, gloamy fatness which was the result of rich food in a sunless country. As for Parveen— he called her Pummy—it was said that she deserved the husband she got. Parveen was a kittenish woman with a roving eye which all but the most innocent noticed. She reserved her kittenish behaviour for the shyest of men, like Dr Zoe Miyng from Burma. She had once asked about my love life and when she found that I had never had an affair and was not living with any of the guys, she shrieked with laughter. 'You poor thing,' she said.

Cloud resented people for no apparent reason. When he began to deride the British, I could tell that he had said it all before and was only doing it to shock me.

'Dour lot, the locals. Frozen smiles and frozen lives. Favourite colour, grey. Pastime, solving crossword puzzles or watching football till brain-dead.' He would have gone back to India long ago if it were not for the fact that he was 'personally involved'. He carried on with several nurses while Parveen looked the other way, and referred to his dalliances as 'rape by consent'.

The drive to Birkenhead was forty-five minutes. Cloud was obviously pleased to have got me a little flustered. As we drove through the Mersey tunnel, he kept on at it. 'Merely a goodwill gesture, going to this lunch. Bet it'll be a sit-down meal. The weapons they use, just to eat food. Fish knife, bread knife, meat knife, butter knife . . . Then there's the soup spoon, dessert bowl, wine glass, beer mug.'

'We have our peculiarities too,' I said, rising to their defence. But I could not immediately recall something to answer him with.

He sneaked a look at me and grinned. 'Can't be upsetting the ambulance man. He's smitten by you. Don't do anything foolish, okay?'

'Stan's a good friend.'

'You're a severe prude, I know. Surely, there's been some necking at least? He's a good sort but he's all wet!' He nudged my arm. 'These white males are like dilute coffee—too much milk. No wonder the women come crawling to me. But then, they're for short-term pleasure only, not for taking back.'

It delighted him to see me angry. 'Have fun with as many Stans as you want,' he laughed, patting my knee. 'But say no to marriage. What'll you tell them at home—that you married a driver?' To be sitting there beside him, holding his dish of fried rice and unable to say anything infuriated me. What could I have said in defence of Stan, or myself?

When we got there, I dumped the dish on the seat and got out of the car. For the rest of the evening I avoided Cloud. He tried to annoy me with crude and pointless jokes, and ribbed Stan about his Indian romance. Fortunately, once into his third drink, he forgot about it. Stan sportingly tried a spoonful of the fried rice before giving up. His parents wisely said they would have it for dinner.

Stan's mother liked my gift. 'What a lovely doll,' she said, and was about to place it on the mantelshelf when Cloud stopped her, with, 'It's a heathen god, not a doll.' Her hands stopped midway. She tried to say something nice but her words faltered.

'Jesus may be offended,' Cloud said. 'This one is not armed with weapons, but almost any Indian goddess can kill.'

Stan rose from where he sat and took the Saraswati from his mother. 'It's beautiful,' he said. Placing the figure on the mantelshelf, he sat down and picked up his drink.

Being the only one without a date for Christmas night, I had offered to do the night shift. I came back from Stan's lunch just in time to start work and had no time to change out of my sari.

Road accidents and injuries from drunken fights poured in steadily until four in the morning. One of the last to arrive was a couple, both with gashed heads. They were very drunk and just about managed to tell us that they were Dot and Ted. Dot was a big woman who carried herself with the elegance of a queen, even when drunk; Ted, though bigger, had had the worst of the marital fight—a deep cut on his forehead and a black eye. Every bed and stretcher being in use, I sutured him while he sat on a chair. Dot, who sat opposite, kept up a constant chatter. 'Is this a hospital or some stable . . . it reeks like a cowshed.' She looked carefully at me. 'My, you're pretty. But what you wearin'? A curtain?' Ted said something which infuriated Dot. She leapt off the chair and would have assaulted him if the nurse had not stopped her. The local anaesthetic which I had injected into her scalp had begun to wear off and when I sutured her wound, she felt the last suture go in. 'Fuck off, you curry-face,' she shouted, pushing me with her big, strong hands.

If it had not been so funny, I might have resented it.

There were times when my inexperience became obvious. Having disposed of some latecomers, I was seated at the desk when a group of young people came in. They hesitated near the door, arguing. From the tone of their voices I could tell they were tense and keyed up. A boy and a girl walked towards me and the rest, still talking, walked away. The boy—he looked about nineteen—leaned on my desk and asked if I was the doctor. In spite of the long overcoat over his jeans and shirt, he shivered. Producing a syringe filled with bloodstained fluid he said, 'Gimme this . . .' His breathing was laboured and his pupils pinpoint; the hand that held the syringe shook violently. I smelt trouble.

'I can't . . . without knowing what it's for . . .'

'Jus give it to 'im,' the girl snarled. She was bigger than the young man, and older. I hesitated. Next moment she had hauled me roughly off the chair. '*Come on!*'

They smelt ill and they smelt different. I was scared. Nurse Mackay, who had appeared at the door, signalled that I keep cool. Fighting panic I got up, took the young man into the cubicle and prepared to give the injection. He raised his shirtsleeve and offered his elbow, dotted with puncture marks. He shivered again when I touched his arm and I felt it burn with fever. By then the nurse had summoned the security guards and after an initial scuffle he was led away to the de-addiction ward. He smiled weakly at me as he went. The girl scowled.

When I finally went to bed, I dreamt of Stan standing in the porch with Ajja. Stan was dressed in a dhoti with a red dasavala tucked behind his ear. He was telling Ajja something about me, but I could not hear what he said.

The next morning I was still dead to the world when there was an urgent knock on the door. Cursing, I got up and opened the door to find Parveen standing outside. 'You have a lipstick in frosted pink, don't you?' she asked. Yes, I had two. 'So it's your lipstick I found on my husband's shirt last night,' she sneered.

Too sleepy to argue, I shut the door in her face and went back to bed.

≈

I took on my future with everything I had; I jumped in and started to swim. The initial adjustments over, I was settling down nicely. No blurred edges, no unpredictability in work. I even managed to find some time to write in the red diary. At first I wrote every day, but then I became erratic. I made an occasional entry that was pages long or just a paragraph, phrase or sentence. Some days, too tired to write, I turned the pages, read and remembered.

I thought about the village hospital and about Appa's talk the day before I left. He worried about other people, like the man picking out food from garbage, but it was he who needed help. He had only a year before retirement and the family fortunes had been declining. When his salary stopped coming it would be more difficult.

I had been saving money, and when there was enough sent two hundred pounds to Appa. It was a lot of cash. I hoped it would help the family to get some things, things that were tasteful and smart. I remembered the cowdung floors of the house, the bench in the porch, the old, old kitchen table, Appa's creaky bicycle. The money could buy a Formica-topped table and chairs, curtains, and maybe a new cycle for Appa. I imagined and savoured visions of their joy and their grateful letters. I waited impatiently for a reply.

When Appa's letter arrived, there was no mention of the money. A few weeks later the money came back, the whole two hundred pounds, without a word of explanation. I was shocked and very hurt but I had the feeling that for Appa it had been worse.

I had settled down but I never ceased to wonder and exult over my good fortune: of being there in England, thousands of miles from home, of training in an esteemed university to be a surgeon, of being comfortable in trousers and boots, of earning in pounds not rupees, of having grown accustomed to the British strangeness, politeness, the thank yous, hello luvs and *good* mornings. Oh, the British! How I would mimic them back home, at the kitchen table. 'It's true! They drink coffee and tea without sugar . . . they *don't* drink water . . . they like *boiled* cabbage . . .' I played it all to myself in my mind and smiled at the thought. Inevitably, I became too confident.

I was enjoying myself at work and otherwise when an episode jolted me out of complacence.

I was on duty that night. Usually it stayed busy until one or two in the morning by which time the drunks with bleeding heads and punched noses would have been attended to and the last tramp would have been coaxed into bed. When everything was quiet, the casualty officer could have a nap. That night I was nicely asleep when the nurse called. 'Two lads with cut heads. One needs suturing.' It was never easy to get out of bed at three in the morning. I went through the motions mechanically. A quick, cursory examination. One had a deep, two-inch laceration over the right temple but was otherwise all right. Four stitches, a tetanus shot and painkillers to take home. He was to report after five days for the sutures to be removed, or earlier if there was any problem.

Late next morning, the shrill sound of the telephone shattered my sleep. 'Yes?' I said crossly. It was only ten and being off duty, I wanted to catch up on sleep. A male voice was at the other end. 'You the casualty officer last night? This is Martin Rose, senior reg, Neuro. You sutured a young boy with a cut head and sent him home. He was brought here this morning at six, unconscious. An extradural. I've just done a burr hole.'

I stammered something about being sorry to have missed it. 'Not good enough,' he snapped. 'If you'd bothered to take a careful history, he'd have told you. He had flaked out for a few seconds when he fell. He nearly died, thanks to your negligence.' He banged the phone down.

I had sent home a head injury without taking a proper history. I hadn't thought of an X-ray and overnight observation in hospital, a standard procedure for anyone who has lost consciousness even for a few seconds. I had missed an injury that caused a dangerous clot pressing on the brain. He was lucky to have reached the neurosurgeon in time.

I felt like a criminal. I avoided the television room and went to eat when the others had finished. Everywhere I went I imagined accusing glances and whispers.

Sushma was worried. 'I've heard of doctors having their registration cancelled by the General Medical Council,' she said.

If I lost my registration, what would I tell them back home? The only person who could be of help, if at all, was Professor Ferguson. Early next morning I called his secretary, Dawn Armitage, and asked for an urgent appointment. 'He has a busy week,' said Dawn. 'Is the coming Thursday all right?'

'It's very very urgent,' I said. 'Please. Do something.'

She must have read the distress in my voice. 'He has a post-grad lecture in twenty minutes. If you can make it here before that . . .'

The professor's office was in another building, some distance away. It was very cold outside but there was no time to get my overcoat or gloves. Clutching the collar of my white coat around my neck, I ran all the way. I made it just as the professor was gathering his papers for the lecture.

'Sir,' I said. 'Please give me another chance . . .'

He looked puzzled. 'I . . . don't know what you're talking about.'

'The extradural, sir. The young boy who came on Tuesday night.'

He heard me out. 'That's bad. It shouldn't have happened, of course. Now put it out of your mind and get back to work.'

I returned to work and study, determined not to blunder again.

25

When I cleared the first part of the FRCS in May, Walter Mountain baked a special cake and Stan took me out to dinner at the Adelphi. I decided not to write home about it until I had passed the finals which would take much more time. My stint as a senior house officer in casualty was over and Mr Ferguson posted me in the surgical wards. I was to work for two senior surgeons, Selby and Bianchi.

It took some getting used to. Mr Selby never passed up an opportunity to needle his colleague. We were on ward rounds and had stopped near the bed of a fifty-year-old with a colostomy.

The cancerous growth in the colon had been removed six weeks earlier and the two ends of the colon sutured together. A colostomy was fashioned as a temporary diversion for faecal matter, to be closed when the joined ends of the colon had healed well.

'About time it was closed,' observed Selby, peering into the wound. 'Leave it any longer and you'll have problems.'

'Don't like hurrying things,' said Bianchi, smiling mildly. 'I'll wait another week.'

'The poor chap's been here long enough. Time for closure, I'd say.' And Selby walked cheerily to the next bed.

Morning rounds started in the male surgical, a long, well-lit ward with twenty beds, plus an annexe with four beds for infected cases. The rounds were tedious and with arguments cropping up between the two surgeons, it could go on forever. It was just after nine on Monday with every one of us glum at the prospect of another week. Bianchi had a total gastrectomy, a spillover from the previous list, to do that day. Dave McFarlane, the registrar, was to assist him. As we walked down the corridor between male and female wards, Dave stopped me. 'Do me a favour,' he smiled. 'Give Bianchi a hand with the case. I've a sigmoidoscopy lined up and then the outpatients'.' I protested that I had to go to the clinic. 'Not to worry, I'll manage the clinic,' he said, walking away. 'The gastrectomy won't take more than three hours. Or four. Or five.'

An endearing man and a brilliant surgeon, William Bianchi worked without haste or panic. His slow ponderous style of operating was the bane of Theatre staff. It was a stale joke that by the time he put in the last stitches in a wound, the other end would have healed. Assisting Bianchi meant staying back till late.

The subtotal gastrectomy for cancer involved cutting off a major portion of the stomach and joining the remnant cuff to the duodenum. We started at ten. I mopped blood, snipped sutures and pulled at the retractor. Hours passed.

'Don't dig with your retractor, you'll tear the duodenum!' Vexation in Bianchi's voice, and he wasn't easily vexed. 'Sorry.'

Mustn't let tiredness get me, I told myself. Stand on one foot and then the other. Lift shoulders, drop them. Where was I aching? Biceps, latissimus, glutei, quads, the foot, the back of the knee? Flex the toes, extend them. Flex, extend. I tried recalling the names of all the muscles in the sole of the foot. Four layers . . . flexor digitorum longus, flexor digitorum brevis, flexor tibialis posterior, flexor tibialis anterior . . . Damn. What did it matter when the entire foot was one aching mass?

'Nellie, was that your tummy?'

That was the scrub nurse. I did not like her calling me Nellie. It was past lunchtime and there was no chance of getting finished before three or four. If only I could sit down, rest my throbbing back and drink some tea.

My mind teemed with questions, but it was easier to hold the retractor and do as I was told than to reveal my ignorance. Finally I picked up the courage to ask: Why is catgut used inside the gut, and linen on the outside? Bianchi paused to explain. The anaesthetist cursed under his breath and the scrub nurse glared at me. Lunchtime came and went; the scrub nurse handed over the instrument trolley to another and went off duty.

Late afternoon: 'Cover the wound with a sterile mop,' said Bianchi, walking away from the table. 'I'll just stretch my legs and get some coffee. Ten minutes.'

At last Bianchi finished. My back screamed but I was past caring. It had taken exactly eighteen minutes short of six hours. 'Put in the skin stitches, will you?' he said, slipping off his gloves. I struggled with the slippery nylon to suture the wound that skirted around the umbilicus. When I finished, the navel was a good inch to the left. 'I'll take out the sutures and do it again,' I whispered to the scrub nurse. But the anaesthetist was already waking the patient and the nurse was eager to finish. 'Enough flab there, it won't show,' she said. I covered up my guilt with a generous wad of gauze and suffered all week. I did the dressing myself every day, diverting the patient's attention with breathless conversation. I waited for the day when Bianchi would discover my clumsy deed. On the ninth day I removed the sutures and the wound looked fine. No one complained.

I longed to be back at my job in casualty where I had a lot of time to do what I wanted between shifts. Now it was an endless round of clinics, Theatre days, ward rounds and call duties. I walked past the casualty department and saw the Sri Lankan who had taken my place chatting with the nurses. I eyed him resentfully and went back to the wards.

Three times a week, on Theatre days, I changed like everyone else into the green scrubs and stayed in them until the list was finished. Theatre started before daylight and when work finished, it was dark. I learnt with agonizing slowness, practising in my mind the steps of every surgery. When asked to do the simplest case, I fumbled. I got the knots wrong, tied them too tight or too loose and dropped instruments. Between cases, I sat in the surgeons' room listening to the others and drinking endless cups of tea. Water would have been fine but no one drank water, so I made do with tea.

I managed somehow, assisting and learning. But nervousness blunted my faculties and I became clumsy. My shoulders developed a permanent stoop; laughter belonged to another time. I recollected every blunder and punished myself with more work. The sound of the pager going bleep-bleep-bleep set my nerves on edge, even when it sounded in someone else's pocket. If on call duty I was awake half the night, expecting the bleep to go off. Anxiety enfeebled me. While others grabbed at chances to do cases, I waited timidly to be offered a chance. I did a few appendicectomies under supervision, closed wounds and cut out some simple cysts with Dave picking on every fault. 'Surgery isn't like peeling onions, y'know.'

Of all the surgeons, it was Richard Selby I feared most. He was a swashbuckling Tony Curtis look-alike with three-inch-long sideburns. The collar of his white coat was pulled up to cover the nape of his neck and his coat was always unbuttoned. He kept his hands deep in the pockets of his trousers until he was required to use them. Every morning Selby jogged to work, in tracksuit and running shoes, and then showered and changed in the hospital in time for work. He played tennis in the evenings. On weekends he took part in quiz shows and played the trombone for a local band. Selby made friends easily, charmed the women and had the juniors hanging on to his every word. When he entered the ward and stood with his hands on his slim hips, tired eyes lit up, backs hunched so long in despair straightened, and drooping mouths relaxed into smiles. Like the lead dancer in a troupe, he drew attention to himself without trying too hard. Selby could do a gastrectomy in forty minutes flat and a gall bladder in twenty. He matched his speed with a temper.

Seeing me in the tearoom towards the end of a long operating day, Selby asked if I would assist him. 'Perforated duodenal ulcer. I'll show you how to do a perf, on this slim little beauty.'

The woman was fat, bronchitic and a high risk for anaesthesia. The anaesthetist wanted us to complete the surgery as quickly as possible. I made a midline incision but not having steadied the scalpel, it veered crazily over the spongy abdomen. 'Disfigure her tum and you'll have her chasing you for the rest of your life. Place the knife firmly on the skin, steady the wound between fingers. Clean and sharp. Once the knife touches the skin, don't lift it until you've made the full incision.

'You can't get at a perf through *that* incision. Wounds heal from edge to edge, not above downwards, so don't skimp. Go all the way down through fat to the fascia . . . stop! That's the fascia, dammit. Here, I'll hold the edge with an Allis forceps, while you cut.

'I don't have all day. There's the perf. Anterior. Nice and easy. Two-zero catgut for the closure, yes. *Don't* poke around the abdomen with that needle, we'll have more work—shhh . . . ugar! That's not the way to take a bite. One sure poke, no second chance, you'll *kill* tissue . . .'

Selby taught the basics of technique better than anyone.

I made friends with some of the nurses—Fiona Mackay, Pat Nesbitt, and Angela, lovely in her blue uniform with the starched white apron, frilled cap and sheer black stockings. Angela was forever on the lookout for a 'beautiful piece of meat'. When she was on duty the tearoom reeked of cigarette fumes. And there was Stan's sister, Hilda, the head nurse in the male ward. She was so unlike her brother: tall, with strong arms and a quick temper. She was stern but gentle with the patients. 'Come on, love, here we go!' she said (which also meant 'do as I tell you, or else'), heaving up a decrepit patient and propping him on pillows. Patients adored Hilda.

Stan came every Saturday and we went out for a coffee or a drive. From my window I could see him waiting outside the newsagent's near the hospital gates, in his brown corduroy jacket and soft cotton cap; it was not like him to come knocking at my door. I would wear a sari just to please him. Seatbelted and snug in his red Mini, we talked about my work and sometimes his. Stan was a great listener. I often wondered what drew me to him. Perhaps it was his austerity and a cleanness of spirit that resembled Appa's.

I told Stan about my fears. 'You'll be all right,' he said, with complete faith. It pleased me to hear him say that. I told him about home and about Angheri, about Appa's debacle in school, about the charming life of a medical student. He never interrupted me with 'Amazing!' or 'Fascinating!' the way others did. If I probed Stan to tell me about himself, he shrugged it off with, 'There's nothing much to say, really.'

Once, I was in the canteen with brother and sister, and Hilda said, half-joking, 'Watch out, Nalli. Our Stan has a soft corner for you.' Stan turned carrot-red and sat with his hands on his knees, looking unhappy and embarrassed. The tea went down my throat in noisy gulps and I prayed for Hilda to shut up. From then on, a shyness came between us; his visits became less frequent and when he took me out he was more reticent and aloof.

Hilda was engaged to an Irish doctor and they were to marry that summer. Every weekend, he came from Dublin or she went across in one of those steamers that took passengers across the Irish Sea. One time, she came to work after a three-day break and when I asked about her fiancé, she said, 'Oh, we fell out.'

'The water must have been very cold,' I sympathized.

'I mean, we fell out with each other. Had a spat and broke off.' She didn't seem troubled by it.

I was in the midst of a busy clinic when Bianchi sent for me.

'Mr Slater, from Devon,' he said, introducing the patient. 'He's here on work. Severe pain and vomiting since morning. Do the work-up and let me know.'

Slater lay on the examination table clutching his belly. He was obviously in pain. He told me that he had been operated upon no less than seven times and his abdomen was criss-crossed with scars. 'I don't mind another scar, doctor,' he said. 'Just make the pain go away.' His family was in Devon but it was all right. 'They're used to it,' he said with a weak smile. 'I'm in and out of hospitals all the time.'

The X-rays were not very helpful but I was convinced that Mr Slater had a bowel obstruction. I reported my findings to Bianchi. 'It could be due to adhesions from previous surgery,' I said.

'What do you plan to do?'

'I'll try conservative treatment. Intravenous fluids and pain-relieving drugs.'

'Waste of time. He needs a look-in. You won't find anything. It'll be clean inside.' I was baffled. 'See . . . his abdomen is a battlefield. The diagnosis is written there. Hospital Addiction Syndrome. Ask him and he'll tell you he's seen different surgeons every time, in different hospitals. Nothing short of surgery will satisfy Mr Slater. An open-and-close.' I was hesitant, so he said, 'If you can convince him otherwise, that's fine.'

I was not keen to open an abdomen and then close it, merely to satisfy a quirky patient. I admitted Mr Slater, put up a drip and told the nurses to give him painkillers when he needed them. By evening he was rolling in agony. He spent all night, and the day after, in excruciating pain. In the end, admitting failure, I did a laparotomy. A quick in-and-out. A clean abdomen, just as Bianchi had predicted. Next morning the patient was sitting up in bed. 'Thanks very much, doc,' he said, grateful. He was pain-free. 'It'll cure him for now,' said Bianchi. 'Next time, he'll go somewhere else. See if you can get him to meet a counsellor. Hospital Addiction is the result of a deep-seated need for attention.'

Bianchi was not through with his surprises. Who would have thought that it was a surgeon's job to treat faecal impaction? Tracy was a fifteen-year-old suffering from cerebral palsy, with the problem of not having a bowel movement for weeks. Nothing worked except a manual removal of stool in hospital, under anaesthesia. Tracy would not allow it otherwise and, every six weeks faecal disimpaction appeared on Bianchi's Theatre list. Some of us tried to avoid Tracy by applying for leave when the time came up, so Bianchi cleverly set up a rota system for us to do it by turn. Gloved hand in and out two dozen times until a basinful was cleared and the surgeon and anaesthetist staggered out of the room, olfactory senses assaulted. 'Good for the soul,' Bianchi said.

My first big lesson while working with Bianchi came in the form of a beautiful woman with a papilloma above her right eyebrow. As I cleaned the operating area with hibitane I admired the lady's symmetrical face, the sweeping lashes and arched eyebrows. She was a beautician, and all set to go to Majorca on holiday the following week. I made small talk and, under local anaesthetic, excised the warty growth. Too late I realized I had excised too much skin. My sutures had pulled the eyebrow straight, in a horizontal line. 'Thanks very much doctor,' the woman was saying. 'You didn't hurt me at all.' I dressed the wound and she left, with my blunder concealed beneath gauze and plaster. I waited guiltily for her to come back. When she did not, even to have the sutures removed, I was sure that she would sue me for disfiguring her lovely face. But as other disasters followed the incident slipped out of my mind.

Sometimes, it seemed I looked for a chance to make a fool of myself. One Saturday evening I was called to see a fourteen-year-old girl with retention of urine. The bladder distended to the umbilicus, the girl was in considerable distress. Her anxious mother hovered behind the screen. On rectal examination I could feel a firm, almost hard horizontal ridge along the front of the rectum. *Bladder tumour*! Triumphant at having chanced upon a rare case I wrote the diagnosis in bold letters on the case record, and phoned Selby. 'A young girl with a bladder tumour. Advanced stage, with retention of urine. It seems to have spread all the way across . . .'

'I'm coming,' he said. I called the girl's mother aside and conveyed the unhappy news.

Twenty minutes later when Selby had seen the girl, he called the mother and spoke to her. Turning to me, he said with a deadpan face, 'Get the Theatre ready for a suprapubic. We're about to deliver a thermometer from the bladder.'

The girl had been 'playing around' with a thermometer. My precious bladder tumour and a lot of my ego went with the suprapubic cystostomy—in which the bladder was opened and the thermometer removed.

As if that was not enough, a worse crime was due. I had assisted Dave on a hemi-colectomy and was closing up after him. The scrub nurse had left a junior to help me and gone off on her lunch break; a couple of eager medical students who had been posted in Theatre asked questions. Flattered, I expounded on the layers of the abdomen and the superiority of silk over catgut in wound closure. A nice feeling, to be the know-all.

It came back to me all of a sudden that evening in my room. The swab on the right side of the abdomen, under the liver—had I taken it out? Had the scrub nurse verified that the swab count was correct? I could not remember. I phoned Theatre. The nurse was off duty and would be back only in the morning, I was informed. I called the ward. How is Mrs Hind? She's complaining of pain; analgesic given an hour ago. Is the pain severe? Is it worse than usual? The staff nurse was not amused by my sudden concern for Mrs Hind. 'Why don't you come and see for yourself?' she asked.

I cornered the scrub nurse next morning and confirmed the worst. The nurse had declared that the swab count was correct but did not remember if I had removed the one beneath the liver. We eyed each other with silent accusation and thereafter she avoided me. To worsen matters the patient was febrile all that day and the next. She retched and looked ill. On the evening of the second day I went to Bianchi. As he listened, his normally relaxed face became worried. He called the ward. 'Get an X-ray on Mrs Hind and send it to my office.' An X-ray would pick up the telltale white line of a gauze swab.

'I wanted to ask for an X-ray but . . .'

His eyebrows came together in a frown. 'No doctor—*ever*—wants to make a mistake,' he said. 'The only way to cope, other than give up surgery, is to confront it. You should have taken that X-ray as soon as you had a doubt.'

After what seemed like ages, the X-ray came. It was clear. I found myself grinning with relief. Thanking Bianchi, I got up to go but he motioned to me to stay.

'I'm glad the X-ray is clear but we need to talk about it.'

'I wanted to do an X-ray,' I said. 'But I was afraid.'

'Of what? Of the swab being found and your reputation being affected?' I had to agree that was true. 'Think of the consequences. Mrs Hind would have suffered and we'd have had no clue why. Not for a long time at least.'

I sat there, unable to look at him, I was so ashamed.

'Indecision is usually born out of fear and that is the worst curse.' It was commonly said that a surgeon should have the courage of a lion, eagle-eyes and the delicate hands of a woman. But it was not so simple. Diagnosing and treating an illness were complex. 'There is the analytical thinking that we learn about in college. But there is also intuition, which comes with experience. When we look at our mistakes honestly, we sharpen intuition.'

He must have noticed my misery. 'Mistakes happen. A fellowship of the scalpel does exist. Every doctor worth his degree will, at some time, protect another and in turn be protected. There's a difference, though, between defending a doctor who's had a problem and covering up for negligence. I can forgive your neglecting to do a proper swab count at the end of the operation because now we know it's all right. But what if you had left a swab inside?'

Bianchi had never talked to me like this. 'See how the mind

works. When a diagnosis is made, the mind reasons; it uses intuition and decides in a split second, juggling facts and cross-checking with past experience. It pauses only for a fraction of a millisecond. By the time the diagnosis is written down or spoken, it's precise. This, or That. You have appendicitis. You have lower respiratory infection. Is it any surprise that we often go wrong?

'Medicine is an imperfect science and doctors who practise it are more imperfect. See how surgery has evolved, step by painful step. A hundred errors. Not every technique is learnt from books or from other surgeons. One learns on one's own. How long an incision, how tight a suture, how deep should the needle go, how big or how small. Every case teaches.'

There was a knock on the door—the matron wanting to discuss some ward matters. 'Half an hour, Ms Wilson. I'm busy.' He settled back in his chair. 'I worked in orthopaedics for a year as a junior,' he said. 'I found it tough. I was slower than I am now, so you can imagine the frustration of the Theatre staff. I was trying too hard. I struggled through an Austin Moore's prosthesis for three hours and it dislocated next day— came right out of the socket. One of my colleagues took the woman back to Theatre and set it right. The patient said I shouldn't be allowed to put a knife on any one. She said it in front of the entire team, in the ward. Her wish almost came true. I stayed out of Theatre and did not want to operate, till my boss dragged me back.'

It was hard to imagine Bianchi in such a predicament. 'It happens. The ego gets abraded, sometimes badly dented.' He smiled wryly. 'For a surgeon, contentment is out of reach. Our work depends on the scrub nurse, the assistant, the anaesthetist, the time of day, the state of our digestion, the dozen aches and pains that lurk in the body. Anything can affect the equilibrium. But of all drawbacks for a surgeon, the worst is indecision.'

Chastened, I went to my room.

Six p.m. I had scrubbed six times and was getting ready for the last case. I picked up the soap and squirted povidone iodine on the bristled brush in my hand. My legs ached, my eyes burned. I wanted food and sleep.

Bianchi came and turned on the tap next to mine. 'Bile duct, next?' he asked, cheerfully. 'I'll show you how to explore it with bougies . . .'

I had waited for months to do a bile duct. But at that moment, every aching muscle tugged at my resolve. With Bianchi helping me, I would be there all night. 'I wanted to ask . . .' I blurted. 'If you could excuse me for the next case. I've got an upset tummy.'

'Off you go then,' he said, kindly. 'Send in an intern.'

I slunk away, unrepentant of my fib.

I had to go through it the following week. I had done gall bladders but not one with stones impacted in the common bile duct. The previous month a registrar had cut right through the bile duct during surgery and Selby had to be called to repair it. I was nervous, and had prayed all week that Bianchi would forget it was my turn.

The anaesthetist, a new senior registrar, switched on music to 'relax the patient and the surgeon,' he said. It set my already fragile nerves on edge.

I had rehearsed the surgery in my mind the previous evening and now with the abdomen painted and draped, I made the right paramedian incision four inches long and to the right of the midline, extending a little below the level of the umbilicus. Bianchi mopped away the blood and helped with artery forceps and cautery to stem the bleeding, talking all the time to the anaesthetist, something about the music. I cut the white layer of fascia in a vertical line and lifted the rectus muscle, exposing peritoneum—the thin glistening layer of tissue which envelopes the digestive organs.

It was going like a dream. Lift up between forceps, snip and cut. First up and then down and I was in the abdomen, with the healthy pink loops of small bowel prolapsing into the wound. 'Pack it away,' said Bianchi and I was already doing it with a large mop. Bianchi placed a smooth metal retractor on the right edge of the wound and the purple, jelly-textured liver came into

view. Beneath it was the gall bladder. I grasped it with forceps.
'Take a look now,' Bianchi was saying. 'Below the edge of the
retractor . . .' And there it was, a greenish-blue tube the size of
my little finger. The common bile duct. The CBD.

'Feel the stones?'

No more hunger, no more aches. I sutured with catgut to
lift up the tube, followed it up with a gentle snip and the orange
bile seeped through. Bianchi suctioned the bile out of the
wound. I probed the CBD with bougies. One, two, five little
stones—olive green, and wondrously hexagonal as if cut by a
jeweller. I flushed the bile duct with saline, placed the T-shaped
tube made of latex inside to prevent seepage and sutured the
duct with fine catgut. Then I was closing. I had done it! A CBD!

26

The advertisement for registrar posts in the university appeared
in the *British Medical Journal*. I applied for the job, more in
order to comply with the professor's advice than because of any
confidence I had in myself.

A few weeks later I got the call for the interview. It would
be held in town in a building called the Strand, ten minutes
away by bus. Dressed in a sari and my purple coat I set off, well
on time. The bus stop outside the hospital was deserted except
for an elderly lady on her way to the shops. I asked her about
buses. 'The Strand in Bootle? Number 11, luv. Here it comes!'

The journey was more like forty-five minutes and when I
got off at the Strand, my watch said five to nine. I went to the
lady at the reception and asked where I should report. I showed
her the letter. 'It's the Strand in town you want. This is Bootle,'
she said. 'What will I do?' I wailed, as if it was somebody else's
fault. The lady looked at me for a moment, tight-lipped, and
then picked up the phone. I listened to her explain that a doctor
had lost her way and landed at the Strand in Bootle. Replacing
the receiver she said, 'Take a cab back to town. Hurry!'

I appeared for the interview and was selected to fill one of the twenty-one registrar's posts. The only other woman was from Guy's Hospital, London. I was pleased with myself.

The next day after the rounds the doctors gathered in the duty room for coffee, as was the usual practice. Coffee over, I was about to leave for the clinic when there was a call. Dawn Armitage on the line. 'The professor wants to see you,' she said. 'Can you make it by eleven?'

Thoughtful of the professor to want to congratulate me personally. He was one of the interview committee and I thought he had looked rather stern. I had not had the chance to speak to him afterwards. I went through the main foyer, stopping at the hospital shop which sold flowers, fruit and chocolates. I had a pound in my pocket. I picked up a box of Black Magic for the professor, paid quickly and ran.

I went into his office and he pointed to a chair. 'Sir, I'm most grateful . . .' I began, unable to hide the smile in my voice.

He stopped me. 'You know you got the job because I was on the board?'

I was aghast.

'Why do you think we take the trouble to hold an interview? If you're asked a question, any question, you speak. Show that you're the best person for the job. You grab the chance to project yourself. If it's yes-and-no answers, where's the need to call fifty candidates from different parts of the country? We'd simply select the best from the CVs.' At work too I was diffident, he said. 'If you stay in the background and expect someone to hold your hand, you'll never make it as a surgeon.'

My throat ached with sobs. I hated Professor Ferguson.

The new job would start in three months. Until then I was to continue working with Bianchi and Selby. There was a lot to learn and I was now more in earnest. Slowly, painfully, I had begun to follow the professor's advice. I had gained confidence and was enjoying my job. And I was learning to laugh, even at myself.

The two surgeons were fiercely opinionated and their approach to cases was as different as their natures. They disagreed about a lot of things. Bianchi believed in inserting a drain in the abdomen after every surgery; Selby said, no way, how can a piece of rubber sticking out of the wound drain anything? You simply agreed with both and did what each wanted. 'Is this a Bianchi case? Give me a drain, then. Selby? No drain, and make it silk for the skin.'

Selby thrived on speed. He was naturally showy and wanted to better his speed and technique. After each case his eyes moved to the clock on the wall. He would stop by in Theatre on days when Bianchi had an operation list to see how he had fared. 'You just finished the second case? You'll be here all day, Bill. Want me to take a few cases off your hands?'

His feverish pace and skill swept patients off their feet. But there were those who found it unnerving and went to Bianchi. The two rivals—I had come to expect this of the best doctors— genuinely liked each other. If one had a patient who developed a complication of some sort—so common in surgery—the other defended him.

In the end it was the younger, quicker, smarter, surer of the two who needed help in a big way.

Brian Haggart was fifty-two. Occupation: painter of hoardings. Diagnosis: Peripheral Vascular Disease, with unhealthy ischaemic ulcers on both feet; Right worse than Left. From the outpatient clinic I sent him to the ward in a wheelchair. I did not elaborate on the grave nature of his illness. That would be done later, on evening rounds.

It was Selby's admitting day and Brian got a yellow label over his bed. Bianchi's patients got blue. Brian was put on antibiotics, dressings, and drugs to increase the flow of blood to his legs. A few days later Selby did a sympathectomy on both sides, cutting the nerves which exert a constricting effect on the vessel wall. The surgery helped the blood flow to the right leg which had been the less healthy to start with but the left then grew worse and the pain from it intense. The ulcer turned purple at the edges and the foot a mottled blue. Selby ordered a special X-ray after injecting a radio-opaque dye into Brian's lower limb arteries and it revealed 'end artery disease' in the left leg and a major block in the right. Sitting on the edge of Brian's cot, Selby explained the problem. 'We've found something positive to work on,' he said. 'With a graft to bypass the block in the right leg, we can have some good blood trickling into the foot. The ulcer will heal, the leg will be good and strong.'

'And the other leg?' asked Brian, suspicious.

'I'm afraid we've tried everything, Brian. It's no use. The block is in the small vessels of the foot and no bypass is possible. The leg is already showing signs of gangrene. It'll have to go.'

Brian Haggart was a handsome man, and gregarious. He had been an instructor with the Boy Scouts for a number of years and the outdoor life made him look younger. He could be seen at all hours propelling his wheelchair along the ward, ribbing patients, flirting with the nurses. But the day Selby told him, his wheelchair was stationary. Brian stayed in bed. It took him a day to agree to the amputation which had to be done before the bypass on the other side.

'I need to climb ladders,' he said to Selby. 'Will I be able to climb ladders?'

'We'll see about that,' said Selby gently. 'When we get the right leg good and strong, the artificial one will be easy to manage.'

I assisted Selby in the case. Having scrubbed and gowned he walked towards the operating table. It was normal practice for the to-be-operated side to be marked with indelible ink by the intern on the morning of the surgery. This was to avoid errors and was practised religiously for every operation, in particular for limbs and groin hernias. The black arrow was clear, pointing downward at the hip. Selby showed me his technique for an above-knee, and finished in half an hour. 'The next amputation that comes is yours,' he said as he wrapped the pressure dressing over the stump.

The list over, we went to the wards to see the patients. Just then the intern walked in, pale as death. 'I—I made a mistake . . . I marked the right leg. It should've been the left.'

Busy in the morning with getting patients ready for Theatre, he had checked the case record and seen my entry on the first day: right leg worse than left. He'd surmised that the right leg was to be removed. And the leg Brian now had was a dead leg. He became a bilateral above-knee amputee. The smile went out of his eyes.

Stan asked me later, 'Nalli, how could you all forget which leg it was?' Perhaps only a surgeon would understand. Too much work, too many patients and too little rest had caused an inexcusable crime for which we were all to blame. But Selby, the surgeon, was the obvious target.

He was suspended from his job, hounded by the press and vilified as the 'maverick surgeon for whom tennis, quiz shows and jazz were more important than a patient's leg.' Through the sustained efforts of Bianchi, Ferguson and others, and letters from many grateful patients, Selby was reinstated after six months. Brian Haggart gave newpaper and television interviews in which he said 'it was nobody's fault.'

Time helped us cope with the grievous error that cost Brian Haggart his legs. Selby was as brazen and superfast as before, but there was an unmistakable sadness underlying everything he did. The memory of this one terrible mistake would always stay with him. I recalled my own failures and fears and wondered why we become surgeons at all, when we have to die so many deaths in a single life.

My registrar's job started and I moved on to join a new team. I had two anaesthetists—Peter Wise on Mondays and Soh-toun on Fridays. Peter was a good anaesthetist, and a tease. If I opened a case for acute appendicitis and found it to be normal, Peter said, 'Not another lily-white appendix?' Flushing beneath the mask, I defended myself. 'It's inflamed at the tip and turgid. If I'd left it till morning . . .' Peter grinned. 'No need to grovel. I'm used to being dragged out of bed for non-existent problems.'

One busy operating day, I failed to notice that my green Theatre trousers had come undone and were sagging at my ankles. The sterile surgical overgown had hidden it and no one noticed. The case over, I walked away from the table and took off the surgeon's gown. For a split second I stood there with the trousers at my feet; and then realising what had happened, pulled it up and ran. 'Lots of excitement in Theatre,' Peter said at lunch. 'What with surgeons who undress while operating . . .'

Once we quarrelled. On Christmas night, I was on duty. At midnight a young boy was admitted with peritonitis. I called Peter for an urgent laparotomy. When he came he was quite drunk.

'Ask your senior registrar to do the case and go to bed,' I told him.

'Jesus. You think I'm drunk?' He walked into Theatre and plonked himself on the operating table. 'Only had six drinks. I can work all night.'

The Theatre Sister tried to reason with him in vain. I called his senior, who marched Peter off to bed and took over. Peter was angry and did not speak to me for two days.

Dr Soh-toun was an affable Burmese, and passionate about his work. When on call he paced the corridors listlessly, the pockets of his white coat jammed with instruments, needles and tubes which he might need in an emergency. He hung about the wards and the ICU inquiring if there was any case which might require his attention. When there was no work, he was glum. He said he could not understand how I sat watching television soaps when on duty.

His method of anaesthetizing a patient was unique. 'Good morning, Mrs Hill . . . How are we today?'

'Very well, thank you, doctor.'

'I'm putting you to sleep. Okay? Nothing to worry, I have lots of experience. Eight months. See this needle? I poke it in your hand. Good. Now, I give this injection. It will put you to sleep. And then I give you another injection which will make you stop breathing . . .'

'*Stop breathing?*'

'Yes. It will paralyse you from head to toe. Then I put this tube into your windpipe, through your mouth, and pump in gas . . .'

'Doctor . . .!'
But Soh-toun was a safe anaesthetist.

I was learning to think. 'How will you manage a sixty-year-old vomiting blood?' was a likely question in the exams and not 'What are the six causes of haemetemesis?' The focus was on what you would do, not what could be done. Surgery was common sense.

I never stopped thinking about the exams. The leather-bound file that Bansali had given me was as clear and succinct as any of his lectures and I was grateful to him for having lent it to me. Having finished with Part 1, I was in a hurry to get through the finals and become a Fellow. I bored Stan with endless descriptions of the surgical world I lived in and even resorted to history lessons: 'The Royal College owes its pedigree to the Society of Barber Surgeons.'

'You're kidding.'

'It's true. Physicians scorned surgeons with their crude instruments, knives and hammers. They thought themselves superior, because they healed with the clever use of medicines. When the Royal College of Surgeons was formed in 1800, the surgeons were not addressed as doctors; they had to be content with being called Mr So-and-So. It's still Mr or Ms for a surgeon. And we're proud to be different.'

I read about great men whose names appeared in textbooks and about those who had instruments and operations named after them: Babcock, Halstead, McBurney, Billroth. Especially Billroth, the Viennese surgeon who was the first to excise a portion of a cancerous stomach, a hundred and fifty years ago. His method of joining the two ends together was called Billroth's gastrectomy and was still the technique used by surgeons everywhere. He lived in a time when surgeons operated without anaesthesia or antibiotics. He was heckled on the streets if a case went wrong. I took to silently invoking Billroth when I scrubbed for any surgery till it became a habit.

The exams came and went. Theory, practicals and viva. On the evening of the last day, I stood with the other candidates in the foyer of the Royal College and heard my name being called. I had passed. A weight slid permanently off my shoulders.

27

Ms Stevens was a statuesque woman, five foot ten, with ash-blonde hair and kind grey eyes. I was fortunate to land my next posting with her. Ms Stevens did not shout at the staff or throw things. She was never rude. Surgery was not theatrical, she said. Surgeons were. Ms Stevens worked with a calm, unhurried confidence. Watching her, I refined my techniques, learnt again the precise way of throwing a surgical suture and getting the knots square. I trained myself to handle tissues with respect.

She must have noticed the awkward eagerness with which I tried to prove myself. 'Avoid stooping during surgery,' she said, watching me. 'Raise the table to the height that's comfortable for your back, neck and arms.' Ms Stevens did not believe in the heroism of surgery. For her, goals were tangible, the challenges practical. 'It's a lot like dancing,' she said. 'You must have physical grace and you must have inner grace. Only then will you learn to move your body in a certain way and feel it grow free.' Her lessons were invaluable.

Work started when I entered Theatre a little before eight. I slipped into the green trousers, shirt and sandals, twisted my plait beneath the cap, tied on the mask over my face and detached myself from the outside world. It was going to be a good day. No calls after one the previous night, no complications in the wards, no backache. The operating lists for the day were pasted on a board. I scanned them to check if there was anything out of the way, any emergency from the previous night added on. None. I had on my list a thyroglossal fistula in a young girl to start with and then a prostate, a vagotomy GJ, an inguino-scrotal hernia and varicose veins. A nice enough daylong list.

Surgeons and anaesthetists moved about the corridors. The early morning anxiety and a keenness of eye on masked faces mirrored my own. Someone talked about the weather and others bantered in low-toned voices as they moved about. Patients were wheeled in, intravenous drips put up, case sheets checked. My mind was not thinking yet focussed.

The thyroglossal fistula was removed *in toto* without difficulty. As I scrubbed for the next case, I went over the prostatectomy in my mind. Removing the prostate to relieve the 'water-works' problem in men was anatomically interesting and surgically demanding. Extirpate the offending tumour, and the patient is cured. Martin, the intern who was to assist me, was talking about one of the patients in the wards. I began to relax, my mind only half-listening, already in tune with the scalpel and suture, suction and scissors. The gears were being set. The slight twinge beneath the ribs due to a double helping of custard the previous night was forgotten, the back was behaving itself.

I was glad to have Martin as my assistant. He was keen on surgery. That was not an uncommon trend among interns. Surgery seemed skilled, clever and somehow heroic in contrast to the intellectuality of medicine. Most young doctors were cured soon enough. For Martin, his first ischio-rectal abscess could have been the last. The patient, an obese dockworker, had been anaesthetized and positioned with his legs up in stirrups in the ungainly lithotomy position. 'Ready,' said Peter. Martin stood, scalpel in hand. 'Cut deep until you hit the abscess,' I said. 'Then make a cruciate incision.' He cut, and the pus oozed, filling the room with the horrific smell. 'Make the opening wide enough for your finger . . .' I directed, wondering what was taking him so long. His hands moved in slow motion. 'Martin?' His face had turned chalky and he came down, all six feet and a hundred and eighty pounds of him, on the patient. Luckily the knife missed. Fifteen minutes of drama and the procedure complete, Martin was sitting in a daze on a stool. Martin's ischio-rectal would be laughed over for some time, but he was not put off. I was mean enough to make him do Tracy's faecal disimpaction once. His keenness stayed. He had the curiosity, the mental toughness and a certain thick-hidedness that was essential.

As we prepared for the prostate, I thought: Here I was passing judgements on an intern while a part of me was conscious of still being a fledgeling.

The prostate went well. Once the knife had touched skin and dug into the flesh, once that first act of violence was done, a rhythm was set. A quick cup of coffee, a walk up the corridor and back to limber up.

We scrubbed for the next case. The patient for the vagotomy and drainage weighed twenty-two stone. Inserting the breathing tube down a fat neck could be tricky. 'Where do you hunt up these cases?' asked Peter. I cut through the two-inch layer of fat, entered the abdomen and groped for the lower end of the oesophagus where I would find the vagus nerves, which control acid secretion to the stomach. They are divided to help heal stomach ulcers. Since the nerves also control the motility of the stomach, a drainage procedure has to be done after dividing the nerves to prevent food staying in the stomach.

The bleeding started as soon as I divided the nerves. I packed the site with a large swab and got on with the next step—making a wide outlet between the stomach and the small bowel. I showed Martin how to find the upper end of the jejunum, hitch it to the stomach with clamps and suture the two-in-four layers of catgut on an eyeless needle. As we worked, carefully placing the sutures in the slippery pink gut, I told him about the surgeon in Osmania Medical College in Hyderabad who had to perform the same surgery on a patient some fifty years ago. At that time the special clamps used to hold the stomach and the jejunum had to be got from Britain and it took six weeks! Instead of waiting, the surgeon designed clamps out of slit bamboo tied together. They worked as well as the imported clamps.

Martin was impressed with the story, but on the other side of the screen Peter was shaking his head. Was he ridiculing me, or did he think I was making it up? 'It's true,' I insisted. 'I've read about it . . .' Just then I noticed that the gauze placed around the gullet had soaked through and the abdomen was filling up with blood. Martin suctioned, and I tried to find the bleeder. I could not see because of the steady seepage. The blood loss was considerable and I grew worried. The patient was fat, and I was tired. I needed help. Aware that Ms Stevens was away at a conference, I said to Peter, 'Would you call Mr Batey?' Batey was a quick and confident surgeon and pleasant to work with, but that day he was gruff. He had to interrupt a class for medics to come to my rescue. He found a couple of small bleeders, which he cauterized. The wound became dry. 'Major Haemorrhage is easier to deal with than General Ooze,' he quipped. Humbled, I closed the abdomen.

Half past three and two cases to get through. No one liked staying long on a Friday evening. Peter read the *Daily Mail* and ate his sandwich in angry mouthfuls. Barbara the scrub nurse drank tea, saying it was too late to be eating lunch. I looked at my sandwich, the creamy egg sandwich that I liked best. That day it tasted like glue. I told Peter that the patient with the hernia had a groggy chest, hoping he would want it postponed. No problem, he said, he'd give an epidural. Weariness seized me. I looked dumbly at the newspaper. Better not to get too comfortable or it would be a struggle to get out of the chair. Martin had been called to the ward to attend a case of severe burns and I would have to manage without him.

The two cases were easy, the monotony of operating soothing and unhurried.

'Going out somewhere for the weekend?' asked Peter.

'Catching up on sleep.'

'What you havin' for dinner?' That was Barbara, always thinking of food.

'Cheese pasty with peas. Cream trifle.' Lies, of course. It was rice and beans sprinkled with Pathak's chilli powder. I was happy on a diet of rice (lots of it) and baked beans. Pathak's chilli powder I finished by the tinful, increasingly needing larger amounts to please my palate.

'I've cooked an Irish stew. Can't wait to get home. Tomorrow I'm doing a casserole.'

Snip. Suck. Cauterize. Ligate. Barbara could not tempt me with her casseroles and stews. My own dinner always tasted divine.

The day was over at seven. A quick visit to the post-op ward to check on my patients, and I was in my room. Bone-weary but the mind clean and sharp, as after a long walk. Everything—even boiling water for tea—was a pleasing, noble act. I was in tune with all that had happened. I did not want anything different, even the problem with the vagotomy was all right. The rest of the evening held no excitement. Next day could be worrisome but for now all worry was edged out of the mind. The clock which monitored my day ticking on the shelf ceased to matter. My body filled with delicious aches and pains. Sitting before the TV and watching *Poldark*, I was aware of a restful uncoiling of my mind.

After the failed research with ankle sprains in casualty I had shied away from writing academic papers. Ms Stevens persuaded me to try again. So I wrote about the incidence of recurrent pulmonary emboli and the post-phlebitic syndrome, more to please my boss than out of any real interest. I far preferred the practical challenges of surgery to the theoretical. My paper was published in a journal and I was asked to present it at the weekly surgical conference. I planned carefully, rehearsed before the mirror and deliberated on what I would wear.

I spoke as I had planned, faultlessly, moving my eyes towards the projector screen and back to rest on the audience. No jerky movements, no fidgets and stammers. I was proud to be among surgeons who wrote academic papers. When the conference was over and we filed out, Martin, who had been sitting in the third row, said, 'You should've spoken louder. Couldn't hear a word you said.'

I spent the happiest of my surgical days working for Ms Stevens but blunders were never far away. As part of my job, I had worked in the cardio-thoracic unit where the on-call registrar had to sleep in a room next to the Intensive Care Unit. One cold, dull weekend the senior surgeons were away for a conference in Edinburgh and there were no patients in the ICU. Ms Stevens was in charge until Monday morning. By Sunday afternoon it was obvious there would be no work that night. It had been a miserable day with incessant rain and sleet. The duty room was cold and I decided to sleep in my room instead. I told the switchboard operator to call me if I was needed. It was past midnight and I was just climbing into bed when the phone rang: Ms Stevens on the line. 'I'll see you in the ICU in five minutes,' she said.

I changed and ran, grabbing my coat. 'We have certain rules and they're to be followed,' she said. 'A surgeon who does not understand discipline is of no use to the patient.' She stood up. 'You'll be on call all of next week.'

I deserved what I got.

The next time, it was different. On a Sunday night I was called to casualty to see a man who had fallen off a ladder and complained of chest pain. An X-ray confirmed my suspicion. Fracture rib with a pnuemothorax—air had collected outside the right lung and compressed it, thus interfering with his breathing. The treatment was to insert a tube into the outside pocket of air and empty it, allowing air to flow easily into the lung. I showed the X-ray to the patient, a middle-aged bricklayer. 'I'll give you local anaesthetic to numb the area where the tube goes in,' I said, pointing to the spot a little below his arm. 'Once the air comes out, you'll feel a lot better.'

He pressed his lips together and looked away from me, at the casualty Sister. 'I won't let a bloody immigrant treat me,' he said. 'This is the NHS, isn't it? I want a British doctor.'

I walked out hoping they would not find another surgeon. Half an hour later the Sister called to tell me that the patient was a lot worse. Her voice was anxious. 'Will you come? I'll get him to apologize later. He's in no state to . . .'

'He was okay when I spoke to him,' I said. I refused to go.

I worked myself up until my arrogance and sense of hurt were magnified many times over. Bloody immigrant, indeed. I would show him. Some time passed and I thought maybe I would relent if the hospital administrator asked me. An hour later, when nothing happened, I went to casualty out of curiosity. Ms Stevens was standing beside the patient ready to put in the tube. There were three nurses, helping with the drip, the oxygen and the instruments. The man's breathing was laboured, his face had a dusky tinge. Lack of oxygen. A grave emergency.

Ms Stevens had come all the way from Birkenhead, where she lived. She injected the local anaesthetic and inserted the tube, connected it to the underwater seal drainage in a glass bottle. I stood there feeling useless, my arms hanging by my side. I followed her to the main exit and mumbled an apology. She shook her head. 'If you were a shopkeeper or a waitress or even a driver on a bus, it would have been excusable to insist on an immediate apology. But in hospital, in casualty . . .' That was all. She patted my arm and left.

Next morning, I faced the hospital administrator in his office. Mr Hallam was an officious little man, with a fat, pink face and gold-rimmed spectacles, the type who know a lot about management and little about doctors or patients. He asked me for an explanation. When I started to tell him, my reasoning sounded feeble. Anger made my voice and me nervous, tremulous. 'He called me a bloody immigrant,' I said.

Mr Hallam made a clicking sound with his teeth. 'He shouldn't have used such language, of course.'

'It's not the language,' I said. 'He called me an immigrant. I'm not an immigrant. I . . .'

'The patient could have died,' he said.

Somehow, hearing him say it made me defiant and unrepentant. Later that day, in my pigeon-hole in the doctors' room, I found a written warning cautioning me for negligence.

I related the episode to Stan. 'As if the patient insulting me wasn't enough, I had to be pulled up by Mr Hallam,' I fumed, 'and then cautioned. It's there in my record now. Forever marked.'

'I can understand how you must feel,' said Stan. 'But it's a fact. You were in the wrong.'

He did not understand. 'I'm not a bloody immigrant,' I said. 'The trouble with some people is they think every Asian wants to stay on here. I don't want to. And those who do stay, it's not because they love it here or anything. It's circumstances. Good money to take home . . . that's all.'

Yes, yes, said Stan.

⌒

For six months after that I worked in orthopaedics. It was hard. Nowhere else did skill and judgement, or the lack of it, show up quite so clearly. The X-ray told the story. In general surgery, minor mistakes could be glossed over. The abdomen could hide errors and provide the doctor some breathing time to rethink strategy. Orthopaedics demanded honesty. Acquiring the skill of reducing fractures and setting them in plaster was gratifying but I was clumsy with drills, screws and nails. My weak back and the lack of physical strength made it more difficult. What took ten minutes for my male colleagues took me thirty or more. I backed off, but learnt enough to manage fracture reductions and operations that did not require the use of heavy instruments.

As a junior surgeon you were expected to follow the techniques of your boss. Selby used silk for skin, Bianchi used monofilament nylon, with Dave McFarlane it was continuous nylon mattress, with Stevens subcuticular dexon. Some preferred vertical incisions on the abdomen, some transverse. If one used subcutaneous sutures beneath the skin, another omitted them all together. Working with different surgeons was good experience, but not every senior was worthy of imitation. Phil Carver was a case in point. A senior registrar, he had the ability to mess up every case he operated on.

Carver was popular with patients. Red-lipped, curly-haired and blue-eyed, he talked to patients, held their hands and laughed with sick children. He loved to operate and was miserable on days when his list was short. 'I've only five cases today,' he would say gloomily. Everyone loved Carver, but assisting him was hell. The simplest surgery got bungled. Five minutes into a case and there was blood on the floor, on his gown and even on the faces of the scrub nurse, the assistant and Carver himself. Once he dropped his spectacles into the incision he had just made for repair of an incisional hernia. He did what only he could have done: picked them up, positioned them over his nose and carried on with the blood-spill.

The juniors wisely got blood ready for every case that was to be 'carved'. Once while doing a gall bladder, he spilt a lot of the red stuff and was soaked through when he finished. Peter saw him on his way to the changing room. 'Been having a period, Phil?' he asked.

Carver made up for the most dreadful complications with his positive approach. Rubbing his hands together, he would tell the unfortunate patient who had developed a complication: 'You've now got a fistula through which fluid will leak for a couple of weeks. Never mind. It'll be hunky-dory in no time,' or 'We had a bit of a bleed during the surgery. That's why you've got a nasty little infection inside. Not to worry. You'll come through.'

Thank you, Mr Carver, was what the patients said, bravely.

Carver was a devout Methodist and taught at his local Sunday school. He once said that the church was his first calling. 'If I hadn't been a surgeon, I'd have been a priest,' he said at the bedside of a patient. Quick as a flash, the patient responded, 'Would've been a good thing for all of us, Mr Carver.' Phil laughed his good-natured laugh and moved to the next bed.

Leslie Springer was equally dangerous. He was a humourless surgeon who levelled his eyes at no one in particular, spoke his clinical findings into a dictaphone during the rounds and was unconcerned with the person behind the disease. Every registrar despaired of being on call with him. He could never make his mind up about a case and would not let anyone else do it. It was usual practice to phone the consultant and brief him about the case that you were to take to Theatre. The consultant usually told the registrar to go ahead with the surgery and intervened only if asked. But Springer always offered to come and have a look. He would go through the patient's history, prod and shove endlessly at a belly already sore, or examine a limb or rectum already inspected, increasing the distress of the patient. He sat in the duty room with the case sheet and lab reports, trying to decide what to do. He asked that the surgery be put off and examined the patient several times in the night. The patient, the nurses, the doctors all ended up nervous wrecks.

So many surgeons, each unforgettable in his or her own way: Nick Batey with his silken deftness and irascible good humour, who never failed to dig out a joke at the worst of times; John Lee, the utterly calm but superb urology surgeon with his dignified patience and faultless technique; Mr Bickford, the thorough gentleman even with a knife in his hand. Bianchi, Selby and Ms Stevens; Carver and Springer. I learnt from them all.

I had come to that stage in my career where I knew how to use my faculties. I diagnosed with my eyes and my hands and my mind, confirmed with X-rays and scans. I assessed for myself the length, breadth, toughness and friability. At surgery, I snipped, cut, clamped and tied, confident of my judgement, my ability to get the thing out and sew the cut ends together. When I finished, I straightened my back and walked away from the patient, with pleasantly aching limbs and the comforting knowledge that I had done it. It recharged my batteries like nothing else.

28

Appa's letters were full of news. He had retired from the village school. In forty years, he had watched it grow from a single room of mud and thatch to a tile-and-brick building. He had ensured that the youth of Angheri became literate. Forty years of doing something he loved and the Maestru still had the zeal for another mission.

The yet-to-be-built hospital had become a collective dream, Appa wrote, and Naganna Gowdru had declared he was willing to sell the half-acre of land for a reasonable price. The plan for the hospital had been discussed with contractors and an engineer in Mysore; Jai had sent his suggestions by post. If everyone agreed on the plans, construction would start and the roofing would be finished before the monsoon next year.

Appa wanted me home. I was still hurting from his rejection of the money I had sent. I had made up my mind to ask him when I returned: Wasn't my money as good as his? My years in England had brought a change in our relationship. Appa became more tolerant, I more honest and less afraid. There would be no more of standing before him in his office with my hands nervously clasped behind me, no more passive listening. I would pose questions, clear doubts. There was so much to tell him, the certificate of the Royal College to show, and the photographs. I missed Appa more than I did anyone else.

For now, I would keep my success in the exams a secret. My training in England was far from finished.

The last six months of my registrar's job, I was posted in a seaside resort a half an hour's bus ride from Liverpool.

Perhaps due to the smallness of the hospital—a hundred and fifty beds—and fewer doctors, it was less stressful. The two senior surgeons dealt with everything. Cases which could not be handled by them were sent to Liverpool but rarely before Mr Burgess, seven years retired, had given his opinion. After thirty-six years, during which time he had moved up from house officer to registrar, senior registrar and consultant, he was still very much a part of the hospital. A big man with a wonderfully lined face, silver eyebrows and bat ears, Mr Burgess came every day. For those of us who had never seen him operate, it was a wonder how his big stumpy fingers could handle delicate structures, how they could throw a surgical knot.

Mr Burgess belonged to an era of kindness and courtesy. He was armed with good humour and wisdom. Every morning he left his hat and coat in the alcove near the entrance and went to the surgical wards, pausing on the way to speak to someone he met—a porter, cook, doctor or nurse. Mr Burgess had all the time in the world. The surgeons asked him to see difficult cases. Picking the Burgess brain, it was called. His presence in the hospital comforted patients and reassured the doctors. As long as he was around, nothing could go wrong. He never operated or took over the treatment of any patient. He would look over the shoulders of the younger surgeons and offer his advice. 'I'd do an end-to-side anastomosis'; 'I'd use silk sutures there, two-zero silk.' You could defend yourself by using him as a shield: 'Eusol will be ideal for this ulcer. Mr Burgess used eusol'; 'Mr Burgess preferred linen mattress for the skin'; 'Mr Burgess always said . . .' To listen to Mr Burgess talk to a patient, to observe his unhurried examination and to take part in a bedside discussion was worth more than a day's work.

Sometimes I met him in the alcove as he came in and we would exchange greetings. 'Good morning, Mr Burgess!' 'Good morning, my dear!' A few minutes with him helped wipe away any work-related strain.

I soon grew to like the hospital and the little seaside town which was so much smaller than Liverpool. The only Indian shop in town was Sharma's. Messy, throbbing with unceasing confusion, yet efficient. On Sundays, while the locals stayed home and watched football or swilled beer, the Sharmas—like the Rafiques and Patels elsewhere—were open all day. They made money, invested wisely and sent their kids to university. Their growing prosperity was sometimes resented but there was little anyone could do about it.

I loved the Sharmas' shop, where onions and bhindi spilled out of bags, bottles of mango pickle and packets of papads stood angled precariously on corner shelves, the odour of garam masala and hing, jaggery and garlic drenched every cranny. I stood before the counter displaying Indian sweets and sniffed greedily. Ignoring the barfis and laddus I settled for my favourite— the gummy, rich sohan halwa bejewelled with kaju and kishmish. It was funny how I always said 'kaju' and 'kishmish' and not 'cashew' and 'raisins', just because the sweets were Indian.

Mrs Sharma, fat and shining in a flowery salwar kameez, was a fixture behind the counter. She sat immobile while the knitting needles in her hands beat a steady rhythm. From her perch she instructed the young lad who served. 'Arre, aam ka achaar idhar, adrakwala udhar! Teri khopdi kidhar hai?' She talked sweetly to the customers, throwing in a 'luv' or a 'my dear' to make them feel more welcome.

The Brits were embarrassed when they shopped at Sharma's. They grabbed what they wanted and left.

'I'll have one of those sweets, thank you,'

'That will be tenna penas, please . . . thank you,'

'Beg your pardon? Oh . . . *ten pence* . . . here we are, thanks very much,'

'Thank you, dear.'

'Thank you . . .'

The exhausting round of thank yous and pleases over, Mrs Sharma would settle back with her knitting, pausing to yell at the young boy who served in the shop: 'Arre, sambhal ke!'

The irrelevant overuse of 'thank you' and 'please' had annoyed me from the time I first came to England. I was considered ill-mannered because I did not say it every time.

'I want a coffee.'

'*Please* . . .'

'What?'

Sushma had convinced me that it would not hurt to throw in the courtesy words. She told me she had once assisted in a hysterectomy where thirty-two 'thank yous' and forty-one 'pleases' were exchanged between the surgeon and scrub nurse.

Sushma and I had kept in touch on the telephone. She had become a senior registrar in Birmingham. Ambili had moved to Wales and I did not hear from her again. Romeira had married the American and gone to New Jersey. A few months later she returned, bitter, and eager to make amends to herself. It was not difficult to guess what had happened. She recovered quickly and went back into training to make up for the precious months she had lost.

Whatever the work, the Indians did well, mostly. The ones who did not fare well blamed it on prejudice. I went for the Diwali, Pongal and Ugadi Nights and listened to conversations about the shocking plight of people back home. Or the discrimination practised by the whites. Few managed without guilt and resentment.

Radha and Krishna were one such blessed couple.

They had come to England soon after internship. Radharaman had been a year senior to me in college—a shy, unassuming chap I had never spoken to. Krishnaveni had been a year junior. The Radha–Krishna romance during our college days was no fleeting affair. Radha planted a jasmine creeper at the back of his room to grow flowers for Krishna. He wooed her for six years and before he left for England talked to her parents. The day Krishna finished internship he was there to marry her and take her back. After two years of working in junior jobs at district hospitals, both of them opted for general practice and settled in Wycombe, near London.

Radha was a craze with the cleaning ladies, shop assistants, housewives and most other women who flocked to his clinic. He knew that the key to pleasing a woman was to compliment her about something—her earrings, the colour of her cheeks, or her age. 'Fifty? You? Not a day older than thirty-five, surely . . .' 'Linda, you can't go to Greece without me. Will you take me in your suitcase? Paul needn't know.'

They were a generous couple. Countrymen in need of help would head for their utterly disorganized home. Krishna kept the house in a clutter; Radha cleaned up. Their fights were habitual, loud and predictable, about trivial things, like poorly cooked rice, the colour of Radha's tie, Krishna's reading habits (she loved cheap thrillers), his aftershave or her lipstick. They screamed at each other, banged doors and stamped out of the house. I spent an occasional weekend with them and watched their fights and the making up.

I understood the reason for their popularity over a weekend I spent with them. A friend who was a general practitioner called at nine in the evening and asked if Radha would do a domiciliary visit for him. 'It's Cathy,' Radha said as he put down the receiver. He bolted down his dinner and got ready to go. Cathy was a thirty-year-old with Down's Syndrome, married to Harry Talbot, also afflicted. Cathy was myopic, hard of hearing and mentally handicapped; Harry slightly less so. They had lived in a nursing home from their adolescence and married some years ago. Harry could not stand his wife being slighted in any way. He often became quarrelsome and violent. A year ago, Cathy developed cancer of the cervix. She went through several sittings of radium treatment and chemotherapy, but declined rapidly. A few days earlier she had developed a lung infection; the doctor started her on intravenous antibiotics. That evening she took a turn for the worse and the doctor on call, not wanting to be confronted by Harry, asked Radha if he would go.

I asked if I could go along. It was a few days into the new year and bitterly chill. I shivered all the way during the thirty-minute ride. Radha drove in silence. When we reached the nursing home, I followed Radha inside. In spite of the medication and oxygen, Cathy was not doing well at all. The matron led us through a corridor to the Talbots' room and peered in through the door that was slightly ajar. 'We'll have to wait a few minutes,' she said. 'Harry's doing her hair.'

Harry brushed and curled Cathy's hair twice every day. He had a drawer full of clips, curlers and ribbons for her. It was a blue-ribbon day: Cathy's blonde hair was in ringlets and tied with blue ribbons above the ears. She was an enormous woman, filling the sofa she sat on, gasping for breath. She struggled with the nursing attendant who tried to hold the oxygen mask in place. Her face was dusky and her eyes terrified. When Radha went near her she pulled the oxygen mask off her face and made an attempt to rise, knocking the oxygen cylinder over. Harry let out a yell as it landed on his foot. It took some time and a great deal of coaxing for Cathy to let Radha examine her.

'It's bad,' he said. 'We can try shifting her to the hospital but . . .'

'What you fuckin' doctors going to do for her?' yelled Harry. He was a strong man with blunted features and serious, troubled eyes. 'Every time you give her fuckin' medicines, she gets worse. I haven't any faith in the fuckin' crap you feed her in hospitals. You treat her here and make her all right, you hear me?' His voice rose to a threatening pitch and he caught Radha's arm in a violent grip.

'Harry,' Radha said quietly. 'Either you cool down and listen to what I have to say or I'll go straight home and to bed. Which do you want?' He put a hand on Harry's shoulder and added, 'Can we talk?'

When Harry sat down, Radha explained. Cathy had reached the stage of no return. Moving to hospital might prolong her life by a short span but it was not much use. Harry pressed his eyes with his fists, got up and took a few purposeful steps towards Cathy, then he came back and sat down. 'You mean nothing can be done for Our Cathy,' he said, miserable. 'You mean . . . she's . . . going to go. But there must be something *I* can do. There *must* be.'

'Show her you love her,' said Radha.

The scene stays with me: Harry propped up on their bed, holding Cathy's enormous body in his arms, his hands soothing, stroking. Radha, the matron and I seated in a far corner of the room. Harry spoke to Cathy about things they had done together as children. How they had picked daisies, fought each other with snowballs, and how they had eaten ice-lollies on hot summer afternoons. 'Your favourite was Mr Men, lemon flavour, and mine was Dracula with those coloured bits of sugar strands on it.' Cathy listened. Her face relaxed, the terror went out of her eyes and a smile quivered on her thick lips which were slowly turning blue. Two hours later, Cathy breathed her last. 'You're all right, Cathy,' Harry whispered. 'I love you . . .'

Radha was quiet on the way back home. He drove the car into the garage, switched off the engine and wiped his eyes with the sleeve of his shirt. 'Tired?' I said, needlessly. He shook his head.

The other couple I knew from college were Dr Shankar, the registrar in medicine, and his wife Shanta. He was a physician, smoothly handsome and distinguished-looking, with prematurely grey sideburns and an inerasable Tamil accent, now fused with a local one. Shanta was pleasing and homely. The red bindi on her forehead, the gold chain and bangles did not go with trousers but she was not the type to worry over such things. She was the forever busy perfect wife and mother who went about her cooking-cleaning-washing rituals, happy to care for her husband and sons. She had a PhD in Sangam poetry. When she told me, her husband smiled and switched on the TV.

Did she regret lost opportunities? She was grinding a chutney in the mixie when I asked. Her face tensed, just a little. 'The kids must grow up,' she said, making an excuse to herself.

The Shankars spoke about the lack of Indian culture in Britain. They took their boys, four and six, to Ugadi and Pongal parties and spoke to them about the greatness of their past. On Sundays the boys read aloud the Amar Chitra Kathas in their British accents and watched the hideously produced mythological dramas, specially taped and sent for them all the way from India, on video. For the rest of the week they lived British lives in British schools.

Shankar and Shanta urged me to equip myself with essentials like a washing machine and vacuum cleaner. They advised me to buy a house on mortgage. Shankar was a member (an active one) of the Indian Doctors' Association, and concerned about me. Why would I want to go back? He cited grim examples of friends who were languishing in the Public Health Centres in remote villages, or frustrated in cities. The roads were treacherous, the filth disgusting; his kids always got diarrhoea when they went home on a visit. And did I know, they still had those old-fashioned telephones with dials on them? Their fingers hurt to use the wretched things.

'We can do more for our country by staying on here and being successful,' he reasoned. 'It's not just the money we send home. If each of us can pull out three or four people from India and help them start life here, it would be a service. These white bastards. They must be taught a lesson. We'll rule them one day, on their soil.' He laughed. 'Just joking.'

Listening to him, I was eager for home.

➥

My love of England had begun to pall. I had had enough of sunless winters. Something must be done before the frost settled in my heart. And yet it seemed inappropriate, ungrateful to long for home when everything was going so well for me. Three years since I left home; the family would be waiting. It was easy to love them from a safe distance, from where they could not constantly nudge me towards marriage. Meanwhile there was work: patients to see, tumours to cut out, cavities to evacuate of pus. Every act gave me the feeling of something done the way it should be done. The little victories added up. I was vaguely unhappy, but not in a hurry to dislocate myself.

It was a Sunday, and having nothing to do I walked into town and through the shopping malls. The wind was strong, gusty. My eyes and nose streamed from the cold and demanded attention. I had my usual supply of tissues. When they were used, I moved them from the right pocket of my coat to the left. An hour later, I had had enough of walking; I sat on a stone bench in front of a kiosk selling sweets and cigarettes.

The sky hung low, hugging the buildings like a grey-and-white quilt. My mind was thinking, not thinking, empty. I felt cold. Tea, I thought, that's what I need, I would have some tea. With the paper cup in my hands, I came back to the bench. I warmed one hand and then the other on the ribbed outside of the paper cup. I drank in quick gulps to warm my throat and chest. It was not good tea but what could I expect for five pence?

People were walking in an unceasing stream. Shops bulged with goods. I tried to pry into the sounds of people but there was nothing to listen to. I looked at the crowds, trying to find something new, something different to rest my eyes on. The people became a blur of marching figures; I felt dizzy.

The tea finished and I was cold again. My nose streamed, I used up more tissues and sat with my cold hands pressed between my thighs. God, I said. God, tell me what I must do. It had been a long time since I had last addressed the heavens. I wished I could find out what marks I had earned for myself up there, if I could have a progress report of my life. Silly, silly. I must decide for myself what to do. I will shut my eyes tight and open them—the first thing I see will be a revelation of some sort, I told myself. When I closed my eyes and opened them, they fell on an old woman, really old. She staggered out of the huge swing doors of a shop, with carrier bags in both hands. Her back protruded in a hump through her coat. I tried again; this time the backsides of two girls, plump and busy in tight jeans, walking away from me. I tried a third time and opened my eyes to a young man with long hair stopping to light a cigarette.

Well, what? I wished I could prise open my future and peep in, and find out if everything was going to be all right.

Damn the weather. The sameness of my life annoyed me. I wanted noise and abuse, colour and chaos. I longed for the sight of lungi-clad men with curious eyes, of saris billowing in shops, of sweaty strangers in buses, for the din of filmi songs. I wanted smells and sounds that worried my senses a bit.

My friendship with Stan had firmed into something steady and comforting but I could not define where it was heading. We met often for lunch and tea. He despaired of my eating habits, my lack of taste in clothes, my stupidity with money, my fear of the cold and my inability to stay sober after two glasses of wine. Also of my increasingly irritated nerves. The predictability of everything had begun to vex me. I cribbed about silly things.

'You call this rain? The only thing you have is an ooze from the sky. You see proper rain back home.'

'Okay.'

'Darkness fell, you say, but it never *falls* here, it creeps up on you.'

'Okay.'

That was Stan. Not wanting an argument.

'The British are colour-blind. Even women prefer men's colours. Blacks, greys and browns. They haven't heard of magenta, violet, yellow, and pastel shades like tender pink and aqua blue.'

'Maybe we're colour-blind. But those colours you mention, they'd be wrong, unsuitable.'

'Frightened to experiment, that's what. And the British politeness, it isn't natural.'

'It's natural for us. And, Nalli, will you stop baiting me, please . . .'

'There! Why the please? And I'm not baiting, just stating facts.' All of a sudden, just like that, I was miserable. I wanted to cry. Hiding my face with my fingers, I said, 'You don't understand how different it is for me.'

He understood. I knew. It was Stan to whom I reported my success and disaster at work. It was Stan I called from London when I passed my exams. I told him about my family, about Jai and the hospital. He listened without being intrusive.

'Nell's a deep one. She's dating Stan, the ambulance driver,' the nurses said.

Stan had not kissed me, except once. That was after the Christmas party when he held me close for a split second and whispered something about love. He took me out for drives or when I needed to buy some fruit or go to the laundrette. I wondered what he felt about me. Was I a mere filling in of some void in his life? When would he say something, when would it happen?

It was a Sunday. We had driven to Cheshire. The day was delicately warm, the greens, blues and yellows at their sharpest best. Stan stopped often so we could take in the scene. And I, for no reason at all, began thinking of home. Of all things, the wrinkles on the faces of Ajja and Ajji. Ajji's wrinkles were fine and fragile. You did not see them unless you went close. It looked as though her skin would tear if you touched it. I used to feel dizzy peering into her face and tracing the lines on her skin as they curled and curved around her eyes and mouth. Ajja's wrinkles were firm and dark. They sprang to life and danced when he talked.

'Stop for a coffee, Nalli?'

I thought about Budhi and his talent for slurping. He was a master slurper. He slurped pumpkin sambar and mango juice with the liquid trickling down to his elbows. The divinely sweet plantain, milk and honey nectar doled out in the Peggala temple dribbled down his chin, and he drank the coffee from his steel tumbler without his lips touching the rim. In acknowledgement of his slurping abilities, Budhi's tumbler was filled to the top every time. If you forgot, he sat silent until you filled it.

In the photograph the family had sent me, they looked so complete that I felt disappointed. Sujju beautiful, with a strand of hair which had slipped out of place, Ajja morose as always in photos, Appa stern, Amma composed, Budhi smiling. And Vishnu. The real change was in Vishnu. Each time I looked at the photo, my eyes were pulled towards him. Memories of long ago pinched and nibbled at my brain. Why, why, why did it happen? Why, why, why did it not?

When I showed the photograph to Stan, he said Appa was handsome and distinguished. Appa, handsome! He said the way I talked about Appa, it made him jealous. Stan said strange things like that.

We stopped at one of those places off the motorway where they serve coffee and snacks. I asked for a cheese sandwich without wanting it. Through the window I looked out at the gentle loveliness outside and thought, all this is nothing without the nearness. I looked sideways at Stan's honest face, at the defencelessness in his slight frame. It filled me with a longing that was not entirely sexual. I wanted to run my fingers over that chin and stroke it into a firmer, stronger chin of determination and strength. Whenever I dreamt of Stan, the dreams were sexual, a mingling of memories of a long-ago desire in lampless darkness, with the erotic smell of the wick just burnt, the touch of hardness and softness and a terrifying realization that *this* was it. What should not have happened had become a reality which I pushed away with one hand and pulled with the other, and the pull was stronger. But that was long ago.

A few people stood outside, drinking coffee from the vending machine. The steam rose from the paper cups as they drank and their voices rang thin and sharp through the warm air. I looked without looking at a man standing near the window and then suddenly saw him and sat up. With a squeal of delight I jumped up and ran. He had finished his coffee and was walking away. His hands were deep in the pockets of his overcoat and he was heading for his car among those parked outside. I ran and, when I was within three feet of him, cried out, 'Appa!'

When Stan came out five minutes later, I was leaning

against the rails, fumbling for a tissue in my bag. 'What's up, Nalli? You haven't finished your sandwich . . .' Seeing my tears, he pulled out a tissue. I told him how I had mistaken a stranger for Appa. I had run after him and called out, and when he turned around it was someone else. Of course it was someone else. Appa was thousands of miles away. I was ashamed to be crying. Stan waited patiently until my sniffling was over and then reached out and touched my arm. 'Nell . . . I think it's about time . . .'

'. . . that I went back,' I said, finishing the sentence for him.

He looked at me, a queer expression around his mouth, and nodded.

That evening I sat looking at the one photograph I had of Stan and myself together. Hilda had clicked it during a 'do' at the hospital, a going-away party for a senior Sister in the wards. It had me laughing over something, giggling perhaps, and Stan looking at me with a smile on his lips. Stan had brought me the photo. 'Lovely, isn't it?' he said. Hilda told me later that he had framed the photograph and kept it in his room.

I looked entirely happy in that photograph though I could not remember what I was amused about. So did Stan. That smile of his, it said so much. I could not remember a single moment of unhappiness when we were together. He had asked me all about home and about my future plans. We talked of everything under the sun. We argued and disagreed and still remained close. I had thought . . . We had left it unresolved and unsaid for too long. We had held on to our innermost feelings. Now it would never happen.

All of that day and the next I planned my going back, but by evening I knew I was not ready yet. Appa would understand and so would Jai, who was too busy to write. I must do more gastrectomies, at least one procto-colectomy and some rectal surgery. It would take me another year, I wrote. Appa would not be pleased to read the letter but when I went back and told him everything, he would forgive my delay in returning. Then I received the news that Ajji had fallen and broken her hip and Budhi had developed severe stomach pain that stayed for days. They had been taken to Mysore.

Three and a half years after coming to England, I returned.
But abruptly, for a reason that had nothing to do with Ajji's
broken hip or Budhi's stomach pain. A greater sorrow was
waiting for me.

29

I left without farewells or gifts to take home, with hurried
goodbyes over the phone and messages sent in haste to friends.
Stan had offered to drive me to Heathrow, but the need to be
alone with my sorrow was overwhelming. I would not share it
with anyone. Not even Stan.

I hauled my various bits of luggage on to an airport trolley.
I had mixed feelings about Britain. Three and a half years of
learning and adjusting to politeness and punctuality. Three years
of autumn leaves and long twilights, raw winds, smell-less
flowers, the cold glow of the sodium vapour lamps, and shops
that made me dull with indecision. I was happy to be rid of long
winters, fussy rain, endless layers of clothes, and of saying
'please' and 'thank you' more often than I wanted. I had thought
I would feel some wrench at leaving, but I did not. What
awaited me at the other end consumed me and I left without
regret.

It was a perfectly beautiful summer's day. Stinging blue
skies, a soft breeze and bright sunshine. Bare-chested men and
scantily clad women, old dears in shorts and straw hats were
everywhere. HEAT WAVE—the papers boasted—the hottest day in
twenty years. The temperature was 102 degrees. Almost forty
degrees back home. Having no confidence in the British weather,
I put on my sweater.

In the airport I heard someone call my name. Stan. Stan,
with Walter Mountain. This was unnecessary. I had wanted so
much to be by myself. They should have understood. Walter
pressed a bunch of flowers into my hands. We sat on the cold
airport seats and drank coffee from a vending machine. I
listened dully to their sympathetic words and answered their

queries. Strangers walked past dragging their chattels with the single-minded purpose of getting away. Yes. Flight was the precise word.

'I've got a friend who works here, in the cargo section,' Walter said, rubbing his nose. 'Mind if I go see him?' He looked at his watch. 'Be back in half an hour.'

Stan handed me a paper parcel—a light brown Shetland sweater, his going-away gift. 'You owe me dinner, remember,' he quipped. 'Shan't let you get away with it, even if I have to come all the way to India.' Stan moved my hand baggage from the seat between us and moved closer. 'I wanted to talk to you alone. Walter's friend in the cargo section, he doesn't exist.' He spoke with effort, trying to find the right words. 'I'm so sorry that you have to go like this . . . thought we had a lot of time . . . there's so much I want to say.'

It was easier to talk with the noise and clutter swirling around us. Stan cared deeply for me but was not sure if it would work. Talking, he took my hand in his. In spite of the grief that engulfed me, it felt good, quite natural, to be holding hands. There was no nervousness. 'I wanted to ask—may I visit you in India? We must get to know each other more.'

'Of course.'

I watched him push the hair back from his eyes. If my years in Liverpool had not helped us know each other, why would it happen in India? Stan could not see what it was like for me. For a split second I was transported back home, listening to the litany of crickets in the evening and seeing the hills by day, so sharp, so real and wrapped in a shroud of mist. Stan was not the type to take risks and it was a risk—hoping that we would understand each other better at home.

'I wanted to tell you,' I said. 'Knowing you was the best thing that happened to me here.'

He grinned. 'And surgery?'

'Surgery first. You second.' Our hands were pressed together in a deep embrace. I was so happy. Whatever else happened, nothing would take away this feeling I had for Stan.

It was a cheerless flight. When I came out of the aircraft in

Delhi, the warm, muggy air was familiar and comforting. I
stuffed the sweater into my bag and once out of the airport
headed for the exit where taxis waited. A doctor had given me
the address of a guest house which he said was clean, and the
prices reasonable. I went there and was told they only took
Europeans and Americans. How did one handle discrimination
in one's own country? I had no energy—to fight, argue, protest.
Easier to find myself a room somewhere else for the night. In the
morning I took the flight to Madras and from there a day-train
to Bangalore. The train was packed and the air slimy with the
stagnant heat of August. My back hurt and I needed sleep but
the seven-hour train journey passed swiftly. Seated on my
suitcase near the toilet, with people constantly brushing against
me, I ate a dosai, drank too many cups of coffee and inhaled the
harsh, dubious, congenial smells of a long ride.

A bus ride from Bangalore to Mysore and I would be nearly
home. After an endless wait in the station I climbed into the
local bus and found a seat. The bus spluttered on its way and
I fixed my gaze towards Angheri. The sky was overcast, the
clouds dark and determined. When the rain came, it pelted the
glass windows and beat angrily on the gutted roads. After a long
while it slowed. The hills were invisible, sequestered behind the
mist. The bus bumped along for another hour before it took the
familiar turn around the bamboo grove.

Vishnu was waiting at the bus stop. He had filled out a
little; his voice was deep and manly. I felt that inexplicable
attraction towards him, like an ache, and was ashamed. We left
my luggage at Raghavendra Stores—we would collect it later—
and walked home, talking as we walked.

Ajji had died quietly, without fuss. Ajja had given her a
glass of milk, changed her clothes and combed her hair as he did
every night. In the morning he went with a chombu of water for
her to wash with and she was gone. Ajji, who had dominated
Ajja's life for over fifty years, had died not from the broken hip
but because she had lost the will to live. In the last few months
her face became darker, her mouth puckered, her hair dry and
voice rough. She became more querulous and blamed Ajja for

not doing enough. She refused to talk of anything other than her illness.

I tried to imagine the front room, bare without Ajji's bed, without the chamber pot which she used at night and which Ajja emptied every morning; without the smells of ointments and oils, and the smell of imaginary ailments which pervaded her world. The family had adjusted itself around her illness. Her sickbed had been the fulcrum around which everything turned.

We walked past the coconut grove. Clouds, ragged and dishevelled, hung in the sky. Vishnu stopped to tell me the rest.

Even after retirement, Appa had kept himself busy. There was not a single day when he did not go out on a visit or an errand of some sort. That Sunday he had gone to the santhe and then cycled on past the school to visit Sompa. Near the school gate, a bus loaded with Sunday morning santhe-goers overtook him. It veered too close and its rear end struck him. The passengers later said they heard a sound like a shot from a toy gun. Chellaiah was the driver. In the minute that it took for the bus to stop and people to rush to his side, a crimson puddle had formed around Appa's head.

We stood beneath a banyan, its snarled, jutting roots clenching the earth. I leant against the tree trunk and felt the rough bark on my back. The rain had quietened to a drizzle and the sun was out, sharp as nails in my eyes. Drops of rain, alight in a fury of colour, hung from the leaves; a squirrel rustled in the undergrowth and on the topmost spray of branches a bird sang shrilly. Vishnu stood waiting, his arms crossed in front of him.

At the gate, a tearful Sujju greeted me. In the background stood Vishnu's wife Harini whom I had never met, and Budhi. Amma came and asked if I had eaten, would I like some tiffin? Ajja would not step out of his room. 'He says if you hadn't gone away you could have saved them both,' Sujju said. 'What were you a doctor for if you couldn't be there when we needed you?'

Ajja was seated at the window, his goose-like neck bent. When he saw me, his shoulders shook with inconsolable anguish. I felt it the most then, a physical pain that cut me in two.

In the night, a strong wind licked at the doors and windows. I got up, felt my way to the front room and lit a lamp. I watched as the flame shivered and did a short, giddy dance before the wind snuffed it out. The bamboo clumps behind the house creaked and it sounded like Ajji groaning. The wind shook the doors and pounded the rafters. Sleep eluded me. My neck ached from the journey. Some time during that long night I heard the owl—gnnn . . . gn . . . gnnn . . . gnnn . . . gn . . . gnnn—like a very thin line scratched into the night. A scratch with a long-short-long pattern and a maddeningly slow rhythm that I could not help but wait for although there was such pain in the waiting, such resentment at the happiness in that gnnn . . . at a time of sorrow.

I rose early and sneaked back to Ajja's room. He was up already, praying to his deities.

'The gods are angry with us,' he said, seeing me. 'I don't know why, but they're angry.'

He looked small and defenceless in the darkness of the early morning, with the lamplight playing on the trembling contours of his aged face. I sat by the window and, rubbing the sleep out of my eyes, looked out. The mist which had curtained off the trees and swallowed the hills now lay at their feet. The sky was a loving blue and the light spread in a thin sheet of silver over the tallest peak. Dark and holy the hills stood, consoling me with their strength.

Budhi showed me the scar from his surgery. When his stomach pains did not go away with medicines, the doctors had operated. They found nothing. I was not sure if it was shyness in the presence of Vishnu's wife or because of the tragedy at home, but Budhi had become quiet. The days passed slowly, painfully, in so much silence. There was no joy in watching the sky turn pink behind the guava tree or in seeing the russet wings of the chembooka or in hearing the owls which had increased from three to five.

We sat at the kitchen table and ate in silence. When we talked, it was about Appa. After Ajji's death and during the mourning no one had been to the market. That day, Amma had drawn up a list of things to be bought. Appa ate his breakfast—upittoo with mango pickle—and had a second helping. He sat in the porch and read the front page of *Prajavani* and, before he left, asked Ajja if he wanted snuff. With a bag slung on his shoulder and another on the handlebars, he cycled away. On the bicycle which I had so often cleaned, snatching the chore from Budhi. I loved the feel of the metal, the smell of oil, the sight of spokes turning, the chain slithering. The cycle, which had escaped, stood leaning against the wall, as if ready for Appa to wheel it away. If I closed my eyes I could hear the diurnal creaking of the wheels, I could see Appa, noble as a king on his throne. How could a stupid bus kill him who preached safety on the roads? Fracture skull, haemorrhage—both intracerebral and external—cerebral oedema and cardio-respiratory arrest. All in a few seconds. I could not have done anything. The sharp edge of the bus had struck him. Two inches. Just two inches between life and death. They heard his skull crack; they saw him come slowly off the cycle and hit the ground. His arm twitched for five seconds and then blood poured in a red stream towards the school gate. Chellaiah lost his job and his swagger.

Neighbours, friends and relatives had all come, first when Ajji died and again for Appa. Sompa, Shanku Master, Gowdru, Bhimasena Nayaka, the Vaidyar, Akkamma Teacher, Beach Aunty and Fat Aunty, as had teachers, students and old students. After Ajji's death, Amma had performed the special puja for which she had to fast all day. She bathed and, wearing a wet sari, cooked a meal for the ritual feeding of six sumangalis from the village. This was the way married women paid their last respects to another, fortunate enough to die a sumangali. Twelve days later, Amma had ceased to be one.

Amma, without the bright red kumkum. No matter how untidy her clothes from daylong work, how dishevelled her hair or how sweat-stained her face, the kumkum stayed, a velvety drop on her forehead. I used to watch her put a dot of vaseline and then the perfect circle of crimson over it. She kept the kumkum in a little leaf-shaped metal box. Once, she had found me dipping my finger in it.

'Not now,' Amma had said, taking away the box. 'You'll wear it when you marry.'

Amma removed her black and red glass bangles, the ear, nose and toe rings and the mangalsutra. But it was the loss of the red, fragrant drop of kumkum on her forehead that said everything.

Ajja could not face a life without the grinding routine of Ajji's needs, or without Appa, whose love for him remained unchanged even when they quarrelled. The fight had gone out of Ajja. He was meek before the gods, religious in a pathetic, grovelling sort of way. Now he always tied his hair in a grandmotherly knot at the back of his neck and spent all day in the porch. He had given up his easy-chair and instead sat on the bench, staring into the front yard. He made pickles and preserves, sold bananas and vegetables, because there was nothing else to do. When would death come sniffing at Ajja's door? I prayed that it would not take him away unawares, that it would not finish him like some insect, the way it had Appa.

My mind wound itself around death in useless circles and robbed me of sleep. Death was not the opposite of life. A stone does not live, but we do not say it is dead. Did death mean that the person was permanently extinguished? That was what I dreaded most. Was Appa no more? All of medicine was about warding off death but we knew nothing about death itself: passed away, reached heavenly abode, laid to rest; expired, like some drug past its date. Were we all labelled—to last until ___?

I was angry with Appa for having left me when I needed him most. Appa had inspired me, steadied me, asked me to come back to Angheri and when I was all ready to get started, he went. As if I could, as if I would do it without him. And I was angry with myself for my stupidity. If only I had come back earlier. A year had passed since I cleared my exams and I had jealously kept it a secret. Wrong decisions, thoughtless actions and thoughtless silences. They glared at me.

I had to give strength but had none to give. Amma went placidly about her work; she did not break down or weep even once. She talked about Appa in an unsentimental way as if he had just cycled off on some errand. I resented her calm because it enforced a calmness in me, when all I wanted was to sob my heart out. Neither did I have the energy to start treating patients like I had done years ago. The village left me alone and I was glad for it. It was easier to stay unhappy. On the jackfruit tree, high up on the trunk, a giant fruit ripened and rotted. The sour smell filled the air but no one thought of having it cut down. Worms finished it slowly.

A framed photograph of Appa and one of Ajji were put up on the wall in the front room. Time demanded to be filled. Every day at four, Sompa came, to sit in silence, and left when there was just enough light to see him home, his tall figure stooped with a permanent weariness. Then he stopped coming.

Vishnu, only Vishnu was able to carry on unaffected. Occasionally he would get on Appa's cycle and go to the village. I ached at the sound of the creaking wheels just as I did when I sat in Appa's office and wrote in my diary. I wrote copiously, with the pen that used to be Appa's.

Vishnu had been teaching at the school and had been awarded the prize for the best teacher. Strange that Appa, the best teacher Angheri ever had, never won any prize. After Appa's death, Vishnu gave up teaching to look after the farm and do some 'business'. He was more efficient than Appa and his taking over the responsibility meant more money.

Vishnu and Harini stayed in the same house but lived a life of their own. It would not be long before they would move out. Vishnu had added a white-painted gate in front and a low wall around the house. The pillars in the porch, which were once black, were painted blue; a sink was fixed in the kitchen. Everything was bright and new and solid. But in my eyes the house was no longer as solid or as strong as it once had been.

There was also a radio-cum-tape recorder on which Harini listened to film songs and hummed in her sweet, tremulous voice all day. She was a nice girl, but indifferent to anything that did not concern her. Sometimes, in the evenings, I saw Vishnu watching his wife with eyes that were drugged with lust. He tapped his fingers on his thigh and looked at her. I felt a rage tearing through me as I watched him. I need not have envied Harini. She would soon be an unhappy wife.

One morning Amma asked me to take a tumbler of coffee to Vishnu who was to leave for Mysore on work. Harini had finished her bath and was out in the yard drying her hair. Not finding Vishnu in the porch, I went to their room. The door was open and Vishnu stood before a mirror that hung on the wall, combing his hair. He was smiling as he combed his hair and then the two winged lines of moustache on his upper lip. This he moistened with his tongue and ran the comb through. I walked back to the kitchen with the coffee in my hand. Moments later Vishnu appeared. I sat sipping my coffee, not understanding why the sight of Vishnu admiring himself had hurt. He reached for his coffee. 'Why were you spying on me?' he asked.

He talked of taking loans to buy a tractor and a diesel generator for electricity; of building a cement yard round the house to dry grains; of employing workers to help in the fields. Amma wisely let him run the farm. Ajja acquiesced to everything with a timid nod of the head. 'Nin ishta, kano. Your wish.'

Amma was the first to recover. She started going to the paddy fields with Vishnu, she sat at the sewing machine and stitched something or the other. One evening I sat in my room, not reading, not thinking. I could see Gaja husking paddy in the back yard and the dust rising from it in curling loops as she waved the basket up and down to separate the husk from the grain. Amma was in the kitchen and from there came fragrant smells of patte, lavanga and elakki being fried. Nothing but the simplest food had been cooked since the mourning began. My senses swam with the stinging pleasure of anticipation. I went to the porch to see Ajja wipe his nostrils vigorously, fighting the aroma. Amma came carrying a vessel and Budhi followed with the plates. 'Payasa,' Budhi said. He and I sat on either side of Ajja, and Amma served. We ate silently, reverently, minds tuned to the sweetness of the payasa. Amma sat on the ledge with the vessel by her side and she talked. 'If a bullock cart gets stuck on the road, it will block the path. It must move on and work must be done. The paddy has to be cut, the cows have to be milked, the plantains are ready to be sold and there are things to be bought. The cart must keep moving.'

Ajja looked at her. His nose was red and his eyes belligerent. He got up and washed his hands. Next morning he went to the paddy fields with Budhi, and then to the stream. When they came back, Budhi held an injured crow in his hands. They had found it on the bridge made of wooden planks strung across the stream. They spent the rest of the day nursing the crow and feeding it. Late in the evening they left it on the hedge near the gate. It took a few steps and then, flapping its wings awkwardly, flew away. 'Come, let's see if the cows have enough water for the night,' Ajja said, heading for the cowshed.

The cart had begun to move.

A week after my return, Vijai came with her husband and two-year-old son. Their second child was due in two months. They had settled in Mandya and her husband commuted to Mysore for work. Vijai was comfortable in her life and still uninterested in my life in a way that got me frustrated.

I went with Vijai to visit her parents. Shanku Master was courteous, meek. His wife's face wore the same expression of sorrow, without pride in Jai's success or in Vijai's family. Their house now had an extra bedroom with a bathroom, the walls were whitewashed, doors and windows painted. There was new furniture in the living room, a steel almirah, tables and chairs. Shanku Master spoke guardedly; he appeared to be ashamed of the wealth that Jai had provided and preferred to pretend it did not exist.

Every day I told myself I must think about my future. But I had no desire to do anything. Sorrow had taken the edge off my ambition. I was surprised when Sujju told me that I should go back to England. 'Appa's idealism wasn't practical,' she said.

I asked her if she knew that I had sent money to Appa and he had refused it. Sujju smiled. 'He said he would not stand for such vanity. But don't feel bad about it. I think England suited you. You've put on weight, become fairer. Don't stay here because Appa wanted it.'

'No.'

'Go back and work there for some more years. Make enough to get the family out of this village.'

'Why should we get out of here?'

'There's no money in farming. See what Jai has done for his family. They're so proud of him.' There was envy in her voice.

I argued that Angheri was a better place to live in than any city. We talked back and forth. 'When we were children, everyone said that I would cause problems for the family, never you. It's turned out otherwise. You've been the problem. First you refuse marriage. Now you don't want to help the family.'

I was silent. 'You must have met nice men in England,' she said. 'Doctors, surgeons. Tell me if there's anyone.'

'There isn't.'

She eyed me closely. 'I guessed right. There *is* someone. Don't give it all up, Nalli. It doesn't matter who. I can convince the family.'

'Then why don't you convince them that I've no desire to get married? If I can be a doctor, why can't I decide not to marry and choose where I work?'

Sujju was angry. 'I never had your opportunities, but I made the best of what I got. I married Kaviraj. If better luck had come along, I'd have grabbed it. I used to envy you for being clever, but not any more. You're not clever.'

With Appa gone and Jai far away, the village hospital was not talked about. No one asked me. Was that all it took—the death of one man—to divert them from a purpose? I went for walks, taking care to avoid meeting people. Peshwa, the tortoise which Jai had given to Budhi, kept me company with his uncomplaining presence. When hungry he would brush against my legs, stretch out his neck, which was like Ajja's, and look at me with trusting eyes. One day I decided to walk to the stream and get some of the yellow flowers which Peshwa loved to eat. Stepping carefully on stones that were slimed over with moss I reached the strip of water. I hitched my sari to my knees and tucked it in at the waist. Standing with my feet apart, I bent forward, straining my calf muscles to steady myself, and picked an entire bunch.

How strange that a little thing like plucking those flowers should raise my spirits and my confidence, but it did. It connected me with the Jai of my childhood and with the dream I had held on to all this while. I began to notice things: how thick and long Harini's hair was, the delicious avalakki at breakfast, how like a delicate scarf the mist wrapped itself around the hills and how the leaves on the banana trees waved their clean feathery leaves that were spliced and shredded by the wind.

'I'm going to Madras to meet my professor,' I told the family. 'And then to Bombay to talk things over with Jai.'

30

Jai had sent two telegrams and a letter to condole the deaths. He was going to Switzerland on a four-week fellowship in advanced endoscopy. When he returned, he wanted to talk. Typical of Jai to make such statements without saying how and when it would be possible.

I booked my ticket to Bombay. I would stop in Madras for two days and meet Bansali. But first, there was one person I had to meet in Mysore. I found Sridevi in the male surgical, adjusting an intravenous line. She finished attending to the patient and then greeted me with, 'Is it time for coffee?'

We went to the canteen. Sridevi was eager to hear about my training in England and life in a foreign country. When I told her my plans, she was happy. 'I'm glad you're not joining here,' she said. 'It's too bad now.' An hour later I saw her to the wards. As she walked away, I had the strange feeling of being back there in the male surgical, struggling with blunt needles and intravenous lines in my inept hands. Toppi. Sabari. Shiva. Ponnamma Matron. Don't forget, don't forget, I told myself as I made my way to the railway station and boarded the train.

At Madras Central I managed to get one of the retiring rooms inside the station. Having bathed and changed, I came out of the station and stood at the entrance where autos stopped to deposit passengers.

An auto came soon enough. The passenger inside got down with his luggage and was fishing in his pockets for his wallet. I recognized the back of his balding head. 'Nigam?'

He turned around. The face looked so different, I thought I had made a mistake. 'You!' he said, grabbing my hand. We jabbered excitedly until the auto-rickshaw driver yelled that he could not wait all day for us to finish talking. Nigam paid him and then we stood there talking about the years since we had last met. Nigam had moved to Madras soon after his internship. He was a lecturer in medicine, and a partner with three others in a polyclinic in Nungambakkam. He had lost weight and his chubby face was thin. I used to think he would look good if he was slim but seeing him now I realized that some people were better fat. I teased him about it and asked whether he remembered the Mysore bondas in the canteen. 'Get me a Nigam Special,' he used to tell Srini. It meant three bondas, the size of cricket balls, each decorated with a sprig of coriander.

He laughed, obviously embarrassed. 'I'm more refined now. The cigarettes are down to 16.5 a day.'

I looked hard at him, hoping to see something of the old Nigam. He asked about my work. 'You stayed with surgery and I did not,' he said. 'It happens. I too wanted to go abroad. Instead I got married. We have a son, and now it's difficult. When are you going back to England?'

I told him about the hospital in Angheri and my plans of working there. 'That's good,' he said but the tone of his voice was disapproving. It was as if suddenly there was nothing more to talk about. I began to explain a little more, when he cut in: 'Why don't you join us in the polyclinic? We need a surgeon.' He said it half-heartedly as though he himself was unconvinced. He was going to Salem on some work and it was time for his train. We said goodbye, knowing that the next time we met, if we did, we would be less chatty. Nigam melted away into the

crowds heading for the platforms. I got an auto and went to college.

Bansali looked older but his movements were lithe, the poise in his small frame intact. His right forearm was in plaster: fracture both bones, from a fall outside the OT a week earlier. We sat in his office, the same office where a few years ago he had spoken to me plainly about my objectives. I told him about Liverpool and the infirmary where he had worked twenty-five years earlier. And about Rose Mountain. 'Oh, Rose . . .' he said, grinning. I returned his leather-bound file of notes, aware of the privilege that had been bestowed on me. It had been a useful ally. No matter which surgical book I read, I had referred to his notes for reassurance.

He scratched his chin with his plastered hand. 'You're here till Friday evening? Good. You can do my list for me tomorrow.'

I looked frantically for an excuse. 'I have to catch the train at six.'

'Gurudakshina,' he was saying. 'My assistant's away and I don't want to subject the patients to any of the trainees. You'd better see the cases now.'

The small hope that Bansali was joking faded when he introduced me to his juniors and announced that I would be doing the list. I had not expected that I would have to prove myself to him in this way. 'There's nothing much,' Bansali said. 'A vagotomy-GJ, a below-knee, a Psoas abscess, and a few its and bits.'

Psoas abscess? I had never done one before. As a student I had seen a few cases but knew nothing of the surgery. I examined the eighteen-year-old boy with the tender lump that extended from his loin to the groin. An X-ray of the spine showed destruction of the twelfth thoracic vertebra. The abscess had formed from the pus that tracked down from the diseased bone. A classic textbook case of tuberculosis of the spine, and I did not know what to do: an FRCS ignorant of a surgical procedure. I could not possibly sneak up to the library and read.

Bansali had guessed. 'The Psoas abscess, in case you haven't done one, is simple. Lumbar incision.' He showed me on a piece of paper. 'Extra-peritoneal approach. You'll find several litres of pus in there. But mind you, don't go into the peritoneum.'

He gave me a lift to the station in his green Ambassador with its worn-out seats and broken door handles. 'Come home for lunch when you finish the list tomorrow,' he said. 'You know my place. It doesn't matter what time.'

The Theatre next day was dismal. Surgeons walked in without a change of clothes; a lady doctor came inside wearing a sari, her plaits swinging behind her. Most cases were done without the surgical gown, with only mask and gloves for protection. I tried not to show my surprise when coffee and vadais were brought into the side room, or when the anaesthetist strolled in for a case with the coffee cup in his hands. I was unused to working without cautery, and the vagotomy took twice as long as in England. The surgical gown clung to my chest and sweat poured down my face. After the first case I relaxed. The Psoas abscess went off well. The its-and-bits were done with patients sitting in the corridor.

It was half-past four when I reached Bansali's house. He was not surprised that I had taken so long. When I had eaten, he asked about my plans and I asked his advice.

'I'm interested in your future but not in the decision-making. Did you wonder why I never asked you to join me here?' I had been hurt, but I denied it. 'Or why I wanted you to operate in our Theatre? Not out of any great regard for your skills. I wanted you to see things as they are.' He sounded bitter. 'There is no will, no purpose. We have a committee for every problem but the problems don't get solved. Meetings twice a week—drug committee meeting, waste disposal meeting, medical ethics meeting. We even have a committee for revival of old values. Nobody cares. I'm a carping old man, so I protest.'

He spoke to me as if I were a colleague. 'It hardly matters whether you work in a city or a village. Clever doctors are as easy to find as flowers in a garden. Good doctors? Talent means taking risks. If one doesn't have talent, that's all right. But to not use talent is—a life wasted.'

For some reason, I remembered Selby and his terrible

disaster with Brian Haggart. I told Bansali. He leant forward and thrust his face belligerently at me. 'A surgeon is entitled to only one type of fear, and that is surgical fear. Without it, you can get too complacent and then mistakes happen. Don't ever lose your surgical fear. You must learn to carry it around without losing your confidence. About everything else, be fearless.' Then he said, almost gently, 'What I mean is, you must take risks, even with your future. You're far too young to worry about money.'

Before I left he gave me a box covered in black leather, inside which was an elegant set of instruments—a needle-holder, a pair of long dissecting scissors and fine tissue forceps, toothed and non-toothed. 'Cutlery for the surgeon,' he said. 'Bought them in London twenty years ago. They've seen the insides of hundreds of patients, cut into VIP bellies even. You keep them.' He paused and added softly, 'You're at the beginning of your career and I'm nearing the end of mine. I won't say anything so smug as "They'll bring you luck." You can bet they won't grant any favours. I'm only trying to pass on something important.' He bid me an abrupt farewell.

I thanked him and walked away, clutching the box of fortune in my hands.

Bombay. Everything about the city was familiar. The resilience and energy which I had warmed to earlier cheered me again. Jai was thinner and sported a moustache. Bela was lovelier and more fragile. They had moved to a bigger flat in Colaba with three bedrooms and a balcony. Their son Nakul had inherited Bela's looks and Jai's nervous energy. He had the arrogance of a child who has too much too soon. He rode his tricycle, ate his breakfast, played with little motorized cars and worried the maidservant, all at the same time. Bela claimed proudly that he was a difficult child.

'You're brave,' Jai muttered, touching my arm when he first met me in the station. I had expected him to talk more about Appa, and not just for my sake. Appa had moulded an entire generation in the village. Every one of us was beholden to him. But Jai did not talk about him.

He asked if I had met his parents. Were they well? Did they get the new furniture he had ordered from Mysore? Did his mother employ a servant in the house? Had the roof leak been repaired? He seemed concerned about them.

He was one of the most sought-after surgeons in the city. A year ago he had split with his boss and set up on his own. But he still went to work at six and came home after nine in the evening. On the first day of my stay he told me that he had had an endoscopy list that morning. 'Three thousand for two hours' work,' he added casually. He operated almost every day, even Sundays. In Zurich he had acquired the latest gastroscope, with a video camera. 'It's made a huge difference to my practice,' he said. 'There's nothing a patient likes more than seeing a picture of his insides, even if it's only blobs of red and yellow.'

The never-fading sounds of the city woke me early. I got ready and carefully walked around the new carpet which had replaced the beige one. It was a soft, succulent green. I got myself coffee from the kitchen and went into the sitting room, determined to talk to Jai. He was ready for the day in neatly pressed trousers, full-sleeved shirt and tie. The maidservant brought him a bowl of cornflakes, milk and sugar on a tray.

'Sorry. I've to leave early,' he said, pouring the milk into the bowl and sprinkling four spoons of sugar on it. 'There's a bile duct at seven, an incisional hernia and then a breast.'

'Is that your breakfast?' I asked.

He grinned. 'Packed with vitamins and iron and easy to eat.' His eyes flickered from me to Bela, who sat trimming her nails, and then back to me. 'Don't mind my rushing like this,' he said, shuffling through some papers on his lap. 'I've a PG lecture in the afternoon.' Balancing his bowl of cornflakes on one knee, he began to read.

How about lunch, I asked. 'He'll grab something from the canteen,' said Bela, not looking up from her nails. 'Problem is, he fills himself with coffee instead of food.' Her tone was appreciative; complaining. She looked tousled, sleepy-eyed and beautiful. 'Want to come home for lunch today, Jai?'

'I'll get some lemon rice. Why don't you two go for a movie?'

Bela and Jai felt that I needed to enjoy myself. What do you want to do today? Shopping? Movie? Beach? Aquarium? In the evenings when Jai returned from work we went out to dinner. We slept at one or two, but in the morning Jai was away at six. When he was home, the phone rang constantly.

They did everything to make me feel at home but there was a restraint, an embarrassment between me and Jai. He was always in a hurry and I was in some way pushing the 'talking to Jai' to another moment, another day. His mannerisms bewitched and annoyed me: the way he stroked his moustache as he talked, the secret amusement around his mouth. And the way he still glanced sideways with that look of inexplicable dread in his eyes.

There was little time. I told Jai that we had to talk and he said, 'We will. What's the hurry?' Three days went by. I would be leaving on the fifth evening. I asked Bela how she felt about settling in Angheri. In her impractical way she believed that they would live the way they did in Bombay. They had visited the village twice together and everyone had liked her. She took to Jai's parents without strain. I knew the strain was entirely on Jai, who was anxious to prevent any discord with the family.

On the fourth morning Bela said there was a party to attend. 'It's at Singhania's. You'll have to come,' she said. Singhania was the CEO of a major drug company. Jai had operated on him for gallstones. I protested that I was not keen, but she was insistent. 'You've come for a short time. We must pack in as much as possible. And Singhania's parties are not to be missed.'

The parties I had been to in England paled in comparison to what I saw that night. It was held on the terrace of a flat in Malabar Hill. Bar, liveried waiters, barbecue, a ghazal singer and exotic food that was widely praised and sparingly eaten, it had it all. The guests were few and chosen to retain the air of snobbery. I only knew Bela and Jai so I was content to shrink into the background and eat the food, which was very good.

Singhania was a big man with thick silver hair he was proud of. His hand often moved up to smooth it in place. He was expansively courteous, the way people are when they do not have to worry about details or expense. With a flick of his wrist or a lift of his eyebrows he would tell the waiters whom to serve, and what. His wife was slim-built and heavily jewelled. She would have been beautiful if her upper lip was less rigid. She was conscious of this defect and had a habit of thrusting her tongue against her cheek to get a comely expression. It was sad to see her struggle. When she managed to adjust her features, her smile was perfect.

Everyone was trying in some way or the other to appear like someone else. Only Bela did not need to. In beige trousers and a black sleeveless top, with a gold hair clip as her only ornament, and gold dust on her cheeks, lashes and shoulders, hers was the one untroubled face. She had no need to impress, and of course, she was married to Jai. Jai moved between the guests, his shoulders neat beneath his jacket and on his face an expression of polite boredom.

I was enjoying myself in a voyeuristic way when a man, whom I had noticed earlier because of his pedestrian appearance, accosted me. His small face was all mouth and eyes, and remarkably mobile. He walked with a pronounced stoop, strange in someone so young. He looked ordinary and, like me, lost for company. He had headed straight for the bar, and stayed there. 'You need a few drinks—do ya teen—to get you through this farce,' he said, and offered me a rum and cola. 'Best drink in the world. Phikar mat kijiye . . . they're all too busy impressing each other.' He was easily the most garrulous person I had met, but I was grateful to him for having guessed my need. A few sips of rum and I found myself listening intently.

'Who has brought this punishment on you?' He made a face when I told him. 'Ah, the blue-eyed couple. The best place to be at such a party is behind the bar. Hai na? I'll protect you from being devoured by this unmentionable trash.' He would not keep his voice down. We had talked for a few minutes when he took his hand out of the trouser pocket and extended it to me. 'Salim Yusuf. Jai's one-time chela and paon-pakad.'

When I told him I was a doctor, he said, 'Whatever you do, don't work here. A wicked trap, Bombay. A snake pit for the young and innocent. That's what I was when I came ten years ago. Mathura se aaya . . . Kishanji ki janam bhoomi se. Socha tha bahut chaalu hoon. Lekin ullu tha main. Slogged for my MS and what did I get? A coronary at thirty-five. Inferior wall infarct. Kishanji ki kripa se. All this grey hair isn't hereditary. In Bombay, it's a waste of time being good at one's job unless you're blessed with luck *and* talent. Like Jai. After my coronary, I chucked it and joined this X-rated drug firm, as one of the directors, if you please. Mahaneeya Director Saab. In other words, a ghatiya drug peddler. I'm doing well, considering I do so little.'

As I listened, I saw as if in a blur the beautiful women and men gliding about. Silken shoulders, iridescent smiles, cultivated laughter. Perfumes mingling with the smells of cigarettes and whisky. People were always so different at a party and they expected you to be different. But Salim did not expect anything of me. He only wanted to talk.

'Working for a drug firm must be easier than being a surgeon,' I said.

'Suniye ji . . . kisi se bolna mat.' He looked over his shoulder and smirked. 'I spend a lot of time at high-level meetings and conferences, cooling my backside at airports to catch a flight to Delhi or Hyderabad or Madras. I'm also, fortunately, a member of two top-level committees that work towards perfecting every aspect of our beizzati company, namely Committee for Reorganization and Positivism, and Men for Engineering Simple Solutions.' His eyes did a nystagmic dance behind his spectacles. 'CRAP and MESS, you'll have noticed. Our conferences are held in Panchmarhi, Panchgani, Mussoorie and Munnar—where we're insulated from any disturbance. We work all day and finish off with tennis or billiards and go on to more serious discussions behind the bar. The minutes from these conferences run into hundreds of pages.'

He gulped his drink, and helped himself to another. I was not sure if he was just pulling my leg, but he was good company so I continued to listen. 'We're coarse business folk, selling medicines. We know that doctors don't listen to anything we say about the efficacy of a drug. They don't read the scientific bakwas we give away free. All they want are freebies. A ball pen set, a flashy scribble pad, a calendar. Flashier the better. You offer them something and they'll order your cough syrup even if it's rangeen paani, or capsules filled with chalk dust. Some get greedy. They know they're worth more than ball pens and calendars. They're the ones who bring us the profits. They ask you to sponsor a medical conference where they can meet and eat and we can later cheat.'

I protested. 'In Mysore I knew at least three or four who would never do such things.'

'That's what. You can count them on your fingers.' His eyes narrowed. 'You think I'm exaggerating? I can show you drug stores with shelves full of antibiotics which you would never prescribe. Bechte hain paanch, dus rupaiya ke liye, but they cost fifty paisa, no more. A doctor prescribes 1000 capsules, he'll get a table fan delivered home. Ten thousand, and he'll get a TV or a music system or a holiday in Goa. And then, why blame the companies when every one of us is ready to swallow medicines like food? It's quite touching, the way the public *ask* to be suckered. So my boss can buy his BMW and I my Ambassador. I know of a highly reputed company which makes 200 per cent profit on vitamin capsules which most of the people in this room swallow every day. They inspire third-raters like us to emulate them. Phate Nirodh ke aulaad hain hum sub.'

Below us the city glittered; the sea was a crouching expanse of darkness and the stars in the sky subdued. I wondered why it was that I could put up with the strain of being at a party with strangers but could not talk to Jai, the one person I had always been close to.

Jai, who was watching, walked up to us. 'Food's been served,' he said. 'You must be hungry.'

'Chhod yaar,' Salim said, shoving Jai with his elbow. 'There was a time when this guy was worth something. Now all he thinks of is his goddamn practice, can't get him interested in anything else. When the Test match against West Indies was on, and the whole of Bombay was glued to the transistor, he never listened. Isn't that creepy? Get out of this snake pit while there's time. I'm in this narak myself, but at least I know it. I'll be getting out soon.'

Jai laughed and walked away. 'He won't be staying here much longer either,' I said. 'He's starting a hospital in our village.'

Salim spluttered into his drink. 'Village practice and Jai? I'll believe it when it happens.' He paused to get himself another drink. 'I think he's had too much too soon. Kamina is obsessed with work and that's a bad sign. Most successful doctors are afflicted with this sense of mission. Wringing out their guts to impress others. Me included, until the bloody clot got stuck in my coronary. Dekhiye . . . this society, it will love you only if you're either successful or virtuous. I'm incapable of either. But Jai, the bugger's too disciplined. He knows that by doing something well and sticking it out, success is assured. Maybe I'm jealous.'

Salim brought me a plateful of food which I ate gratefully. Just as dinner was over and I thought we could leave, Salim, who was drunk by then, got into an argument with Singhania. 'You know something, you and I ought to be in jail,' he said. 'Your firm plugs drugs to doctors, institutions, hospitals, governments and they in turn fling them at the unsuspecting public. Own up, now. Sach hai ki nahin?'

The CEO laughed his hearty laugh. 'Come, Salim. What you need is food.'

'Fuck your food. The only place for me is behind the bar but today I found this nice young lady to talk to.'

Jai tried to tell Salim that he was being rude.

'And when did *you* become refined? You used to be a decent bugger but that was a long time ago. You had something in *here*,' he patted his chest. 'Now you're a behenchod glamour boy. I can't stand it!' He turned to the CEO's wife, beaming. 'Fine evening, ma'am. Excellent rum. I must have had some eight or nine. I came only for that, really. Your rum beats anyone else's and it makes up for the rest of the shit . . .'

31

I was up early but not early enough to catch Jai before he left for work. Bela phoned the hospitals he worked in to check where he would be. She sent me there in her car. I reached the hospital and told the driver not to wait. I would be returning with Jai.

Twenty-four-hour emergency service. All Specialties, said the luminous blue-on-white board outside. Dr Jayanth, Surgeon and Endoscopy Specialist, it screamed on top. He was in Theatre, on the third floor. An hour of hanging around and I saw Jai emerge through the swing doors. He was in a crumpled green Theatre shirt with the buttons missing and green trousers held at the waist with a drawstring. The Theatre mask had left deep marks on his cheeks and nose, a sign that he had been there a long time.

'I've come to speak to you,' I said. As if it was not obvious.

'Can't we talk at home?' He could not hide his irritation at my having trapped him. 'I'll be back early. Before nine.'

'I must talk to you alone. You've got to make the time.' I tried to control the frustration I felt at the way this conversation had been put off. Four and a half days wasted, and me right there in his home. It looked as if he would refuse. But the frown faded and he relaxed. 'Could do with some coffee,' he said. 'I'll see the ward patients later. Wait a minute while I get changed.'

We went downstairs and across the road to a restaurant, an upmarket place where coffee cost five rupees. Extra strong, I said, so the waiter brought some instant powder. I emptied it into my cup until the coffee was a respectable colour. The place was crowded; the babble of voices and the tinkle of cups seemed to create a space just for the two of us. Sitting there with him, I began to feel a sense of order and peace. The words came spilling out of me.

'You know,' I said, looking around us. 'We should have thought of this earlier. What time is it? Twelve. You can stay here till two, at least? Gives us enough time. Last night, at the party, I was watching all the strangers. I was comfortable talking to that chap, Salim Yusuf. How much easier it should be with you. Me and my stupid fears. As if marriage or the city could have changed you. I like Bela a lot. And Bombay. I don't agree with Salim. Bombay leaves you alone. I mean, it doesn't tamper with what you are.'

An unfathomable look flitted across Jai's face. He glanced at his watch; he held a cigarette in one hand while the fingers of the other drummed the table.

'So, let's talk,' I said. 'All these years when I was away I kept the image of the hospital in my mind, like you explained the first time. You remember? Now, after Appa's accident, everything's come to a halt. I've taken so long to talk to you. You must have wondered what was taking me so long.' The chairs were deep and I hunched forward as I spoke. 'We must plan our budget and get the work started. Make a list of the equipment to be bought and nurses to be hired. I've got savings. It'll be hard for me without Appa but he would not have liked me to waste any more time.'

'You're allowing yourself to be influenced too much by your father,' he said. 'Maestru was too serious. Forever on about poverty, inequality and justice. He was too serious.'

'Not always. He could be great fun. When we were small he used to dance to *Kaggalappana kanive olage* and make us laugh. Really.'

'Imagine remembering something like that. What I mean is, he was too bothered with things that didn't concern him.'

Oh. The old argument. 'He believed that poverty was everyone's business,' I said. 'If we spend too much, someone else will have less.'

Jai shook his head. 'Shows how little he understood about money. By spending, we drive the economy. We provide jobs. It's like this: The new suit I bought last week helps the garment worker in the factory keep his job, it helps the tailor who stitched it earn a living. When I give it to be dry-cleaned and spend twenty rupees, that's someone else helped. Every time I buy something for myself, I'm helping others.'

We were veering away from the issue. 'I stayed in the village for three months before internship, remember? I have first-hand knowledge of the problems there. And I don't think *just* like Appa. I disagreed with him often. He called me his problem child. But he was the biggest influence in my life.'

Jai looked handsomer than ever that day. 'I've been meaning to talk to you,' he said. 'An accomplished surgeon like you will be snapped up like *this*. Wherever. But there's no place like Bombay. I've seen the best hospitals in Switzerland, I've heard all about working in England and the US. This is the place to be in.'

'Not for us,' I said, softly. 'We're close to realizing our dream.'

He covered his mouth with two fingers as he spoke and looked at me without focusing his eyes. His voice was barely audible. 'I have sort of made up my mind. I mean to stay on. I'm a good surgeon, one of the best around here. I have so much to give.'

He twirled a spoon on the tablecloth. Alarm bells rang in my mind. I remembered Carol's game of twirling a spoon to predict the future. If the handle falls facing Jai he'll come to Angheri, I thought. The waiter came and removed the coffee cups and the spoons.

Jai spoke quietly. 'We never imagined surgery advancing like this. Endoscopy. Scanning. Angiograms. There will be more sophistication, more gadgetry. Unless we understand machines, we'll be left behind. And keyhole surgery is all set to become very popular. Our hands will become redundant.'

The word surgery came from 'chirurgia', which meant to work with one's hands. There was no use telling Jai that. 'Angheri can't afford the gadgetry,' I said.

'It'll become affordable in due course.'

I tried to reason. 'In Angheri, there have been cases of malaria. Cows are kept near the houses, the pond is filthy. There is no drainage system. Women stay in bed for forty-five days after delivery. They're fed ghee with sugar but no milk. We have to change all this.'

'What do surgeons have to do with such things?'

'You know what happened to Muruga? He was in school, in Budhi's class.'

'I don't want to know.'

'You have to know. Muruga fell off a tree in Nayaka's coconut grove and landed on a sharp-edged stone: ruptured urethra. In Mysore, nothing could be done without money at every step. He ended up with the urine leaking through a fistulous opening in the scrotum. He came back to Angheri, stinking like death, stayed two weeks and then disappeared. Went away to die.'

His voice was sharp. 'If I go back to the village, I can't bring back Muruga. And what makes you think that things are any better for the poor folk in Bombay? I can do service here too.'

'You know what I'm saying. All the doctors crowd in the cities and forget the villages where most of our people live. Something like seventy or seventy-five per cent. If we don't go to Angheri, no one will, except quacks.'

'Exactly. And we'll be misfits. Let the village improve. Let the villagers show that they can keep a surgeon busy. If you go now and work with the quacks, they'll say it's because you're not good enough for a city. And the hospital—it won't be easy for you to handle the construction. Contractors, builders, engineers, then buying the equipment.'

'It's difficult but possible.'

'Who cares about our miserable village? If I achieve something there, no one will know. I like to have someone to compete with. Someone looking over my shoulder and applauding. In my most desperate moments, when we were in the dung heap, I wanted it. I was madly jealous, even of your family. The way I worked in the fields, and lived on rice and buttermilk. Dig, plough, sow, reap and carry heavy sacks meant for beasts twice my size. By the time I was thirty, I'd be fifty. What for? My sisters sewed the gunnysacks of paddy for sale, using monstrous needles until their hands were as rough as jute. I want to give them something better. The village is proud of me, even though *you* don't say it. Last year I was honoured at a school function as the most outstanding student. Our own Jayanth is a big doctor in Bombay, they say. I have no illusions. Any ordinary doctor can work in a village.'

I tried to control my panic. Did he really mean all this? 'Gowramma's niece died of worms blocking her gut. Karim Darzi's daughter Subeida bled after her third child and no one in the village could save her. Narayana's older brother died of a bleeding ulcer on his way to Mysore. If we set up our hospital, cases will come not only from Angheri but other villages, right up to Mysore.'

'Your friend Gowramma's here, in City Hospital.' He had not thought of telling me till now. 'She phoned me once. She has more sense. She knows what Bombay has to offer. We have to bring our villagers out of their coarse existence. Look, I really meant it when I talked about the hospital. I wanted to give our village so many things. Health, education, a chance to earn and live better. I didn't know then, but I know now that there's no point investing in a village. They will cease to exist, and rightly so.'

I must have known it all along somewhere in my heart, that Jai would back out. 'You're a traitor,' I said. 'You had given your word.'

He seemed, momentarily, to lose his cool. 'You're getting emotional and that's bad for a doctor. We change as people. And our dreams change too. Sure, as a young boy I had certain dreams. Small, ridiculous dreams. They changed, thank goodness. Try to be calm, Nalli. Your head is full of this honesty-goodness thing. You must stop thinking of these things all the time.'

'And start thinking of profound things like money.'

'Life isn't like that.'

'It used to be.'

Anger rose inside me, but I was beginning to tire. I let him speak. 'If you had been as close to poverty as me, you would understand why I want only the opposite of poverty. Yes, the opposite. In everything.'

'How do you decide when you've arrived at this opposite?'

He closed his eyes. 'Going to buy a house in Bangalore.

Palace Orchards. For once- or twice-yearly visits. Maybe get a flat somewhere, as investment.' He leaned forward, suddenly earnest. 'Nalli, I'll do things for the village, I promise. I'll introduce the people to good business. Show them how to boost the economy.'

'I can see it,' I said bitterly. 'Jayanth Talkies, Jayanth Petrol Station, Jayanth Hotel . . .'

'Your training in England hasn't changed you,' he said, his voice taking on an accusing tone. 'Look at me. I want never to have to worry about money. Maybe then I'll start a hospital.' He lit another cigarette, with deliberate slowness, sure that now he was in control. 'We must brush aside anything that may come in the way of being good surgeons. I'm not trying to discourage you or dismiss your talent, after all your professor picked you out. But you lack ambition and scientific curiosity. Doctors need both. If you have any respect for the profession, you'll strike root in a city. You're impractical, that's been your problem, always. The one person who must take the blame for setting our country back is Gandhi. Glorifying villages. He set us *fifty* years behind. We could have been up *there* with America, England, Japan. They're never satisfied with what they have. That's the key. Not to be satisfied, never to say I have enough. To crave for something bigger and better. You don't want me to turn my back on my talent, do you?'

I remembered what Bansali had said about talent. I had scribbled it down in my notebook and read it many times. It was the ability to work on a mere hunch. It was having an audacious belief in something no one else believed in. Jai had skill. I was not so sure about talent.

'You can't leave Bombay except for a very big reason. It is *the* place for a surgeon. We're worshipped here.'

Worshipped. Like the deities in Ajja's room, standing forever on the mantel, choking with the smell of incense, listening to ceaseless demands.

'I want to send every patient home with a smile,' he said. 'Customer satisfaction. Have I told you how I manage to do so many cases?' He had trained Shivkumar, his driver, to assist him in surgery. He drove to the hospital ahead of Jai, set up the equipment and started the case. Jai took a taxi and reached in time to do the important bit. Shivkumar could open and close most routine cases. 'Unlike junior doctors, he knows his limits. And I don't have to pay him a lot. Of course, I keep him happy. Bela buys gifts for his kids' birthdays . . . sends sweets for Diwali and New Year.'

He finished his coffee, caught the waiter's eye and tapped lightly on his cup. The waiter hurried forward to pour fresh coffee. I refused a second cup.

'We need money. What do we need gratitude for when we have money? Look at your father with his principles. I'm not sneering at him but what did he achieve? He got a lot of gratitude but money would have served him better. Went around on a bicycle till the end.'

A long time ago, Jai had punished Rumba with his mindless violence. Now he was punishing me. The silence hung between us—it seemed so long but could not have been more than thirty seconds. I heard a customer ask the waiter for a tomato omelette. My mind dwelt uselessly on the omelette he would soon eat. Jai resumed talking and I heard, momentarily, the Jai of my past, the Jai who had filled my universe. 'This is where we will build our hospital, Nalli . . . here we will have the OT, here the outpatient complex and there the wards. Patients will come from everywhere . . .' My mind was backing away, running to the past when we had chased a dream together. When we were children, Vishnu had kicked the hospital I had built into a shapeless lump of mud. Now Jai was trampling on it. It was ridiculous to feel hurt, but I was devastated.

'I do good, too,' Jai was saying. 'Once a month, I operate at a charitable hospital. Fifteen hundred for a gall bladder. Good for my reputation. In Jaslok I charge five thousand.'

'It's against the law, what you're doing, getting a driver to assist. You could get juniors, or medical students. You could teach them . . .'

'I care two paisa for medical students,' he said coldly. 'I've come up the hard way, haven't I? Slogged for two years and my boss paid me a measly thousand. Four of us shared a room at the hospital. Two beds, two to a bed. Clothes slung on a rope, shoes, books, soap-dish and razor on the floor. That's the life I had for two years. Did my boss feel guilty? Last month when my earnings touched fifty thousand, I treated the Theatre staff— that's fifteen including the ward boy and ayah—to cold drinks and samosas. How happy it made them.'

'Your parents will be disappointed,' I said feebly.

His eyes became hard. 'You said once that you did not like my father. I hate him. Now he's trapped. I'm the provider.' He smiled, not a false smile but an unnatural one. 'For all his brahminism, he's always been greedy.'

Jai's hands trembled as he lit another cigarette. 'You're too self-righteous. The way you talk, trying to make me feel guilty about success. And when I give you some good advice, you dismiss it.'

Jai was trying to acquit himself. He transferred the blame, if there was blame, on to me. It was I who had wronged him. 'Never mind,' he said. 'Can't we leave our differences and be friends?'

In spite of myself, my heart melted. We sat tight-lipped for a few minutes, each feeling sorry for the other and helpless because we could not change things. Jai remembered that patients would be waiting. I got up, determined to walk away with dignity. A sob wrenched me as I went. Jai's eyes were on my back. I did not look back at his eyes asking that I understand. I would not. I would not.

～

The City Hospital was in the same part of the city and I could get there in twenty minutes if I walked. It was an obviously poor area. The hospital was on the seventh and eighth floors of a multi-storeyed building near a busy intersection next to a temple. I saw a group of nurses going home after the day shift and asked for Gowramma. Someone phoned her ward and she came quickly. She was stouter; the nurse's frock was tight around her arms and middle. Her hands were sweaty as she clasped mine, her gong-like laughter loud. She changed quickly and insisted on taking me home.

We went by bus. 'We're lucky to have a good house,' she said. 'It's very difficult to get one here. Gopal is a nightwatchman in Juhu, he has contacts. He drops me at the hospital on his moped every morning and I go back by bus.'

Gowru was impressed that I was staying with Jai and Bela. 'Must be a posh house, no? He came to City Hospital once, for a special consultation. But I didn't disturb—he's so busy. Only once I phoned. He was so nice.'

I told her that he had let down the village by going back on his word. 'How can he work in Angheri?' she asked. 'He's famous here. One of the best.'

'He promised.' I explained what it had meant to me, to Appa and the village.

Gowru didn't say anything more until we reached their home, near Mahim. It was a slum house of two rooms and smaller than their thatched hut in the village. In a corner of the room she lit a kerosene stove and made tea. While we drank it, she grated coconut and chopped onions.

'Jai can do so much here, in Bombay,' she said. 'This city has everything to keep a good surgeon happy. Lots of diseases, lots of money, lots of poor people. In Angheri I wasn't even aware that we were poor. Here we're aware of it all the time. Money is just round the corner, speaking in a very loud voice. Rupees slipping through the fingers of other people. Another world, but right here. I know a doctor's family, they own three cars, and they're four people. That's wealth. Jai won't want to go back.' She sprinkled a heap of dry avalakki on the chopped onions and mixed briskly with her fingers. 'But, if he does start a hospital . . . you think I can get a job? I'd like to go back if there was a job. In Angheri, I could have a small garden in front of the house.' Her eyes grew dreamy.

'The hospital will start,' I promised. 'And you'll be the head nurse.'

Her children, Neeraja and Asoka, came home from school in time for the baale murukku and fried avalakki. Gopal was giving tuitions to high-school students. He would be back at seven to eat, before setting out for work. Gowru wanted me to meet Gopal. We walked to a house not far from where they lived. It was a smaller house than theirs, with about twenty students crammed inside. Gopal came out, stood with us for a few minutes and went back to his students. At half-past six Gowru took me to the bus stop where I would get a bus to Colaba. As we waited for the bus, I said how hard it must be for them to live in a slum.

'Slum?' Gowru was taken aback. 'This isn't a slum, these are respectable middle-class homes. Professionals live here. Teachers, lecturers, bank officials, nurses. We have all the facilities. We get water for half an hour, morning and evening. Electricity all day. We have a computer training centre and a beauty parlour. Come, I'll show you a slum.' I protested that I would be late but Gowru was insistent.

She led the way behind the cluster of shacks to a narrow road. On the opposite side was a large maidan piled high with garbage. 'Come.' We walked along a narrower mud path across the maidan. 'Cover your nose if you don't want to vomit,' she said cheerfully, stepping over a puddle of water thick with scum. Five minutes later we were on the other side: dreary clusters of sacks and tin, tyre and plastic; palsied huts that shuddered in the wind; thousands and thousands of shacks as far as eyes could see. 'It goes on for miles,' Gowru said. 'Someone wrote in the papers that these were the insect millions who ruined the beauty of the city. But they too pay rent . . .'

In Angheri, Gowru and her family had lived away from the rest of the village, in the ukkada, on a barren stretch of land below the hills. There was a small pond adjacent, where they washed their clothes, their cows and buffaloes. Their house was better than many others. With a potter's sense of the aesthetic, her father had built a low mud wall enclosing a narrow strip of earth—about one-fourth the size of our porch. Here Gowru tended flowers—dahlias, rajakirita, jasmine, sampige, kanakambara and dasavala. A small patch was marked off with stones for three rose bushes. Gowru watered and manured her plants with love. In the evenings, after school, she went out to collect dung. She carried it home, mixed it with water and left it overnight. In the morning before the sun was out she watered her plants with the nourishing mix of dung and water. Her roses, small and pink, bloomed all through the year. Gowru never asked me home but once I had strayed across. I could not imagine anything more beautiful than those tightly whorled, fragrant roses on sparkling well-fed bushes. From then on, I would plague Gowru to tell me about the flowers in her garden. With her irrepressible grin, Gowru, who sat in the fifth row in class, would communicate with me in the second row across the room. I waited for the teacher to busy herself with correcting answer papers. Turning around, I mimed my question to Gowru: *How many roses?*

Gowru showed me with her fingers: *10+10+1 . . . twenty-one roses*. She confirmed this with vigorous nods.

Bring me one.

I'll bring two. Roses the colour of your langa day before yesterday. Such generosity.

If there was one person I wanted to change places with, it was Gowru. Everthing about her, the gong-like laugh, the oiled plaits, her wonderful garden, were enviable. Even now, after seeing her in her slum house, which she preferred to call a middle-class home, I was envious.

That night, Bela said, 'It's wonderful the way Jai and you can have such an argument and be friends. If he doesn't want to go back, you shouldn't feel hurt.' Jai promised to help me settle in the city, make contacts, get attached to a hospital or two. He spoke of the wide range of surgery we could do between us. He had the money to buy more equipment. Bank loans would not be a problem. I could stay with them as long as it suited me.

On the fifth morning I was up early, too early, but the traffic was already a din. I sat on the bed, scowling at the carpet which mocked me with its likeness to the green of paddy fields. A few hours later I boarded the train.

When the train reached Madras I found a room in a lodge near the station where I stayed three days. I did not want to meet Bansali, or anyone else. I sat within the timid confines of the room, staring at the cream-coloured walls and the door that led to the corridor. I did not look at my watch, for I had entered a cul-de-sac that was outside of Time. The hot rays of the sun slanted onto the bed and, later in the evening, shadows crept along the floor, telling me that it was the end of another day. I imagined someone weighing my happiness level each day— today it's 2 kg, tomorrow 2.01 kg, yesterday 2.02. Would the state of my mind affect the sum of all the happiness in the world? Nonsense.

Memories as thin as air and hard as nails. I wanted to reach out to Appa and talk to him but all I got was the vision of the young man foraging for food in the garbage pile. I struggled to shake myself free from such wretched images but the state of my mind reinforced it. The only thing is to not forget, Appa said. Why? I wished I could forget that young man and also the stupid dream I had dreamt with Jai and build a life altogether new. Jai had built a new life and made a success of it.

During the day I made forays from my room to a tea-and-dosai stand near the station and filled my flask with tea. The young man who served the tea was always busy. There was a patch of wet ground for about three feet around the shop from washing the cups. I stood outside that radius and waited for my flask to be filled. After the first few rounds of flask filling, he would simply reached for my flask and ask, 'Three or four?' I never bought less. He was always busy, boiling tea, serving, washing the cups. If he did not have too many customers he made special tea for me with a pinch of cardamom, even though I never asked for it. On the first day he charged me fifty paise for a cup. Later he cut it to forty paise. He kept buns, biscuits, mixture and roasted groundnuts in glass bottles. The buns were thirty paise when fresh and twenty when stale.

The dosai stand, which was open only in the evenings, was a huge metal drum with an opening for coals to be put inside. On top was a tawa fixed to the mouth of the drum. The young man poured a small cup of dosai batter on to the hot tawa and spread it with another cup. It cooked instantly. He lifted it off and slapped it on to a plate with some chutney. A young girl, perhaps his sister, sat on the ground washing plates and slicing onions. His family lived in the two dark rooms behind the shack. Late in the evenings his father delivered a stack of bread-omelettes wrapped in newspaper to the stall. Sometimes a woman came out of their house and stood looking curiously while I got my tea. The men who frequented the stall must have wondered who I was. Once in a while there would be catcalls and whistles from some youth and the young man in the stall would silence him with his eyes.

By the time I filled my flask and walked back to the room my body was muggy with sweat. I was trying to prove to myself that I could live cheaply if I had to. I ate a bun for breakfast, vadais for lunch and bread-omelette at night. It cost twelve rupees a day and would have been cheaper if I did not drink so much tea.

I decided to find out something about Carol and Suguna. I had lost touch with them a long time ago. I got a list of old students from the college, spent precious money on telephone calls and finally traced Carol. We had a long chat over the phone. She was married to a doctor and had settled in the outskirts of Bangalore. They had two kids. A year ago Carol had given up her practice and started a hairdressing saloon. 'I earn more now than I did when I was doctoring,' she said. Carol wanted me to go over to Bangalore and stay with her. I promised that I would go, but some other time. I did not want to see an older Carol. Neither of us had been eighteen for a long time . . . But the real reason was that my life suddenly seemed to be in disarray. I needed time with myself.

On my last day in the city, when I heard his mother call him, I found out that the young boy at the tea stall was named Afsar. I should have told him that I was going, but I simply took my flask and walked back to the lodge.

～

Something within had impelled me, even as a girl of five or six, to stand before the gods and ask for *that* thing, not knowing what it was I asked for. Give me *that* only, God, and I won't ever ask for anything else. I'll do everything right. I'll face whatever problems I have to if you give me that. Please.

It was afternoon and only Budhi and I were on the porch. I got a piece of charcoal from the kitchen and drew the squares carefully.

'Are we playing with the marble, Akka, or with the bille?'

'You're not playing, Budhi. I am. Just watch as I jump and stop me if I land on a line, all right? I have to hop into a square every time, and not touch any line.' Closing my eyes and balancing myself on one leg, I jumped.

'What are you whispering, Akka?'

'Nothing.'

'If you don't tell me, I won't help.'

'I'm saying a prayer.'

'You can't pray jumping on one leg!'

'I can.'

'I'll tell Ajja . . .'

I opened my eyes and grabbed him by the back of his neck. 'I'll tell you about it but not a word to anyone.' Having got Budhi's promise, I told him. 'I'm asking God for *that* thing. When I jump on my left leg, if I get the square right twenty times, or if I jump on my right leg and get the square right twenty-five times, God will give me *that* thing.'

'What's *that* thing?'

'If I tell you, I won't get it.'

Budhi understood. I got the square right nine or ten times but not more. 'Why don't you reduce the number of squares?' Budhi asked.

'I can't cheat.'

'Then you won't get it, akka.'

'I will, I will, I will . . .'

The first thing I did when I got home from Madras was tell the family that I would start the hospital on my own. I had money saved. With loans from the bank, I could build a small place.

Five beds. I would start with minor surgery and allow the hospital to grow.

Amma said there was no need to rush into it. 'This isn't the time, Nalli.'

Ajja only said, 'Ask Kamu. Kamu will know what to do.'

Vishnu was more direct. 'It won't work.'

We were in the kitchen. Vishnu rose from his chair. 'Come, I'll tell you,' he said, and walked out. Standing beneath the parijata tree, on a carpet of white flowers, he smirked, 'So Kulla ditched you?'

I turned around to walk away. 'Wait.' He was amused by my anger. 'There's been a lot of talk going on here, I might as well tell you. Most people in the village feel that you're not competent enough to handle a hospital.'

I did not believe him. 'You're just saying it to put me off. I'm being practical. Five beds. I can help the people here. I'm a good doctor.'

'That's not what the villagers think. When you were in England, many women here followed your advice and went to Mysore for delivery. They were admitted in filthy wards, cut up when there was no need. Sarala—you remember Sarala?—was left unattended during the delivery. Her womb was torn as a result and it cost them nine thousand rupees and two months in hospital.' Vishnu paced up and down as he talked, as if he was delivering a judgement. 'They blame you for having advised the women to go to Mysore when they were better off delivering at home. The villagers feel that you want to work in Angheri so you can feed the doctors in Mysore with patients and in turn get paid by them.'

He stopped my protests. 'It's not that we believe you'll do such a thing. But—you're a woman. It's difficult here. It will be better for you, and us, if you work elsewhere.'

Long after darkness fell, I sat by the window, straining my eyes to see the hills. The night was starless and deep; dry twigs on a branch of the guava tree snapped and crackled in the wind. The flame of the lamp which Ajja had lit for puja had guttered and the smell of burnt wick filled the air. The people of Angheri had rejected me. They could manage without me.

Appa's death. Jai's refusal. Now this. What reason did I have to hang on?

In the morning I went to meet the Vaidyar. He was heating a mixture of oils for someone with joint pains but came out when he heard I had come. He had thinned with age but his face was sharp and his eyes keen. The fleshy earlobes which had fascinated me as a child seemed to have lengthened. They almost brushed his bony shoulders. We sat in the small veranda in front of their house. I told him everything.

'Why should you let other people decide your worth?' he asked. 'You know how good you are.'

'I want to work in Angheri but they don't want me,' I said.

'It is their ignorance that makes them say these things,' Vaidyar said. 'It is the most paralysing of all diseases. You will have to give them more time. Go as far away as you dare, find a place where the people need you. And dip your hands in work.'

part three

One should travel with a companion of equal mind, or one who has a better mind; one had better travel alone than travel with a fool.

—The Buddha

32

It was a bumpy ride, over four pothole-ridden kilometres from the railway station. I clutched the scorched blue Rexine seat as the cycle rickshaw veered sharply through the hospital gates. A swami waited at the steps to greet me.

Keshavganj was four hours south-east of Delhi, two days by train from Madras. I had seen the job advertised in the newspapers and applied. Until then Keshavganj was just the name of a town I had read about somewhere. I could not remember what I had read; it did not matter. I felt no curiosity about the place where I would work.

There had been no arguments against my going; the family was used to farewells. Ajja and Amma saw me off at the gate, and Vishnu and Harini came up to the bus stop. Before I left I asked Amma for the Pilot pen which had belonged to Appa. In the train, I sat with the red diary on my lap and the pen in my hand. I opened it, haphazardly, to a blank page somewhere in the middle of the diary and wrote in big, bold letters: NOT GOING BACK. Then I put the diary away in my bag and looked out of the window as the train sped on its way. The unending expanses of fields, the muddy villages and the seething jungle of disordered towns were not concerned with my life. They dragged my mind away from my thoughts.

The ambulance from the hospital was to meet me at the station. But it had developed a last-minute snag and so the driver—a garrulous youth named Bishan—came to escort me on a rickshaw.

'This is a holy place,' he explained, climbing into a second rickshaw with some of my luggage. 'Sri Krishna grazed his cows in the scrub forests around Keshavganj. People come for darshan at the temples and foreigners come to take pictures.' Cows led by present-day cattleherds grazed on dust-choked grass on the sides of the road. A bus spilling over with passengers overtook our rickshaws. Rickety cycles, bullock carts and a two-wheeler with four passengers went past; barefoot men and bald, kyphotic women shuffled along. The riches of poverty were everywhere.

The hospital itself comprised several single-storeyed buildings spread over two acres of land. It had a neat garden, a water tank and a vegetable patch. Set apart from the hospital was the monastery where the sadhus lived and the mandir with a statue of the swami who had founded the monastic order a hundred years ago. I had been allotted one of the four bachelor houses: veranda, living room, kitchen and bathroom-toilet. The swami who met me at the stairs said I could eat in the dining hall until I was settled. Some of the hospital staff ate there every day. I sat, like everyone else, on a low stool and ate rice, chapattis, sookha sabzi and dal, curds which were naturally sweet and a banana. A quick meal eaten in silence, after which I washed my steel thali at the stone sink in the corner.

The secretary, also known as the Big Swami, was Vishwananda, a diminutive man of about fifty, less than five feet in height. He had pleasing manners and an agonizing shyness with women. He took me to his office, passing through the main administrative section: a room with four desks, and swamis in saffron and brahmacharis in white typing and filling registers. Milling around one of the desks was a clutch of people, money in hand, paying hospital bills. A swami was explaining why he could not reduce a bill any further. The Big Swami approached and the crowd parted like a curtain. 'Doctore, this is assistant secretary,' he said. The swami behind the desk bowed courteously and got on with his work. He was large and heavily muscled, with protruding teeth and a voice that sounded like sandpaper at work. He was the Small Swami.

The secretary told me that the hospital had started seventy years ago as a dharamshala. Their guru (whom he referred to as Thakurji) along with two disciples used to dispense ayurvedic medicines from the front yard of the dharamshala. In the sixties, a retired medical practitioner joined them and they began to dabble in allopathy. A twenty-bed hospital was built at that time. Twelve years ago came a doctor with an MBBS. More doctors joined, the hospital expanded and they now employed a part-time surgeon from Agra. 'The people here are religious, they visit temples every day,' he said. 'There are two hundred temples but this is the only hospital.'

On the train I had heard that the town had acquired a name for harbouring criminals. Was it true? A minor problem, Big Swami assured me. 'A small number of people take to crime— rival gangs which have fought each other for decades. They don't harm the hospital.' He seemed comfortable with the fact, so I let it rest.

Service was the motive of the sadhus and the hospital was called the Sevashram. Treatment was subsidized because of donations, but the money was never enough. 'I don't know what your reasons are for joining us,' the swami said. 'We don't pay much. Fifteen hundred rupees, with Thakurji's blessings.' Much later he told me that he had wondered if I was an incompetent surgeon in need of a place to hide. The Sevashram had suffered many such doctors. The better surgeons never stayed more than a few months. The hospital was able to cope because of Dr Trivedi, a senior surgeon from Agra Medical College, who came on Saturdays to operate and went back the next day. The resident doctors did minor surgery and what they could not handle was referred to Agra.

That evening I met the other doctors. Dr Narayan, a shy young man from Andhra, looked after the surgical patients and assisted Dr Trivedi. Dr Vanaja, who treated the women, was middle-aged and obese, with an unsmiling button mouth. She had retired from the Army Medical Corps as a Colonel and was doing 'seva' at the hospital in return for food and a place to stay. Dr Singhal, also retired, dealt with the medical cases. Dr Dharma Tejus supervised the lab, X-ray and Theatre, besides giving anaesthesia. The Swami asked him if he would show me the Theatre and explain how they functioned.

Dr Tejus was thick-waisted with a barrel-chest and a neck that gave an impression of strength. His hair was speckled white and his smile exasperatingly unhurried. He walked clumsily, as if his joints did not work, and listened with polite unconcern to the swami tell him that I was a surgeon trained in England. Smoking all the while that he showed me around (except in Theatre), he gave me the details in a lazy monotone. Work at the hospital started at seven with ward rounds, after which there was outpatients' until eleven. Patients came in tractors, carts and tempos. Those very ill were brought on stretchers made of bamboo. Some came across the Yamuna in boats. All the patients paid a fifty-paise fee to see the doctor. Blood tests, tablets and injections came free. There was a constant clamour for sooiyan—penicillin, streptomycin or B-complex injections.

Early next morning I opened the door to a frantic knock, and in walked Sapna, the eleven-year-old who would clean and cook for me. Sapna was disrespectful and unafraid but good at her job. She scrubbed and cleaned with energy, constantly wiping her blunt nose on the sleeve of her dress and laughing with her mischief-filled eyes.

'Didi! Baingan banaoon ya bhindi . . .?'

'Baingan. And don't shout so loud.'

'Adrak daloon . . .?'

My Hindi sent her into giggles. In the evenings after work she was a child again, playing hopscotch with Bishan's children. The only work Sapna did not do was clean the toilet. That job belonged to Raghubir, an old man with stick-thin thighs peeping out of khaki shorts. He came dragging his broom and bucket every morning and cleaned the toilets in all the houses. For five rupees a home, each month.

Wednesday was market-day in Keshavganj, and the weekly off at the hospital. Persuaded by Dr Singhal's wife, I went to see *Jai Santoshi Maa* at the local theatre on my first day off. After enduring such films for a few months, I found that the nurses were smarter. They went to Mathura and watched films starring Amitabh, Mithun, Rekha and Hema Malini. In spite of the worn-out seats, creaky fans and the unpredictable power cuts (a noisy generator spluttered into action after fifteen minutes), it was three hours of fun. We followed it up with tricolour barfis and samosas.

The people of Keshavganj were maddeningly frank and inquisitive. I lost count of the number of times I was asked, 'Bachche kitne hain?' I had no children, I told them, and hoped that would be the end of it, but it never was. The next question was inevitable. 'Shaadi hokar kitna saal hua?' 'Shaadi nahin . . .' I mumbled and, before they asked the reason for my not being married, steered the conversation back to the patient. The women touched my sari appreciatively and asked where I had bought it and how much it cost.

It took them much longer to accept me as a surgeon. On outpatient days, the number of patients waiting to see me was pitifully small. Once, in the ward, I offered to show a junior nurse how sutures should be removed, when the patient said, 'I want the dacter to remove my sutures.' He looked at Sukhdev, the ward boy, who he assumed was the doctor. I stood, scissors in hand, furious. When the nurse finally managed to explain to the patient, I went ahead, conscious of the smirk on Sukhdev's face.

As I got to know the people I saw that their lives were harsh. Most were kind and caring to the sick, especially children. Parents took turns to sit up with a sick child. Men missed work and wages for weeks to be there when someone was ill. If a patient died the husband or wife and other relatives would squat near the entrance and rock back and forth, groaning softly. Others would join in to comfort the bereaved. It would go on for hours, the circle of mourners and the din growing all the time until someone helped the bereaved to their feet and led them away.

On my third day at work I was in the plaster room applying a cast for a fractured wrist when Dr Narayan hurried in. A woman had been brought from Barsana: acute abdomen. I washed the plaster off my hands and went to the ward.

Savitri was nineteen. Two days earlier she had developed severe pain in the stomach, with vomiting. She was moribund, with a frail pulse that galloped at a hundred and twenty; her facial muscles were stretched and rigid—the appearance which had classically been described by Hippocrates and was referred to in textbooks as the Hippocratic Facies. She was dehydrated and when a catheter was passed a mere 50 ml of dark urine trickled through the tube. I palpated the abdomen, listened with the steth. No bowel sounds. In all likelihood, it was peritonitis—infection trapped within the abdominal cavity. Only surgery could save her. I explained this to her father and instructed the nurse about the intravenous fluids, antibiotics and blood tests. 'Send for Dr Tejus,' I added, just as he appeared.

Leaving him to see the patient, I went outside the ward to speak to the relatives. One of them asked if Savitri would be able to have children after the surgery. That was the least of her problems, I said. The girl's life was at stake. As we talked, I heard Tejus tell the Small Swami that it would be better to refer the patient to Agra.

'But the doctor, she says she'll operate.'

'She won't be able to handle it.'

'She's well qualified, she's an FRCS.'

'One operates with a scalpel, not a degree. They don't see typhoid peritonitis in England and this one's more than a day old.'

I walked in. 'I can handle it,' I said.

Tejus smiled grimly. 'You may have the confidence but not the competence. How many typhoid perforations have you done?'

I hadn't considered typhoid as the cause of peritonitis. I hadn't seen or done a single case of typhoid. 'You only have to put her to sleep,' I said, aware that Sukhdev was listening with suppressed elation.

'This is no place for bravado,' Tejus said. 'What do you want to do, risk her life?'

'I will operate, unless, of course, *you* lack the competence to anaesthetize her.' Savitri was as much a challenge to the anaesthetist as to the surgeon.

'She'll mess it up,' Tejus told the Swami. 'We should send the patient to Agra. I can phone Dr Trivedi . . .'

'Doctores, please! Do not fight!' implored the Small Swami.

In the end he wisely let the relatives decide, having explained how risky it was to operate on such a sick patient. Without the surgery, she would surely die. Sending her all the way to Agra meant a delay of several hours.

An hour later we were in Theatre. Anger and nervous excitement compounded my unpreparedness. The only blood tests we could do confirmed that the girl was anaemic and toxic, with millions of dangerous bacteria teeming inside her. She had improved with the intravenous fluids and antibiotics, but just a little.

'We'll use a right paramedian,' I said to Narayan, scrubbing my arms with the tiny piece of carbolic soap. I knew that an organ had ruptured and spilled its contents into the abdominal cavity. I could handle that. I prayed that it was not a case of typhoid perforation only because I wanted Tejus to be wrong.

It was my first major case in Keshavganj. The light did not focus, there was little choice of instruments and sutures, the scrub nurse and assistant were not used to me. Worse, the anaesthetist had no faith in my skills.

My fingers trembled as I made the incision. Faecal fluid poured out as soon as I opened the belly. 'Keep suctioning,' I said to Narayan and then realized that it was a manual, foot-operated suction which sucked with a slow whirr. The fluid from the abdomen seeped over the green drapes and on to my feet. I lengthened the incision upward and found, to my horror, faecal matter floating high up in the space below the diaphragm. Tejus had by then taken over the foot suction and was pedalling steadily. I asked for two litres of saline and poured it into the abdomen, while Narayan dipped the suction nozzle into the mucky fluid, sucking it away into a large bottle on the floor. The saline wash would clear away the faecal matter and enable me to see. When it was reasonably dry, I checked the loops of bowel and found gaping holes at different spots along the twenty feet of small intestine. Typhoid. There were six perforations, all of them in the last few feet of the small intestine. The usual pale pink lining of the bowel was now an angry red, pouting at the edges of the holes through which faecal matter oozed. My mind seemed paralysed.

Dharma Tejus was peering in over my shoulder. 'Shall I give her a dose of Chloramphenicol?'

The drug of choice for typhoid. I nodded, grateful, and raised my eyes from the mess for the first time. 'I'll have to resect several feet of ileum. She'll need two units of blood, at least.'

'It's on its way.'

Carefully, I marked out the segments of bowel to be removed. The process of clamp-cut-ligate went on until the damaged bowel was freed from its blood supply and divided between clamps and the four feet of now-black intestine lowered into a basin. I sutured the ends together with catgut and placed two rubber drains inside the abdomen. After irrigating the peritoneal cavity with more saline, I began to close.

The green gown stuck to my body, my cheeks were wet with sweat. 'She's okay,' said Dharma Tejus, as I peeled off my gloves, and added, 'I've sent for some tea.'

I was elated at the thought of having proved Tejus wrong about my abilities but I had to give him his due. 'You were right about it being typhoid,' I said. 'Of course I was,' he retorted. 'History of ten days' fever preceding the pain. Typhoid is the first diagnosis.'

For several days admiring, grateful glances met me everywhere. Savitri improved steadily. Then on the fifth day, when she was started on liquid food, she began to discharge fluid through a drain site. Faecal fistula, a dreaded complication caused by the suture line giving way. I stopped the oral fluids and hoped it was a small split that would close. When three days later fluids were tried again, the discharge became copious. To make it worse, Dr Trivedi came on his weekly visit from Agra and saw Savitri. He was extremely courteous with me but implied that the complication had occurred because of my inexperience. 'You did the anastomosis in four layers? Hmm . . . You used atraumatic clamps? Hmm . . . She will soon go into septic shock . . .' Very kindly he advised me not to venture into major surgery but to assist him until I was proficient. It was futile to try and defend myself.

There was only one thing to do: wait, and hope for a spontaneous closure of the fistula. Such patients could be kept nourished on high-calorie intravenous fluids but it was impossibly expensive. Given her condition, Savitri's recovery was unlikely. Each morning I steeled myself to inspect the dressings soaked with thick brown fluid. There was no sign of healing, even after five, seven, ten days. The relatives who had looked at me with gratitude now eyed me in rebuke. I relived many times the steps of the surgery. Why had the sutures given way? Rough handling. Tension on the bowel edges. Poor technique. Was I guilty of any of this, or did the complication arise because the woman was already ill and anaemic?

Savitri's father was a tall, spare man in a dhoti and banian with a green towel wrapped around his waist. He was there every day, waiting for me to tell him that Savitri was better. But she was not better. I explained that although 'everything' had been done, Savitri was not likely to pull through.

'You do your work, jajjan memsa'ab. She will live,' he said.

Persistence paid. The fluid discharge slackened little by little, the pain lessened and the number of dressings needed went down from five a day to two. The signs of recovery became visible. Savitri started to drink and then to eat. Thirty-eight days after the surgery Savitri left the hospital.

I was anxious to do well and therefore frustrated and unhappy with the condition of the hospital. I pestered the Big Swami about the lack of drugs, the poorly trained staff, the ill-equipped Theatre. He listened quietly and said, 'Do something, doctore.'

The Big Swami had been an engineer before he joined the monastery. Whenever I made a suggestion, he asked questions and, if convinced, acted on it, even if it meant a trip to Delhi for a purchase. He could be persuasive and cunning. And he could bring any conversation to a close with, 'I won't take up more of your time, doctore, I know you're busy.' He was staid but his cheeks held an irrepressible mirth and when he laughed his small frame shook alarmingly and his eyes shone with tears.

The Small Swami was deeply involved in the hospital routine and the problems of every patient. He did not appear too interested in his religious duties. In the evenings after the arati in the mandir, while every other swami stayed for the bhajans, he went back to work. On rare occasions, like Thakurji's birthday, he played the tabla in accompaniment to the singing, his massive shoulders moving with grace. He had a good grasp of medicine and an unusual insight into the outcome of an illness. He was always around, his broad shoulders stooping over a bed, speaking to relatives, or listening to a doctor or a nurse.

A massive bunch of keys constantly jingled in the Small Swami's kurta pocket. Every once in a while a brahmachari would come to ask for it. If the swami had to talk to one of the doctors, he stood near the hedge that skirted the quarters and stared intently at the doctor's house as though willing him or her to appear before the swami and complete the conversation. He had an abiding curiosity in all matters. He was interested in my family, my views on religion, in the quality of garam masala sold in town. When I got to know him better, I asked questions: How did the swamis survive on their monotonous diet? Did they really bathe in cold water in winter? Why did they allow people to touch their feet; were they not in danger of enjoying the sense of superiority? I ranted; the Swami listened. I said religion was futile and he asked with a buck-toothed smile, why, was someone trying to force religion on me?

The Kitchen Swami was devoted to the task of feeding people. Three times a week he went to the market in a cycle rickshaw and returned with sacks of vegetables and provisions. Wheat, mustard and sugar cane were grown in the land behind the monastery. If anyone on the campus ran out of chillies or potatoes it was all right to borrow from the ashram kitchen.

The Stores Swami was lean, with a skeletal grin and a nervous shaking of the head, coupled with an absurd timidity.

As a result, those who helped him in the drug store were lazy and disorganized. The store was an ill-managed godown but if you asked swamiji for a drug he could get it within minutes. There was never a day when a doctor did not stamp down to the drug store with some grievance about a medicine that was not available. The swamiji would listen to complaints with a frightened look in his eyes, his head shaking in a maddening rhythm. He also had the habit of repeating everything you said before replying to it.

'Swamiji, this ointment for burns, it's not what I asked for.'

'It is not what you asked for . . .'

'I said, two-way Foley's catheter, not plain rubber.'

'You said two-way Foley's catheter, not plain rubber . . .'

'Will you get it? Urgently?'

'Get it . . . urgently . . . yes, yes.'

He bungled on, saved by humility and an absolute lack of ill humour. The Stores Swami was also the Mandir Swami, in charge of the day-to-day affairs of the temple. In his spare time he wrote his own compositions. Twice a week, when the evening arati was over, he sang bhajans in his nasal voice. It helped in some way to make up for his clumsiness in the drug store.

The plump, puffy-cheeked swami with light eyes and pupils as small as mustard seeds managed the finances. He was known to be interested in the paranormal and the occult. When not working on his massive registers, he sat poring over some big tome with a title like *Self-Hypnosis*, *Paranormal Visions* or *Occult Experiences in Daily Life*. I did not meet him often. When I did, I was struck by his unblinking stare and the mustard seeds jerking restlessly as he worked out something in his mind. Was it the accounts which preoccupied him, I wondered, or did he actually see other worlds. Months later I would try to find Appa through his voluminous, dog-eared books.

In the hot summer months before the rains, stories were told and listened to. Dr Singhal's wife, my own Sapna and the nurses—sharp-eyed Radhamani and giggly Jessy Kutty—were always full of tales. I heard that Accounts Swami had once disappeared from the ashram. Searches were conducted but there were no clues to be found. He was supposed to have left the monastery and resumed his ordinary life in some secret place across the river. Some said it was his connection with the occult; others associated it with something even less savoury. Three months later he reappeared. After a two-hour debate with the senior swamis, he came back to his job of accounting as if he had returned from a long leave.

One night, Accounts Swami complained of severe abdominal pain. X-rays showed that he had multiple stones in the gall bladder. I said he would need antibiotics. When I started to advise him about a low-fat diet and the possibility of surgery, he quickly got off the examination table. 'I will be all right with an enema and something to ease the pain,' he said.

I tried again to convince him. He listened to me explain that the stones could cause an infection in the gall bladder, or one of them could block the bile duct and cause jaundice. A fat-free diet was the best protection against such complications. 'No fat for three months,' I said. 'Then we can decide about surgery.'

The swami talked, suddenly, volubly, the way patients sometimes do. 'All my ailments are a result of my excessive love for food,' he said. 'Ever since I can remember, I've had a continuous longing to eat.' It was a strange confession from a swami. The few times I had seen him in the dining room, he appeared greedy, almost gluttonous. Sitting across my table in the clinic he looked like any other patient. He had noticed my embarrassment but it did not make him self-conscious. 'Food is not just soothing on the tongue and stomach but a salve for daily strife, for suffering of the soul.' He was still uncomfortable with the pain and was pressing his belly as he spoke. 'I worried about my indulgence much before my parents became anxious. I joined the monastery, hoping that the austere food habits would help me renounce greed. It did not happen. Next to Thakurji, I can't think of anyone, anything that gives me peace and contentment.'

At this point Sukhdev, whom I had sent to the lab on some errand, walked in. The swami shooed him away with his eyes. 'That boy, he likes to gossip, he will go about telling everyone,' he said, with a sad smile. 'I live from one meal to the next. At night I take a sleeping tablet so I can last till morning. You must wonder how such a decadent man can be of any value in a monastic order. May Thakurji forgive me. I have no malice towards anyone.'

'Swamiji,' I said. 'I've told you there's a problem. Gall stones. If you're not strict with yourself, food will give you ill health and worry, not contentment.'

'Can I be strict with a friend? Food is my steadfast, uncomplaining friend. When my stomach is satisfied, I meditate. I transform myself into the bird in the sky, the lizard on the tree trunk, the bee on the champak flower, the dog at the rubbish pile. I listen to the heart of the universe. I am an island of peace. The thought of hot kachori, samosa, rabdi or even a simple dal, makes my spirit content. Doctore, I cannot follow a diet and I will not need the operation. I'll manage.' He was back at work next day.

I asked the swami to lend me one of his books on the other world. 'If I want to communicate with someone who died, will the book help me do it?' I asked. The mustard seeds were still for a while. 'First, you must believe that you can do it,' he said.

Tejus told me that he was the most interesting of all the swamis. 'You have to be careful, though. He thinks too much.'

Among the doctors, Tejus was the most popular. Gaswallah Dacter they called him. His attitude confused me—he was too lazy to stir out of his house soon after a meal, but was willing to stay all night with a patient whose condition was serious. But I had to admit that he was good. He had devised his own modification of a stethoscope, with which he could monitor the patient even when he was several feet away.

Dr Trivedi had favoured Sukhdev as his assistant and allowed him to do minor procedures while he lounged in the tearoom. Sukhdev took his cut from every patient and Trivedi fleeced them with his high rates. Even so, considering that the hospital had only five doctors, eleven nurses, a compounder, a ward boy and three watchmen-cum-helpers, it was efficiently run and affordable. Three months after I joined, Dr Trivedi's services were dispensed with. Sukhdev indulged in minor surgery in a drug store in town. Sometimes a problem occurred and the patient was brought to hospital. But Sukhdev continued to have his clientele.

On Saturdays, the doctors met in a small room adjacent to the plaster room. An aluminium kettle of hot, sweet tea and a plateful of glucose biscuits would arrive from the kitchen at four-thirty. At these weekly meetings, cases were presented and discussed. I dreaded Saturdays because of Tejus. He rebutted me every time, hinting that my foreign degree was not of much use. 'It's not like that in India,' he would say, dismissing my comments. Because of Tejus, I found myself developing a complex. When I went past his quarters, I imagined his mocking glance pursuing me. Bossy and foul-tempered, he was my only problem. He was a favourite with the nurses and the only doctor who got a cup of tea from them at night. That really rankled.

But for Tejus, my life in Keshavganj was almost good; I did not mind the monotony. In the mornings as I combed my hair and smoothed the pleats of my sari, I told Sapna what to cook. Aloo sabzi, sookha lauki, daal or kadi, day after day. Lauki was sometimes replaced by tinda, bhindi or baingan. In winter when the variety of vegetables improved I ate better. Sapna's mother, anxious that I should retain her daughter, would sometimes send puris or mooli rotis. They came in a steel tiffin box which Sapna placed near the kerosene stove, announcing, 'Ma ne bheja hai.' I thought it fit to protest against this largesse but only mildly. I looked forward to seeing the glint of the steel tiffin near the stove.

When the cleaning and cooking were over and on days when she had no one to play with, Sapna lingered, feeding me gossip from Radhakunj, the area where she lived. She told me about the sadhu with the powers to make a childless woman pregnant by feeding her a mango, the witch who tempted men away from their homes and the man who turned into a donkey every full-moon night and brayed till dawn. My curiosity encouraged her, and she had lots more to tell me every time. I had things I could give away to Sapna's family: a pair of slippers, a sari, petticoat, or some trinket. On those days, Sapna's work progressed at top speed. When she finished, she raced off as fast as she could, clutching the packet.

On Sundays, Raghubir paused after his toilet-cleaning ritual, to talk. He greeted me with a namaste, laying down his pail and broom. He had two sons he was trying to put through college and a wife who worked like him. Their colony was exclusively for sweepers, he said. They were planning to build a Hanuman temple there. Why, when already there were so many temples in Keshavganj? 'We cannot go inside. Some temples are good, they allow us to stand outside and pray.' Why did they not protest? 'Aisa hi hai,' he said, explaining the obvious.

⌒

Eight-year-old Sona was the first of the many peculiar cases I encountered in Keshavganj. The girl walked into my clinic hunched over with pain. Her mother was a sharp-tongued dehati who clearly kept her children on a leash. 'Stop your nakhra and get on the bed!' she screamed at the girl. To me she simply said, 'She eats stones.'

The girl climbed on to the couch, more out of fear of her mother than awe of me. Her dark eyes were big on a face that was thin and pinched in pain. She did not let out a whimper as I examined her. Sona was the youngest of eight children. She walked six kilometres from her village to her school. Her mother said that the other children saw her pick up stones along the way and swallow them. Beatings and threats did not work. She had started having severe stomach pains the previous day and had passed some of the stones. The mother produced a rag in which she had them, about a quarter-kilo of gravel, each the size of a gooseberry. Yes, they came from the girl. 'Bahut ziddi hai, dacter sa'ab. Stubborn as a donkey.'

I tried to tell the mother that there was some reason deeper than stubbornness that made the girl eat stones. The mother looked impatient. Just do your work, her eyes said. I did an internal exam: The rectum was full of stones, packed so densely I would not manage to manoeuvre them out without damaging the delicate inner lining of the rectum. I took an X-ray. The rectum and the lower portion of the large intestine, about twelve inches of it, were packed, the stones forming an opaque white pattern like some crazily designed vase. I admitted the girl and attempted to take them out under general anaesthetic. It was not easy and I had to do it in several sittings, stopping each time there was bleeding. When her bowel was reasonably clear, I prescribed liquid paraffin which would ease the remaining stones out in good time.

When Sona went home, I asked her mother if I could keep the stones. She looked at me as if I was mad, took her daughter by the hand and walked away. I never saw them again.

33

The temples ran to full houses, the town overflowed with pilgrims, tourists and wandering sadhus. It was the tumultuous week of Janmashtami. After a busy outpatients' I was heading home for lunch and had stopped to discuss a case with Tejus when the sharp, loud burst of firecrackers reached us. 'Gunshots,' Tejus said and marched back to the wards to alert the staff. Another of his wisecracks, I smirked, and headed home. Ten minutes later, Vedram the watchman was at the door. 'Goli maar,' he shouted and sprinted back to the wards.

I rushed out. Crowds jammed the corridors. Tejus and Narayan were seeing the four casualties: a nine-year-old boy with gunshot wounds in the abdomen, his small bowel prolapsing through the wound; a pregnant woman with a bullet graze to the forehead and another bullet lodged in her knee; a young man with a shattered femur. The fourth, with a bullet in his back, had been rushed to X-ray. I heard whispers that this man, the one with the back injury, was a criminal.

'The child first,' said Tejus. I agreed. A crowd had clustered around us, making work difficult. Two men wore shawls beneath which were visible the contours of guns. A man with a curving scimitar of a moustache and a red rumal on his shoulder was apparently their leader. The hostility was evident in his eyes and his stance.

'Bhai sa'ab,' I said, timidly. 'Will you ask everyone to wait outside so we can attend to the patients?'

'Who is the jajjan?' he asked, ignoring my request.

I took a deep breath before admitting that I was the surgeon. The scimitar quivered and he tugged at his rumal. Stepping back two paces, he stood, hands on his hips. The crowd fell behind him. Mindful of their scrutinizing eyes, I helped Narayan set up the drip and put in a nasogastric tube for the child. Tejus was telling the nurse that Theatre should be ready in ten minutes.

The man with the red rumal coughed. 'Can she handle it?'

'She can,' said Tejus. There was authority in his voice. 'But we need some peace and quiet. If you want any of them to survive, you better reserve your questions till after the surgery.' The leader shifted on his feet and a hand went up. He signalled and the crowd melted instantly.

Inside Theatre, I confessed to Tejus. 'I've never seen a gunshot wound before.'

'There's always a first time. The boy won't survive the journey to Agra.'

The decision made, my nervousness vanished. The bullet had bored through the boy's intestines and lodged in the muscles of the back, missing the kidneys. In the midst of the surgery, a nurse came with the news that the man with the wound in his back had died in the X-ray room. When we finished the other three cases, it was night. Two cups of tea and I was ready to talk to the men who came with the victims. I was confident that all three would recover. The man with the red rumal was polite, almost respectful. No one will cause any trouble, he said. I will see to it. And he did.

My desire to prove myself, especially to Tejus, caused needless stress. I had a volatile temper and was not very dignified when flustered. When I argued with Tejus, which was often, my voice became high-pitched and tears started in my eyes. Tejus was loyal to the swamis; I ridiculed their self-denial and austerity and was against their free-treatment principle. I complained spitefully to the swamis about Tejus and picked faults where there were none. Tejus enjoyed good food; I made it a point to disturb him when he was deep in the enjoyment of his dinner.

He did not like my apparent calm before a difficult case. 'You're not holding the scissors properly!' 'How can you assess the tumour if you raise the table so high?' 'Hey, there's a bleeder!' 'Watch it, the carotids are just beneath your scissors!' I refused to listen to his suggestions, even when they were good. Some days I woke in the morning hating him, went to bed hating him and watched in a huff as he walked to the wards, his white coat flapping around him.

It erupted as expected, in the midst of an operation on a young man with a maxillary fracture. The treatment was interdental wiring: bits of wire hooked between the teeth which would hold the upper and lower jaws together. The patient could not afford to go to Agra and asked if I could do it.

I had no experience of facial fractures except what I had learnt from a registrar in maxillo-facial sugery just before my FRCS exams. He had explained the various grades of the fractures, and their treatment. I decided to read and learn the steps and made a bold entry in the case sheet, mainly to impress Tejus. Diagnosis: LAUGH-OUT FRACTURE.

Later that day, when I saw Tejus, he asked, 'Did you really mean *Laugh-Out* fracture?'

'Yes. This is a Grade Two Laugh-Out . . .'

'It's *Le Forte's* fracture, for God's sake!'

My operative surgery book quickly proved him right. Next day, as I scrubbed for the case, he muttered, 'I hope you know what you have to do with your Laugh-Out fracture.'

He watched closely as I passed bits of wire between the teeth on the upper and then the lower jaw before wiring them together. 'Don't pull so hard, you'll damage the gums,' he said. 'Watch out, you'll poke it into the tongue.'

He made me feel like a student being taken through the

steps of the procedure. I was less than halfway through when I lost my cool. 'If you know everything, do it yourself,' I said, putting down the instruments and peeling off my gloves. Tejus started to apologize. I walked away, changed my clothes and stamped off to my room, crowing at the thought of Tejus being stranded with the patient. There would be apologies and missives imploring me to return.

Ten minutes. Thirty minutes. Two hours. It was not right what I had done, leaving a patient in the middle of an operation. Why hadn't I been called? I had been bull-headed like this in England once, when a man with a chest injury had insulted me. Ms Stevens had quickly taken over and put things in the proper perspective: A doctor letting pride come in the way of work would set patients' lives at risk. I suffered now for not having learnt my lesson. I waited until I could wait no longer, then walked into the men's ward. The patient had been wheeled back an hour earlier. Tejus had finished the case. My ego was mauled.

Next morning, we sat in the office facing the Big Swami. 'Doctore! Was it right what you did? A patient's life, doctore! You cannot be childish.'

'He was meddling in my work.'

'I was being helpful.'

'If I needed help, I'd have asked.'

'Contused pride, that's what it is.'

'Would he like it if I told him how to use gas?'

'She doesn't know a thing about it.'

The swami finally had both of us acknowledge our stupidity.

I realized I had been petty. The patient did well and Tejus did not boast about it. The episode took the edge off the rancour between us. We argued and fought, but without the bitterness, and a nettlesome friendship developed. I called him the Light of Righteousness; he called me Jajjan. He dropped in at home quite frequently and even accepted my offer of tea. Relieved to find that I did not mind him smoking, he talked amicably.

Having heard that Tejus hated films, I bought second-hand copies of *Stardust* and *Filmfare* to annoy him.

'I bet it does you a world of good to watch pious mothers and insipid heroines,' he sneered. 'Why do women accept such roles?'

'For the same reason that men take on the macho act,' I said. My sympathies were with the vamp, I declared to an amused Tejus. Her role was single-dimensional, with no scope for complexity: She had all the wiles and no virtue.

I was walking back from the wards one evening after seeing an emergency when I noticed Tejus sitting on his front steps, looking glum. Judging from the number of cigarette stubs lying at his feet, he must have been there quite a while. There had been a death in the medical wards—a girl had died from poisoning—and he had watched the mourners. The crowd was bigger than usual, and the wailing women and children a heartbreaking sight.

'I have no one to grieve for when death happens,' Tejus said glumly, as if talking to himself. 'I'm not close to anyone.' The cigarette in his hand dropped ash on the ground and he rubbed it roughly into the mud with his foot. I could not imagine a life like his, with no one to grieve for.

Tejus had come to Keshavganj out of curiosity, and stayed on because work was here never dull. He could not stand it in city hospitals with the gadgets which coughed up the diagnosis before you could think. He said it hurt his ego. 'Here it's not just anaesthesia but the quackery I practise which interests me,' he joked. 'I spent two extra years in medical college, that makes me more learned.'

Tejus was a good doctor. Those unhappy with the treatment of other doctors inevitably ended up outside his door. His clinic was next to mine and I observed with envy the gaggle of patients who waited their turn.

There was a neurotic young man who found himself impotent after marriage. It was the fault of women, who were all dirty, he said. They had defiled his body. His wife was unclean for four days a month and he could not stand it. He had done his round of doctors, now he only talked of suicide and his wife was distraught with anxiety and guilt. They had come to me and I could do nothing to help. I saw them outside Tejus's door the next day.

Tejus had listened to the young man describe his problem. 'I don't dislike women, only their bodies,' he said. 'And mine.'

'A difficult problem,' Tejus told him. 'There's only one tablet that can cure you. But it doesn't work for everyone. Tell me, do you have a silver lota?'

'I can get it from my mother-in-law,' the young man said.

'Good.' Tejus gave him thirty vitamin tablets. 'Take one a day, after ablutions, with a silver lota-full of milk at seven in the evening. In three days, if you feel an itching in your eyes, it's a good sign. You'll be cured within a month. It shows that you are an assertive, virile man and very attractive to your wife. But if you feel the itch around your mouth, it's a bad sign. It means you're feeble, unattractive and without sexual vigour. The only way out is to become a monk. Are you willing to try?'

A week later the man returned, itchy-eyed and jubilant. 'Ab hum theek hain,' he said happily.

Tejus had a good opinion of some of the quacks in town. 'It's better to work with them than against them,' he said. He himself was a super-quack. I argued: Quacks used antibiotic cocktails and dangerous steroid preparations. 'You're convinced that they're ignorant and don't notice the good ones,' he said. 'If Dr Ramesh in Balaramkunj sends you a patient with meningitis or appendicitis, you better believe him. I've never seen him get it wrong and the only training he's had is as a peon in a government hospital.'

I cavilled about the nurses being untrained. How could the swamis expect an FRCS to work with them? 'No fault of the nurses that you drag a four-letter word around after your name,' said Tejus. 'The swamis have tried to get trained nurses but who wants to work in a crime-infested town where you must travel four kilometres to watch a movie? *You* can teach the nurses. Swamiji has some books he could lend you.'

'It's not my job to teach nurses.'

'Then stop whining.'

Finally, seeing the wisdom in his suggestion, I teamed up

with him. We had a room cleared, put in chairs and a blackboard. Big Swami bought an articulated skeleton (for eight hundred rupees, from Delhi) and it made a world of difference. The nurses had learnt haphazardly to give injections, put up drips, do wound dressings and assist in Theatre. They had worked without any concept of the body and its functions. After several arguments, we agreed that I would teach anatomy and physiology, Tejus the OT techniques and nursing arts.

My job turned out to be easier than his. He had to read up the nursing arts: bed-making, giving the bedpan to an immobile patient, feeding the unconscious, administering enemas—none of which was taught to us in college. Tejus grumbled, but once he started teaching he was very good.

In an exam held six months later, the girls did well enough. The Big Swami was pleased and gave us all lunch, with barfi and rasgulla from Motihari Mithaiwalla.

34

Distance, I found, was no aid to romance. My friendship with Stan settled smoothly into occasional aerogrammes that we wrote each other.

The letters from England were welcome, but each week it was the blue inland slipped beneath my door by the postman Madho Singh that I really waited for. Ajja's letters were voluminous and without zest; Amma's short and full of concern. Sujju, whose twins were in school, had started a small business in Mysore making decorative flowers. From her, I heard about Budhi.

Budhi had failed high school. He refused to try again and instead worked, desultorily, on the farm. He had been happy until Harini came. Now he sat around the house, moody and truculent. He grumbled about everything Harini did or did not do: 'Athige wears too many bangles'; 'Athige wasted the balekai palya on her plate'; 'She uses perfumed hair oil.' He watched her listen to film songs on the cassette player which Vishnu had bought. The tinkle of film music irritated him. Even Ajja, who was at first indifferent, had begun to drum his fingers to the music. Amma paused to listen and when a song appealed to her, asked Harini to play it again. Budhi said that his head hurt and his ears ached when the music was on. When things came to a head with Budhi refusing to eat if played music on the radio again, he was sent to Mysore to stay with Sujju and Kaviraj and a five-hundred-rupee fee was paid to get him admission at a polytechnic there. The family hoped that if Budhi learnt some skill he would settle down.

I had been in Keshavganj for over a year. It was time to go home on leave. For a year I had thought little about my family, but as the day of my going approached I became restless. I bought my ticket, packed and got ready. I would miss some of the intolerable heat, get a break from seeing patients night and day, eat good food.

Alone in the train, I took out my red diary and pen and looked at the pages filled with words. I could not remember when I started writing with Appa's Pilot pen instead of the one Jai had given me. I did not write often enough because of the pain I felt, whether I used Jai's pen or Appa's. If Appa had been alive, I would have worked in Angheri without Jai. Each time I overcame a difficult surgical case, I thought of Appa. He would have listened, asked questions and urged me on.

I had brought with me a book, *Conversations with the Dead*, which I had borrowed from Accounts Swami. During the two-day journey, I read the book from beginning to end and then reread it. It had everything—theories about the soul, real-life experiences, techniques. It said that the only requirement was that you must truly love the soul you wished to communicate with. I was excited by the possibility of speaking to Appa, of telling him all that I had been longing to. If I could converse with him just once, find out what he expected of me, I would make amends. Everything would be all right.

I reached Angheri late in the afternoon. It was a few days before Ugadi and the house had been newly whitewashed, doors and windows painted. Budhi was home and came to meet me at the bus stop. He was leaner and more cheerful.

How did he like studying in Mysore?

'I've left, akka,' he said with an engaging smile.

Why? It was less than six months since he had joined.

'Akka . . . I'm getting married.' He looked anxious. 'Are you also angry with me?'

Violet, his fiancee, was the sister of a boy at the polytechnic. One hot afternoon Budhi had visited their home and Violet had served them lime juice. After that, he took to going there whenever he felt the heat. Her parents did not mind. He asked them if he could marry Violet and take her back to Angheri, and they weren't angry. 'You should go home and think it over,' they had said.

The family tried to dissuade Budhi from a hasty marriage. I too said he should complete his two-year course at the polytechnic. He listened to everything I said and ended the conversation with 'When can I get married?'

We were all worried, except Amma. 'Budhi has always been sensible,' she pointed out. 'There is no reason why we shouldn't trust him now.'

Budhi told me that the scar from his operation was growing nicely. Growing? He pulled up his shirt and showed me: He had developed a hernia in the incision, a big one. The inner sutures had probably given way before his tissues healed. Budhi coughed to show me how he could make the hernia swell until the lump was visible through the shirt. He was offended when I said that he should have it operated on. 'I'd like to keep it,' he said. He made a habit of showing it off whenever he had the chance.

Akkamma Teacher, who had moved to Bangalore with her son, visited once when I was home. I was saddened to see my beautiful teacher so changed. She had shrunk and her skin had become rough. She looked like a fruit which had fallen from a tree.

The village, which had been immutable during my childhood and youth, had been transformed. The youth who had migrated to Mysore or to prosperous Coorg in search of work came back with visible signs of modernity. Noorumane was now just a memory. Brothers no longer shared homes, parents were slowly eased out, each family prided itself on its own dwelling. A sign announcing a toddy shop had appeared a few years ago, and now there was Sri Laxmi Wines next to Raghavendra Stores, a cinema house and several hotels with 'Meals Ready' signs outside. In the market on a Sunday, the sour smell of arrack hung in the air. Ajja went to the market dragging a bag along and stood sad and solitary, watching the waves of change sweep through Angheri.

For me, Angheri was different not just because of changing times but because of the fading away of the permanence of my childhood. It had slipped away, somehow, while I was not looking. Appa was gone and the hills, with their vigilance and strength, were too distant and unconnected with living. A darkness settled in my mind and refused to go away.

I missed Appa terribly and told Amma of my desire to try self-hypnosis, which would enable me to call his spirit. 'He died when I needed him badly,' I said. 'I had so much to tell him and make him happy. It's very hard for me, amma. I want to speak, just once.'

She looked down, I think to hide the sorrow in her eyes. 'Ajja and I, we too have to bear the burden of life without Appa. What if we too, like you, tried to speak to him?'

But my desire had become an obsession. Amma could do nothing to convince me otherwise. Every day I read the book and learnt the steps of self-hypnosis. I spent hours in Appa's office room with the door closed and the single window covered with black cloth, so the room was entirely dark. I sat trying to focus my mind on an imaginary sun. I excluded every thought from my mind until there was emptiness. I tried for days, until I thought I felt the sun like a fiery ball near my forehead. Maybe I did feel it enter my mind. I had kept a notepad and the Pilot pen on the table for Appa to write with, but nothing seemed to happen.

With each failure I became more determined. I could not sleep. One night I woke in the midst of a feverish sleep to the sound of commotion in my room. A scuffling, slapping and thudding that drove me crazy with fear. The only thing my half-slumbering mind could imagine was that I was being taken to the land of the dead. I wanted to be alive and meet Appa. I closed my ears with my fingers and wrapped a sheet around my head but the sound pierced through and made me sick with terror. In the morning I saw that it was a pigeon that had flown into the room and died. Death had been there after all.

I became frantic in my efforts and the family was concerned enough to advise that I consult a 'mind doctor'. For once Amma objected to what I was doing, seriously and strongly. We were in the kitchen, she pouring jaggery coffee from the chombu near the fireplace and I sitting on the low, three-legged stool. It had become a habit with the two of us now to drink coffee together in the morning. Vishnu and Harini would be in their room and Ajja at his prayers, which started earlier now and dragged on for more than an hour. Amma told me I should stop troubling Appa. It wasn't right.

'Appa won't like you wasting your time,' she said, in that quiet, honest way of hers, as if speaking to a child. She sat on the window sill with her coffee and traced the outer ridge of the chombu with her fingers. 'Dead persons can be respected only by the manner in which we live after they're gone.'

On my last night at home I dreamed that I was in a long dark tunnel and Stan was calling me from the other end. And then I heard Sapna crying from inside a well. Her left cheek had been burnt, she said, by the water in the well. Get me out, didi, get me out, she cried. Wait a minute, I said, and wandered down a maze of narrow streets where little wayside shops sold scissors. Scissors of all types and sizes, stacks and stacks of them. My shoulder bag was full of scissors but I kept wanting more. Soon I was running, with the bag heavy on my shoulder; I was running across paddy fields where the paddy had been harvested and the just drying hay lay in thick sheaves on the ground. My feet thumped softly and easily on the hay and I could hear the sound of another pair of feet, alongside me but faster. How could I mistake the sound of those feet when Jai and I had run just like this as children? It grew dark quite suddenly and I was aware of someone throwing stones at me. They fell softly on my head and did not hurt. I looked around and saw Appa. He had his hands crossed in front of him but it was he throwing the stones, and talking. I just could not understand what it was that Appa was trying to tell me.

Next morning I put away the book the swami had given me and decided not to trouble Appa again. Instead I would live my life the way he had lived his. He had taught with passion, I would do my work with passion.

35

It was a Saturday night. I was wrenched out of sleep by the light of the watchman Fakira's torch shining on my window. 'Ek goli maar aaya hai!'

It was one of those lucky accidents where the trauma turned out to be minimal. A single entry point in front, the bullet lodged in the man's stomach and the surgery happily uncomplicated: Open the stomach, take out the bullet and close. I was back in bed by four. Compared to most cases of goli-maar it had been a low-key affair. So I was surprised when, next morning, a doctor from Agra came to see me about the patient. He came with a gift of fresh river fish. Patients sometimes gifted vegetables, fruit or fish but this was a doctor I had never met. He said he was from the same village as the patient.

'You will be giving a police report?' he asked.

All gunshot wounds were medico-legal and had to be reported to the police. We had already informed them. The typed report would be sent on Monday.

'I have a small request,' the doctor said, looking warily towards the window. 'Please do not mention the bullet in your report.'

'But the bullet was in the stomach.'

He shifted uneasily in his seat. 'If you can say that it could have been due to a household accident with a sharp object . . . no one will question you.'

The report cannot be altered, I said. He pleaded some more. 'A doctor must not be stone-hearted. Your statement to the police will put a young man behind bars.' He almost succeeded in making me feel guilty for doing my job.

Next day Vidyut Singh who owned the telephone booth in town visited me with a tokriful of choice, juicy Nagpur oranges. Someone who claimed to be the patient's relative sent mango pickle. It was embarrassing but impolite to refuse such gifts. The same evening, when I came home from the wards, Vidyut Singh and the doctor from Agra were waiting at the door. For over an hour they tried to persuade me. This time there was a perceptible change in their demeanour.

'We're only advising you,' said Vidyut Singh. 'Aap ko pareshan nahin hona hai. Isliye. It shouldn't become a problem for you . . .'

I said something about having to see a patient, and they left. The cold gleam in the doctor's eye filled me with foreboding. Each time I passed by Vidyut Singh's telephone booth my steps quickened. I went ahead with the medical report to the police. The fruit and pickles stopped coming as promptly as they had started.

Religion and crime coexisted in a crazy, dangerous harmony in this town. For months there would be peace and just when we got used to it the shots would be heard—too rapid, too fierce and too brief to be crackers. After the first gunshot victims who came during Janmashtami, the man with the red rumal became my aide in times of trouble. And trouble there was when any patient, however serious, succumbed in hospital. Angry crowds blamed the doctors and threatened to burn the place down. Every time, the man with the red rumal would be there, standing a little apart, waiting. If I looked at him, he stepped forward, listened to what I had to say and then talked to the relatives. Inevitably they cooled down, apologized for their behaviour and retreated with salaams.

In the evenings after work, ignoring Tejus's taunts, I walked quickly round the campus, twice. It felt good to be slightly out of breath. When I trudged back sweating virtuously, Tejus called from his window: Was my conscience nagging me, like a carious tooth? I advised him about the need to exercise, to stop smoking. 'Every puff is killing you,' I said.

'It's this doctoring, the wrenches of everyday decisions which enslave me to this reed.' He pulled deeply at his cigarette. 'I'll give it all up one day. You may even see me walking around the campus.' He clutched his middle at the dismal thought.

I had started out on my walk one evening when a pregnant woman was brought in with a painful foot. Ten days earlier she had stepped on a thorn while collecting dung. Her foot had become dusky and swollen, with an ink-like stain spreading up the leg. A closer look revealed blisters from which a mucky fluid oozed. The girl was visibly ill. Her blood pressure was low, the temperature high and the pulse feeble.

Gas gangrene. I explained as gently as I could that the offending part would have to be removed. The girl was nineteen and it was her first pregnancy. Her husband—also very young— and her two brothers were furious. 'We will take her to another hospital,' they said and took her away, refusing to even let us give her a shot of penicillin. Next morning they were back. The gangrene had spread to mid-thigh and the girl was in delirium with a raging fever and a runaway, thready pulse. Septicaemia had set in.

Do whatever is to be done, jajjan sa'ab, the husband said between sobs. You must save her and the baby.

The girl was in her ninth month of pregnancy and the baby slightly premature. There were no labour pains. A Caesarian was the only way of saving the baby. But it would take up precious time while the infection seeped through her blood. If I did the amputation first, the anaesthetic would depress the vital functions of the baby and put its life at risk.

'How about a guillotine?' said Tejus. 'It'll only take a few minutes.'

The barbaric method of amputation called a guillotine was used before the advent of anaesthesia and in times of war. The surgeon cut through the limb in one swift movement while an assistant gave chloroform through an open mask and several hands held the patient down. If he survived the terror and the pain, if infection could be kept at bay, the wound healed over agonizing months. The modern practice was to raise skin and muscle flaps to cover the raw surfaces of cut bones. The muscle and skin provided a soft cushion which could support an artificial limb.

I did not believe in reverting to this older method. 'Why don't you just do your work and let me think . . .'

Tejus persisted. 'I've seen it done once, in an emergency. The surgeon cut the skin and muscles at the same level as the bone. He used skin traction to gradually pull down soft tissue, and sutured it over the cut end of the bone after a few weeks.'

'It's brutal. I won't do it.'

'I'm putting her to sleep. You'll have to think fast.'

The patient was *in extremis*. The Gaswallah Dacter became a man transformed. His movements became swift, his temper quicker. He yelled at the scrub nurse and she burst into tears. I shouted at him to stop bullying her. The Small Swami, waiting at the door to Theatre, rushed in. 'Thakurji will save her, doctores!'

'Will you shut up and leave us to our work?' screamed Tejus.

I picked up the scalpel. The amputation first. A guillotine. Skin, subcutaneous tissue, fascia, muscle. Was I quick enough? Arteries, nerves, veins, the bone. Blood vessels ligatured, the raw surface covered with thick wads of saline-soaked gauze and the stump firmly bandaged. Seven minutes. The Caesarian followed.

'Her pulse is stronger now and the blood pressure is more stable,' said Tejus. 'They'll make it, the two of them.'

When it was over, I pulled off my mask and grimaced at him, more out of relief than anything.

With traction on the skin around the amputation, the wound began to close. Many times I saw the young husband squatting in the passageway near the ward with his head between his hands, weeping. The girl was stoic and did not flinch even when the dressings were done, concentrating instead on her baby lying in a crib next to her. The wound healed in four weeks. What we could never cure was the other pain she would have to endure for ever, of living with one leg.

〜

'Abhi na jao chhod kar . . .' Rafi was crooning one of my favourites from *Hum Dono* on Vividh Bharati at three in the afternoon from the transistor radio near me when I saw Fakira at the window. 'Sweet shop Kanhaia,' he said, breathless. 'It looks bad.' Pulling on my white coat, I ran.

Kanhaia, an inoffensive giant of a man, worked at Motihari Mithaiwala's. Motihari's was the only sweet shop in the area which used pure ghee and the sweetest of milk from the cows of Vrindaban not far away. It was no secret that the mithai shop did roaring business because of Kanhaia. He had many offers for work elsewhere but his loyalty stayed with the little hole of a shop where he had learnt his art as a slim lad of eighteen. His steadily increasing girth (a sumptuous hundred kilos) was proof enough of the lavish hand with which he blended ghee and milk with sugar to create unforgettable sweetmeats.

Kanhaia came to work well before dawn. By the time the milk—two hundred litres a day—arrived in huge, clanging aluminium containers, he had the gargantuan kadai on the fire. He toiled all day in the kitchen, turning out kaju-studded laddus, wickedly sweet jalebis, saffron-flavoured barfis and 'never-before' pedas. He enticed customers from as far away as Barsana and Nandagaon; vendors on railway platforms sold imitations by invoking his name. Even the swamis splurged on Motihari sweets for special events like Thakurji's birthday.

There was one stain on Kanhaia's otherwise pristine reputation: It was rumoured that he had a weakness for the not-so-sweet meat. The boy who supplied the eleven o'clock chai claimed to be a witness. He had seen the Malayali cook in Brothers Hotel adjacent to the mithai shop handing out fried meat to Kanhaia on a ladle through his kitchen window. Kanhaia crammed the meat into his mouth and returned his compliments in the form of a couple of golden laddus. When his employers confronted him with this salacious bit of news,

Kanhaia said, 'You think I'll let my brahmin stomach be defiled by meat?' He offered to quit if it was proved to be true.

A sly meat-eating brahmin he might have been, but Kanhaia was venerated in Keshavganj. No hostility could be imagined to this big, soft man who seduced everyone with sweet creations. And yet one evening, in an unbelievable act of wickedness, gunmen fired at him near the sweet shop and sped away on a motorbike. A few days earlier certain persons from Agra had approached Kanhaia with an offer: a job in the city for twice the money he got at Motihari's. The bullets pumped into his abdomen were the price of refusal.

Minutes after Kanhaia was rushed to hospital, the crowds began to pour in. I pressed my way to the stretcher, aware of the shrill cries entreating us to save him. There were four bullet wounds on the wide expanse of his belly. Two had passed through to the other side and two were lodged inside. Though sweating profusely, he was calm. In his eyes I saw the question I have seen too often in the eyes of one who fears for his life. Joining his palms together he said just one word: 'Jajjan.'

'You'll be all right,' I said. 'Definitely.' Saying it, and seeing his face and body relax, filled me with an instant thrill. The blood hummed in my veins and every cell in my body sang out in elation: The gift of saving this life was mine. I felt the surge of confidence that comes to a surgeon facing a hyper-acute emergency. Tiredness fell away and I squared myself for the challenge. For a challenge it would be to open the bullet-ridden belly of this obese young man.

I went into Theatre, changed and scrubbed, mentally visualizing the battered landscape inside that corpulent abdomen. Tejus had trouble getting the endotracheal tube down Kanhaia's fat neck. I had the table lowered and stood on a stool so I could look inside the belly. Kanhaia's small bowel was riddled with four star-shaped rents and faecal fluid bubbled out sooner than it could be sucked out. Sitting at the mouth of one of the rents was a chunk of barely-chewed meat. Five more chunks were removed, along with the deadly metal bullets. A bullet had grazed the left kidney and just missed the spleen; another had come out on the right side, missing the liver but having got the edge of the lung and broken three ribs. Blood had collected in the chest and would have to be drained. There was so much fat in his abdomen that two nurses—in addition to Narayan—had to scrub up and hold the retractors. My fingers were greasy with fat and I wiped them again and again on the drapes during the surgery. Resection of gut and anastomosis. About the secret in his belly which the bullet had pried open, only a few of us knew. We could keep it to ourselves. When it was finished, I was pleased with a job well done and ready for the grateful admiration of those waiting outside. My happiness at the thought of this little glory was no doubt tinged with conceit.

I was walking towards the sink to wash my gloved hands when I heard Tejus shout the dreaded words: 'Cardiac arrest!'

The tube in his windpipe removed, Kanhaia had been lifted on to the stretcher when his heart suddenly stopped beating. Tejus—detecting it instantly because of his custom-made stethoscope—was at the head end, giving mouth-to-mouth. I put my gloved hands over the heart and pressed down in coordination with Tejus's breathing into the lungs. We were trying to squeeze the heart back into action and drive some oxygen into his lungs. The pressure of my tired hands over the massive chest wasn't enough. Narayan took over from me. Tejus, meanwhile, got the tube back into the patient's windpipe and delivered full-strength oxygen. Driven by panic and frustration, I moved from head end to chest to wrist where, through the intravenous line, we were pushing medicines to revive his heart.

Ten minutes. Fifteen minutes. Twenty minutes. Twenty-five. It might have been a clot driven into his lungs, an acute coronary which blocked the blood supply to the heart, or respiratory failure. His heart refused to wake up. Kanhaia died within an hour of the surgery. For a brief moment I stood looking at his naked body, devoid of all modesty at death; the abdomen which had been rent open by bullets now scarred with sutures; the blood stains of my gloved hands still fresh on his chest; tube in his windpipe, tube in his veins, tube in his stomach, tube in his bladder. Sucking out, pumping in. What did it matter how much we had struggled, how hard I had tried, or how well the operation went?

With tubes, catheters, pipes and bottles dangling from his massive body, Kanhaia was wheeled out of Theatre. I followed through the swing doors. A clutch of his close family and the sweet shop owner came forward from among the hundreds who waited. Pulling the mask down from my face, I spoke to his brother. 'Bhai sa'ab . . .'

The next few moments were like an explosion. I cannot remember the details, but can recall Tejus pulling me back into Theatre, closing the door. Outside there was commotion, people screaming, yelling abuse. I stood there within the aseptic sanctuary of the operating rooms, the exultation of a few moments ago slumped at my feet.

Kanhaia's death caused an uproar the likes of which the hospital had never seen. For once, the man with the red rumal could do nothing. Doctors, nurses and the swamis watched stupefied as the mob let loose its anger. Tables and chairs were smashed, windowpanes broken and oxygen cylinders sent crashing to the floor.

'Why did she operate if she couldn't handle it? If she had told us, we would have taken him to Agra.'

'He was talking when he was brought to hospital. It was not such a serious wound. The jajjan isn't good enough.'

They had seen too many serious cases come in and go out restored. Now they could not accept my failure to save their prized citizen. Tejus did something only he could have done. He took my face in his wet, just-washed hands and said, 'Steady. I was watching, don't forget. You handled it well. Now get changed, go home. We'll manage this.'

The next day a local newspaper which was always on the lookout for cheap sensational news reported Kanhaia's death as the lead story. Having described the shooting incident in colourful detail, the article said that 'a murky doctor with murderous intent' had killed Kanhaia 'through negligence'. The incident was 'a black dot on the forehead of the Sevashram'.

It had the desired effect. For weeks afterwards, angry

protestors congregated in a chai shop near the hospital, exhorting patients not to subject themselves to my hands. 'Dacter nahin hai woh,' they said. 'Yama hai, Yama.'

Tejus was angry enough to implore the Big Swami to sue the newspaper. The swami called me to his office and explained why it was not a good idea. 'How long will street dogs bark? Can you boil brinjals in a pot when the water dries up? That newspaper is nothing but a gossip mill. Do not stoop to their level. Ignore, doctores. Ignore.'

We did. And yet, I began to feel like my head had been tonsured for some monstrous crime. When I picked up the scalpel I was tense and awkward, as though operating with two left hands. I stopped my evening walks, sat at home in the evenings and was miserable. Surgical Fear. Not fear of smashed furniture or physical violence but that other fear. The one fear that every surgeon knows and no one else understands.

I was tired of operating on bullet wounds, of tearing myself away from sleep to spend hours in Theatre, and of talking to relatives in the middle of the night. If I had known earlier how savage life could be in that town, I would have gone elsewhere. I told Tejus. He said that I should stop grumbling and be grateful for the opportunity to do unique cases.

Soon after the tragedy with Kanhaia came another incident which involved two young men. Rival gangs in a neighbouring town had had a shootout and the two youths, trying to get away from the scene, were snared in the crossfire. They were brought in a tempo driving at breakneck speed and reached the hospital within half an hour of the incident. Both happened to be on the left side of the road when it happened and the bullets that sprayed out of the AK-47 rifle had got them in their left flanks. The injuries appeared to be equally serious but one looked paler. He might have lost more blood so I decided to take him up first. I looked at his face and wondered if I had seen him before. There were two gold rings on his fingers and a gold chain around his neck which the nurse was removing. At least he could afford the expenses of a long stay in hospital.

The injuries were grievous: a rent in the spleen causing the abdomen to fill with blood; a perforation high up on the left colon; a small tear in the left dome of the diaphragm; a bruised left kidney; fractured lower ribs. The treatment required would be elaborate. Splenectomy, closure of perforation and repair of the rent in the diaphragm. Irrigation of the abdomen with several litres of saline. A rubber drainage tube inserted into the chest to pre-empt the collection of blood from fractured ribs.

When the wound was being closed, the scrub nurse told me that the youth was Chopra Medum's son, Kethak. Medum worked at the revenue office in Mathura and was infamous for her corrupt ways and her rudeness. She was hated and feared. The son had inherited some of his mother's traits. He had once shown his high-handedness in the ward. I had asked the visitors milling around a patient's bed to leave the ward during doctors' rounds as it interfered with work. The boy said that he did not care for two-paisa doctors like me and then complained to swamiji. He went unpunished and continued to strut about the hospital whenever it pleased him.

'Why did no one tell me that it was him?' I said, looking at the drugged face on the table. 'I could have done the other case first.'

'He was more serious, you said so yourself,' Tejus reminded me.

I was confused and frustrated. 'Let's break for tea,' I said, wearily. 'The other case will take just as long.'

'A young lad bleeding away and all you can think of is tea,' said Tejus. 'Ten minutes, while I put him to sleep.'

The trauma the second youth had suffered was identical to the first. Spleen, colon, diaphragm, kidney and ribs. Not any worse and not any better. I came out of Theatre and found distraught relatives waiting. Chopra Medum was there. 'My son, doctor,' she said, worried. 'You must do your best for him.'

'I do my best for every patient,' I snapped, needlessly.

The boys lay on adjoining beds. Every day I saw them, checked their wounds, medication and intravenous fluids. I found myself taking a little extra care of the second boy, hoping his recovery would be quicker, that he would not develop any complications. The antibiotics were expensive and the nurse told me the relatives did not have enough money. Could they give him penicillin, which was cheaper? 'No, I'll pay for it,' I said, aware that my gesture was not out of goodness but a mean desire to help him more than Chopra Medum's son.

But things did go wrong. He developed breathing distress on the fifth day, went into an irreversible shock from sepsis and died on the tenth day. Chopra Medum's son recovered and she expressed her gratitude with a box of mithai.

⁀

Training in England, it had never occurred to me that male patients might feel embarrassed to be examined by a woman. There I had done sterilizations under local anaesthetics, and some of the patients would joke: 'Mind the waterworks, miss.' In Keshavganj it was otherwise.

The first thing I noticed when I saw Makkan Singh was the aggression in his eyes. He was from a village not far away, where physical fitness was more important than religion or money. Boys barely nine years old were trained with exacting discipline. Their bodies were toned with asanas, pranayama, meditation, weightlifting and wrestling. They lived on a diet of milk, bajra, ghee and pigeon's meat. It took eight years of regimented training to become a pahalwan. The young men from the village won every contest in endurance in that region. Makkan was one of the best but for the last several years he had been plagued by a strange illness.

Tejus brought him to my clinic. Makkan was a handsome man of about forty with muscles like rippling silk. He came with a burly companion who stood behind him and eyed me coldly. It took a great deal of persuasion to convince them that I was the surgeon. With some prompting from his friend, Makkan told me that he had a problem with his 'loha'. He had noticed in the last few years that it had been getting shorter. It was also 'teda', it swung to the left when he willed it to be straight. This happened every time he had tried to 'be' with his wife.

'No other problem,' said Makkan. 'It just won't go in. Just

straighten it for me, and make it a bit longer.' Having made himself clear, he lay back on the examination table with his hands behind his head. He had come to get it fixed.

His friend chipped in, 'He used to be perfectly all right. He has four children to prove it.'

I examined Makkan and found no defect whatsoever. I avoided looking at Tejus. 'This is a different sort of problem,' I said, with a straight face. 'I'm only a surgeon . . .'

'That is why we've come. We know that medicines won't cure him.'

Tejus had needlessly put me in an embarrassing situation. 'You explain to them,' I said between clenched teeth.

'Jajjan memsa'ab wants some time to think,' Tejus told them cheerfully. 'If you will wait outside for a minute . . .'

We sat facing each other across the table. 'You know he needs to see a psychiatrist.'

'His friend said he's seen enough of those.'

'Let him go to a sexologist, then.'

'Think,' suggested Tejus, tapping his head. I hated him when he did that, making out that he was clever, and I was not.

'The Light has gone out of your head, it looks like,' I fumed, rising. 'I'm going to tell them.'

But he was serious. 'Listen to me. He has a bipolar disorder with delusions. It can get worse if he's not handled properly. He's tired of medicines, doesn't believe in them and has faith only in surgery. You have to show him he's right.'

'Meaning?'

'I put him to sleep and you make clever-looking incisions on his loha.'

'He won't be cured by incisions on the skin.'

'It's worth a try.'

He talked me into doing it. We admitted Makkan and told the other staff what we planned to do. I explained to Makkan that it was major surgery and his wife would have to be summoned from the village to look after him. The morning of the surgery, he was given an enema and a drip was set up. Dressed in a long, shapeless hospital gown, he was wheeled into

Theatre. Under anaesthesia I made three elaborately curved incisions on his penis and then sutured the skin with multiple, fine sutures. Tejus kept him in the recovery room inside Theatre for a needlessly long time and then he was taken to the post-operative room where patients who had major surgery stayed for a few days.

It was the first post-operative day. Makkan lay in bed, looking very much the courageous martyr. His wife stood by with the look of overwhelming gratitude that you see on the faces of relatives after a major surgery. I checked Makkan's pulse, the wound dressing, his urine output and blood pressure. 'Is it very painful?' I asked him.

He moved his hips carefully and winced. 'Never mind the pain,' he said. 'I will never forget the seva you have done for me.' His tear-filled eyes moved from me to Narayan and each of the nurses. His hands were folded in a namaste. 'Bahut, bahut shukriya. May God bless every one of you with happy marriage and many, many children . . .'

Radhamani, the nurse who had assisted at my fake surgery, giggled in the background. Having advised Makkan about his diet, we moved on to the next bed. Later I ticked off Radhamani. No giggling and giving the game away, I warned.

We kept him on intravenous fluids for two days. I inspected the wounds daily, changed dressings, discussed his progress at the bedside and prescribed a different coloured vitamin each day. His dutiful wife attended to his needs and Makkan lolled in bed, luxuriating in his well-earned post-operative pain (I had carefully avoided painkillers). On the seventh day the sutures were removed. Makkan was allowed out of bed and then sent home on a strict diet.

Three months after leaving the hospital he came back to tell us that he was cured. 'Ab hum theek-thaak hain jajjan sa'ab,' he said with a wide smile. 'Gharwaali bhi bahut khush hai. My wife is very happy now.'

The success of Makkan's operation brought others to my clinic. You know a patient is more anxious than usual when he starts clearing his throat outside your door. I heard the repetitive, exaggerated coughs, and a young man walked in. Something in that lower, secret part of his body was worrying him. He sat on the edge of the stool. He was dressed in trousers and shirt, shoes and wristwatch. His hair was oiled and styled in the latest filmi fashion. He was studying law and, like many educated young men in rural areas, particular about speaking in English.

His problem?

'One cock.'

'Sorry?'

'I'm having only one cock.'

I looked helplessly at Phalguni, the nurse. She looked blank. I tried again. 'What exactly is the problem?'

He shifted in his seat. This doctor was a bit dim. He had to be explicit. 'Everyone has two cocks,' he said, splaying two fingers. 'I'm having only one.'

I asked him to lie down so I could examine him. Perhaps he meant he had one testis. I usually made sure there was a male attendant around when seeing a male patient but that day, with the outpatients' being busy, I was unable to get one of the watchmen. The young man had come alone. I still had several patients to see, so I decided to examine him with the nurse in attendance. It was an unkind thing to do. Phalguni, with her large-framed spectacles and an intense, serious face was not among the brightest. She peered closely, with earnest scientific curiosity.

The young man undid the top button of his trousers and, sweating profusely, lifted the seam so I could take a peek. 'I can't see,' I said, ignoring the surprise on Phalguni's face. He lowered his trousers and underwear by inches until at last I could check him out: a single testis which was enlarged because of a hydrocele. The atrophied remnants of the other testis, which had not come down to the scrotum during early development, could be felt in the groin. Sadly, it had been neglected in childhood. If the defect had been noticed when he was three or four, it could have been operated on and brought down to the normal site.

I explained all this to the young man and advised him to

have the hydrocele operated on. His sexual life would be normal. All went well and he went back, hopefully, to studying law with his manhood and his pride intact.

Makkan's friend, the man who had brought him to hospital, came a few months later. 'I have a problem, a very small one, with my loha,' he said, in an anxious whisper. 'A boil that won't go away. I'm a good married man,' he added. 'Sirf ek baar paav phisal gaya tha. That was a long time ago.'

The hard everted edges of the ulcer were unmistakeable: Cancer affecting the shaft of the penis. Glands in the groin. It had nothing to do with his 'foot having slipped' once. A biopsy proved malignancy. Nothing short of total amputation of the penis would save him. If things went wrong, I would be blamed. I pretended to be busy, contemplated falling sick, tried referring him to Agra. In the end, I had to do it. It was a bloody procedure and he needed two pints of blood. Following the surgery, his personality seemed to undergo a change. The reality of having a female perineum was difficult to live with. He looked so miserable I wondered if it would have been better to have saved the penis and opted for radiotherapy which in his case was the second-best option. I felt unhappy when I thought of the wrestler with his masculinity removed.

One busy morning, having finished outpatients', I was leaving my clinic, thinking happily of the nimbu pani waiting at home when the watchman Vichitra wheeled in an emergency. On the stretcher was a man who looked well enough and stared at me with unblinking eyes. No anxious relatives with him. He could not be too ill.

'Kya hai?' I asked brusquely.

The man lifted one hand and threw aside the towel wrapped around his neck. His throat was sliced open with a clean slit, cutting through the trachea. Air whistled in and out through the wound with a peculiar sound. His eyes urged me to do something. With the trachea severed, the voice box, which was just above it, failed to function and he could not speak. The wound had missed the jugular vein and the carotid by millimetres.

The slit was sutured and a tracheostomy fashioned lower

down to enable the windpipe to heal. He recovered well. When he could finally speak, I asked what had happened. 'Chhath se gir gaya,' he said. 'I fell down from the roof.' It was not worth telling the truth.

No more complicated cases, I said to myself. I had had enough to last me for some time.

36

Tejus sent the nun to my clinic. Sister Philo was dark, with lively eyes and a scar on her chin. She shook hands with me and said she was fit, except for the pain in her stomach. She had lost ten kilos in six months. The grey-and-white habit hid her real thinness. There was nothing to be found on checking her and Tejus had already put her through the deworming and anti-amoebic treatment. 'You'll need some tests,' I said. 'A sigmoidoscopy and a barium enema, to check for other pathology.'

'Other pathology?'

'Tuberculosis or a tumour in the bowel. Stay on a light diet for two days and take this laxative tomorrow night. Come back Thursday, on an empty stomach.'

Two days later Sister Philo walked into my clinic and placed a glass jar on the table. 'Could this be a tumour?' She was laughing. A tapeworm, pale pink and several feet long, lay curled inside. With treatment, the pain stopped and she was soon back to normal.

Sister Philomena came from Tirunelveli in southern Tamil Nadu, a couple of thousand kilometres away, and belonged to an order of nuns which had their mother house in Holland and regional house in Bombay. She was a trained nurse. Religious life bored her and a few years ago she had asked for permission from the church to work independently. She had opted for a village ten kilometres away from the hospital. Years of drought, famine and bad planning had snared the farmers in a life of debt and want. Philo lived in a hut like the rest. She delivered their babies, taught the dais and got young people to dig drains and build wells. She went about on a bicycle and talked to the women about spacing their pregnancies. Being a Catholic, she was averse to any other method of family planning. When I came to know her better, however, she admitted that the Pope would soon have to reconsider his dictum. Sister Philo received a regular allowance of five hundred rupees a month from Bombay. Her needs being few, it was usually more than she could spend. With the money saved from her allowance she bought second-hand books whenever she went to a city.

We became friends. I admired her for the brave woman she was, living alone in a far-flung village. She once fell off her bicycle on a bumpy village road and cut her chin. Being too far away from any doctor, she sutured it herself, standing before a mirror in her room. If she was needed somewhere at night, no matter how far, she thought little of setting off alone on her bicycle. Was she not afraid of dacoits and criminals? Yes, she said, matter-of-factly, as if she were talking of the heat of summer or the bitter cold of winter. Sister Philo was different from the nuns I had known. She thrived on her irrepressible optimism. She spoke in sudden spurts and weighty silences. I asked why she did not wear saris like most nuns. She stood, plunged her hands deep into the capacious pockets of her habit and said, 'Baggage space.' In her pockets she always carried tablets, ointments, dressings and a sewing kit, little bottles of herbal pellets which she made herself, and a book or two.

Philo treated village folk for simple maladies. With every prescription she advised the patient to drink vegetable juice— hibiscus, bel, carrot, beetroot, ginger, dhania or cucumber. She was specific. Beetroot for blood pressure and falling hair, ginger and dhania for flatulence, cucumber for the heat, carrot for memory and eyesight, gooseberry for preventing a cold. 'I try to make them spend their money on food instead of expensive medicines,' she said. She did not dismiss village remedies without trying them herself. From the villagers she learnt that sugar applied locally was excellent for prolapsed piles, honey for burns and rancid oil for varicose ulcers, and drinking pomegranate juice for anaemia. But when they clung to ideas which were harmful, she tried to dissuade them; like their belief that drinking milk caused infection in a wound.

I had thought Tejus had become less harsh and a bit pensive of late and I was happy about it. But when Philo came he reverted to his old self. She was one more person to argue with, though unlike me Philo could hold her own against him.

'Sister, did you know Nalli reads only the headlines in the newspapers?'

'It's only political news, and that's boring,' I said.

'Politics is tearing the country to shreds and Nalli finds it dull.'

'It *is* dull, isn't it, Sister?'

'Anything that changes society should concern us. Try reading every day, Nalli. You'll begin to feel involved.'

Tejus, of course, unhappy at my being let off so lightly, took off: 'She's no different from cultured people everywhere. Living in homes with "Beware of Dog" signs, getting in and out of cars. Mouths nicely buttered, thank you. Wince at a murder here, a rape there, or at a bloodbath somewhere else and go back to your fuck-eat-work-sleep routine. Sorry for being coarse, Sister. I'm really . . . I take that back. I'm not being coarse.'

He went on till Philo asked him to stop. 'You're just trying to sound clever,' she said. It shut him up. Why wasn't I able to handle him like that?

Tejus carped about religion and used swear words to test how Sister Philo would react.

'Nice to be bald, Sister? You don't have to spend money on shampoo,' he said.

Sister took off her wimple, revealing thick, curly tresses that had been cut short just below the ears. 'Soap's just as good as shampoo,' she said.

Tejus the bookworm was surprised to find that Sister Philo was better read than he. In her huge pockets she carried, from time to time, Wodehouse, Chandler, Asimov, *Stories of Tenali Raman*, or the Bible. Tejus quizzed her, hoping he would find something good which she had not heard of. 'You haven't read Brautigan? My God. Here, read *In Watermelon Sugar*. It's divine.'

She returned the book the following week, shaking her head in disapproval. 'You said divine.'

When Philo heard that Tejus had not read a particular novel that was admired by everyone, she offered to buy it for him. 'I'm suspicious of a book which no one has disliked till now,' he said loftily. 'Someone said reading it was like swimming in chocolate. I won't pay to swim in chocolate.'

One day Sister Philo came to my clinic as I was finishing with the last patient. 'I've heard the strangest bit of news,' she whispered. 'I'll wait till you finish.' When the patient left, Philo came in and sat across the table. 'Wonder if you know this: Tejus used to be a Catholic.'

I had heard rumours but did not believe them. 'If it's true, you shouldn't mind it too much. The way he swears, he'd be a bad Catholic.'

'I'm curious,' said Philo, as we decided to find out.

It was Saturday. Tejus had asked us home for coffee and bondas. He was having something stronger. Rum, with pomegranate juice to 'detoxify' the system. He had been drinking for a while and was in a malevolent mood.

After a few minutes I managed to turn the conversation towards religion. Turning to Philo, I said, 'Christianity must be a dull religion. All those disciples following Jesus Christ, hanging on to his every word.'

'Listen to her, just listen to her!' Tejus cried, jumping to his feet. 'Did you hear that, Sister? Aren't you going to defend yourself?'

'I'm not criticizing,' I said, primly. 'It's a fact, isn't it? I mean, even the Bible is monotonous.'

He glared at me. 'Beautiful book, the Bible. Nothing as practical as the Sermon on the Mount. And the Song of Solomon—you haven't read it, of course—is lusty, beautiful poetry.' A smile spread over his face. 'I know. I used to be a Catholic.'

'You weren't!'

'Really?'

He was pleased with the effect. 'I change my religion every five or six years—before I became Dharma Tejus I was Gonzales. When I "embraced" Hinduism five years ago, the swamis were worried. I wasn't doing it to impress them, just roosting where I wanted. Next year, soon after Ramzan, I'll be Dr Naqvi.' He gulped his drink. 'Buddhism I've reserved for when I'm older.'

'He's joking,' I said.

'You want proof?' He went to his bedroom, rummaged in his desk and came back with two passports in different names.

'I'm surprised that a good person like you failed to find answers in the Bible,' said Philo.

'Don't bullshit, Sister dear. All of life is double standards. Doctors, especially doctors. We're in a cesspool of vice. Piddly surgeons and arsehole anaesthetists. Chipping away at the minuscule and taking credit.'

'That's not true. We work hard.'

'Nalli here cribs about the difficulties of being a surgeon. I tell her surgeons have been through harder times. The whale surgeons, for instance, operated on dead whales under the waves. Managed to sever the head from the body with precision.' He looked fiercely at me. 'Ask Nalli if she's ever done something worthwhile like help build a latrine, or deliver a baby . . .?' He refilled his glass. 'As if there are any good persons left. The last one went out with that sweet old man, Gandhi.'

'Changing your religion seems so pointless.'

'Jesus goddamn Christ. You don't understand. I have a superiority complex. I won't cling to one faith. It hurts me, hurts me . . .' He started to sob. 'You must know by now that *everything* has ulterior motives. Even charity. In your case, if it isn't with a view to converting people, it's to go to heaven. No need to blush, it's no better with the sadhus. In this land of Sri Krishna there's a lot of humbug. When did the gopis who pranced with Krishna milk the cows, do housework or clear away the dung? How did the Virgin Mary deliver in a stable with the sheep and the muck and stay spanking clean?'

'He's drunk,' I whispered.

'Not drunk. *Drinking*,' muttered Tejus. There was no stopping him. 'It's always the same. First the self. Then family, community, caste, country and mankind. Of course, animal-kind is strictly for the activists.'

'There's a lot of good being done for animals,' said Philo.

'Hah. We butcher them and then start anaemic little organizations. What crrrap, Sister. You're stupidly innocent and that's dangerous. You're the sweetest person I know next to this dumbo here, but you're stupid.'

He rose on unsteady feet and staggered mournfully around the room. 'We admire fish trapped in bowls believing that it's good for our stressed nerves. We leash dogs, cage parrots and slaughter sheep. We harpoon the whale, the poor whale serenely spouting seawater, because the sperm oil can give us light and what-not, the bone can be used to make artificial legs and decorative vases, which of course are all more important than the whale.' He sat next to Philo and put an arm around her shoulder. He pulled out a rumpled kerchief and blew his nose. 'We say the tiger is cruel. Which tiger would have butchered as many as you or me, Sister? Oh, to be a tiger . . . To have lived a good Tiger Life. Or to be a turtle, moving uncomplainingly beneath her shell with fellow turtles, laying eggs in the sand for a hundred years. He sat there with his back hunched, staring into his glass. Every once in a while he looked up at me or at Philo, as if reading our faces. He drained the glass and gave it to me. 'Will you . . .?'

I placed it on the window ledge. 'Thank you,' he bowed and then turned to Philo. 'Shall I tell you what I would like to do? I'd like to start a College of Quackery and Common Sense. Don't look at me as if I'm crazy. We doctors are selling ourselves to technology so we don't have to think. Whoring. And then we earn so much that we die of stress ulcers. In this Quackery College, I'll teach about the body, about diagnosis and treatment. To any person who's school-passed. One-year course. It'll include suturing wounds, setting fractures and setting up intravenous lines, the side-effects of drugs . . . Start a

Quackery College in every district and see the miracle revolution. We doctors can all fuck off to . . . Sister . . . you listening?'

He stumbled into his bedroom and crashed on to the bed.

'I get mad when he speaks rubbish like that,' I said, rising. 'He'll sleep now, let's go.'

'Such a lovely man,' Philo said, wiping her eyes.

Next day I needled Tejus about his grandiose idea and he said, 'What Quackery College?'

Philo wanted us to visit her in the village where she lived, and we went by bus. Tejus sat in the back so he could smoke. Two hours later when we got off, he was grumbling that this was not how he wanted to spend his weekly holiday.

Philo showed us around and chatted to the villagers, slipping easily into their dialect, a mix of Brijbhasha and Hindi. One hut boasted the sign SCHOOL FOR ADULT LITERACY. It was a school Philo had started, where men and women learnt to read newspapers. Most of the huts had a drain, a soakage pit and a vegetable garden. Later we sat on the floor of her two-room house, drank tea and ate the upma she cooked on a chulha. She took a piece of chalk from her pocket and drew sketches on the ground to show how the village was laid out and how the local youth helped with simple projects. 'There has been only one case of polio last year and none of cholera or tetanus. It's an improvement, but it isn't enough. We still have malaria, typhoid, tuberculosis and infant diarrhoea. They can be wiped out if clean water and hygiene are taken care of.' She sighed. 'You doctors should do something to educate the people about health.'

Tejus chuckled. 'We won't, because we're too damn clever. I can roam about on a cycle preaching cleanliness, digging soakage pits and spraying DDT but who'll pay me? How will I buy my Maruti, how will I go on a pilgrimage to Nainital or Mussoorie or Ooty? How will I give my daughter a decent marriage? Diseases are our livelihood, we don't want them to go away. Death, diarrhoea, falling hair, acne, weight gain and weight loss. We work hard, find new medicines, and attempt to cure everything, but we don't want it all to *go* away. A tightrope act, balancing compassion with having a fat bank balance. We have to con the public.' He turned to me. 'God help us if Sister becomes the health minister.'

'She'll be very good,' I said, overcome with admiration for Philo. 'You talk as if you know the motive of every doctor, but you don't.' It was natural that the village should remind me of Angheri. I told them about the hospital which we had planned to set up and how it had been buried in disappointments.

Tejus stood up. 'If it's more of glory-to-village business, I'm stepping out for a smoke.'

'You sit right there and listen,' said Philo, angry. I made it a point to direct my conversation at Philo. 'You should do it,' she said when I had finished telling her.

'You really believe she can manage a hospital single-handed? It's not like cutting up people, you know.'

'You can join her.'

He got up. 'If she has the gumption, let her do it. At least it'll be a splendid failure. Now I do need a smoke. Do you mind?'

When we were on the bus going back, Tejus said, admiringly, 'I like that Sister. She's brave.'

I resolved never to speak to him about Angheri again.

37

The name on the outpatient slip intrigued me. Rimzim. I recognized her as the young girl who helped in her father's sari shop in town. She was plain-featured and big, with a bigger problem camouflaged beneath the dupatta that she wrapped over her kameez. She fussed with the voluminous garment while her mother sat on the stool meant for the patient and leaned towards me. 'Her breasts are growing,' she whispered.

The girl had the self-consciousness of one who blames herself for whatever's wrong with her body. She came from a family of big-bosomed women and, in her case, the breasts kept getting bigger and bigger. She hid her shame in loose clothes and wore home-made bras because the size was now an alarming forty-eight inches. 'Her marriage has been fixed,' the mother said, then added, lowering her voice, 'thoda sa kaat deejiye.'

Reducing the size of the breast wasn't merely 'cutting off a bit', as the mother had suggested. It was a complicated job and had to be done one breast at a time with a gap of seven days in between. During the long and painful post-operative period, the girl never complained. 'I'm all right,' she said and submitted to the painful dressings and injections. Slowly, as the girl realized she was as normal as anyone else, she smiled, her movements became lighter and her face radiant. Rimzim.

Two months later, the wedding invitation came by post.

*

'Humko bachado dacter sa'ab,' said the woman in a low, defeated voice. 'Please save me.' But that was later.

At first, she did not speak at all. She was attractive, with deep, dark eyes and clear skin. Her sari was a pale blue and she had flowers in her hair. She stood a few feet away but the mephitic smell had already filled the room. The patients waiting outside did not hide their disgust. She stood before me with the pallu of her sari half-concealing her face.

The man who escorted her had curling whiskers and a jaunty stride. He said that he had brought her to have her insides fixed. I must examine her, I said.

'You won't be able to bear the smell. Just tell me if you'll operate and put it all back.'

'I can't, unless I look at it. And I have to speak to her first.'

'I'm her devar, you can ask me anything.'

The man needed to be convinced. I spent several minutes explaining that there was no need for his sister-in-law to be shy with me. Reluctantly, he agreed to leave her with me and wait outside.

'Humko bachado dacter sa'ab.'

I closed the door and helped her on to the couch. Her vulva was swollen like a melon and the skin was scarred and corrugated

like the bark of a tree; the urethral opening was pulled forward
and urine leaked in a trickle over her thighs. As I examined her,
the woman's eyes became glassy with tears. She told me that her
husband had disowned her and her three children refused to
come near. Cut it away, cut it away, she begged. I don't care
what happens, just do it.

Elephantiasis of the vulva: a hideous thickening of the skin
and subcutaneous tissue which eventually became waterlogged
and infected, seen often in the leg and sometimes the scrotum,
but very rarely in the vulva. Why did such problem patients
keep coming? No book would tell me what to do. If something
went wrong, no one would defend me. And here she was before
me, pleading.

Her haemoglobin was six grams. She had to be transfused
a pint of blood before surgery. Tejus settled for a spinal
anaesthetic which would numb her tissues below the waist
without putting her to sleep. It was cheaper than a general
anaesthetic and, in his hands, safe. The indurated tissue bled
steadily as I cut. Four scalpel blades were blunted before I was
through. To my dismay I had a large gaping wound before me,
with no skin cover. Two weeks later, with skin grafted from her
thighs on to the wound, she healed. A month later she returned,
this time with her husband. My wife is fine now, he said, folding
his hands in gratitude. Wordlessly, the woman placed a handful
of jasmine on my table and left.

The delicate scent of the flowers stayed with me all day; I
smiled easily. The same night I dreamt of someone giving me a
string of jasmine so long that after I had pinned two lengths on
my hair there was enough to wind round my neck, wrists and
ankles. I could not tell if it was Ajja who gave me the flowers,
or Amma, or the jasmine seller. Or Jai.

I wished I could talk to Jai. The last time we met, before I
left for Keshavganj, he had said that we must not let our
differences come in the way of our friendship. But we had not
even exchanged letters since. Putting aside resentment, I wrote a
long letter of seven pages. I described my life in Keshavganj and
the cases which fascinated me. He replied promptly. Hurry

disfigured his otherwise neat hand but that was only understandable. He was busy, busy, busy. He would love to tell me about his practice but where was the time? 'One of these days, I'll dictate a long letter and have it typed, I promise. Our second son, Abhijit, came five months ago. Bela sends her love.'

I wrote back to congratulate them. I did not hear from Jai again.

Chandrika came heavily laden with bangles, chains and anklets. She was attempting, with the clatter of ornaments, to hide the gurgle in her bowels, a sound loud enough to be heard in the next room. This 'tummy gurgle' or borborygmus is the sound of peristaltic waves of contraction as food is propelled down the intestine. Chandrika's bowel for some unknown reason produced gross, cacophonic sounds which embarrassed her. Three surgeons had operated and found nothing. It was futile to try once more and Chandrika left my clinic unsatisfied and uncured, her ornaments jingling sadly as she went.

But with Sudha there was success. When I saw her squatting before me in the clinic, I thought it was hopeless. Most cases of serious burns were difficult to handle, given the limited resources at the hospital and the little that most patients could afford. Sudha's burns were three months old. Severe flexion contractures as a result of poorly managed burns had resulted in her being unable to close her mouth or straighten her knees. She had an ugly scar beneath the left eye and a webbed, splayed-out heap of tissue on the neck pulling down the lower jaw. Thick scars behind her knees had drawn her knees back until they were completely bent.

Sudha retained her dignity and composure although she came alone, dragging herself on her haunches. 'I want to walk,' she said. She would go through any amount of pain. Her knees were her priority. Her face came second.

How had it happened and why had she delayed it so long?

'I'm a teacher in middle school. I teach maths,' she said. 'My husband didn't like my going out to work. If I missed the bus and walked the five kilometres from school, he would fly into fits of rage. That day I had walked back and was lighting the kerosene stove to make tea when he kicked the stove in my face. It was several minutes before the neighbours heard my screams. The first thing I said was that I would live. My husband was terrified. He fell at my feet and begged me not to tell anybody; he took me to the government hospital where I stayed for two months. What was the point in telling the police? They would only make a tamasha of it and never even try to find out the truth.'

She withdrew a bundle of tightly folded notes. Eight hundred rupees. 'It took me all this time to collect the money,' she said.

I went to talk to Big Swami.

At the first surgery, I cut away the dense scar behind the knees, taking pains to avoid the blood vessels and nerves, until the knees could be straightened and held in place with splints. Five days later I took her back to Theatre for skin grafting. The following week I excised the scars on her neck. Sudha was in hospital for more than a month; she bore cheerfully the pain of dressings, injections and surgery. When the immediate post-operative disability was over, I discovered that she liked to talk.

'My naani always told me that we women need wiles in order to survive. She survived two attempts to kill her, my mother one. When I was burned, I thought that if I give up it will be a stain on the family. I'll tell you, dacter sa'ab, how I collected the money. The two months I stayed in hospital I was treated kindly by everyone. They were sorry for me. I dragged myself to their bedsides to talk, to hold a baby in my arms when the mother ate or went to the bathroom. And I stole from patients, nurses, doctors, anyone, in the night, when the duty nurse and ayah never came anywhere near us and everyone was asleep. My need was greater than theirs, dacter sa'ab.'

Her lips contorted in an attempt to smile. Once or twice a week her husband came and peeped through the window of the ward to see if she was dying. 'I'm not afraid to be his wife. But he may no longer have the courage to be my husband.'

Sudha did not become completely normal. But she could

walk, close her mouth and lift her head. She would teach more than maths to her middle-school students.

The three-bedded ward for burns was always taken up by young women, not more than a year or two into marriage. The alleged cause was predictably similar: accidental bursting of a kerosene stove while cooking. It was always a young wife and never an older one who got burned, and never an unmarried girl. And no husband or mother-in-law ever got burned attempting to save the young woman. The girl on the bed opposite Sudha's had not been lucky. Her parents argued with the husband's family about the payment of bills. Each said it was the responsibility of the other. The girl made the decision for them. She succumbed without a fight.

38

It was a cruel summer, and the monsoons were more than a month away. The Kitchen Swami sent sweet-and-salt lassi to Theatre instead of tea. For the doctors' meetings on Saturdays he sent bel juice to cool irritable stomachs and tempers. Dr Vanaja, along with other women devotees of Thakurji, doubled their efforts at prayer and bore platefuls of special offerings to the mandir. I stayed away in spite of Dr Vanaja lecturing me on piety and its benefits. But in that wretched heat I found myself listening to the sweet sounds of chanting and bhajans that floated from the mandir.

The only thing to do after work was wait until a tired breeze stirred in the neem, ashoka and tamarind trees. I wished I could work nights, like the watchmen, when it was cooler. The watchmen, Fakira, Vichitra and Vedram, fought for their turn to work at night. Morning work was much more arduous (they did every sort of hospital work and even doubled up to help in emergency deliveries). At night it was easy to tell which of them was on duty. Vedram went round the campus sounding the rap-rap-rap of his stick as he walked. Fakira surfaced two or three times to announce himself with his sharp whistle and went back to bed. Vichitra was the smartest: he was seen lurking near the nurses' duty room at eleven when the night nurses came on late shift. He disappeared for the rest of the night and emerged again at five, grinning genially at the nurse who boiled tea on a kerosene stove for the night staff.

The tedium of the long summer was broken by the news of a cardiologist joining the hospital as the medical superintendent. He had served in the army for some years, was an MRCP from London and had a thriving practice in Gwalior. Big Swami had been looking for a person who would transform the Sevashram into a modern centre. At a welcome function, the swami said that Dr Pasricha had given up his lucrative practice to devote himself to selfless service in Keshavganj. He had pledged to turn the hospital around to reach new heights of excellence.

Dr Pasricha was lean, with quick movements and an excess of nervous energy. Though sixty, he moved with the swiftness of a young man. He smiled only when it was necessary to smile and his facial muscles were taut, as if forever under some strain. He always came to work in full-sleeved white shirt, tie, knife-creased trousers and dazzling black shoes.

At a meeting with the doctors and staff on the first day, he stressed the need for punctuality and neatness. 'We are dignified members of society,' he said. 'We must be decorous at all times.' He looked pointedly at Tejus, who wore his white coat directly over his vest in summer and sandals instead of shoes. After the meeting, Tejus went to the Big Swami. Whatever the others might do, *he* wasn't going to change the way he dressed. The swami tried to convince him. An argument ensued and Tejus walked out of the office. It was the first and only rift between him and the swami.

Pasricha, with his knowledge and his flair, was an instant hit. Even when called to see a patient in the night, he was depressingly cheerful. He urged the doctors to read foreign journals, write papers and understand the need for constant progress. He had the pragmatic *Problem? Solve it* kind of approach, which I had seen in England. At the Saturday meetings, Tejus could not trip him up the way he did me. Not only did

Pasricha have an answer to every question, he could even quote effortlessly from journals and books.

His manners were impeccable: 'Will you get me a tongue depressor, please, Sister? Thanks *very* much.' 'Would you be kind enough to meet me in the office at 1000 hours?'

Dr Miltry, he was called. Work started at 0700 hours and finished at 1730 hours, with a half-hour break for lunch. The screws tightened quickly. Nurses stood in a row every morning and spread out their hands for inspection. Nails clipped. No nail polish. Hair in a bun. No bangles, lipstick or flowers. Meetings were held several times a week to lay down yet another protocol, of which now there were many. Committees were set up. Nurses started to come in their free time to catch up on paperwork and maintain registers. 'Off-duty work,' it was called, and they fell over each other to do it. Slouching ward boys, gossiping ayahs, noisy relatives and unruly staff were ticked off. Floors sparkled, windows and doors were scrubbed clean, cots were painted, toilets reeked phenyl. Patients lay in regimented rows on their neatly made beds, believing that anything done with such efficiency must be good for them.

The crowds outside Tejus's OPD shrank rapidly. Every patient wanted to see the specialist. 'Dil ka dacter is very clever,' they said.

In spite of myself, I was impressed. Discipline, punctuality, decorum, neatness, good manners, it was easy to lose touch with all this in Keshavganj. I decided to pattern myself on Pasricha, at least in some things. If only he could slow down a little, I could catch up. I secretly exulted over the fact that he was the opposite of Tejus. Mine was a superficial sort of spite; I did not realize then the harm it could do.

Light of Righteousness was uneasy. It showed in his indifference to everything Pasricha did, his excessive smoking, his constant picking on me. Copying Pasricha, I started doing my evening ward rounds at three in the afternoon. Tejus heckled, 'No siesta, Ms Busy-busy?'

'It's a lazy habit we have, sleeping in the afternoons. They wouldn't dream of doing it in England.'

'You've been a puppet of the West long enough. What next? Joining the army?'

Meanwhile, Big Swami launched into a fury of buying. Every week some new equipment was unloaded from a truck: a new ECG machine, plastic spittoons, synthetic blankets, a motorized brush for swabbing floors. The next step, Miltry said, would be to start an ICU with cardiac monitors, defibrillators and respirators. Fully convinced, the swami prepared to go on a fund-collecting mission.

Mrs Pasricha—no one knew her first name—was a thin-lipped woman, visibly older than her husband. She went to the market once a week with Fakira's daughter walking behind her, basket in hand. Farida selected the brinjals, onions, dhania and bhindi. Mrs Pasricha paid and ticked each item off her list. She did everything as seriously as her husband pursued his job. Working for them, Farida, who was the same age as Sapna, became quiet and melancholy.

The Pasrichas were veteran walkers. Every evening they emerged from their house to walk around the campus. 'Dr Miltry is on his chakkar,' we said. After three rounds, his wife went back into the house, and then the doctor's pace quickened. Faster and faster he walked, checking his watch after each round. Ten, twelve, fourteen. It was fascinating to watch him. When it rained, he walked with an umbrella, his shoes squelching in the mud. Chakkar after chakkar.

Miltry believed in honesty and transparent values. A new rule proscribed anyone other than a doctor from speaking to patients' relatives about medical matters. The Small Swami, who had always been a mediator in the wards, became redundant. Pasricha made surprise visits to the hospital to catch those who might be defying the rules. Spying became a virtue and Sukhdev Miltry's trusted aide. Miltry would summon a nurse to his office and hint displeasure towards another. She would then blab. The atmosphere in the hospital threatened to turn sour. The nurses smiled rarely and Tejus retreated into a major sulk.

It was in the drug store that Miltry met his match. When he saw the unique chaos with which it functioned, he came away mopping his brow in disbelief. The same evening he went back to have a long chat with the Store Swami. The swami listened, his doe-eyes perplexed. Systematize, Miltry told him. Maintain registers for daily drug indent, stocks, weekly indent, purchase and expiry. Thirteen registers to be filled every day.

The swami and his helpers worked bravely, moving shelves, sweeping, dusting, pulling down cardboard boxes and throwing away waste. Rusty bedpans, broken sputum cups, chipped ounce glasses and reels of frayed gauze were bundled out. In the mandir, the swami's voice trembled. He sat with his head bowed in prayer after a single bhajan and a brahmachari took over. In the mornings he walked to his cell and worked away until late evening.

Everything went awry. The drugs reached the wards several hours late and patients went without medicines until the forenoon. Wrong drugs were issued in haste. Miltry assured us that everything would soon fall in place but it did not. His master plan for the drug store was a failure. The swami quietly reverted to his original jumbled efficiency and things were back to normal. The drug store debacle had a strange effect on Pasricha. He wilted, just a little, as if he had shed some of his military blood. Failure did not suit him.

The nurses had the worst time of it, with Miltry determined to make them as efficient as the nurses he had worked with in England. The Nurses' Daily Report on the patients was carefully scrutinized, spellings and other errors encircled in red. Mistakes like 'the patient's fever is normal' or vomiting spelt with a double-t ('vomiting however severe is spelt with *one t*') were punished with a fine. The nurses steadily lost one or two rupees a week. When Jessy Kutty sent the call book to Dr Narayan with the note 'Ramprakash in bed 22 cannot pass urine. Please come and pass urine,' Narayan laughed it off, but Pasricha chanced upon it the next day and fined Jessy five times the usual.

Miltry instructed the nurses to wash the bedpans themselves and not give them to the ayahs. 'The nurses do it in Britain,' he explained. 'Defecation is a normal body function and the cleaning of excreta is a noble act.'

Upset, the nurses asked Tejus and then the Small Swami to intervene but the two men firmly said they could not. Big Swami found himself confronting the eleven nurses in his office early one morning. Lilly Kutty, who was their leader, spoke. 'Sir is asking us to wash the bedpans,' she said. 'He says it is a noble act. Maybe it is in England, but here in Keshavganj . . . the patients pass so much hexcreta . . .' and she burst into tears. The bedpan washing stayed the way it had.

At times like this even the swamis were disconcerted by Pasricha's unstoppable momentum, his single-minded aim to excel. But how do you find fault with efficiency, discipline, dogged work and gentlemanly behaviour? I was confused. I hoped that once the new rules were firmly in place, Miltry would relax a bit and things would sort themselves out.

All things considered, Pasricha was very much in favour. The changes he brought about in the hospital were visible and praiseworthy, and his name spread beyond the hospital. Within six months of coming to Keshavganj, he was made the president of the Indian Medical Association, local branch.

From the day he took over as president, the members of the IMA had no time to fathom what had hit them. There were weekly meetings, case presentations and scholarly discussions. Soon Pasricha announced his plan to organize a district-level medical conference. Keshavganj came alive with bustle. Drug companies swooped down and offered to sponsor dinners, lunches and the gifts needed for a two-day conference.

The people of Keshavganj, long used to the tranquil nature of work at the Sevashram, were bewildered. The Big Swami rushed to Delhi every week, sometimes with Pasricha. There was much to do: invitations, travel and staying arrangements, shamianas, drug stalls, free gifts, slide projectors, sound systems, entertainment. A week before the conference, the routine work at the hospital was abandoned and only emergency cases were treated. Pasricha was like an engine that could not be switched off.

Pasricha said I should present a paper on abdominal trauma. My experience was modest, but by following his advice of using slides, graphs and statistics I found my confidence growing by the minute. Tejus called it a mindless extravaganza. Uncaring of the disruption around him he sat in his outpatients' and saw the few patients who trickled in. I felt sorry for him. He had isolated himself from a great event and would surely regret it.

The delegates—more than a hundred—started to arrive the evening before. They stayed in the hotels in Mathura, and in the morning a stream of cars and buses drove in through the gates of the Sevashram. Fakira, Vedram and Vichitra worked overtime: 'Salaam sa'ab! Idhar sa'ab . . . udhar memsa'ab . . . naashta wahan hai . . . Jaaiye! Aaiye . . .!'

The conference went like a dream. Papers were presented and lectures delivered. The drug stalls, which were cleverly positioned in the eating area, did brisk business, luring doctors with free gifts and persuading them to buy the 'best' suture material, tablets and injections. Doctors and families moved about bearing 'with compliments' packages. The chief guest, a cardio-thoracic surgeon from Delhi, praised Pasricha's efforts to modernize the rural hospital and promised support. He would be happy to set up a unit for heart surgery in Keshavganj, he said.

Tejus was there, sitting a little apart from the smartly attired delegates. In the afternoon, full of mind and body fatigue, I trudged to my room for a rest. On the second day I saw Big Swami take the seat next to Tejus. He looked worried. The reality of the conference with its drug hawkers, the bountiful food, the music and entertainment (on the first evening a Kuchipudi dance performance, on the second a music recital) had begun to wear him down.

Pasricha had reserved his presidential address for the last. He appealed for the cause of progress and swore that he would bring open-heart surgery, brain, kidney and keyhole surgery to the villages. 'We will strive to push forward the frontiers of knowledge. The day will come when Keshavganj will be no different from any big city in medical technology. Villagers will be made to shed old beliefs and embrace modernity.

'We will not ignore the common problems here,' he said, adjusting his blue silk tie. 'I'll give you an example. Malnourishment. It's rampant here. Even second- and third-degree malnutrition is common in children. The average diet of a villager is miserable—hardly any protein, vitamins or minerals. We will attack these age-old concepts and start them on the road to modern . . .'

Tejus was up on his feet. 'Before you do that, have a good look at what they eat,' he said. 'Dr Pasricha may not know it, but the villagers eat better food than the poor in cities. Yes, they live on chapattis, dal, onion and green chilli and chew a raw mooli or carrot afterwards. Some families buy a metre-length of sugar cane at the market as a Sunday special. Roasted wheat, groundnuts or cucumber with salt serve as snacks. They drink tea, once a day in summer, twice in winter. They eat what they can get and they're healthy. If they fall ill and come to hospital, they sell a goat or cow to pay for treatment.' He looked pointedly at Pasricha. 'How will they be able to afford the specialized services you mention? Does a conference with fancy stalls and clever speeches do anything for them?'

There was a commotion as delegates stood up to defend Pasricha. A few said that Tejus should be allowed to make his point. The MC, a young doctor from Lucknow, tried to plead into the mike. Pasricha stood stone-faced and immobile.

'No, I'm going to have my say. Last month the hospital spent a lakh on equipment. Where's that money going to come from? Swami struggles to get donations, but it won't be enough if the Sevashram is strangled with more purchases. The patients' bills have been creeping up. As for this conference and what Dr Pasricha was saying, he should think before talking about food habits. The poor man's diet . . . What do you know about the poor man's diet?'

I shifted uncomfortably in my seat. Wasn't he taking this a bit too far? But they would have to let him finish.

'I had a young patient,' said Tejus, 'who told me he never washed his hands after eating, he simply wiped them dry so the smell of food lasted until the next meal came. This is the problem of millions of villagers everywhere. The bonded workers in Bihar for instance live on sattu, which, if you don't know, is roasted, powdered channa dal carried in a twist of cloth. To this they add water and maybe salt and chilli, and it is a ready meal. Sattu. They put in a hard day's work, day after day, on sattu. It doesn't spoil, so it's never wasted. There are the mushahars, a rat-eating people in Bihar. They live on field rats and eat house mice and termites on festive occasions. I have an excellent recipe for rat fry, if anyone is interested. Whether it is sattu, rat meat or chapattis, the calorific value of their diet is 1500 calories a day, plus or minus 200. They put in eight hours' work in the fields on this diet and return home to cope with housework. I learnt in medical college that an average healthy diet for a working man is 3000 calories, for a woman 2500. Who are they talking about?'

I sat in the fourth row, drinking in the scene. All these knowledgeable experts from big hospitals in the audience, and Tejus holding his own, slipping in the barbs.

'Last night a doctor I know well ate and drank enough to please the drug company which hosted the dinner, and then vomited it all out in the garden at the back of this hall. While he was thus lightening himself, a few feet away two children and a woman were picking up half-eaten rotis, chicken bones and crumbs of laddu from a pile of used plates and stuffing it all in a plastic bag—their festive meal.

'May we please have a long and mindful discussion about the true meaning of malnourishment and its causes? In college I learnt about first-degree, second-degree and third-degree malnutrition. Seeing those children pick through the garbage for food last night, I thought instead of first-, second- and third-degree murder. Who is guilty? One more point and I'll shut up. In two days, food worth thousands has been wasted to feed us. If it had been simplified . . . I mean the number of dishes cut down from fourteen to eleven, we could have given milk to a hundred pregnant women for three months. You want to do research, come and figure out how these village folk manage, as our big doctor says, on a meagre diet . . .?'

Any questions, asked the MC. Someone cleared his throat, out of embarrassment. No questions. We quietly filed out of the hall to have tea and samosas and then wait for the closing ceremony. Tejus stood near the water cooler, drinking glass after glass of water. He looked crestfallen. 'There was no response,' he said. 'Absolutely none. I thought that at least a few might appreciate what I was trying to say . . .'

The whole thing was wrapped up in an air of awkwardness. With his ranting and invective, Tejus had ruined the conference. I was angry, but not as angry as I was confused.

Late that evening, Tejus dropped in. 'Care to speak to the pariah?' he said, carefully choosing a cigarette from his pack. 'Pasricha has given an ultimatum, in writing. It's me or him.' A smile snipped across his face. 'He says he will be honoured to remain the swami's humble, obedient servant if the obstacle in his path is removed.'

I was angry. 'All these months when Pasricha was working so hard to improve the hospital, you carped, but did nothing,' I said. 'You waited until you were sure of an audience, took his one statement about malnutrition and blew it out of proportion. It was unfair. I know what you said was true. But the way you attacked him. You're jealous.'

Tejus smoked his cigarette through and stubbed it on the ground. His mouth twitched. 'I *have* been playing foul, but not because I'm jealous. It's frustration at seeing something so diabolical happen in the Sevashram.' He looked miserable. 'Fuck,' he muttered and got up. 'The swami will tell me to apologize. I won't do it. I cringe from defeat just as much as Pasricha does. If swami wants me to leave, I'll go.'

I spent an anxious night, not knowing what would happen. Tejus should pay for his outburst against Pasricha. But what if he was made to leave? Who was more important for the Sevashram? Tejus the loud-mouthed, abrasive Gaswallah or the highly competent dil-ka-dacter who would turn the Sevashram around until it was unrecognizable?

Next morning the news came: Pasricha had resigned. He left quietly two days later without wishing any of us goodbye. He had done many good things for the hospital; it was cleaner, smarter. He was a good doctor. But somewhere his vision had fallen short and marred everything he did. He left behind him a trail of deranged nerves.

Tejus did not crow about his victory. 'He taught us something,' he said to me. 'Let's leave it at that.' He was trying hard to overcome his own prejudice.

The chirpy voices of the nurses were again heard in the hospital, patients laughed and Small Swami returned to the wards as friend and advisor.

It was back to the usual.

'Kya taqleef hai, bhai?'

I'm gastric, dacter sa'ab. I'm appendix; I have urine trouble; I have piles; boils; chest pain; burning in the head; burning in the stomach.

Sweet words.

39

Having watched me sweat through an orthopaedic operation for a fractured femur, Tejus pronounced an unpalatable fact about my work.

'You're not cut out for this.'

We were in the tearoom and I on my second cup. Narayan had just left to see an emergency and there was no one else around. I was furious. He resents my doing orthopaedics, I thought. He wants women to be rose petals sweating dew.

In England, when I had worked briefly in orthopaedics, I had liked the common-sense approach required to fix bones. A good orthopaedic surgeon was a combination of skill and common sense. No bone surgeon could hide behind vague remarks and reassurances, or use medicines to set right a mistake. I had got used to the electric drills, reamers and the image-intensifying television screen which showed you where to place a nail or a pin during surgery. In a small hospital like ours, besides manual skills, you had to be good at using drills, nails and screws, which I was not. Though I hated to admit it even to myself, the problem I had faced in England became more acute here: I did not have the physical strength required to reset human bones.

Tejus wasn't going to soften the blow. 'I've watched you operate for a long time now and I don't need to tell you that you're good. But when it comes to bones, you lack that three-dimensional vision which is so important.' He shrugged. 'I'm telling you because it's better not to deceive yourself, especially about the big things.'

I sat there a long time, playing his words back in my mind. I had been deceiving myself, especially about the big things. It was the protective ploy of my subconscious to retain happy memories and blot out the unpleasant ones. After a complication or a failure, I suffered intensely, but just long enough for the next problem to come along and obliterate the first.

However, some mistakes were impossible to forget; one case in particular, where I stubbornly stuck to my own reasoning and rued it in the end.

I had been suffering from a severe cold for days. Having dosed myself well with cough mixture, antihistamines and ginger kashayam, I went to bed early. Vedram's knocking woke me from a fevered sleep. Urgent, the nurse's report said. A full-term pregnancy with pain all day. The baby's heart sounds could not be heard. Walking across to the wards I thought of all the people sleeping peacefully in their beds, their dreams not rudely interrupted by night calls. Being ill was even more reason for me to have had a decent night's sleep. Cursing and full of self-pity, I entered the ward.

It was a case of rupture of the uterus, a dire emergency. The foetus, which cannot survive outside the uterus for more than a few seconds, was predictably dead. At the operation, the uterus was found lacerated all the way down and bleeding profusely. It would have to be removed to save the mother's life. This I did and was about to close when Tejus pointed out that the urine in the bag connected to the catheter in the woman's bladder was heavily bloodstained. Had I checked for bladder injuries?

'I've had a good look, there's nothing,' I said. 'The bladder's bruised, that's all.'

'Checked the trigone?'

The trigone, or the base of the urinary bladder which closely adheres to the lower part of the uterus, could be easily injured in a ruptured uterus. 'It's fine,' I bluffed and started closure, but not before taking a sneaky look. My reasoning was that if there was a rent, urine would have seeped into the wound during the hysterectomy. I could not have missed it, and anyway I did not want the Light of Righteousness telling me what to do.

The patient recovered and went home. A month later she was back, with urine dribbling through her vagina. Working in the fields had become impossible and she was unable to go anywhere. 'She knows very well why it happened,' her husband said. 'She's been eating chillies.' It's not because of the chillies, I said, but did not have the courage to add that my negligence during surgery had brought about this complication. She now had a fistulous opening between her bladder and cervix.

That evening, I told Tejus. 'Why're you crying to me now?' he said harshly.

'I've come to eat humble pie. I'm thinking of . . .'

'No! Send the woman to a urologist. And as for the humble pie, I've just made papdi puri, if that'll do.' He was being sarcastic. I could see how angry he was.

I felt sheepish and did not quite know how to overcome it. 'I guess one has to accept,' I said, unneccessarily, 'that surgery isn't all intellect and science.'

'Hardly *any* intellect or science is more like it.'

'Sometimes a surgeon's work is a lot like that of a tailor. Or a barber, or a butcher, or potter . . .' I was only saying it to show how modest I was.

'Leave the potters out of it,' he quipped. 'Pottery is graceful. And skilled.'

Back in my room, I pulled out my diary and began to jot down all the errors I had ever made in my surgical work. When I finished, I had filled three pages. I stared in disbelief and despair. Once again, serious doubts assailed me. How did my work compare with that of other surgeons? What would my grading be? True, I did well most of the time, but in a profession like a surgeon's were so many errors permitted? I, who never forgave Chellaiah the driver for the way he had wielded the steering wheel of the bus the day my father died, how was I better than him?

No more mistakes, I told myself. But the more I tried, the more I fumbled. A suture too tight, a plaster of Paris cast too loose, an incision too curved. My errors glared back, mocking. I suffered.

Weeks went by, and one day a scrap of paper was slipped under my door.

Who do you think you are, Jesus Christ? Imperfection is your strong point. PS: Dinner at 9.30 p.m. Pav-bhaji special. Coming?

How dare he call me imperfect? But pav-bhaji . . . I wiped my eyes, washed my face and went, ready, as much for the pav-bhaji as the duel.

In the morning we were discharging Kethu Ram, a querulous man with a malignant stomach tumour. He had agreed to the surgery and bravely stayed put right up to the moment when, dressed in a loose gown, he was wheeled into Theatre. Radhamani, her face partly covered by a mask and her hair beneath a cap, took charge of him. Tejus had started to wrap the blood pressure cuff around his arm when Kethu Ram struggled free and leapt off the stretcher. He ran out, through the corridors and out of the hospital. He had reached the hospital gates when his brother caught up with him. After a heated argument he was led back with the tubes hanging from his nose and arm. When persuasive words did not work his brother shouted, 'How will you work in the fields, how will you feed your wife and children if you don't get cured?'

Kethu Ram recovered from the partial gastrectomy to remove the cancer in his stomach. He was thinner and paler, but had the confidence of a patient on his way to recovery. As I gave him last-minute advice on his diet I happened to look at Phalguni, the nurse who was with me. She watched Kethu Ram with a radiant smile on her lips. Phalguni was a junior nurse and not very bright. She was reprimanded often for her mistakes and had even considered giving up nursing. But seeing Kethu Ram going home after a serious illness had made her happy. She was pleased to be a part of his getting better.

That evening I sat in my veranda, the sun's warm rays touching my forehead. In the kitchen Sapna washed vessels with her customary din. From the mandir the sounds of chanting drifted in. I closed my eyes and leaned my head back, stretching my neck to ease away tiredness. So many years of training and work. Had it been easy, or difficult? After that first case, the gluteal phlegmon, it had been easy rather than difficult. Straight lines and foreseeable outcomes. Shapes I could define, edges, consistency, the rough and the smooth, the hard and the soft, the tender and the non-tender. Find a lump, cut it out. See a cut, suture it. Pus, drain it. Offending bit of something, remove. Quick results, without the waiting for drugs to fight atoms and molecules. Surgery was easy. And *that* was the problem. Patients believed that a doctor thought about their illness alone. But the mind had to swing free from a hundred thoughts that cluttered it. There was doubt, lack of confidence, overconfidence, hubris, jealousy and tiredness, all vying for attention. But it had been all right to be on my feet ten, twelve, sixteen hours a day, to sleep for five, and worry about one patient or the other. That was my lot. To see a hard day's work end in failure, to look at the gloomy face of death and suffering side by side with triumph. That was my lot. It was hell sometimes, but it was the life I had chosen.

I felt a certain sadness about my friendship with Tejus. Our arguments were honest but they hovered above the real, like some inane, childish squabble. I wanted to understand him; I wanted him to understand me. Each time we talked there was this yearning, this hunger for plumbing the depths of his thoughts and my own. It never seemed to happen.

For some reason Tejus did not talk much about his past. Any curiosity about his personal life irked Tejus. He went to

Delhi on short breaks and invariably returned after a drinking
binge that took a day to get over. Very rarely did he go home,
to Wayanad in Kerala. He dragged his past along like a
mysterious shadow. He kept his house sparsely furnished, except
for a beautiful clock with a rosewood frame and a musical
chime he was proud of and an ornately carved desk with several
little drawers which he had paid four thousand rupees for. There
was some talk that he was married, that there was a daughter.
Once, on my way to the sink inside to wash my hands after
eating with him, I saw two drawings on the wall. They were
framed and mounted in glass; one of a dog, titled Tommy Bow-
Bow, the other a donkey, titled Ulta-Pulta. The words were
scrawled in crayon below the drawings, obviously done by a
child. I could imagine Tejus with his little girl.

Small Swami witnessed innumerable fights between us and
often stepped in to resolve the issue. 'Did you hear what she
said, Swamiji? Did you *hear* what she said?' Swami would smile
his toothy smile and jingle the keys in his pocket. 'It's nothing,
nothing. She's only saying.'

Tejus would blow smoke rings and smile at my anger. The
way the smoke curled, it looked like the thoughts unfurling from
his brain. When he was upbeat, he blew the rings upward, and
when depressed he looked down and blew the smoke towards
his feet. It was most peculiar. When a particularly difficult case
was done, we sat in the tearoom. I loved that moment, when my
body was full of aches and pains and my sore back was pressed
comfortably against the chair. I waited to hear the tinkle of the
cups and the aluminium kettle in which Govind brought the tea.
The tea was always sweet, and perfect. Sometimes we sat late
into the night, in Tejus's house or mine. In the nocturnal quiet,
all the acrimony of the day seemed to wash away. We would sit
silent for long stretches, when the only sound we could hear was
the soft scratch of a match being struck and the rustle of the
flame as Tejus lit another cigarette, or the spiteful hum of a
mosquito in my ear. Tejus was quiet and ruminative, sometimes
answering a question many days after I had asked. Once I asked
about his family and he shut me up with a cold and furious
glance.

In his desire to get through all the religions in the world, he had wanted to be a sadhu. But he was not accepted by the monastery because he had asked for the freedom to leave when he was seventy.

'What can you do after seventy?'

It was raining and we were sitting in my house. An insect, the size and shape and colour of a groundnut fried in oil, fell into the saucer in his hands. It beat its wings in frenzy and swam in the coffee that had spilled into the saucer. Tejus picked it up and chucked it out through the window. He watched it crawl bewildered on to the sill and lie there, wings fluttering feebly. 'Plenty,' he said. 'You think that all this smoking should finish me off early. I fight it mentally. Have you ever heard me cough? I have clean lungs. Health is up here.' He tapped his forehead. 'I'll start achieving after seventy when my greed and my attachments are spent. No one pays much attention to an old man. I'll have the time and the peace of mind to meditate.'

'You don't even go to the mandir. And don't tell me you don't enjoy being a doctor.'

'We become doctors so that we can belong, to this group or that. I'm an executive, I'm an artist, I'm a doctor. We choose, like everyone else. Birds fly miles to reach where they want to go. Even a rat will find a sewer to his liking.'

He was strange.

'You're a good anaesthetist,' I said.

'I'd be good at anything,' he said, gruffly. 'The thing is, all my unhappiness has to do with my relationships with others. Alone, I'm perfectly happy.'

I was surprised when a few days later I came to know that Philo had been writing letters to Tejus. I heard from Madho Singh who brought in the post. Why was she posting letters when she could talk, I asked Philo. She hesitated, but then came out with it.

'He's unhappy,' she said. 'He'll be all right when he marries and settles down.' She looked meaningfully at me.

'Don't look at me.'

'He's a wonderful person, you two would make a good match. In fact, I've tried to talk to him.'

The letters had been an effort to get us fixed up. I said I would not dream of it. 'Keep an open mind,' advised Philo. She talked about mental compatibility and the need to find the other person interesting.

It was true that Tejus and I had a good friendship, but what else? About others like Stan, Vishnu and Jai, I knew what my feelings were. I liked Stan; I disliked and feared Vishnu; I adored Jai. With Tejus, I could not tell what I felt. He was overweight, slothful and had hair growing out of his ears. He smoked and drank too much. I found myself thinking about what Philo had said. What did Tejus think of me? At first I was merely curious and then I became anxious. The other day in Theatre, seeing me sweat, he had reached over and wiped my brow with a piece of gauze. 'Thanks,' I said, but he had already turned away and was adjusting the intravenous line. I had stopped paying much attention to my appearance a long time ago. I only had two shades of lipstick. I decided to get some more; and maybe some blush-on and nail polish. Foolish of me to have ignored my looks for so long.

Tejus was drinking more and it was noticeable. Philo was upset. One day after an argument with him, she came away angry. 'I've had such a shock,' she said. 'A terrible, terrible shock.'

Tejus had told her that he had a woman in Delhi.

Philo was very apologetic. 'I'm so sorry,' she kept saying to me.

'He's not worth it, Sister,' I said, keeping my voice calm.

40

It was late April and Keshavganj was already in the grip of a vicious summer. I was escaping on my yearly holiday and had comfortably settled in my berth—a pillow for my head, magazines, a flask of tea and a packet of murukkus within reach—when the train stopped at Jhansi. Two passengers got into the compartment; only one of them had a reservation. The other, a young girl, was thirty-sixth on the waiting list. She walked up and down glancing ruefully at the passengers.

She stopped by my side, flushed and slightly out of breath. 'I don't know what to do,' she said, lowering her bags on to my seat. An angelic, pure sort of prettiness, I thought, envious. 'I *have* to travel today. I've to be admitted at the hospital for a heart operation.'

I swung my legs down and shifted to make place for her. With some pushing and shoving I managed to fit her luggage next to mine. I explained that I was a doctor and, trying not to reveal my concern, checked her pulse. A hundred and ten. Respiration twenty-six, forehead bathed in sweat. Had she taken her tablets that morning? The girl searched everywhere before she discovered that she had forgotten to bring them. She had mitral stenosis, a disease of the heart valves which often results in poor pumping of blood by the heart. Two days was a long time to do without tablets. I considered stopping in Bhopal and having her admitted, but the girl—Amrita—would not hear of it. Her family had spent so much and they would be waiting. She had to reach Madras.

Amrita was a quiet sort. She accepted the food I offered her, ate quietly and spent most of her time staring dreamily out of the window. I gave her my pillow and let her sleep in my berth; I dozed, sitting. Several times in the night I woke to check on her and was relieved to find her sleeping peacefully.

After an anxiety-filled twenty-eight hours, we reached Madras. I had aching limbs and a headache from too little sleep but I was glad that Amrita was no worse. Her parents would not be able to come to the station, she said. I got her an auto and helped her in with her luggage. As the driver started the engine, she squeezed my hand. 'I'm sorry to have troubled you so much,' she said.

'It's quite all right,' I said, and wished her luck for the operation.

'Actually . . . I was faking the illness,' she said. 'I could not bear the thought of travelling without a berth. This was the only

way.' She was a just-passed medic and had used the ploy a few
times with success.

I stood there stupefied as the auto sped away.

⤴

Back again in Angheri, I prepared myself to face the many
changes both in our home and in the village.

Budhi had married and settled at home with Violet. She was
a plump girl with a square, determined face, strong arms and
hair cropped above her ears. Her face spoke of hard work and
honesty. Sujju and Vishnu were mildly scornful of Violet, and
Harini was a little afraid. Ajja would have none of her friendliness.
He scowled at her and stopped talking the moment she appeared.
Violet asked Amma tearfully why Ajja did not like her. Was it
her dresses that he objected to? They talked for a long while and
then set to work: they opened every one of her dresses and
sewed them into salwars and kurtas. Amma gave her saris to
wear when she went out. It worked like magic.

I liked Violet. She had a mind of her own. She pointed out
that the family had no expectations of Budhi. We showed our
affection by indulging him. If there was extra coffee, it was
poured into his cup. If there was extra rice, palya or a chapatti,
Budhi got it. Violet grumbled to me. 'Why not keep some pigs
instead? It isn't good for him to be treated this way.' I was
ashamed at the truth in her words. Budhi himself was
unconcerned. He had taken to discussing politics with me.
Shaking his head sadly over some depressing incident in the
papers, he would say, 'This is kaliyuga, akka . . .'

One evening, while I sat in the porch with Kapi the second
on my lap and stroked the deep furrow between his shoulders,
Budhi came and sat beside me. 'Akka . . .' he said. 'What
happened to *that* thing? Did you get it?'

'N-no,' I was taken aback that Budhi remembered.

'You should have reduced the number of times you had to
get the square right.'

'I couldn't have done that, Budhi. And anyway, it doesn't
matter. I don't want *that* thing any more.'

In the evenings Violet sat in the porch with Budhi, listening to him read news from *Dinajyoti*. She had persuaded him to buy the one-page newspaper, so he could finish reading it. When Sompa's brother Ganapa offered Budhi a job in their corner shop, Violet made him take it. Sompa was by then drinking heavily and not much good in the shop. His brother was hard-pressed to manage on his own and willing to give Budhi a try. It worked. Budhi clearly remembered which customers owed money to the shop and how much. And he never made a mistake in counting the change.

The house which had been the mainstay of my childhood was constantly being improved. The bars on the windows had been removed and wire mesh put in their place; the floor was cemented and smooth. The atta, filled with old books, utensils and junk, was inhospitable. In the front yard the jackfruit, guava and parijata trees had been cut down. It was the only time Ajja had protested but Vishnu had his way. The sky looked bald and the hills desolate. The yard was cemented, to dry the pepper that Vishnu had started to grow, and in the afternoons it gave off an angry white heat that was different from the scent of sun-baked earth.

Vishnu I believed was to blame for everything. Angry and aggrieved, I watched him go about his day. He was still slim, with a small paunch that rose offensively above his belt. He dabbled in 'business' and was in and out of Angheri. He brought his associates home; they went to his room and talked behind the closed door but their presence in the house was like some invasion—impudent and unholy.

I protested to Amma. It was evening, and we were at the kitchen table. Amma poured coffee from the aluminium kettle that had replaced the brass chombu and handed me a cup. Vishnu was changing things too fast. The changes were eroding our family life. On the blue plastic sheet that now covered the kitchen table were small squares of cardboard to put the hot vessels on. I longed to pull the plastic sheet away and run my fingers along the grooved edge of the wooden table. I longed to dig my nails into the comforting crack that ran along the middle where two pieces of jack wood had been joined to make the top surface.

I watched Amma as she listened to my many grouses against Vishnu. She had became more comely with age. Her movements had slowed a little, adding a grace which she had lacked in her youth. The artlessness of her honesty had spared her the wrinkles she would never have tried to hide. Not having resorted to creams and lotions when young, she had no need of them now. With Vishnu being away a lot, Amma managed day-to-day work on the land. She could handle Ajja's mood swings and his dejection. Sometimes they travelled to Mysore and stayed with Sujju, more for his benefit than hers.

Amma let me talk, and then said quietly, 'You're not happy.'

'Vishnu's hacking away everything without consulting you and Ajja.'

Amma poured another half-cupful of coffee for me. 'It's something else,' she said. 'Is it your work?'

I looked down at the brown coffee swirling around and around in the cup and did not answer her. The family listened attentively when I talked about Keshavganj, but they did not ask me to come back. The village hospital was all but forgotten. I saw Appa in my dreams, seated on the shoulder of Donkubetta, observing me with his silent, headmaster eyes.

The monsoons had come and gone, the weather had cooled. Three months more and I would complete three years in Keshavganj. I was happily settled. The Big Swami had called me to his office and said that he was pleased with my work; he wanted to give me a raise. My salary was now two thousand rupees.

That evening I spent a long time thinking. It felt good to be appreciated. Three years of work; glorious triumphs had dimmed the anguish of failures, sleepless nights had been rewarded with a difficult case cured, a life saved. Everything was good. Why then the discontent, the strange aching desire for something more? The swamis liked me, the patients were happy, the nurses were my friends. I worked well with the doctors, even Tejus. What, then, was the problem?

I remembered my conversation with Amma. She had suspected that my unhappiness was in some way connected to my work, perhaps to my frustration about Angheri. I wanted my village to want me but they didn't seem to. Violet had put it wonderfully: 'You expect them to invite you with music and drums?'

My discontent grew. I found fault with everything: The weather was muggy, the house was damp, the swamis were blinkered, the patients ungrateful, the pharmacy in a shambles, the doctors mediocre. Simple satisfaction eluded me. One thing was clear: if I wanted to find the reason for my discontent it would not do to stay on. I had to chase after the problem until I was face to face with it. Then we would see. There was only one person who could help me make my mind up.

It was a Saturday and the clinical meeting had just got over. Tejus was in his veranda, legs up on the parapet, reading.

'I've decided to leave,' I said.

He was about to light a cigarette. He paused for a moment, the match unlit in his hand. Then he struck it and lit up. 'When?'

'There's the three months' notice period, so it will be end of August. I haven't told Swamiji.'

'Better do that soon. And get that thyroid out of the way. And the prostate.'

'Not even a "How Sad"?'

A glimmer of a smile and it vanished. 'How sad. Does that make my sorrow true or false?' He lowered his legs to the floor. 'Sure, we'll have the nurses in tears, the swamis upset, the patients wailing. But you've got as much out of this place as you've given.'

'It's nothing against anyone or the swamis. I just feel . . . I'm rusting.'

'Then you must be derusted.'

'You haven't even asked me where I'm going.' I had looked

up advertisements and found an opening in Madras. The family had financial problems, I had told them. I had to help.

'You're not going to start that hospital in your village?'

'Not yet.' I hated him then, for not trying, for not making it difficult for me to leave. I picked up a book that I had come for. 'Okay then.'

'Just one thing I wanted to say and get it over with.' His voice was hoarse, his eyes angry. 'I'm fond of you.'

I blushed. 'Don't get me wrong,' he added. 'I'm relieved that you're going because I understand you too well. I used to be like you. Trying to invest everything with meaning, not knowing that it's the easiest, most facile thing to do. You end up with all sorts of superficialities and become too judgemental.' He threw up his hands. 'I've probably confused you now. Sorry. I got over my stupid idealism long ago . . .

'Look. Forget all this,' he continued, almost tenderly. 'You're one of the few persons I can have a decent fight with and that I'll miss. You understand? And you have a type of selfishness that's vital. You must guard it.'

He gave me a fierce hug. I walked slowly back to my room.

For a short while I nursed a spiteful glee at the distress I was leaving behind. Big Swami sent emissaries and, when that failed, he talked to me in his office. I piled reason upon reason for having to go. The truth was I had had enough of everything and everyone: the scorching summers and the sameness of the food cooked by Sapna, the swamis and Tejus, the nurses, the man with the red rumal, patients like the woman with the football between her thighs, Rimzim, Makkan, the little girl who ate stones by the fistful. There was too much pain everywhere and I wanted to flee. Go somewhere more pleasant.

Small Swami was the most offended. We had worked well together. He was the best mediator, the voice of reason when emotions ran high. A few days before I left Keshavganj, I met him and the Stores Swami near the rose garden outside the temple.

'It is really hard for me,' I said, lamely.

'So hard for you . . .' said the Stores Swami.

'I want to work in a bigger centre.'

'Yes . . . a bigger centre.'

'My mother is getting old. I shouldn't be staying so far away.'

'Mother getting old . . . yes.'

The Small Swami did not say a word.

With Tejus, I had a talent for getting it wrong. Having decided to take lightly everything he had said, I asked a local tailor to make a kerchief with 'Gaswallah Dacter' embroidered in a corner. The day I was leaving, I rang his doorbell and gave him my farewell gift. A scowl appeared on his face and then a smile fought its way through. He was looking at me without meeting my eyes. It made me shaky. I sat down to compose myself.

'Thanks,' he said, crumpling the kerchief in slow motion. Then he twisted it into a narrow strip, and spun it by its two ends like a cord. 'I'm really grateful you told me what I am. I gas the patients to sleep so you can trim and patch them.'

'Tejus . . . You're one of the best.'

'Fuck. You're trying to cover up for speaking the truth. I'm a stupid gaswallah and you a stupid jajjan. Nice team we make, hiding here in Keshavganj. Now you're running away. Brave of you.'

We were back to our usual spats and I was sort of relieved. 'What's wrong with wanting to set something right?'

'After a while you find yourself in a cul-de-sac and want to back out. That's the price we pay for taking ourselves too seriously. We, especially doctors, have an ego so strong we cannot imagine a world without us. Humanity is being hacked at all over the place and I'm content to gas people, you to snip and sew. Suddenly you pick up a little foolish courage and run to Madras. Great.'

'This isn't fair. I want to stay in touch with you.'

He was tying the kerchief around his neck in a tight knot. 'Just go.'

I did not think he would come for the farewell, but he did. It was a warm send-off. Gifts, a lunch with the swamis. 'You're welcome back any time,' Big Swami said. He sent a group of nurses to see me off at the station in Mathura. Some of the doctors came too, and Tejus. I waved from my seat and scores of hands waved back. Tejus stood a little apart from the rest, cigarette in hand, aiming the cigarette smoke towards his toes, from where, resolutely, it curled up.

41

I was determined to change the course of my life, to fill the vacuum caused by that one thing which eluded me. My dreams had faded away and I came to Madras wanting something different.

I tried to get in touch with Bansali but he had retired a year ago and gone back to his village near Rohtak. I joined a privately owned hospital in Madras, a family concern, the type that had started to flourish in the cities. It was equipped with a CT scanner, an ultrasound machine, a computerized lab and a spanking new Operating Theatre with piped oxygen. There were forty visiting consultants. I joined as a junior surgeon, an assistant to the Medical Director, who was a surgeon himself. I would earn four times as much as in Keshavganj. I would work with top surgeons and improve my skills.

The hospital authorities had found me a place to stay: a single-bedroom flat on a second floor, a fifteen-minute walk from the hospital, at a steep two thousand rupees a month. It was in a peaceful neighbourhood where the sea was near enough for the breeze to rustle the curtains by two in the afternoon. I walked to the hospital for a few days, but the traffic and the cluttered pavements prompted me to take a bus.

In the evenings I stayed in the flat. I had a gas stove instead of a kerosene one. I was looking for a part-time maid to help but in the meantime discovered that I quite liked doing the housework myself. I swept and swabbed the rooms, shopped and cooked. Madras, altered immeasurably since my college days, offered many comforts. I liked being a part of the fast-paced city. I liked the sounds and the presence of too many people, all of which I had missed out on by shutting myself away in Keshavganj.

It was convenient to avoid making friends. The few colleagues I got in touch with, I did as an obligation. Then I stopped doing it, bluffing that I was busy. In the evenings I went up to the terrace. It was peaceful to sit alone, engulfed by city sounds and breathing in the sea air. I shared the terrace with an old gentleman who lived in the flat downstairs. His servant came to the terrace every day to hang up the washing. Very rarely, the old man climbed up the stairs, with the servant carrying an armchair for him. He sat on the terrace until daylight faded into night. If we met, he greeted me with a civil 'Good evening.'

A few days after I joined the hospital, between cases in Theatre, the MD invited me to share his lunch. It was an elaborate meal despatched from his home in several hot cases. The ward boy had spread out the feast on a table. The Chief talked as we ate. 'All the money that my father-in-law blessed me with has gone towards building this hospital,' he said. 'I added to it my sweat and blood. I made my name in this city. Now I work, work, work with the devotion of a saint. People love me because I care for the poor.' A few weeks after I joined, a full-size portrait of the Chief (with a rose in his buttonhole) was put up in the foyer. He explained that it was in response to requests from the public.

He was a heavy-jowled man with restless hands and large, protuberant eyes. I surprised him by asking for a day off every week. He said it was unheard of among good doctors. 'You have the potential to be a famous lady surgeon,' he said, spooning kesar halwa on to my plate. 'Think only of work.'

Visions of being a Ms Stevens rose before my eyes. I muttered an apology and agreed to work on Sundays. I assisted the Chief in his clinic and in Theatre. It was mostly watching, listening, filling in case sheets and directing patients to the lab, to the X-ray or for a scan. I was given simple cases: hernias, haemorrhoids, cysts and boils. I consoled myself that it was only the beginning, he would soon trust me with more.

Work was effortless but every day I trudged home tired. The

five-storeyed hospital churned out health. There was an administrator, a marketing manager and a public relations officer to advise the doctors. Patients were clients. The duty of every doctor was to ensure client satisfaction. I got used to computer-printed lab reports and exorbitant bills. The doctors were hardworking; they seemed to possess a never-tired energy propelled by haste. They were always in a hurry to finish here so they could be there. I saw them in a blur as they sped from one hospital to another, flicking wrists to check the time, adjusting ties, clicking shut executive cases, greeting colleagues as they rushed past.

The Chief was given to maniacal mood swings. He was charming one moment and foul-tempered the next. More dangerous was the fact that he never once thought that he could be wrong. His cronies—the loyal assistant Dr Charles Raja, the secretary Pappachan, and Miss Kumuda, the senior nurse—were always around him. Dr Raja was genuinely admiring of the Chief and obeyed him without question. The sister fawned over him. Pappachan was wily. He was trusted by the MD and could more or less run the hospital in official matters.

It was hard to believe that the MD was a qualified surgeon. Dr Carver back in Liverpool was silken-fingered in comparison. A few days into my job he told me he would demonstrate his technique for repairing an inguinal hernia. He made it look difficult. He cut through the skin and fat and began to search for the hernial sac. He peeled away tissue as if it were a cabbage and muttered, 'Here's the sac!' 'Here's another one!' 'There's one more . . .' He ended up perforating the bowel and hastily left on some errand, leaving me to fix the damage.

There was a cramped little ward, the 'free ward', built on a portion of the terrace and roofed over with asbestos. Even the brief moments we doctors spent there during ward rounds were enough to burn the skin. Luckless patients who had suffered the Chief's bungling and who could no longer afford the fees were carted into this hot-air oven.

In my letters home I described the flat, the neighbourhood and the myriad attractions of the city. I said I had an exciting job. The truth was, with the Chief's bullying presence never far away, I did little surgery. He allowed me to see only women patients with minor ailments. When I did a hysterectomy, the gynaecologists were angry. If there was a surgical patient with high blood pressure, diabetes or a migraine, they were seen by the physician, diabetologist or neurologist. Patients were bounced off from one doctor to the next, from one hospital to the next.

The Chief told me that he was planning to do an elbow replacement and showed me the X-rays. The elbow had been severely damaged in an accident a year ago and the patient, a middle-aged auto-rickshaw driver, was unable to move it more than a few degrees. The Chief discussed the surgery, a procedure which even a skilled orthopaedic surgeon would approach with caution. I tried to dissuade him by relating fictitious instances where I had seen the surgery go wrong, but he was not put off. 'The patient came begging me to give him an arm he can use,' he said. 'I assured him that I will. Sunday morning, at ten. I want you to see how I do it.'

We were in Theatre till late on Sunday evening. I watched him struggle to get one part of the joint to fit the other. While preparing the ends of the bones, he had sheared off too much of the humerus. The prosthesis would not reduce into position. Unwilling to admit that he should seek help, he told his hapless assistant Charles Raja to close the skin over the prosthesis.

Predictably, the skin edges split open in a few days, exposing the steel of the metal elbow. This was covered with padded dressings and the patient put on antibiotics he could ill afford. Each morning the man would ask if his elbow would be all right. The error had been a major one and his body refused to accept the attempted camouflage. When the sheen of metal gleamed through the dressings and the patient supplicated us with tears in his eyes, the plastic surgeon was called to cover the dreadful mistake with a pedicle skin graft. Having sunk a fortune in the surgery, the patient opted to shift to the Hot-Air Oven. His wife and their three children stood outside, staring at the doctors in bafflement. They knew that the poor could not expect the same treatment as the rich. But, for this surgery, nothing had been spared. The patient had sold the auto rickshaw he once drove, his wife had taken money from her parents who had not much to give. They were confident that the twenty thousand rupees would suffice. A month went by. The patient finally went home with a stiff, grossly disfigured elbow. The Chief gave him a discount on the exorbitant bill. The patient said he would sue the hospital but the case was dropped after a payment exchanged hands.

I was infuriated. How was it possible for a hack to survive in a city and consider himself a saviour? In fact, not only did the Chief survive the disaster, he did worse. A young man was admitted with a severely shattered arm following a road accident. Both bones of the forearm were broken in two places and the brachial artery severed just below the elbow. The vascular surgeon said he would do a vein graft to bridge the gap between the severed artery at the elbow and the wrist. 'Do it first,' the Chief told him. 'I'll fix the bones after your procedure.' No one, not even the vascular surgeon, dared suggest that the bones be fixed before the delicate surgery on the arteries: to fall out of favour with the Chief might mean fewer referrals. When the vascular procedure was completed, the Chief started to fix the bones with plates and screws. He gripped the newly laid out graft with his clumsy fingers, drilled the bones and screwed on the plates.

In the morning I went to the ICU to check on the young man. He looked well enough but the fingers of the injured arm, peeping through the dressings, were cold and pulseless. The vascular repair had failed. I informed the anaesthetist and Theatre staff that an amputation was likely. When the Chief came to know of it, he was furious. 'How dare you talk about an amputation when I have gone through all that trouble to save his arm?' he screamed. He refused to undo the dressing and look at the hand.

Every day the doctors gathered around the patient's bed. The Chief told him about the hard work put in by the surgical team to save his arm. He was pumped with antibiotics—Magnamycin, Tobramycin, Augmentin—worth a few thousand, every day. Five days later the arm began to smell and his temperature went crazy. A week after the operation, the young man was sneaked back into Theatre and his arm amputated above the elbow. He was duly grateful to Periya Ayya for saving his life, and touched his one hand to his forehead in a salaam.

Anger and helplessness soured my days. In the evenings I sat with my red diary on my lap, meaning to write, but not having the energy or the courage to turn the pages. Because of the present, everything about the past was painful. From where I sat I looked resentfully at my white coat hanging on the bedroom door. It was a constant reminder of the label, the branding I had to live with. The collar was beginning to fray, the sleeves were begrimed at the wrists and the pockets hung low with the weight of my stethoscope, pens, notepad, hankies and bits of paper. Permeated by the odours of disease, death and disappointments, it had lost its distinction. As a student I had worn it with uncalled for pride; as an intern I walked to the bus stop with the neatly ironed coat draped over my arm. Now its sole usefulness was that it hid my unironed blouses. I got up and opened the door until it touched the wall and hid the coat from my eyes. When I sat down I saw one white sleeve peeping past the edge of the door, mocking me.

I was not enjoying my solitude. I tried for some time to renew my friendship with Stan and with the Mountains. Our letters had dwindled to Christmas and New Year greetings sent in haste. It seemed pointless to try and explain what was happening to me. Would anyone, even Stan, be interested? I spent long evenings on the terrace, watching the myriad lights shivering in the night. Or lying in my bed next to the window and looking out into the street outside. On a clear night the sky was full of stars like pinpricks, pressing in through the window, close enough to touch. But it was not my sky, or my stars. It was not that windowful of sky which I had had to myself at home, with the jack, guava and the parijata, and behind them the hills.

There was a sort of numb reprieve in not belonging, in not having to be accountable to anyone. But it was not enough. I visited the market frequently, walking the one-kilometre distance with a bag on my shoulder. I bought only a few rupees' worth of vegetables so that I could go back the next day for more. If I bought jasmine, I wore it only at home.

Once in the market, after searching my purse for coins to pay for a bunch of coriander, I looked up and saw a familiar face. Badri. He had lost a lot of weight. His yellow-tinged skin hung from his cheeks and arms in loose folds. I recognized his bush shirt, a dark grey now faded to a near white, and that jute bag which he always carried. Only Badri could have kept the bag so long. 'Sir! It's me!' I cried. 'Nalinakshi, your student. Sir, how are you? How's Guru?'

'Guru's all right,' he said, and seeing the surprise in my eyes, anwered my first question. 'Melanoma. With liver secondaries. Guru lets me go out in the evenings. Mostly we stay home.' I walked with him towards the cluster of shops with the low wall opposite. I tried to take his bag from him but he firmly moved my hand away. 'We'll sit here.'

He wanted to know what I had been doing. He was amused to hear that I was a surgeon. 'I thought you'd do something less gross, like paediatrics or cardiology,' he said. 'Did you like living abroad?'

I gushed about my stay in England, remembering only the good things. 'Snow. Boiled meat. Money. That's what I remember. Lots and lots of money with which to bring gifts for waiting relatives.' He sniggered.

He wasn't convinced when I said I had come back for good. 'We all say that. It only takes a trivial annoyance to run away. I almost did. Now, fifty years later, I wonder sometimes. I was too judgemental. Always seeing the black and white in everything. Don't ever think that doing your work well makes a saint out of you.'

He sat up. 'Dr Ali Khan—you called him the Nawab, did you not? Wish he was here now when there is so much time to be friends. He's gone back to Hyderabad . . . my loss.'

People shopping after work walked past us. The market was noisy but the evening cool, with a lively breeze gusting from the sea. 'You like medhu vadai?' he asked, a faint smile wrinkling his face. 'Get four medhu vadais and coffee. Not good for the liver but good for my soul. No food can harm me now.'

We ate, and he talked about himself. 'Forty-two years of anatomy. I believed that all of the world was anatomy and then this stepsister, pathology, befriended me. Had no option but to read everything about it. The primary tumour was in the umbilicus. Can you believe it? Me, a scrupulously clean brahmin . . . but who looks at one's umbilicus? Must have been there for months before I noticed.'

His voice grew sharp. 'Am I talking too much? I *will* talk too much. Am I showing off? I *will* show off. There I was all set to enjoy my retired life with Guru, and these cells were slyly multiplying inside. Anaplastic cells with atypical mitosis and two, three nuclei in a single cell. Runaway delinquent cells with mirror-image nuclei, burdened with melanin. That same melanin which gives the blackness to Tamil skin and African skin and the darkness to Guru's eyes and the head of curly black hair to my niece—the cells ran amuck and formed the tumour. I can remember in excruciating detail the description in Boyd. Now *there* was a good writer. He made poetry out of cells and tissues.'

He bit into the vadai. 'I, a vegetarian and teetotaller.' He shrugged. 'From the perspective of the whole universe it's fair, it's in the order of things that I get this rare type of cancer. I'm just interested in what's taking place inside me. I'm talking about my illness so you get it straight.'

I helped him into the bus and promised to visit them soon.

It happened after three months when Suguna, who lived in Delhi with her husband, phoned to say she was in Madras, staying with her uncle and aunt for a week. I went, suddenly shy, not of my teachers but of my friend. Guru had not changed very much and she was happy to see me. Suguna's age showed in the fine lines around her mouth. She was the same calm, unexcitable person she had been in college. She was a neuro-pathologist and on the faculty for teaching post-graduates. She hardly talked about her husband, and I knew that it was a good marriage. I was envious of Suguna; not so much of her intellectual superiority as her wisdom. She was not the type to show off her happiness, and kind enough not to quiz me about mine.

Jai answered my letters with a phone call. Be persistent and work your way up, he said. Buy yourself a car; banks are good with loans. It is bad for a surgeon's image to be seen in buses and autos.

I wrote Tejus about my frustration and received a prompt reply: 'Serves you right. At least now read my twelve inches of advice.' He was at his abrasive best. 'If you don't care enough, then chuck it and stop moaning.'

In another long letter, he told me everything: The tragedy of his family was that of good people everywhere. The happiness they hankered after was the visible happiness—of beauty, health, education, a good job, marriage and children. Their morality identified all sorts of evil everywhere except that in their own lives. Tejus was spoon-fed goodness. 'I did wrong only to hear my mother say, "Tejoo . . . no . . ." I did things because my father did not do them. Genetically I was clever enough to get into medical college where I picked up some really good bad habits. Then I fled to Delhi with a girl who was in college. A year later, my parents wheedled me back to an arranged match.

'I had inherited their stupidity, after all. I agreed to go through with the farce. A two-day wedding, me in pristine white. I waited for the muhurtam on the balcony of the house where the ceremony was to be held and saw the girl being led towards the flower-decked mantapam below. The wickedness of the sham crushed me. I walked away. I've been home only rarely since. No one can stand me.'

He married the girl in Delhi and they stayed married for five years. It was his fault that it ended. He could not stand her independence. She was *strong*, damn her.

His letters filled me with a longing to talk to him. It had been a good relationship of the mind. What if it had been the other thing? If there had been no other woman and if Philo had pulled off her scheme? Life was so strange. Unfulfilled possibilities, unspoken feelings, touch-button non-decisions. Commitment, confusion, hard work, and the years speeding away.

I was rapidly falling out with the Chief. He accused me of not being interested in the hospital. He had invested two crores in the CT scanner and had to recover the cost in a couple of years. How could he, if the doctors did not oblige and do more scans? All injuries to the head—even the most minor—must have a CT scan. It was the duty of the doctor to convince the patient, he said.

I hated my job.

42

Late one night, I had a call from Jai. 'Will you come over and stay with us for a few days?'

The urgency in his voice made me apply for leave and board the train the following night. He met me at the railway station. How long was it since we had met? Four years? Five? Before Keshavganj?

Their home was bigger, more plush. When he opened the front door with a spare key, we found Bela on the drawing room settee, dozing with the TV on. Jai patted her elbow and she woke, grumbling that she was short of sleep. I could feel her delicate bones when she hugged me. There were dark circles beneath those lovely eyes. I told her she had become thinner and then realized that I should not have said it. Bela was touchy.

Their two boys came back from school, greeted me politely and then kept to themselves. It was not their unconcern or Bela's thinness or Jai's overwork which bothered me as much as the fact that they barely spoke to each other. The TV was on all the time and it did nothing to diminish the unending silence. There was now a live-in cook, a supercilious young man who catered to their individual whims with a barely noticeable contempt.

The next day was Jai's birthday. Phone calls, flowers and

gifts kept coming. Bela gave him a camera. Dinner had been ordered from a restaurant but Jai returned only at ten. The television was on, as always. I said I was switching it off as no one was watching. A little later, Jai switched it back on, to hear the news, he said. It stayed on.

Bela was unmindful of my presence and not curious to know what I had been doing all these years. In the midst of a meal or a conversation she would suddenly disappear into her room. I was sad for them and wanted to do something. 'Shall I make dosais?' I asked one day. Bela dutifully got the rice, urad dal, coconut and til which I needed and left me alone. The dosais were ready on Sunday for breakfast. I watched Jai eat one, three . . . six dosais, and finish all of the til chutney, which I knew he loved. The boys ate a dosai each and then asked for toast and fried eggs. Bela stuck to her mug of tea.

Jai made a pathetic attempt to pretend that everything was all right. He was one of the leading endoscopic surgeons in the city and had set up his own department with machines that cost seven lakhs. He would soon start laparoscopic surgery. He spoke about everything with a dullness in his eyes that alarmed me.

One day he came home very late. Bela was in her room, asleep. I was watching TV and he settled into the settee beside me. Inevitably, he spoke about the rift between them. Bela had become selfish, she wanted him to be home early. How could he come before nine? They had planned a holiday in Goa and when it did not happen she had made a scene. She should find something to do to pass her time, he said, but she was lazy. When she started having a sleeping problem he had prescribed a small dose of diazepam. Now she could not sleep without it. Her family blamed him, but did nothing to help. 'There's no animosity between Bela and me,' Jai said. 'It's just that we can't talk to each other.'

The next day I tried to find out what Bela felt. 'Poor Jai. It's all my fault,' she said.

I sat in my room. The rays of the morning sun slanting across the green carpet reminded me again of the paddy fields in Angheri. I glared resentfully, as if a patch of the greenness of our fields had been snatched away and cut up to make the carpet. Jai and Bela. What could I say to them? I had seen it all along, in the pathetic, fragmented nature of their early happiness, in Bela's mindless extravagance, in Jai's frenzied success, and in the dread that lurked in his eyes.

I watched helplessly and after five days went back to Madras.

～

It happened sooner than I had expected. A patient complained to me that he had been sold a strip of ampicillin by the hospital pharmacy when the drug was past the expiry date. I spoke to the pharmacist who said that in such a busy pharmacy mistakes were bound to happen. I complained to Pappachan.

'We get short-expiry drugs at fifty to sixty per cent discount,' he explained. 'They have to be sold. I know, they should be given only to the not-so-literate patients. I've told the girls at the dispensing counter to snip off the expiry date.'

I spoke to the Chief in private. I thoughtfully closed the door behind me and told him what I had found out.

He looked at me with a mixture of amusement and fury. 'If you don't like our set-up, you're free to leave,' he said.

'I'll send letters to the president of the IMA,' I stammered, furious. 'To the health minister.'

'Good luck,' he said, and stood up.

Two days later a board meeting was held which I was asked to attend, to discuss my insubordination to the chief. The directors (many of them senior physicians and specialists) turned away from me with cold smiles. My conduct, I was told, was unacceptable. My services were being terminated. Half an hour later, having signed the papers, I walked out of the hospital.

My desire for justice was strong; I talked to journalists. When I mentioned the Chief, they said that I would have to produce evidence, consult a lawyer. I knew before trying that no doctor or staff at the hospital would back me. It seemed almost vulgar to be so malevolent against another doctor. Forget it, they advised. After a week I gave up, and concentrated instead on finding a job. Having no credentials of previous service in the city, it was not easy. The word had probably spread that I was a difficult person. Three desperate weeks later I was appointed in a smaller hospital on a modest salary. The director actually congratulated me for standing up to the Chief in the previous hospital. It was a cleaner, happier place and I was temporarily at peace.

When I opened the door and saw Jai, I was not surprised.

'You left in a hurry,' he said. 'I had to come chasing after you.'

I was so glad to see him. I dashed downstairs to the corner shop to buy cake and mixture, and brewed coffee. We sat on either side of a low table in the front room. The breeze lifted the curtain from the window towards him and he pushed it away.

He sat pressing his forehead, not talking. 'Our friendship dates back a long time, Jai,' I said. 'I can and I will say it: You've been unfair. Bela didn't want your success or status, she wanted you. And your parents—they didn't bargain for a trade-off, son for money. You could have had all the money you wanted, and you could have had Bela and your parents.' In my own life, I had done what I wanted when it concerned big issues. Only in little things did I give in, let others decide. 'I know. It's a clever sort of selfishness that I practise but in the end it's better than hurting everyone you care about.'

I got up to offer him cake. 'Sit,' he said. He could still command me. 'You used to care for me.'

'I still do,' I said, proudly. 'It has nothing to do with what we're talking about.'

He spoke with an effort. 'I'll stay all night if I have to and I'll convince you. Don't be angry with me for not coming back to Angheri when you wanted me to. It would not have worked then. But now we can pair up and fulfil our dream together.'

I sat up. For a long time, I had not known a moment as happy as this. He was sitting not more than an arm's distance away. If I reached out I could touch him.

'Jai, how wonderful! Don't worry, we'll involve Bela from the start so she'll be happy there.'

The wind-filled curtain slapped his face. He gripped it with his hand and for a moment he was hidden behind it. Then he thrust it away. 'I didn't mean that. Bela prefers Bombay. She doesn't know any other life, she can't adjust anywhere else. I'll do everything for her and the boys. But I can't stand it any more. I want to leave Bombay,' he said. 'I'd like to practice in Madras until we make plans.' I heard the screech of tyres as some vehicle braked suddenly on our street. 'I won't let you down. I want to help the village. But let the economy pick up, let the roads improve. Let the people feel they can afford us.'

He pushed his upper lip with his tongue to hide his embarrassment. I hated to see him do that. 'Don't blame me for what's happened to Bela. If it wasn't for me she would be worse. She isn't interested in my profession, my reputation and success, which I built with hard work. And you talk as if she's blameless.' At that moment he was miles away, his face was hazy and only his eyes, those burning eyes were close, so close. This was the Jai for whom my universe trembled.

'I know,' I said. 'This is not our dream, it's practicality. You're sick of Bombay and you want Madras.' I felt a deep sadness as I spoke. 'The trouble, Jai, is me. With a few people, one or two, I have to dispense with pretensions. I must not, cannot pretend. What does Madras care about you?'

'I'll be able to attract patients. If you help . . . You're angry with me for refusing Angheri. Why can't you see it as it is? Villages belong to the past. In a village you can't do anything important, you can't be anyone important. Even when I visit, I get sick of the petty problems and inconsequential politics there.'

'You don't mind the big problems and the big politics here.'

His laugh was bitter. 'You never give up, do you? Still the same Nalli. I'm not writing off the poor. They . . .'

'They provide you with an opportunity to do good. Bela told me. She distributes sweets. You do free cases when it suits you.'

'Eventually, everyone will migrate to the cities.'

'If everyone migrates, the cities will collapse.'

'You're pessimistic when an idea doesn't appeal to you, no matter how sound. Cities always find means of accommodating people. Look at Dharavi. Have you seen Dharavi? A million people. They don't mind. Thousands crawl into Bombay every day.' He reached forward and gripped my arm. 'Nalli. Everything is possible! Did you ever imagine that computers would become important? Or that CT scans would make life so easy? I've told you. Lap surgery will become so advanced, it will replace open surgery. Even colectomies, through a keyhole.'

'Voyeuristic and distasteful,' I said glumly. 'I want to use my hands. But that's not what we're talking about.'

'Too late, isn't it? Now I can only do what I do. Better and better.' He showed me a copy of *Lancet* he had brought with him. 'My article,' he said, opening to the page and passing it to me: 'Non-Invasive Techniques in the Treatment of Ampullary Carcinoma'. I looked numbly at the printed words: Abstract. Introduction. Method. Results. Discussion. Conclusion. Jai's accomplishment, a lead article in a prestigious medical journal. But at that moment, it meant as much to me as the lines on a dead man's palm.

Why say it? He was limited by his limitless ambition. Twenty years from now the only difference would be more success, greying hair, spectacles maybe, and a paunch. He said he wanted a more restful practice but it would not happen. He would spread the contagion of work to others. The world loves those who work hard and if it happens to be a doctor, they worship him. He was finished because he had stopped taking risks. 'Go back, Jai,' I said. 'Do what you're cut out to do.'

He nodded lightly, rhythmically, trying to make sense of what I was saying. He got up, went to the window and picked up my diary which was lying on the sill. It had miraculously retained its sheen outside but was twice as thick from use. Then he came back and sat down.

'You got this when you went to college.' He was amused. 'You still write in it?'

'Yes and no.' I hadn't written a word for months. What was the point?

'Let's talk about you,' he said. 'I'm happy you've found your place at last. Keep a firm hold on it.'

'I *haven't* found anything,' I snapped. 'Seven months in Madras and I'm tired. Don't bother trying to convince me that I'll make it.' All the choleys, thyroids and gastrectomies I had done, the hundreds of sutures slipping past my fingers as I tied knots—a thousand times, ten thousand times—none of it meant a thing if I did not do what I wanted to do. I could not explain it to Jai. 'Everything I say, everything I do—I can see the discomfiture in the faces of others,' I said. 'They wish I'd go away.'

The sunlight outside had begun to soften. I could hear the old gentleman, my neighbour, tap his way up the stairs to the terrace. The day melted into shadows but neither of us got up to switch on the light. It was easier to face each other with the darkness hiding our pain.

43

You're in danger of being trapped by your sense of *mission*, Tejus had said. It was not easy to probe one's heart about such things. My mood swung from high to low. Now that I had gained acceptance in Madras, it would be easy to just go on. I could see myself ten, fifteen years ahead: stouter, calmer, more capable, known as such-and-such surgeon. Breast cancer? Go to her, she's good. Was I good? For how long would I continue to walk in and out of wards which smelt of fever, pain, humiliation and death? I picked up my diary and read my first entry, made when I was sixteen, full of impudent idealism. I could hear the squeak of the nib, smell the ink as I wrote quickly, grandly, about going to college. I sat there a long while, flipping the pages, reading.

It was long past bedtime. Opening the door to the staircase, I went up to the terrace. Two nylon ropes were strung across by the servant downstairs, to hang out the washing. Every time I went up I would find some clothes which had been pulled free by the wind lying on the cement floor. I put them back on the clothesline, clipping them along with the other garments. In a corner of the terrace were stored a spade, a hoe and a watering can used by the gardener who came two or three times a week.

It was a cool night; the sky was starless and deep. A grey sliver of moon flitted in and out from behind thin white clouds. Exhausted by the activities of the day, the city breathed quietly. The terrace was too small for walking. But that night I walked, unmindful of the confined space, until it felt like some vast avenue. My mind roamed everywhere but I could not remember much of what I thought. Had I been dreaming? For I was sure I was back home, sitting at the window and gazing through the trees while Ajja whispered his prayers. I thought about an entry in my diary that I had just read, about hunger.

Hunger I associated with the Satyanarayana puja that we held at home every year. Shanku Master was the pujari. With Jai, he took on the entire responsibility including the cooking of a cauldron of payasa to serve at the end of the ritual. The house was in happy confusion for days before the event. Neighbours, friends and relatives came and sat through the day until the puja was done and the five chapters read from the Puranas. Shanku Master as pujari appeared somehow superior to the Maths teacher at school. Even the adults treated him deferentially. Dressed in a spotless white dhoti, with the sandalwood paste smeared in three prominent streaks on his brow, he moved about, instructing Ajja, 'Four annas here,' 'Four annas there,' stretching a pious palm towards clumps of coconut, agarbattis and flowers, which he had arranged with mysterious precision. Jai, very serious and very holy, refused to look at me.

Ajja insisted that we fast till the puja was over. We ate the payasa—sweet payasa made of rice, jaggery, coconut and ghee—after the last of the guests had been served. The waiting was torment. Standing there before the gods with folded hands, the only thing I prayed for was: Let it all be over, so we can eat the payasa. Dum-dum dum-dum, ting-ting-ting-ting, dum-ting, dum-ting—the drums beat and the bells rang, until it felt like someone stamping and dancing in my belly.

When the stories were read from the Puranas, by Shanku Master and sometimes by Jai, I listened listlessly to them repeat after every story that by giving food, clothing and cattle to the brahmins all one's sins could be washed away. Why did no one question it? Shanku Master got a dhoti and a towel, his wife a sari. When Naganna Gowdru performed the puja, once in five years, he presented Shanku Master with a calf.

The stories went on and on while my thoughts were consumed by the acuteness of my hunger. Not a mere hunger for food but a deeper hunger that was as sweet as it was harsh. A hunger which I had sometimes felt when walking back from school very tired and had looked eastward at the hills trembling in a haze or when I looked into Jai's eyes, as deep and black as the water in the well behind the house . . .

I was still on the terrace, pacing. The night had passed swiftly. Rubbing my eyes, I opened them wide and looked eastward. The sounds of traffic stirred somewhere in the city but the neighbourhood still slept. There was a streak of brightness in the sky and then the blue of a pre-dawn light lapped the edges of the night. The sky lightened, and in the distance, blue and purple, grey and black, were the slopes reaching upward. If my eyes were playing tricks, it did not matter.

I went down and made an entry in my diary, the sound of the nib filling the silence as I wrote. Then I started to pack.

acknowledgements

I am grateful for support and enlightenment to the doctors and staff of St John's Medical College, Bangalore; Rural India Health Project, Ammathi, Karnataka; Tata Coffee and Tata Tea Ltd; Ramakrishna Mission Hospital, Vrindaban, Uttar Pradesh; Nazareth Hospital, Mokama, Bihar; The Royal Infirmary, Liverpool; Wycombe General Hospital, High Wycombe; and Nobles Hospital, Isle of Man, United Kingdom.

I am also deeply indebted in big ways and small to my teachers—Drs K. Das and Shenoy, John and Manu Thomas, T. Chandrasekar, Messrs William Beattie, Bickford, Alfred Cushieri, Robert Sells, Malcolm Colmer, Ms Averil Mansfield, Messrs Robert Downie, Nick Batey, John Lee and Denis Powell.

I thank Vijay, my friend, critic and spouse; Ravi Singh, my editor; and Poulomi Chatterjee, for her help with the final draft.